Destiny's Hand

DESTINY'S HAND

▼

Joseph E. Driessen

Writer's Showcase
presented by *Writer's Digest*
San Jose New York Lincoln Shanghai

Destiny's Hand

All Rights Reserved © 2000 by Joseph E. Driessen

No part of this book may be reproduced or transmitted in any form or by any means, graphic, electronic, or mechanical, including photocopying, recording, taping, or by any information storage retrieval system, without the permission in writing from the publisher.

Writer's Showcase
presented by *Writer's Digest*
an imprint of iUniverse.com, Inc.

For information address:
iUniverse.com, Inc.
5220 S 16th, Ste. 200
Lincoln, NE 68512
www.iuniverse.com

ISBN: 0-595-15210-4

Printed in the United States of America

For Christopher

"…It's no longer a question of if. It's a question of when and where."

Lee Silver, reproductive biologist, Princeton University, July 1998, discussing human cloning.

Acknowledgements

I would like to thank my wife, Karen, and my children, for their love and patience in putting up with this project all these years.

I would also like to thank my editor, Ellen Green, of E. B. Green Editorial, St. Paul, MN for her professionalism, patience, editorial skills, good humor, and insight.

All research was done by the author using newspapers and periodicals. Any similarity to any character or aspect of the book is unintentional.

You are the reason I've been waiting all these years.
Somebody holds the key.
I'm near the end and I just ain't got the time
And I'm wasted and I can't find my way home.
     —Steve Winwood with Blind Faith

If love is a red dress, hang me in rags.
If love is aces, deal me a jack.
     —Maria McKee

And it's one, two, three, what are we fighting for
don't ask me, I don't give a damn
the next stop is Vietnam
and it's five, six, seven, open up the pearly gates
well it ain't no time to wonder why
whoopee we're all gonna die…
—Country Joe and the Fish

Above the planet on a wing and a prayer,
My grubby halo, a vapor trail in the empty air,
Across the clouds I see my shadow fly
Out of the corner of my watering eye
A dream unthreatened by the morning light
Could blow this soul right through the roof of the night.

There's no sensation to compare with this
Suspended animation, a state of bliss
Can't keep my mind from the circling sky,
Tongue-tied and twisted, just an earth-bound misfit, I.
—Pink Floyd

Meet the new boss. Same as the old boss.
—The Who

I was born and raised way out west.
But the thing that I like 'bout livin' here best.
It ain't the mountains, the valleys, the hats, or the boots,
It's having plenty of guns and somethin' to shoot.

I don't care 'bout the future, don't care 'bout the past
As long as I've got some creatures to blast
We've got deer, we've got elk, we've got old owls that hoot.
And when I've killed them all, there'll be Yankees to shoot.
— Charles Wall

Fire…fire…life's backwards…life's backwards
people turn around
the house is burned…the house is burned
the children are gone
fire…fire…fire on Babylon
oh yes, a change has come…
— Sinead O'Connor

Other lyrics attributed to the appropriate artist in the book.

Prologue

Monogovody, Siberia
December 31, 1999

"I'm bored..." Lenny grumbled.

Larisa Gritsenko rolled her eyes. "How many times have I heard you say that?" Soaring above the numbing landscape of northern Siberia, the 200-kilometer flight from the city of Salekhard to the Monogovody Research Center offered nothing but snow and emptiness to hold the pilot's attention

"Autopilot?" Larisa suggested, looking up from her magazine, already knowing his response.

The pilot shot her a glance, shook his head, and against the buffeting winds held a steady course. He *could* enable the autopilot, close his eyes, and catch a few minutes sleep. The helicopter's computer navigation system was the best money could buy. But as a pilot in the old Soviet Air Force, Lenny had acquired an intense distrust of high-tech gadgetry.

The knowledge that a series of low-bidding, government-gouging companies had built the helicopter was enough to keep him alert.

His former employers would not have objected to his reasoning. Perpetual diligence was one of their most clichéd credos. During the Communists' troubled reign, however, the threat to Mother Russia was Western imperialism, not the dubious business practices of competing contractors.

Despite occasional boredom, Lenny couldn't complain about his job transporting cargo for Empyrean Technologies International, or ETI, as Yuri Tyrellovich's research consortium was known. The pay was enviable, the hours acceptable, and the benefits such that he was willing to fly through a Siberian snowstorm on the wildest New Year's Eve in a thousand years.

"Any plans for later tonight?" Gritsenko asked, doing her best to entertain her friend.

"Nothing that doesn't involve a pillow." Though he understood the significance of the approaching millennium, after a long week Lenny wanted nothing more than a night's sleep. So much so that before agreeing to deliver a load of emergency supplies, he had radioed ahead to make sure that none of the scientists and guests attending Tyrellovich's symposium had appropriated his private suite. Through luck or his reputed temper, Lenny had received confirmation that the room would be his alone.

Lenny smiled. Even during his tour of duty as a Soviet flight officer, his luck had held. Instead of serving in Afghanistan, where the life expectancy of Russian helicopter pilots hovered between short and nonexistent, Lenny had turned his familiarity with the Baltic coast, from his childhood in Vyborg, into an opportunity to scout for Western submarines instead of Mujahedeen. It was this knowledge and expertise Tyrellovich paid so dearly for.

Some might argue he was overpaid. But as the best helicopter pilot in northern Russia, he—Leonid Nikolayevich Petrov—had the luxury of working for the highest bidder. The law of supply and demand, cornerstone of the free-market system, dictated the obvious: if you want the best, you pay the price. Lenny was one Russian who did not miss the Communists.

Glancing out the cockpit window, Lenny took comfort in the isolation and naturalness of Siberia. Though the world continued to shrink under the relentless advance of civilization, here remained a place too inaccessible for condominiums, EuroDisneys, and government interference.

In every direction was a sea of white. The howling wind and driven snow obscured the horizon, yet on and on the helicopter flew. Inexperienced fliers could hypnotize themselves by staring into swirling reflections of snow and ice in the running lights of a helicopter. The monotony of the Siberian night had taught many careless pilots the importance of staying alert. Remembering that lesson, Lenny blinked hard and turned toward his Ukrainian copilot.

"What are you reading?"

Larisa held up a tabloid: "APOCALYPSE—The End Is Near," the headline proclaimed.

"Bunch of paranormal crap," Lenny opined. On more than one TV news show, he had seen prophets of doom and other lost souls in designer sneakers who, in all likelihood, were waiting in wheat fields and parking lots for flying saucers to swoop down and carry them to the end of the galaxy.

"I don't know, Lenny. A lot of people are worried about this," the copilot said, going back to her reading. Indeed, the sense of urgency concerning the new millennium extended far beyond the paranormal. One could find signs of an approaching maelstrom on paranoiac bumper stickers, end-of-the-world web sites, and prime-time programming. On countless street corners and airport concourses, wild-eyed evangelists ranted and raved, spewing tales of Earth's impending scourge. Global computer failures, earthquakes, boiling seas, falling stars, cities in flame, nations destroyed, and a human carnage beyond imagination.

Apocalyptic rumors ran rife among Southern Baptists, Pentecostals, and other Christian denominations. Shiite Muslims predicted the millennium would herald the return of the fabled "twelfth imam." A white buffalo, portentous omen of Native American legend, had been born on a Midwestern farm.

In Israel, a red heifer precursed the millennium. Not since the destruction of the Second Temple 2000 years ago by the Romans had the Middle East seen such a creature. To devout Jews, it was a presage from God that the Messiah was near. Buddhist and Hindu sects offered their own prophecies of final judgment. By some accounts the dam of civilization was about to burst, and the high ground was dangerously crowded.

"Media propaganda, Gritsenko. Written only to sell magazines and newspapers to people like you who should know better."

Larisa grinned. "So if the sky falls, I can complain to you?"

"Of course," the pilot said. "But you'll have to take a number and wait your turn."

Suddenly, through the snow, Lenny saw a glimmer. He adjusted his headset and looked at the control panel. Soon the helicopter would touch down at the Monogovody freight terminal, and the ground crew could unload the cargo.

Larisa saw it, too. Following procedure, she put away her reading, verified their position, and called to the cargo crew. "All right, you bums, wake-up time," she said, flipping a switch and flooding the cargo hold with amplified music.

Seconds later, O'Leary shouted from below. "*Hey*, you crazy Russian bastards, turn that *bloody* shit off. We're tryin' to get some sleep back 'ere."

"Up and at 'em, gentlemen," Larisa ordered, ignoring the Irishman's tirade. "Mono's on the margin. We'll be touching down in ten, so bundle up—it's minus 25 out there."

The helicopter made its final approach while the cargo crew prepped for landing. Flying over the iron fence of the first perimeter, Larisa remembered that not long ago such barriers had imprisoned some 20 million Gulag internees banished to Siberian wastelands by Josef Stalin.

But times change. Stalin was dead, his doctrines discredited. Free enterprise was the law of the land. The barbed wire of the twelve-foot fence surrounding Monogovody no longer angled inward; its only purpose now to keep out wild animals. Indeed, the remoteness of the facility offered such excellent camouflage that human encroachment never entered Yuri Tyrellovich's mind.

They reached their destination. Through the dancing snow and blazing lights, Lenny and Larisa watched the ground crew prepare for the helicopter's descent in the deadly cold.

With a soft *bump*, the helicopter touched down, and the cargo bay doors opened. With cautious efficiency, the workers drew out and carried away the crates of wine, beer, champagne, caviar, and other items of delectable importance. They had ample reason for precaution. Whatever delicacies remained after Tyrellovich and his honored guests had their fill would go to them and the rest of the service staff.

Rummaging among the pallets, Fertig deftly sliced through the binding tape with a butcher's knife, liberating the object of his frantic search. He cradled the chilled carton and hastened to his table-board. Knowing full well the calamity transpiring in the ballroom, he would not let the celebration be ruined.

Other members of the kitchen staff went about their duties, trying to stay out of his way. They had witnessed the boulanger's agitated pacing as he awaited the helicopter. From across the vast complex, the staff could hear strains of music, while the clock on the wall advised that midnight was near. Wiping the sweat from his forehead, Fertig glanced up at the time. He redoubled his effort, knowing he must not fail.

As the notes of the string sextet faded, Fertig hastened into the ballroom, balancing his creation. With practiced skill, he hoisted an almost-empty tray with his left hand and slid a platter full of sturgeon caviar—gently layered atop a firm yet flaky pastry shell—onto the linen tablecloth with his right. Amid loud conversation and clinking crystal, no one noticed his circumvention of near-disaster.

The revelers began to devour yet another fortune in fish eggs as Fertig stood proudly behind the table, bearing the tired smile of a culinary magician. He'd never seen a group go through caviar like this one. "Then again," he thought, "eggs are the very reason they come to Monogovody."

At the front of the hall, opposite Fertig, six musicians scurried about the stage rearranging equipment and tuning a fresh set of instruments. The enormous digital clock above the stage anticipated the turn of the millennium—11:50 P.M. In ten minutes, the New Year's experience to end New Year's experiences would reach their time zone.

All the world anticipated the final night of 1999. The festivities began at the International Dateline Hotel on the Tongan Island of Nuku'alofa. From that moment forward, on the hour, every hour, over the twenty-four hours heralding the momentous occasion, corks popped, champagne flowed, and lips puckered and pressed.

Though some quibbled that the celebration was a year premature, or that the red-letter affair occurred in the middle of the Judaic year 5760 or the Muslim year 1420, their objections were overruled. Throughout the ages, humankind seldom needed a good excuse to throw a party. New Year's Eve 1999 was no exception.

Partygoers booked and RSVP'd years in advance—from La Tour d'Argent restaurant in Paris, to the Savoy Hotel in London, to Walt Disney World in Orlando. The Monogovody Symposium of 1999 had required years of preparation as well. Despite its location in the middle of a Siberian wilderness—1200 miles northeast of Moscow—all one hundred by-invitation-only guests arrived promptly. They wouldn't have missed it for the world.

Cocktail glasses were filled, drained, and refilled. The revelers—mostly married scientists, scholars, and educators in their late twenties and early thirties—watched the minutes digitize down. Growing weary of discussing molecular structures, embryology, and eighteenth-century philosophers, the crowd was ready for action.

On stage, the musicians prepared to kick off the midnight festivities with something more unbridled than Bach or Vivaldi. Sporting hastily slicked-back hair and pouting lips, the cellist strode to the microphone and waited. Following a cue to the stage manager, the lights dimmed, and the audience howled.

The violinist, now astride a drum set, smacked her drumsticks together once, twice, three times as the dance floor vibrated with the amplified reverberation of the bass and keyboard. Two guitars furnished the rhythm and melody as rock 'n' roll echoed through the ballroom.

The change in tempo electrified the revelers, who found their second or third wind, bobbing and twirling to the rousing beat. Strobe lights pulsated with flashes of shimmering light, and the dance floor filled to capacity.

The crush of tipsy and perspiring dancers pushed their less-dedicated colleagues toward the fringes. One couple, holding each other for support, staggered to their table. The tuxedoed man fumbled in a leather bag picked up from the floor as the beautiful, dark-haired woman kissed him on the neck and ran her hands up and down his sweaty chest.

"Later, my love. Show a *little* restraint," the man teased, pulling a small dark object from the bag. He aimed a palm-sized electronic device at the crowd before realizing his newly acquired gadget did not work.

The man tried to focus his bloodshot eyes on the camcorder in an effort to determine the problem.

"Am I to assume it takes a rocket scientist to operate one of those toys?" the woman oozed, her throaty question tinged with a Russian accent. She reached for the camcorder as the man fingered the proper button and motioned her away.

"*I am* a rocket scientist, my dear, but these infernal buttons are too small."

"My Nyentzi lover is all fingers, no?"

"*Hush*. Tyrellovich warned us never to use that word in public."

"Oh pooh, you know how I am hating of secrets."

"Behave yourself, Olga. Okay, it's working…you're on."

The woman backed up and began to sway to the pounding music. Her hands slid down, around and over her belly; to her crotch, then up and down each leg—slowly, rhythmically, erotically. The man, joined by others nearby, hooted and whistled, urging her on. Above the din of the music and the laughter of the crowd, a chorus of voices began the chant: "*…19…18…17…*"

Amidst the isolation of a Siberian winter, the deafening noise of the celebration, and the shimmering rainbows of light, a crush of humanity witnessed the birth of a new day. With it came the promise the morning, the novelty of a new year, and the sense of transformation of a new millennium.

I

Los Angeles, California
January 7, 2007

Thud.... A morning newspaper landed amidst the weeds and gravel at the bottom of a shallow ravine. The carrier's indifferent toss had carried the daily over sculptured shrubs, pretentious lawn ornaments, and finally over the retaining wall in the southwest corner of a posh Beverly Hills estate. His route complete, the teenager pedaled down the block and out of sight.

On a normal day, the paper would have lain there for weeks. On this perfect southern California morning, however, when much of Los Angeles lay sleeping, a black-gloved hand reached out to retrieve it.

Hidden by the shadows of the dawn, a figure opened the folded paper and read the headlines. It was the Spanish edition of a local publication, as one would expect at this particular address.

A muffled voice whispered, "Hey...Heiple—what's the news?"

"No comprendé Español, mi amigo."

A gesture of command demanded silence. The gloved hand set down the paper as its owner scanned the ravine. Eight figures crouched in readiness, all dressed in ebony uniforms with military helmets outfitted with communication headsets. The only deviation from the black of the fabric was an American flag on the left sleeve and a patch with L.A.P.D. on the right.

A fire-retardant black mask covered every face in the ravine, leaving only small openings for the eyes under the helmets. Bulletproof vests, each breasted with a Velcro-backed, dark gray nametag, completed the stylish ensembles.

The nametag of the figure opening the paper read "Heiple." He checked his automatic weapon for the umpteenth time, listening as the other teams reported. In a few moments, activity in the neighborhood would intensify, and that was fine with him.

Ambulances, fire trucks, an armed police reconnaissance helicopter, and backup squads also waited. They'd evacuated a two-block area around the target house to prevent incidental casualties and to guarantee that their targets—Paulo, José, and Roberto Guerrero—could not escape. Though they were ready for action, if the operation proceeded as planned, they'd be back at their usual assignments before morning coffee break.

Several blocks away was the SWAT team headquarters, in an inconspicuous tractor-trailer crammed with the latest surveillance equipment. Days earlier, agents disguised as telephone-repair personnel had installed the cameras and sound monitors providing the eyes and ears of the operation.

Conspicuously absent was a negotiating team. The time for bargaining had long since passed. Though the occupants of the house were ignorant of that detail, they would find out soon enough.

Inside the command center, FBI agents and local police personnel monitored the phone lines, streets, alleys, and house. Team Leader

Alpha, a sour-faced FBI field supervisor named Felicia Scriff, demanded to know how the newspaper carrier had penetrated the police cordon.

"Inexcusable—that's what this is—inexcusable." Scriff glared at a monitor displaying the image of the teenager pedaling out of sight. "Is this the level of competence we've sunk to? Am I the only one who knows how to do the job *right*?"

Command-center personnel bit their collective tongue, no one daring to suggest that the paper carrier's unexpected arrival might convince the targets this was a normal Monday. Just as well their silence: Scriff was not in the mood for logical argument.

The morning's operation was one of Scriff's many onsite command responsibilities. She wanted it to be her last. At age 50, she was bucking for promotion, impatiently awaiting the desk assignment she thought she deserved. Intolerant at best, Felicia Scriff had few friends. Her only concern was the successful completion of her job—at any cost. Harmonious working relationships were unnecessary indulgences.

Scriff knew the score, just as she knew the Guerreros were not typical entrepreneurs. Busting the their import cartel had been an objective of state and federal authorities for years. From their factories south of the Rio Grande, the Guerreros produced and shipped north vast quantities of merchandise. The problem was not their liberal interpretation of the North American Free Trade Agreement. The problem was the product—methamphetamine.

Known as the drug for the ultimate high, methamphetamine—or speed, crank, crystal, ice—came with a buzz lasting four to five times longer than that generated by other stimulants. Meth cost more, but users appreciated the bigger bang for the buck. Snorted, injected, or smoked, a fix of meth was like guzzling a gallon of espresso in five seconds.

Molecules laden with meth dissolved in the brain, activating intracellular signals and overstimulating the heart. Arteries feeding the heart quickly dilated, adding to the increased blood flow. Heart rates could climb to 120 beats per minute or higher. Body fat turned to adrenaline, allowing the user to work harder and party longer, the body reacting to the high-octane propellant like a combat jet, afterburners roaring, shooting across the sky.

Yet even combat jets run out of fuel. So with humans and meth. What began as a wondrous euphoria eventually turned to desperate cravings, depression, addiction, even death. The warning *"speed kills"* had originated not with a highway safety program but with methamphetamine.

Millionaire drug lords like the Guerreros, while not the only syndicate under attack, comprised one of the largest and most deeply entrenched operations. The profits from their illegal operation had made the brothers obscenely rich. It also made them difficult targets. They owned mansions in the United States, Mexico, and the Caribbean; they traveled with a contingent of bodyguards; they could afford the best lawyers money could buy; and they were seldom seen together.

As expected, however, the fortieth birthday of one of the brothers brought them together for a weekend celebration. The youngest, Roberto, worked as a minor official at the Mexican consulate in Los Angeles. The nature of international law made his Beverly Hills home the site of many family gatherings and, in effect, extended diplomatic immunity to the entire clan. The Guerreros thus could avoid prosecution for parking tickets, aggravated assault, even the suspicion of murder—all found in their extensive rap sheets.

The implications of that immunity was why jurisdiction and overall responsibility for the impending assault extended all the way to Washington, D.C. Months of intense negotiation at the highest levels had secured the Mexican government's permission to indict the Guerreros. But the drug lords' pockets were deep; Mexican officials owed them many favors. In the end, the current administration's threatened veto of a revote of the North American Free Trade Act had ended the deadlock and paved the way for showdown.

All personnel involved in the early morning raid knew the importance of timing. A fax to the Guerrero house, informing Roberto that his services were no longer required by the Mexican consulate, was to be synchronized with the arrival of the warrant at the SWAT command center. Earlier procurement of the warrant—jointly signed by officials in Los Angeles, Washington, and Mexico—would have been unwise, as the Guerreros' influence reached various levels of local government as well.

In the ravine behind the house, Heiple's team leader, whose nametag read "Toner," motioned that assault was imminent. Heiple nodded and did his best not to fidget, but he had drunk too much coffee at the pre-op briefing. If they didn't move against the house soon, the Guerreros wouldn't be the only ones with wet pants.

Toner listened to the latest word from the command center. "Sensors have picked up movement inside the garage," a voice from headquarters reported. "Somebody just placed a call...Wait, they hung up after two rings. Stay low. Either we've been spotted or they've been tipped off. Either way, be ready to boogie."

Increasingly impatient, the team leader whispered, "What's the delay?"

"We're waiting for the fax. Hold on, here it comes...What the hell?"

Confusion on several circuits, then a new voice trumpeted: "All units, this is Team Leader Alpha. Stand down. I repeat, stand down. Do not proceed against the target."

Toner's reaction was immediate. "Whaddaya mean, don't proceed? We can't sit here all morning. The sun's almost up, for Christ's sake."

"We don't have the warrant. The fax is jammed," Scriff barked.

"Big freakin' deal. It's a formality, Alpha Leader," Toner countered.

"It's not a formality. You know from the briefing that the DA's orders were explicit—do not proceed without proper authorization, and that means signatures. So sit tight, people."

Toner was disgusted. "This is ridiculous! The targets will be out of that house and on their way to the border before you can say adios muchachos."

"Team Leader Delta—you have your orders. Your buddies aren't going anywhere. The target area is sealed, and Gourley's on his way with a backup copy."

Toner hesitated. Yes, the order had been explicit. This was one operation that had to go exactly by the book. No one wanted a ten-month investigation screwed up by a belated warrant. But the case against the Guerreros was airtight, the warrant needless protocol. As proximity team leader, Toner assessed the situation and reached a decision.

With the morning rush hour underway, sleepy-eyed commuters flooded every interstate, freeway, boulevard, avenue, and alley. To compound the problem, it was Monday. Hung over, facing another week of drudgery, the eminently hostile commuters likely would not make way for an emergency vehicle with flashing lights and blaring siren, much less an assistant district attorney driving a battery-powered subcompact.

More than ten miles separated their location in Beverly Hill from the DA's downtown office. All evidence pointed to the Guerreros' imminent departure. It was unlikely Gourley and the warrant would arrive any time other than late. Toner knew that if the Mexicans made it out of the house, they could make it over the border.

A great many people had participated in the investigation. If their efforts were for nothing, heads would roll. On the other hand, if they arrested the kingpins, threw them in jail, exposed and disrupted their distribution network, froze their bank accounts, and ran up attorney fees only to set them free on a technicality, heads would also roll. But the Feds might get lucky: one of the Guerrero lieutenants could cop a plea, thinking the case against the cartel was strong.

Last, but certainly not least, Toner knew that in cases involving multiple-team convergence from divergent locations, standard operating procedure was "one for all and all for one." No team would be left hanging. There was only one logical course of action.

"Fuck protocol," Toner muttered after an ohnosecond of indecision. "All units, this is team leader Delta—suspects are attempting breakout. We are proceeding to target—repeat, proceeding to target. Request immediate backup. Okay people, move, move, move."

A roar of approval greeted Toner's decision. Twenty SWAT personnel in three teams complied. The black-clad figures in the ravine rose as one, charging up the retaining wall and into the backyard of the estate.

Team Delta's objective was to secure the rear of the property and remove resistance. To the left was the roar of a diversionary "flash-bang" incendiary device Team Bravo had only seconds before ignited to disorient the house occupants. As the explosion reverberated, shattering west-side windows, the garage door swung open, and an armor-plated limousine accelerated down the driveway.

Team Charlie personnel, who had been hiding in a telephone-repair truck parked on the street, stormed the front of the house. One of the team had strewn tire-piercing protrusions on the driveway. The odd-shaped spikes could not penetrate the reinforced tires of the Cadillac, but once imbedded, they would make traveling at high speeds a precarious endeavor. The limo hit the street with every tire perforated, veering and swaying like a fifty-dollar jalopy in a cross-country road race.

Down the block in either direction, strategically placed moving vans for nonexistent corporate transfers closed the final avenues of escape. The vans had arrived the day before to allay suspicion. The police had even sent the Guerreros an invitation to a fictitious neighborhood going-away party, knowing full well the drug lords would never stoop to mingle with riffraff.

The limousine lumbered down the route to the Interstate as the margin of escape deteriorated. Though he was an expert driver, the chauffeur's optimism dwindled. No amount of skill could compensate for an unstable vehicle and the lack of an open road.

Pedal to metal, the chauffeur aimed the Cadillac at the narrowing space between the moving van and the brick wall guarding the estates along the boulevard. They couldn't escape. The impending crash would be foolishly futile. But better to be a crash-test dummy than not give it a try. The wrath of his employers would be worse than a month in traction.

The impact was anticlimactic. Explosions from the deployment of the airbags drowned out the tearing and grinding of metal against brick. In a deflating instant, the chase was over. SWAT personnel, weapons drawn, converged on the disabled limousine. Stumbling from the wreckage, hands held high, the Guerreros and their chauffeur squinted against the sun cresting on the horizon.

The SWAT teams notified command center: The house was secure, all evidence intact, the suspects apprehended. The fire department and ambulance units on standby could return to normal duty. It was 6:22 A.M. Not a shot had been fired.

Within minutes, the news vehicles approached the site of the bust. In preparation, police from the LAPD traffic division cordoned off the area with bright yellow tape. On the street in front of the house, media techs readied cameras, established uplinks, and set lines of site for microwave relays. Reporters fluffed their hair with practiced precision. No bloodshot eyes allowed, no wrinkled skin permitted, no out-of-place hair tolerated. Intelligence and credibility be damned—looking good for John and Joan Q. Public was job priority #1.

Just then, the Delta Team leader walked out the front door of the Guerrero house and removed the tight-fitting, sweat-inducing black helmet. Toner gripped the fire-retardant mask and pulled it off it as well. Free of the itchy and stuffy cap, the agent was at last able to take a long, deep breath of fresh air and run her naturally tanned hands through her almost shoulder-length hair.

While she reveled in the luxury of the cool morning air, one TV cameramen zeroed in on the smiling agent, focusing on her nametag. Something about Toner had caught his attention—her wavy black hair (parted on the right, a strand over her left eye) or the thin black eyebrows underlining her wide forehead, the long eyelashes accenting her expressive brown eyes, or perhaps the shape of her nose.

The cameraman prided himself on his ability to authenticate genealogy by examining a person's face. He knew the nose was often the defining trait of an individual's ancestry. Still, Toner's nose defied categorization. Not Indo-European, Asian, or African, but rather—the cameraman concluded—the sum of them all. So too her mouth—a thin upper lip, combined with a sultry lower lip. Together, he guessed, they could form a perfect pout or a wide, unforgettable smile. Even without makeup, the agent had a certain elegance.

Not the beauty-queen variety that turned men's heads at every opportunity. Instead, Toner's attractiveness was the kind found in the girl next door—honest and dependable. It might not turn as many heads, but once turned, they were less inclined to look away.

Meeting the requirements for the SWAT team eighteen months earlier had been a major accomplishment for Angela Carmen Toner. She was 32 years old, rebuilding her life after an automobile accident almost ended her life and her law enforcement career.

With a five-foot-five-inch, 130-pound physique—more aerobically trained than muscular—she had to pass training proficiency tests both rigorous and equal in opportunity. Angela Toner had to perform as well as a six-foot-two man weighing 198 pounds. Three-mile jogs in thirty minutes, mile-and-a-half runs in twelve minutes with full gear, hundred-yard person carries, twenty-foot rope climbs, scaling an eight-foot wall, and stringent marksmanship trials were just the beginning of the process of elimination. Thus her employer, the FBI, working in conjunction with the Los Angeles Police Department, weeded out those individuals not able to handle the rigor of an urban search-and-assault team.

Angela applied herself with an intensity that surprised everyone who knew her. In the months since her promotion, the scrappy agent had grown to love the excitement, camaraderie, and danger of her job. Toner blossomed from a competent field agent into a natural leader, eager to be the first one to storm through a locked door or accept a hazardous assignment.

But Angela felt a tinge of apprehension from her early-morning bravado. She knew the decision to ignore Scriff's order might cost her more than a slap on the wrist, as this was not the first time her mouth had run ahead of her intuition.

With the assault concluded, the SWAT personnel prepared to leave the scene, and Toner joined the exodus. The unfolding mass-media spectacle disgusted her. Shaking her head as the vultures jockeyed for position, Angela did not see Gourley until it was too late. The flustered and sweating rookie prosecutor rushed up waving the tardy warrant like a pompom at a pep rally. Fatigued from her 3:00 A.M. wakeup, Toner did think fast enough to flee from the hyperventilating assistant DA.

Gourley thrust the wrinkled document into her trembling hand. "Sorry for the delay, but traffic was *horrendous*. Anyway, here's the warrant. I thought you people were supposed to wait until I got here?"

Toner was speechless. Looking over the ADA's shoulder—eyes wide with shock—she noticed some of the media snoops aiming cameras and microphones in their direction. She crumpled up the warrant, shoved it into her pocket, grabbed Gourley's arm, and walked back towards the house.

"Uh, thanks Phil, but this wasn't necessary," she proclaimed in an exaggerated voice. "We already had a warrant...on site...before the bust. This is just a backup. Sorry you made the trip for nothing."

Gourley stared at Toner in confusion while the flustered agent looked back at the camera crews, hoping no one had captured his statement on tape. Just then, Felicia Scriff charged in, shoving the assistant DA to the side.

"Get the hell out of here, Gourley. I'm sure you've got work to do downtown." Grabbing Toner's arm with a tight, pinching grip, the older agent walked away from the unfolding circus. Gourley, who'd finally acquired an understanding of the situation, left the scene, doing his best to avoid the news profiteers.

Out of harm's way, Scriff continued her tirade, her face taut with anger, her index finger dangerously poised in Toner's face.

"You're in a world of trouble if they got that on tape," she hissed. "You had to be the hero, didn't you? Well, we'll see how much bluster you've got trying to explain your interpretation of protocol to the deputy assistant director. After debriefing, I expect to see you in his office. You got that, Agent Toner?"

Toner met the field supervisor's icy stare. "I've got it." She pulled her arm free and stormed away.

Scriff, her job having just begun, turned towards the crowd of reporters, took a deep breath, and walked to where they waited. With cameras rolling, the supervisor began to answer questions about the drug bust, the Guerreros, and the warrant.

In Moscow, a light snowfall ended shortly after dinner. High above the snow-covered streets, two girls stared at their computer screens. As usual, they'd eaten in their room, stacking their dishes on a tray by the door.

Now they were now back on-line, trying to determine the seriousness of their sister's injuries. Attempts to monitor her condition met with increasing interference—futile attempts to thwart their mission. Slowed by many electronic roadblocks, they nevertheless continued their task.

They'd been told not to meddle. Since when do children listen? Their sister was in trouble; nothing else mattered. What did *he* expect them to do? Let her die alone, anonymous, in a sterile intensive-care unit on the other side of the world? That was simply not acceptable.

They'd known Melissa would be the first to go. They'd always known. They understood and acted, motivated by the obvious truth…

The search for Nyentzi had begun.

2

▼

Road Kill

"Much better," Toner thought to herself. After debriefing, she'd showered, brushed her hair, and put on a navy-blue pants suit. Shuffling paperwork, she was not yet involved in the debate relative to timeliness of the warrant. No repercussions—and there were certain to be some—had trickled to her level. But the word on the street was not good. If heads rolled, hers would be numero uno.

The phone interrupted her musing. "Yes, sir," she said, answering a summons to the deputy assistant director's office on the third floor. Walking down the hallway towards his office, she passed many desks and cubicles. There was none of the usual prairie-dogging—all heads were lowered with no eye contact. Fellow agents went about their business as if Toner's execution had already taken place.

At the end of the hall, blocking the path to her destination, was a large, L-shaped, charcoal-gray desk—the "Checkpoint Charlie" of the Los Angeles District Office of the Federal Bureau of Investigation. Sitting stiffly behind the desk was one of the most dour and imposing women Toner had ever met, her boss's personal secretary, Mrs. Malone.

The secretary wordlessly observed Toner's hesitant approach. Malone had clipped gray hair, pearl-rimmed glasses, and a face displaying thinly veiled suspicion. J. Edgar Hoover had not yet begun his dance in women's lingerie when she started with the bureau—or so the rumor went. Inflexible, demanding, and autocratic, she went by no name but Mrs. Malone. Those in her presence spoke it softly and with utmost respect.

"Hi, Mrs. M," Toner whispered. The secretary had taken a shine to Toner, and she allowed her to forgo certain proprieties. "I take it the Grand Pooh-Bah's expecting me."

Malone managed to smile without a perceptible change in expression. "He certainly is." Her eyes swept the scene to make sure no one listened and continued, "You go right in, honey. That was one heck of a job you did out there this morning. You should be real proud."

"I should be real *shot*—at least that's what I've heard. I don't know what it is, but people have no sense of humor these days."

"Give 'em hell, Angie."

Toner nodded and took a deep breath. She smiled at Mrs. Malone—who winked back—then opened the door and stepped into the office.

Deputy Assistant Director Alfred E. Hatton sat at his desk, in the midst of a heated phone conversation. Field Supervisor Scriff stood at attention in front of the desk. She shushed the new arrival and motioned Toner to join her. For Scriff's benefit, Hatton had turned on the speaker phone. Angela guessed by the tone and subject matter of the dialog that the person on the other end would not like knowing she was in the room.

Toner tried not to listen, but under the circumstances, politeness was impossible. Word that the warrant had arrived after the arrest of the Guerreros had passed through official—and unofficial—channels. Al Hatton, after a quick frown in Toner's direction, continued schmoozing like a game-show host, trying to convince Washington that the brouhaha was a misunderstanding and arraignment of the Guerreros could proceed unimpeded.

"Come on, Chuck...you know how the press is with these things," Hatton, an aging Vietnam vet, said. "Everybody's looking for an angle for the six o'clock news. All we've heard is the typical line of BS, but not a shred of evidence. You have *our word* that the Guerrero bust went strictly by the numbers. We can't help it if some idiot from the DA's office stumbled around with a backup copy *after* the press arrived. We're clean on this one, Chuck, and we're going full bore prosecuting those Tabasco-snortin' SOBs."

"I hope so, Al!" bellowed the voice from D.C. "A major expenditure in assets and manpower—without successful prosecution—will send every bloodsucking politician and reporter hot on our butts. Take the bull by the horns! Put an end to those rumors. *Pronto!*"

Hatton did his best to reassure. "Yes, sir. We all put a lot of hard work in on this one. We're already cleaning up the cartel's operation, so I think we can all sleep better tonight knowing *our* efforts did some serious damage here today."

"Whatever—*just get the job done*. By the way, how're the grandkids..." the voice from D.C. droned on.

Realizing the deputy assistant director would go on for awhile, Toner sighed and let her mind wander. She smiled as she considered Hatton's choice of words to his boss in Washington. With the potential for blame to be passed around, Hatton tended to use words like *we, us,* and *our*. When kudos were in order, all he could manage was *I, me,* and *mine*. Such was life in the food chain.

Toner scanned the mountain of clutter that was Hatton's office. Several open file-cabinet drawers spewed papers and documents. Useless bric-a-brac and office paraphernalia littered the shelves behind the desk. Staplers, folders, procedure manuals, videos, picture frames, an empty Kleenex box, dirty coffee mugs, and other objects vied for space.

On the floor next to the desk was a government-issue wastebasket, bruised and battered from the occasional frustrated kick. Overflowing with used Styrofoam cups, chicken bones, soiled paper products, a crushed pizza box, and too many fast food bags to count, it was testament to society's quest for convenience.

The window ledge hosted a variety of houseplants—all coated with dust and spider webs. Begonias, philodendron, ferns, a schefflera, and several cacti were haphazardly arrayed in the merciless sun. Every plant, except one foolhardy cactus, had long ago given up any pretense of life and gone on to the great greenhouse in the sky.

Looking down upon the disaster that was Al Hatton's desk, Toner pursed her lips in disapproval. The only basket, marked *IN*, overflowed with enough paper to train a puppy. Of the twelve or so pencils strewn about, all needed sharpening; every eraser was worn away.

From experience, Toner knew Hatton's office was a reflection of the deputy assistant director's inner character. His mind had the cohesion of road kill and the organization of a lollapalooza. Standing there, knowing full well the trouble she was in, Toner could only wonder how Mrs. Malone managed to keep her hands off the clutter. No one—not Mrs. Malone, not the janitorial staff, not a team from the Center for Disease Control—dared enter Hatton's personal pigpen with so much as a broom, much less a bulldozer, heavy-duty trash compactor, or flame-thrower.

Toner glanced to her side and saw the disapproval chiseled on Scriff's face. Clearly she had stood there some time. Toner looked down again just as the deputy assistant director ended the call. He turned the speaker off with a hard stab of his index finger and sternly looked up.

"It's so nice to see you again, Agent Toner. Glad you could take time out of your busy schedule to pay me a visit. If I may cut to the proverbial chase, what the hell were you thinking out there this morning? If this were some five-and-dime downtown bust, I'd be screaming 'fuck the protocol,' too. But we're talking about the Guerreros, dammit. You know damn well they've got the best damned lawyers money can buy. Now you've handed them a technicality...and we've lost too many damned cases in the past on damned technicalities. You were briefed, dammit. You knew that goddamned warrant was as political as it was legal, didn't you? *Didn't you?*"

Toner placed her hands on her hips and leaned forward.

"What was I supposed to do, *sir*? Let them drive away in that chauffeur-driven tank?" Refusing to back down, she pointed a finger in Hatton's direction. "The press would've loved that! Nothing like a high-speed chase down Interstate 5 to start off the evening news."

Scriff interjected, "That will be enough."

Toner ignored the field supervisor. "That fax was working fine when Alpha's techs checked it in pre-op, but you know what? It doesn't matter. It doesn't matter whether the fax jammed, whether they were tipped off, whether Gourley got stuck in traffic until after the press showed up. It doesn't matter one bit, and you know why? Huh—you know why?"

Without waiting, without taking a breath, Toner answered her own question.

"I'll tell you why. Because it's an airtight case, *that's* why. We did our homework, like good little boys and girls. Airtight...*sir*."

Hatton scratched his chin and looked out the window as he considered Toner's assertion. "Trouble is, she's right," he brooded to himself. "If she hadn't taken the initiative, those bastards would've been in Tijuana by 8:00 A.M. Smart-aleck-thinks-she-knows-it-all acted just like I would've in her position. And that's the goddamned problem—there's no way I can let her know...at least not today."

Hatton looked up at Scriff, hoping she'd take the initiative in dealing with Toner. Under-standing what he wanted, Scriff refused to meet Hatton's eyes, gazing instead out the window into the noontime haze of Los Angeles. For several moments, the room was silent.

Toner took the lull in the action as her cue. "So, if that's all you needed me for, I'll get back to my desk and finish up the paperwork."

Just a little faster and Angela might have made it to the elevator before they noticed she was gone. Taken aback by her sudden about-face, Scriff and Hatton were almost rendered mute. But the deputy assistant director emerged from his trance.

"Now just a minute," he snapped.

"Oh, is there anything else?" the retreating agent responded. "I thought we were done."

"Listen, we can't have you hanging around the office."

"You can't have me *what*?"

"Hanging around—the office. We can't have you hanging around the office."

"Why would I hang around your office? I avoid your office like the plague."

"Not my office, *the* office—the whole damn building. We can't have you hanging around the building. All we need now is for some scum-sucking reporter to look into the identity of the agent seen walking around the Guerrero house with a warrant that arrived on the scene—*after the fact*. If somebody with a mike or legal pad cornered you with one simple question, you'd spill your guts for sure."

Toner's indignation was immediate. "*I would not*. I can keep a secret as well as the next guy. Besides, I'm not your problem. Gourley is."

Hatton stared at her over the rim of his glasses, unconvinced. Toner's reputation for foot-in-the-mouth honesty was legendary. Everyone knew she was the worst liar and the least effective keeper-of-secrets in Los Angeles County. Obsessed with telling the truth, Angela Toner was incapable of verbalizing nothing less. No matter how brutal the facts, she'd blurt them out—consequences be damned. Anyone needing an opinion about a questionable fashion statement came to Toner. Anyone looking to keep information under wraps kept her out of the loop.

Graffiti in government rest rooms stated that Aldrich Ames kept secrets better than Angela did.

The candid field agent recognized the look and realized her bluff had been called. "No, seriously…I can keep my mouth shut about this. No problem. None at all."

"You said that last time. Remember last time?"

"Yeah…but this is different."

"How so?" Hatton asked.

"This time I mean it."

Hatton jabbed the air with his finger. "*No way*. This case is too big for one of those cross-your-fingers pledges. The district attorney's taken care of Gourley, so that leaves you. Scriff and I have been discussing our options, which unfortunately are pretty limited. But the way we see it, if the Guerreros can afford thousand-dollar-an-hour attorneys, we can pull a few strings, too. We've decided to disappear you—keep you out of harm's way."

Toner started to interrupt, but Hatton's raised eyebrows stated his firm control. She shut her mouth, and her boss continued.

"As a matter of fact, a nice reassignment will work just fine. We've got a case that's so *important*, so *vital*, so *time-consuming*, those pesky parasites from the *LA Times* will have a better chance getting an interview with Elvis himself than with you. You're gonna be digging deep on this one, kiddo. In fact, I wouldn't be surprised if your pretty face began appearing on the side of milk cartons."

Toner's jaw dropped. "Now! You're gonna pull me off the case *now*. I busted my butt on this assignment, and you're reassigning me *now*? Aw, c'mon—not on some *frickin'* technicality! And what the heck's wrong with the DA's office, anyway—they afraid of a little courtroom competition?"

"Courtroom competition has nothing to do with it. I just happen to be a little more concerned about your career than you are. Stop and think of the consequences of another major screw up in light of what happened last year in Long Beach. You're lucky you still have a job, Agent Toner."

"Spare me the speeches—you know the bureau can't fire me."

"You know something we don't?"

"Yeah, slaves have to be sold."

Hatton rolled his eyes in exasperation as Toner continued to argue.

"And I suppose nobody's ever heard of a subpoena," she said. "I'm not that hard to find, you know."

"We have that contingency covered," Scriff interjected. "Article 103.4a of the UCFFFA grants us the authority to assign personnel *pro tempore* to any unit or department within the bureau should there be a requested need for said agent's specialized skills, expertise, or knowledge. You *will* be hard to find because you'll be on assignment out of the building." Scriff leaned over Hatton's desk and retrieved a thick, maroon-colored book—as if the manual's mere existence proved her point. In dealing with Angela Toner, however, rules and regulations seldom sufficed.

"This really makes a lot of sense. One minute I'm a leper with a badge and the next I'm some sort of expert?"

"Bitch all you want—the paperwork's done," Hatton said. After a moment, he continued. "Listen…Angie, you did a great job infiltrating the Guerreros. We all know that. And we're not about to let those scumbags sleaze their way out of this indictment. The evidence is solid, and the case is strong. They're not going to walk, so understand this reassignment—*temporary* reassignment, I remind you—has nothing to do with your performance. We just want you out of here for the time being, for your own good, for the good of the case."

Looking down at her boss, eyes wide, mouth open in shock, Angela displayed some of the acting skills she'd picked up in a theater course at the University of Michigan.

"Are you telling me this has nothing to do with my job performance? You...you mean I get reassigned, no time off, no pats on the back, because you like me, you *really* like me?"

"Could we dispense with the sarcasm just this once?" Hatton barked. "Thank you. Now listen up—this is not a high-priority case, but it could prove interesting." He picked up a small compact disk in a clear plastic sleeve and neatly tossed it to Toner, who caught it with her right hand. "Take the file, review it, get any additional information you need, but be out of the building by 1700 hours."

Toner held up the disk, ready to argue, but Hatton cut her off.

"And once you get into the case, don't ask why you're involved. That file was assigned to the National Security Agency, but it's all I could find on short notice."

"Come on, sir. You know how the NSA feels about encroachment. And what do you expect me to do with a case totally out of my jurisdiction? Couldn't you just rent the video? And please don't give me that song and dance about 'read the file and improvise,'" Toner mimicked, lowering her voice for a respectable impression of her boss.

"There you have it. You've answered your own question. See that, Scriff, she's finally catching on. Yes, read the file and improvise—*figure it out*. Use some of that initiative we're so familiar with. And quit pouting. This'll only take a couple of weeks. You know we've been preparing for this indictment for months. We just need to make sure you're not on any of the witness lists, that's all. And in the meantime, you won't be here, stumbling into reporters and trouble."

Toner looked around, her body trembling with frustration. She looked out the window, at Scriff, and then at the her boss. She knew they had her. Worse than that, she knew they knew they had her.

Her left hand resting on her hip, Toner tightened her grip on the file disk. Slightly pumping her arm, wanting to fling the file across the room, she held her breath and mentally counted to eight. Maintaining her dignity at that moment was the hardest thing she'd done all day.

Hatton didn't help her mood either, leaning back in his chair, hands behind his balding head, the picture of contentment and dominion. Scriff stood by, waiting for the next round of fireworks.

"Dammit. This is *not* fair, and you know it. I worked hard on the Guerrero case and for what? Slam, bam, thank you, mam."

Hatton grinned. "That's life, Toner. Sometimes you're a steel-belted radial—sometimes you're a slow squirrel. So quit yer bitchin'. *You screwed up*, dammit—it's that simple. Now get the hell out of here and back to work."

Muttering under her breath, Toner walked to the door, opened it, and stepped out. She looked back and smiled. Then she gently closed the door behind her. The message was clear—there was nothing she'd rather do than slam Hatton's office door, hard.

3

MADE IN AMERICA

A moment of peace. The way his day was going, Al Hatton knew he'd better enjoy it while it lasted. He kicked back in his chair and thought about the brave new world of interoffice politics. He had a feud on his hands—between Angela Toner, who had left to research her new assignment, and Felicia Scriff, who, after again voicing her dissatisfaction with the younger agent, was off causing trouble elsewhere.

"I ought to quit refereeing and start selling tickets," Hatton muttered to himself. "Let 'em handle their frickin' spats like men!"

But he had to laugh as he thought about ground zero, the impetus for the animosity between the two women. Scriff had been teaching a training session for rookie field agents when she first met the spunky Toner. For some odd reason—Hatton couldn't imagine what—Scriff had taken an instant dislike to the young woman, something about her attitude.

After Scriff confronted her about some ridiculous rule or regulation, the rookie fired off one of her flip remarks. Scriff would have none of that and rebuked Toner for her disrespectful demeanor.

"Oh no, Felicia, you've got it all wrong. There's no way that comment was disrespectful."

"It most certainly was, young lady. What makes you think it wasn't?"

"The dictionary. You see, Agent Scriff, the definition of disrespect is to 'take respect *from*.' For me to be disrespectful of you, we'd have to assume I respected you in the first place, which I certainly did not. Nothing from nothing *is* nothing."

Their relationship had gone downhill from there.

"Smart aleck, know-it-all…" the deputy assistant director mumbled.

Being part of the problem himself, Hatton was at a loss as how best to deal with the situation. Scriff hated his guts, and Toner thought he should have been uninstalled decades ago. In fact, Hatton and other aging Vietnam vets had become lightning rods for the dissatisfaction of the Gen-X-ers. His efforts at mediation were worse than ineffective; they were counterproductive.

Angela Toner and her peers came to the bureau with advanced degrees in law enforcement, criminal psychology, and other areas too numerous to list. The younger generation labeled the older agents—especially the vets—dinosaurs, mongoloids, knuckle-draggers, and Luddites. Angela Toner danced a fine line between sarcasm and harassment with the skill and grace of a Bolshoi ballerina.

As far as Toner was concerned, Hatton's years in the military were nothing more than time spent learning applications of the expletive that so conveniently rhymed with *truck*—not that she was above borrowing the term to suit her labile moods.

"What the fuck does she want me to do?" Hatton mulled. "Run around whooping, 'Oh gosh, we blew the bust. The Guerreros are gonna get off on a technicality. Geezo peezo, won't Washington be angry now?' Geezo peezo, my ass. Goddamn Toner—if she experienced half the shit we did in 'Nam, she'd end up in bed for a month with Russell Stover and a jug of Chablis. God damn, now I'm sounding like my old man! To hell with this growing-old shit."

The deputy assistant director would be sixty in July. His retirement wasn't far off—a thought that excited both Hatton and Toner. But Hatton felt he had a few good years left. Attitude was as important as physical condition. And if he'd learned anything else in six decades, it was that half of being smart is knowing what you're dumb at.

Despite Toner's criticism of his management style, squabby physique, and lack of intelligence, Alfred E. Hatton was smart enough to know his limitations.

He sighed and glanced at the personnel file on his desk. He knew its contents as if it were his own. Shaking his head in wonder, the aging baby boomer had a nagging suspicion that Angela Carmen Toner would be the death of him yet. "She'll probably kill my with her incessant complaining..." he brooded.

Since his discharge from the army in 1970, Al Hatton hadn't heard anyone gripe as much as Toner. She turned the moan and grumble from an annoyance to an art form—and she did it with pride. Toner complained about her job, her pay, her responsibilities, her pay, her clothes, her superiors, her subordinates, and, of course, her pay.

"Well, sir, it's like this..." he'd heard her say. "You've got me working my fingers to the bone for slave wages pulling double duty while you sit on your butt screaming at me to knuckle down get crackin' hop to it put my shoulder to the plow. But I'm pooped out on my last legs ready to drop washed up totally blitzed and whacked out. After all, *sir*, I'm *only* human..."

"Goddamn walking thesaurus. Goddamn black hole of innocence. But enough's enough," he thought, opening the file to finish Toner's transfer orders. Hatton knew it wasn't her nature to be anything but negative. Like the rest of her generation, Angela Toner had been nurtured by the American media. No target was too small, no human too pure.

But he knew Toner better than she thought he did. He knew who her heroes were and who she looked to for guidance and snappy rebuttal. Toner knew the lines and did the impressions to boot. "What the hell should I expect? How can any generation raised on Dr. Seuss, Bart Simpson, and MTV take anything seriously?"

Despite the baggage, Hatton gave Toner a lot of credit—again, more than she would admit. Though her obsession with honesty and fairness was half the reason for his stupid stunt of grabbing the file disk from the NSA, he had to admire the kid. In the six years he'd known her, she'd never wavered from what she knew to be right or wrong. As Toner herself had said, an ethics test is not multiple choice.

Hatton took a personal interest in the young agent's career. More than once he had kept her behind out of a sling—especially after the accident. After Toner recovered and was able to return to work, she was despondent, angry, and about as much fun to be around as Felicia Scriff. There'd even been talk about taking away her service weapon and assigning her to a desk job. That she did not slip into a catatonic depression after that drunk driver killed her husband and put her in the hospital—with injuries including a miscarriage—was testament enough to her perseverance and self-confidence.

Hatton had suggested she make a minor career move. Qualifying for the Southern California Drug Enforcement SWAT team turned out to be the therapy Angela needed.

The Deputy Assistant Director had been impressed with Angela Toner from the first day her file landed on his desk. Old Lady Malone, against all bureau regulations, had already read it and formed an opinion. "Get her on the team. Shut up and do it," she'd ordered. Hatton knew better than to argue.

On her personnel questionnaire, which featured such wonderful clichéd items as: "The book I've been reading is…" and "My personal hero is…" Toner's answer to the race question had caught his eye. Hatton knew the racial classification system to be antiquated, but change came slowly to the U.S. Census Bureau. That being the case, someone reviewing Toner's file might conclude she'd answered to be *cute* (a word she detested) or to score a few *brownie points* (ditto). So Hatton gave her a chance to explain.

While 30 percent of U.S. citizens with Toner's genetic background called themselves *multiracial* and other percentages opting for similar labels, she had simply checked the 'Some Other Race' box and neatly printed *American*. Not for political motives or patriotic ideology, but for the simple reason it got her point across with as little fanfare as possible. It was also the truth.

In their first face-to-face interview, Angela explained her answer. She'd shown Hatton photos of her multiethnic, multiracial family. She proudly told him that if humans were dogs, she would be a consummate Heinz 57.

"Isn't it hard being multiracial? Don't you catch hell from all directions?" he'd asked, wanting to learn more about her character.

The young recruit didn't directly answer his question but pointed to her file. As Hatton read, he understood why Toner was so confident in her heritage. Her carefully scripted response to the question "What is your favorite quote?" seemed remarkably appropriate: "There is nothing so indigenous, so completely 'made in America' as we."— W.E.B. DuBois.

After reading that and seeing proof of the African-American, Japanese-American, Native-American, Italian, and English genealogies flowing through her veins, Hatton knew what she meant. Angela Carmen Toner was, by *any* definition, as American as they came.

Nevertheless, he wished the day would come when she'd admit he wasn't such a bad boss. "Fuck…who the hell am I kidding?" Hatton muttered out loud. He could put on a few pounds, get some fake white hair and whiskers, dress up in a red suit, run around yelling "Ho, ho, ho," and Toner would still give him shit.

He had to laugh, though. He'd overheard her describing the way he decorated his apartment for Christmas as "chalk outlines of a fat guy and eight reindeer. Oh, and a candle."

The deputy assistant director signed Toner's reassignment requisition, closed her file, and placed it on a stack of paperwork for Mrs. Malone. He knew he would have the last laugh, just like his old sergeant did. Sooner or later, Angela Toner would reach the age where she'd look in the mirror and scream, "Oh my god, I'm my mother!"

"And that constant whine of hers about my alleged lack of attention span," he thought. "Well, that's a bunch of…Whoa, look at the time. Better get back to work."

Her face strained with frustration, Angela entered her cubicle, slumped in her chair, and stared at the ceiling. She held the file disk in her right hand while her computer idled. Surveying the small, efficient workspace, her gaze rested on a picture cube containing five photographs. Casually tossing the disk aside, she picked up the cube and examined each photo as if for the first time.

Two of the photos—studies in contrast—were of her grandparents. In one, a lanky African-American man stood beside his young, lighter-skinned, half-Native-American bride. He wore his army uniform with such pride that Toner could not suppress a faint smile, remembering his almost religious sense of patriotism. She treasured the stories he had told her, and she knew that at the time of the photograph, Grandpa St. Claire had just returned from the war in Europe. As a staff sergeant in the all-black 761st Tank Battalion, the medals on his chest were all the proof he needed of his valor and love of country.

In the second picture, Grandma-san Sugihara held her son—Toner's father—while two young daughters clutched at her skirt. Her husband had also fought in Europe during WWII, with the Hawaiian Nisei 442nd regiment. But Saburo (Sam) Sugihara had not been so lucky. He was buried in a small cemetery in France.

Past the difficulty of being a white woman wedded to a Japanese-American, Angela's grandmother never remarried after her hero's death. Raising three children on her own, she had moved to San Diego to be closer to her family, where she'd worked as a cleaning woman. To protect them from anti-Japanese backlash, she'd changed their last name to her maiden name, though she remained Flora Sugihara until the day she died. One of Angela's greatest disappointments was never getting to know her better. Grandma-san had died too young—when Angela was just four.

The blend of ethnic and racial characteristics in her background helped make Angela Toner an effective agent. She could pass for a light-skinned African American, a Sicilian, Indian, or Latino. On the assignment involving the Guerreros, she'd gone undercover, posing as a Cuban-American office manager. Working for the cartel in San Diego, she gained its trust and confidence by eradicating a nasty computer virus from the cartel's mainframe.

What she didn't tell them was that her team was responsible for the infected computer in the first place. The bureau had broken through the Guerreros' bargain-basement firewall. Toner conveniently showed up looking for work at their phony import emporium several days later. After proving her technical skills, they hired her on the spot.

Cautious businessmen, the Guerreros thoroughly investigated one "Maria Nilda Sanchez." The report contained only what the FBI wanted them to know. There was no mention of an Angela C. Toner.

Two of the photos remaining showed Angela's mother, father, and two brothers: One, from 1980, showed the family (Angela at age five in pigtails) crowding the Christmas tree at their home in Ann Arbor, Michigan. The other, taken in 1993, showed them at her high-school graduation.

Angela's smile faded when she shifted the cube and contemplated the fifth picture. Another ceremony, a strong young man of ruddy complexion and straight black hair. He wore a blue police officer's uniform and held Toner's lace-wrapped arm in his. Glued to the side was a small black ribbon, slightly crushed. She stared at the photo until, as if coming out of a trance, she glanced at her watch, hastily set the cube down, and resumed her work.

Inserting the file disk into her computer, Angela waited for the appropriate prompts. Knowing the deputy assistant director as well as she did, Angela understood her disappearing act could involve anything from a ruthless mob of jaywalking geriatrics, to Girl-Scout-cookie fraud. In fact, nothing Hatton did surprised her.

Until now.

Instead of automatically responding to her initial query, the screen remained blank. The opening page of standard bureau disks contained a synopsis of the disk's contents. Dubbed the Basic Biographical Summary, or BBS, the overlay was a separate file, set to autorun, so that an agent could update it without accessing other programs. The BBS contained such information as who and which department compiled the report, a brief assessment, particulars on the subject(s), action taken, and recommendations for future work. That is what Toner should have had in front of her—not an empty screen.

Multitasking to her computer's explorer program, she expected to find a properties message indicating that the disk was blank or defective. It was neither. The disk contained well over two hundred megabytes of data, though no files were visible—no initiate files, no read-mes, no cd.ids. Instead, there were only two folders. Remembering her years of computer training, she shrugged and clicked on the first folder, labeled "Revkin." Consisting of nothing but analogous data, it was not accessible without external prompt.

A click on the second folder rewarded Angela's patience; there she discovered what she'd been taught to look for—the log-on icon. With a quick click, the screen changed, and the disk drive hummed into operation, searching out the hidden information.

While the computer went about its work, Angela reached under her desk and retrieved a battered thermos. She unscrewed the dented lid and poured dark, steaming liquid into a brightly decorated mug sitting on a hot plate next to the computer. The thermos put away, she took a cautious sip of the caffeine-laden brew and scanned the opening report.

She shook her head in bewilderment—there had to be a mistake. The file couldn't possibly be an official government document. The format was wrong; there were no reference points, no signatures, and no clearance parameters. Even the font was wrong. Most federal files used Arial 12-point. She was reading Times New Roman 14-point.

Angela ignored the disk's impropriety, took another sip, and read the opening screen. She could only wonder what Al Hatton was thinking when he relegated her such a vague assignment. Not only was the file improperly constructed, but the text read more like a domestic dispute than a case involving the FBI.

James and Olga Revkin, address simply listed as Los Angeles. James was an American; Olga, a naturalized Russian citizen. Two children, both born in the United States, reference to additional documentation on the oldest, unnamed daughter. The mother, Olga, currently hospitalized at the Beverly Hills Psychiatric Hospital.

Toner sat back and thought about the last bit of information: "BHPH—what a fun place. I can just see the mysterious Mrs. Revkin. Overweight, overstressed, hair in rollers, needing a break from Brownies, PTA meetings, and fast-food kiddie meals."

Mrs. Revkin's extemporaneous vacation in a locked psychiatric unit did not seem to be working. She had tried to check herself out against medical advice. In a counter petition, her husband, James, and an unnamed doctor had obtained a court order for an extended stay. Her rejoinder was an attempt to seek divorce, gain custody of the children, and secure a restraining order against James.

"*Days of Our Lives,*" Toner thought, "but hardly worth the disk space."

And that was it. No mention of Olga's success with her legal struggle, no diagnosis other than that she posed a threat to herself and her family, no treatment guidelines, nothing. The file lacked even a personal history on the Revkins—where they worked, where they went to church, why the bureau was involved.

Knowing there *had* to be other information, Angela prodded the page-down key. She was rewarded with additional notes, but the information was glaringly brief.

Titled "Subject," the next page referred to the Revkins' seven-year-old daughter, Melissa Irina Revkin. Date of birth August 17, 2000: Santa Anita Community Hospital, Pasadena. A list of allergies, with reference to a more complete medical history file elsewhere on the disk. The child was currently hospitalized at the Santa Anna Marine Corps Air Facility, but there was no indication either parent was a government employee or in the military.

Toner continued to read. She learned that Melissa Revkin had been seriously injured in an automobile accident, yet there was no date, location, or circumstance pertaining to the accident. Only the girl's injuries—including severe cranial and abdominal trauma—and the fact she was in a non-responsive coma were listed. Routine brain-wave-pattern tests suggested significant abnormalities, but again the data was incomplete.

As unusual as everything she'd seen, the information at the bottom of the page seized Toner's attention. From all indications, the abdominal trauma would lead to eventual kidney failure. Tissue samples harvested during routine screening for kidney donors showed no match within Melissa's immediate family.

That in itself was not remarkable. But the report of additional testing, including DNA sequencing, opened Angela's eyes. They—whoever *they* were—had determined the girl was not genetically related to *anyone* in her immediate family, despite ample documentation of Melissa's natural birth by her mother, Olga Revkin.

The last line on the third page, which was as far as the baffled agent was able to go, included a vague, unsettling statement: "Priority—verify or refute genetic engineering. Is this NYENTZI?"

Working in a government agency where rhetoric flowed like water and too often secretaries seemed paid by the word, Angela appreciated brevity as much as the next person. The Revkin file, however, was too much of a good thing.

What little of the disk she had seen would give any field agent worth his or her mettle reason to pause and ask for more data. She'd reached the end of her search, and no matter what prompts and queries she tried, she was effectively locked out of most of the Revkin file.

And what the hell was *Nyentzi*?

Angela Toner had been through her share of supermarket checkouts. She'd heard stories about genetic engineering and seen the headlines, the "positively, absolutely authentic" photographs of genetically enhanced and/or cloned humans.

Rumors of mad scientists trafficking in the manufacture and implantation of retooled embryos had been the source of urban mythinformation for decades. Most of the reports, however, could be categorized as sci-fi improbabilities or involving bogus alien-human matings. Only since the late 1990s, with the cloning of monkeys and sheep, had the technology that made genetic engineering a credible science become readily available. Available enough to produce a discipline called bioethics and fuel a movement against genetic research, a movement beginning to supplant anti-abortion as the battle cry of conservative and fundamentalist groups throughout the world.

From an introduction-to-genetics course she'd taken in college, Angela knew that in the early 1990s, while studying the cause of multiple sclerosis, scientists had developed software and technology capable of decoding genetic material twenty to fifty times faster than anything previously available. In eight hours, researchers could decipher as much genetic material as had previously taken a year.

From that point, identifying the location of specific genes had increased with a fast-paced domino effect. Parkinson's, hemophilia, breast cancer, Alzheimer's, immune system, memory, cystic fibrosis, mental retardation, schizophrenia, and thousands of other genes had been cataloged and mapped in a series of multibillion-dollar hereditary blueprints. In the new millennium, even xeno-transplantation—the use of genetically altered animal organs for human surgery—was fast becoming an accepted medical technique.

Angela had no quarrel with genetic research that alleviated suffering and death. But the other stories—the ones involving renegade scientists and secret research facilities—unnerved her. Moving beyond the replacement of unhealthy genes, some researchers had allegedly and illegally set their investigative sights on genetic determinism, on the shepherd instead of the sheep. Unwilling to accept the physical and mental traits proved by nature, science now teetered on a threshold, waiting for the push that would propel mankind into the realm previously reserved for God.

Toner had heard just enough of the whispers to tease her imagination, a belief in the slimmest possibility they were real. The cost of reengineering an organism in an already-established laboratory was negligible. *It could be done.* But no one had produced the slightest legitimate proof that it *had been done.*

Angela glanced at her watch and realized she had one other problem. Deputy Assistant Director Hatton wanted her out of the building in less than four hours. She had better find something—anything—in the Revkin file to justify her existence for the next few weeks. Leaning back, finishing her coffee, Toner remembered something her father, a philosophy professor at the University of Michigan, had told her about such situations: "Nothing is ever lost. Someone just put it where it doesn't belong."

According to her computer, which had never lied before, the disk contained more than two hundred megabytes of data—data that might include complete medical histories, video clips, and other multimedia applications. Angela Toner was certain she had the information she needed somewhere on the disk. She just couldn't access 99 percent of it.

But she knew someone who could—and his office was two floors down.

4

SPUD

Kaloostian didn't hear the soft knock on his office door, or the slightly louder knock several seconds later. But the third knock—he definitely heard that. Not many people had the courage to bother him in his basement sanctuary; it was something important or it was *her*. Whatever the reason, his please-use-the-other-door sign was again being ignored.

He repositioned his wheelchair for a better view of the door's reflection in the mirror above the sink but did not take off the headphones. It was only 12:55, and he still had five minutes left of his lunch break. As an employee of the federal government, Gregory H. Kaloostian had learned to be careful about such things.

When the knocking ceased, Kaloostian hoped the transgressor had gone. A moment later, however, the only door to the room opened and she poked in her head. Pretending to not see or hear her, he closed his eyes to mere slits and waited.

Glancing around the room, Angela Toner saw her friend relaxing in the corner. Her eyes widened with the realization she was interrupting his quiet time. Knowing she had a good reason, Toner slipped into the room and softly closed the door. Biting her lower lip in dread, she tiptoed to an extra chair like a schoolgirl in the principal's office. Understanding Kaloostian's moods, as well as his routine, she looked at her watch and waited for one o'clock to arrive.

Even from forty feet, she could hear the music from his headphones. Her friend was hard of hearing, as were many people who liked earsplitting music. When she'd asked why he liked it so loud, Kaloostian had embarked on an irrelevant commentary about the necessity of drowning out the suppressive voices of modern society—which, of course, was a total crock. In the four years she'd known the slightly off-center Armenian, Angela had learned that many of her questions about his unusual habits, strange behavior, and unique philosophy of life could be answered by the scars on his face and body, the buzzing in his head, and his missing left leg. Since Jake's death, Gregory had gradually become her best friend—and among best friends, certain things can comfortably be left unsaid.

At the moment the music ended, Kaloostian removed the headphones and fully opened his eyes. A still-handsome forty-five-year-old with prominent Middle Eastern features, he had a neatly trimmed black beard and wildly expressive eyes, somewhat hidden behind thick, wire-rimmed glasses. Before the accident that had taken his leg, severed his spinal cord, and paralyzed him from the waist down, Gregory had been five-feet-ten-inches tall, with an athlete's build. His still-active lifestyle allowed him to retain most of his upper-body strength, despite having to spend the rest of his life in a wheelchair.

Pretending just to have noticed her, he glowered, but her impish grin was irresistible. Kaloostian returned the smile with genuine affection and laughed easily.

"Hey Spud, what brings you down here? Got any free samples from that drug bust you orchestrated this morning?"

Angela gritted her teeth and scowled. Other than her older brother, Chip, Kaloostian was the only person who still called her Spud, a nickname dating to childhood. As a wiry four-year-old, she'd had an almost perverse passion for potatoes. One summer afternoon in 1979, Chip took her to see a movie at the old Rialto Theater in Ann Arbor. Safe from the prying eyes of the usher, Angela pulled an uncooked, unpeeled potato out of her pocket and began eating it raw. The connection was immediate. Despite years of protest, the nickname remained.

"I don't know who's a bigger pain in the butt—you or Chip," she said.

Kaloostian shrugged, "Could be worse." He maneuvered his wheelchair from the easy-access workbench covering the back wall of the oversized electronics shop. The bench was loaded with diagnostic equipment, tools, stereo components, and computer paraphernalia. As a government-employed technician, Greg worked to keep a host of electronic gadgets in perfect working order. The sensitive nature of the information contained in the computers he serviced required a top-secret security clearance, as well as an exhausting background check. In an age of ever-increasing reliance on advanced digital technology, competent—and honest—technicians like Gregory Kaloostian were worth their weight in computer chips.

"How was the big New Year's Eve party? You did go, didn't you?"

"Yeah, took your advice: went out and *tried* to have a good time—not much else to do."

"So...?"

"So...so what! I mingled, I schmoozed, sipped sparkling water, got bored, and left."

"With...?"

"Alone, Greg. I left *alone*. Just me, all by my lonesome. That okay with you...*mother*?"

"I just don't want you to spend the rest of your life battling crime during the day and cloistered in your apartment at night. You've got to get out once in a while, for you own good," Kaloostian said with concern. "Enough lecturing…before I forget, thanks again for the can of Spam and the record album."

Every Christmas, Toner bought him at least one item reminiscent of his adopted state of Minnesota. The Armenian had been medivacked to the Twin Cities in 1993 by a local group of surgeons who had done their best to correct the wounds he'd suffered in the Armenian–Azerbaijan War.

"The Spam'll make a great paperweight, and I love the album. You actually found a Stones LP I don't have. How'd you manage that?"

Toner smiled but did not let on as to how difficult an accomplishment her gift had been. Greg had more than three thousand records in his collection, an impressive start considering he'd picked up the hobby only eight years earlier. Angela had learned never to buy him a compact disk, to debate the merits of vinyl versus plastic, or to discuss the technical ramifications of analog versus digital. The rabid audiophile turned up his nose at any prerecorded music that did not emanate from a long-playing, thirty-three-rpm record album.

"Is that what you've just been listening to?" Toner asked.

"On *Monday*? No, the Stones are a bit too rigorous this early in the week. That was the Prague Philharmonic Chorus, performing Dvorak's *Psalm 149.*"

"Say *what*?"

"You know…'Sing unto the Lord a New Song…Opus 79.' Oh, never mind." From the look on her face, Greg knew Toner and classical music were light years apart. "Hey, how'd the big narcotics bust go—other than the technicality over missing paperwork?"

"News sure does travel fast. Yeah, other than the warrant, it was very textbook."

"And I suppose you came down here to avoid all the pats on the back?"

Angela bit the nail on her right thumb, keeping the file disk in her jacket pocket. "Naah. For the most part, people are avoiding me—damaged goods, you know. But Scriff, *whoa*, I don't think she'll ever get over this. Lucky for me, she's all keyboard and no modem. But what I need from you, old buddy, is some of that computer wisdom you're so famous for."

"What's wrong with your laptop?"

"Toto's fine," Toner said, calling her laptop by its pet name. "It's this file disk I'm having trouble with." She retrieved the Revkin file, maneuvering her chair next to Kaloostian at the computer station. "I won't bore you with all the gory details, but Hatton's reassigned me, and I'm having problems accessing most of the file."

"What'd he do that for? If he reassigned you every time you opened your big mouth, you wouldn't be on a case long enough to sign your name."

"Thanks for the encouragement, but I really need your help. Something's not right here—the BBS is nowhere to be found, the format's all wrong, I can't access 99 percent of the information...and yes, Herr Doctor, I used disk verification—the data's there, I just can't get at it."

"Very interestink. Let's see this mysterious file."

Toner inserted the disk into the CD-ROM drive of Kaloostian's computer. As the drive hummed into action, Angela described her earlier difficulty in reading the file, without going into detail on the subject matter. But as she accessed the information from the Revkin file, Greg leaned closer to the monitor, his eyes wide with disbelief. "Holy schmoley, *Olga Revkin*," he exclaimed.

"You know her?"

"I wish! No, I'm just a humble admirer of her work. Olga was a candidate for a Nobel Prize in chemistry two years ago—a pretty well-known lady. Interestingly enough, there was an article about her in the *Times* Internet edition yesterday."

"About what? I pegged her as some housewife bimbo drowning in Prozac."

Greg clicked his tongue. "Olga Revkin is one of the lead biochemical engineers on the Gamma Program at NASA. Everyone knows that—'cept you. According to the article, she's on some sort of sabbatical. And because of her long absence, the entire project's at a standstill. Now you bring me this file. Timely coincidence, hey?"

"Yaaah suuure, you bet*cha*," Toner mimicked, practicing her Minnesotan.

Kaloostian ignored the sarcasm. "If you paid attention to current events once in a while…Anyway, the article restated the news that two weeks ago Olga's daughter was seriously injured in a car accident. Olga took some time off to be at her daughter's bedside. Then the child transferred out of LA General, and Olga *presumably* goes into seclusion. End of story, at least as far as the press is concerned.

"Now in *your* file," Greg continued, pointing to the computer screen, "it says Olga's locked up in a psychiatric hospital! You know the press—that kind of stuff is news. Respected scientists don't generally go off the deep end quite so fast—or quite so anonymously. What else is in there?"

Toner paged down. "If you liked page one, you're gonna *love* this."

Kaloostian glanced at Angela, then began to scan the info on Melissa Revkin's medical condition and genetic dissimilarity with her immediate family. Despite his curiosity, the Armenian said nothing, quickly moving to the final page. When he'd finished, he sat quietly. From the glazed look in his eyes, Angela knew his mind was racing.

"Greg? Earth calling Greg? *Hey,* do you have any idea what *Nyentzi* is?"

"Where did Hatton get this?"

Toner shrugged. "Can't say. He was pretty vague about it. But you know Al Hatton—if bullshit was an orchestra, he'd be the Philharmonic."

"C'mon, what'd he tell you?"

"All he said was the file had been assigned to the NSA, and it was all he could find on short notice."

"*NSA?* What's he doing getting mixed up with them? Is he nuts? If that's the case, it'll be practically impossible to trace to its source. Could be drug-related, immigration, international security…"

"A security leak? To whom?" Toner said. "You're not thinking industrial espionage, are you?"

"No. I can't imagine somebody like Olga Revkin doing anything under the table. And it can't be drugs. Maybe there's some sort of mix-up with her naturalization papers. But that doesn't make any sense, either." Greg shrugged. "And I have *no idea* what *Nyentzi* is. I can't even guess what language. It's not Armenian, Russian, English or Azerbaijan—that I'm sure of. But I do know one thing."

"What's that?" Toner asked.

"We've got to access *all* the data on this disk. We need to see those brain-wave patterns, DNA sequencing, and whatever else is hidden in there. By the way, you notice anything else unusual about the file…besides the font and lack of a BBS?"

"I don't understand."

"Lose the BBS, and all you're lacking is the summary page. You can delete a BBS on any standard bureau file and still have author, dates, recommendations, and all that other junk digitally stamped throughout the text. Those elements are constant and can't be arbitrarily flushed. From what I've seen here, though, none of that's apparent—it's gone. So we need to see what imprints were left by whoever formatted the disk in the first place. Watch this."

Kaloostian fingered a series of keys and downshifted the Revkin file to the taskbar. Next, he accessed the computer's file explorer and right-clicked to the file-disk directory. This gave him a screen full of options to assist his search.

The first tool he used identified the properties of the disk—among them title, file originator, template used, revision number, date of last modification, even total pages and words. The two detectives noted that the only box containing data was the title, which stated the obvious—Revkin. Everything else was blank. As far as the computer was concerned, the file had no author and no template. There'd been no revisions, no dates. The file had come into existence on its own with no apparent help from anyone at any time.

Toner then noticed additional information in the properties menu. "At least it verifies there's only the three accessible pages we've seen."

"And less than a thousand words. Actually, we've confirmed one other thing—the file's a partial copy, and no one's modified it since inception. I just wish I knew whether it had one or multiple sources. That date thing's really freaking me out, though. Even if a computer's battery's dead or the CMOS's corrupted, there should still be a date. The BIOS is stamped on a file no matter what." Kaloostian tapped his right hand on the desk in frustration. "You sure there wasn't anything else with this disk?" he asked, staring at the screen.

"This is all Hatton gave me. Sorry."

"Well…dammit…there's gotta be more."

"What's so important about the format?" Toner said, her impatience obvious. She was not used to her Armenian friend being stumped, especially around anything technical. After several long seconds of silence, Toner changed tact. "Come on, Greg. It's not that big a deal. Personally, I couldn't care less about who, when, and where. I'd be happy with a little *what*. Don't you have any tricks up your sleeve to get into this damned file? I can't believe you're gonna disappoint me."

"It's not that we can't access it," Kaloostian said at last. "Part of the problem with software and operating systems is that they're constantly updated. To make matters worse, a lot of the older programs and platforms were…are incompatible. They can't run without third-party software. Without that, you're locked out—like we are now."

"This isn't old!" Toner countered. "From that article of yours, we know the disk was compiled less than two weeks ago—*after* Melissa Revkin's accident."

"True, but that doesn't mean this file wasn't created with an older word-processing program that our system can't identify. And if that's the case, we're gonna have to cheat."

"Cheat?"

"Cheat. Nothing illegal, but for situations like yours, there's this nifty little software package called *AbsoluteAccess*: Guaranteed to mesh with any word-processing or multimedia program with no loss of clarity, video, or text. Like an electronic Rosetta stone, it'll automatically access the program, scan it, and reformat it in a readable text mode."

"What if there's a password or security blocks?" Toner asked. "I don't have time to run the file through encryption. I need to get in there now!"

"Patience, love. Sit back and watch."

Leaving the disk in the drive, Kaloostian toggled to *AbsoluteAccess* and prompted it to action. He monitored its initial integration with the Revkin directory and waited. In a matter of seconds, the program relayed a message indicating its access of the problematic file. In a few seconds, information began to fill the screen.

"And it's *just* that easy."

"Easy? If that was easy, I'd like to know why I had so much trouble. And if someone wanted the information kept confidential, why didn't they just encrypt the hell out of it?"

"You forget that I do this for a living. As to your second question, you're gonna have to take that up with the author—if we ever figure out who it is. Anyway, let's take a look."

Kaloostian manipulated the page-down key. Obviously, the data had been recently pieced together. Toner and Kaloostian found themselves staring at page after page of jumbled text, charts, and reference material.

The first several pages appeared to have been pulled from depositions involving the girl's birth, including sworn testimonials from hospital personnel. There was also the mother's reiteration of what originally had been reported—Melissa Revkin's conception and birth were thoroughly routine. No records suggested artificial insemination or in vitro fertilization. Nor was there record of complication or cesarean section. The odds that the child had been switched at birth were not even worth considering. Record-keeping had come a long way since the 1930s.

"This is bullshit," Kaloostian swore. "They find a child genetically unrelated to everyone in her immediate family, and all they come up with are some worthless testimonials."

"There's something else we ought to consider," Toner said. "These depositions are recent—meaning somebody's been pulling a lot of overtime doing the fieldwork and asking questions. If it's somebody out of this office, we might be able to track 'em down using the travel logs and time records from the central database."

"Good point. We might even be able to find out who compiled the data in the first place. Too bad that information's under tighter security than a Jell-O factory."

"When's that ever stopped you?"

"I didn't say it was going to stop me. It *might* slow me down, though. For now, let's keep going on this," Kaloostian said, eager to continue. But analyzing a disorganized file with more than two hundred megs of data would take longer than Toner or Kaloostian had time for. There had to be an easier way.

Knowing this, Kaloostian simultaneously fingered the control-and-F-key combo. A menu popped up, with a small box in which he could type exactly what they needed to locate.

"All right. Whaddaya want to see first—brain waves or DNA?"

"I'm kinda partial to brain waves," Toner decided, not well versed in either. She exchanged anticipatory glances with Kaloostian and waited while he typed "brain wave" in the find box.

The computer quickly responded, shifting to the section of the file that contained Melissa Revkin's hospital records, including the brain-wave readouts. Medical notes, as well as the ambiguous commentary of several anonymous filled the screen. In the upper left corner of the screen was the icon for the file's video clip library.

Kaloostian touched the icon and a four-square-inch viewing screen appeared. Below it were the play, fast-forward, reverse, pause, and stop buttons. Before activating the video, Kaloostian lightly pressed the right corner of the small screen. The box expanded to fill the monitor, offering a better view and hiding the rest of the file. With a touch of the play button, a digitized video began.

Toner watched in silence while brain-wave patterns flowed across the computer screen. When the digital tape ended after fifteen seconds, Kaloostian replayed the video. Then he paused the film. "Well, if nothing else, we've found one reason to justify the file's existence. It doesn't explain NSA involvement, but it's a start."

"What do you mean? Excuse my ignorance, but brain waves all look the same to me."

Kaloostian leaned back and gathered his thoughts. "Remember when I told you that before I got my teaching degree, I thought about becoming a doctor?"

Toner nodded.

"In premed, I learned that brain-wave patterns are fairly predictable, especially when somebody's in a coma, like Melissa here. Neural activity decreases significantly, but look at this." Kaloostian pointed to the computer screen. "This gently sloping wave signifies somatic cranial activity for basic life support. It's your typical alpha wave, and since she's in a coma, that's what you'd expect. But this second set of superimposed waves representing neural synaptic activity is *way* out of whack."

"I still don't follow you. What's wrong with them?"

"Angie, this kid's in a deep coma—practically brain-dead, with no external sensory stimulation. That being the case, these waves, which represent the transfer of information *within the brain itself,* should be almost flat. But look, they're jutting damn near straight up and down—they're spikes, for crying out loud. Hell, if I fed you five grams of that methamphetamine you busted the Guerreros for, I couldn't get a response like this. Any way you cut it, Melissa Revkin's not normal—not by a long shot."

"What could cause waves like that?" Angela asked. Her faith in Gregory's computer skills was such that she assumed his knowledge of biology would prompt an instinctive explanation of this problem as well.

Kaloostian did not immediately respond. After waiting a moment, Angela turned towards him, expecting a look of uncertainly, anger, or disappointment. She was surprised to see him twiddling with his glasses, and avoiding eye contact.

Angela had taken classes in nonverbal communication. She'd learned to be sensitive to body language, to recognize the subtle, almost imperceptible hints and innuendoes—clues nearly impossible to suppress. Scrutinizing her best friend, whom she trusted as much as her own parents, Angela felt her stomach go tight. She didn't know why, but she had the queerest sensation that whatever Gregory Kaloostian said next would be a lie.

5

Misconception

They'd taken over the world. From the wallet PC that stored her checking account balance as well as her best friend's email address, to her voice and video telephone messaging service, to grocery scanners, to the desk model she worked on this moment—computers were everywhere. Just as coal-generated steam drove the Industrial Revolution, so did silicon-generated data drive the Information Age.

Modern society relied on the computer like no other manufactured product ever. Modern society also dictated that computer systems and correspondent technologies not only work well, they must work perfectly. The acceptable margin of error had decreased to the point where it simply did not exist. One mistake, one virus, one mistyped command representing less than a single byte of data, could shut down the most extensive network or turn the most expensive, state-of-the-art computer into a paperweight or an end table.

To Suada Sivac, a pleasant-faced, brown-haired, twenty-five-year-old Bosnian expatriate, computers were repetitively familiar. Even during her childhood in the Sarajevo suburb of Vogosca, they'd not been uncommon. Arriving in the United States in 1993 as a war orphan fleeing the carnage of the Balkan Civil War, Suada had thrown herself into her schoolwork. A frightened and lonely child—virtually alone in the world—she'd initially lagged her Manhattan Beach, California, classmates in most areas of study. But in computer applications, she equaled, than eclipsed, her American-born acquaintances.

From grade school through high school, Suada mastered every computer program she could find. Ten years later, after graduating from UCLA at age twenty-one with a degree in computer engineering, she unofficially joined the inner circle of scientifically advanced, socially stunted misfits. Knowledgeable enough to strip a computer to its base components, she could also put it back together. Suada and others of her kind could also navigate, administer, and troubleshoot the industry's most advanced software or network.

Thoroughly Americanized, she could scarcely remember her family or her homeland. The only possession she had from the first ten years of her life was a faded black-and-white photograph of her mother, hidden in a small pendant hanging from a chain around her neck. Suada had last seen her mother, father, and brothers fourteen years earlier. She had learned of their deaths while recuperating from her own wounds in Germany.

While the memory of her family grew dim, Suada often recalled her mother's gentle humor and worldly insights. "Remember Suada," she had said, "opportunity knocks, at times too softly. Be careful to listen—*listen closely*. Adversity, on the other hand, does not knock. Instead, it kicks in the door, beats you upside the head, shoots your dog, and steals all your money and food."

Computers were Suada's golden opportunity, failure the adversity she could not accept. Every system crash, hung application, corrupted file, memory deficiency, or piece of poorly written software was an open door for her troubleshooting skills. Suada cherished the anonymity offered by computers and the Internet. She relished the freedom from human interaction that came with the solitary nature of diagnostic and repair work. And she absolutely flourished in her job as a technical writer subcontracting out of her apartment.

As a firsthand witness to the death, destruction, and dissection of what had then been called Yugoslavia, Suada Sivac considered herself a survivor. Though she was never quite free of the psychological scars from that war, her determination to forget the horrors of childhood sustained her existence in America. Because her youth had been cut short, she knew as an adult that the only way she could retain sanity was to keep a safe distance between herself and the rest of the world.

A poet once wrote that no one is an island, but Suada learned that humans, when necessary, made excellent peninsulas.

Anyone observing her work could not have guessed the importance of the day's assignment. Alone at her computer, her face betrayed no emotion as her nimble fingers flew across the keyboard like a concert pianist's playing Rachmaninoff. She could have been typing a letter to an old friend, not putting the finishing touches on a year-end report.

She would email the final product to the board of directors, various market analysts, and her client's accounting department. Annual shareholder dividends soon would be calculated. Suada's reputation for perfection had earned her the contract.

Suada leaned back, stretched her aching neck muscles, and yawned. She'd been working on the project since 6:00 A.M. Glancing at her watch, she knew she would easily meet the late-afternoon deadline. "One more year of this," she said to herself. "then I'm out of here."

Rising from her chair, Suada walked to the window of her apartment. The final spelling, grammar, and readability tests could be run later; right now she needed a break. She gazed from her twelfth-floor window into the noontime haze, hoping it would rain. Suada was thankful for the winter months in southern California. While only slightly cooler, winter offered the inhabitants of Los Angeles a respite from the smog alerts. Suada didn't care for Los Angeles. Too much of a good thing, or so the natives once claimed. She had other long-term plans, plans that did not include a lifetime of working for others, no matter how idyllic the circumstances.

As an independent contractor for Exemplary Temporary, Inc., she knew what an exceptional employee she was—and had to be. She had one of the hardest jobs to land in all of California, but she would not regret her decision not to renew her contract. Five years would be long enough.

Suada's employer demanded—and received—total loyalty and dedication from its personnel. While some might criticize the authoritarian atmosphere, no one could deny that ETI paid the highest salaries of any temp agency, provided medical benefits, profit sharing, and offered the ultimate carrot—a $50,000 bonus at the end of each five-year contract period. Exemplary also offered its temporaries the opportunity to work for the biggest, brightest, and best companies on the West Coast.

The key to Exemplary's ability to offer such a package was that it charged its corporate clients more per contract hour than any other temporary agency. It could do so because it offered the crème de la crème of the temporary workforce. Exemplary was scarcely able to meet the insatiable demand for high-quality, temporary employees.

Granted, the strings attached to Suada's employment were many, and not everyone collected the bonus. There could be no sick days, no absent days, no unsatisfactory performance, no missed deadlines, no talking back, no complaining, no hanging around. Contract personnel had to be familiar with any and all computer and software systems, any and all word-processing and spreadsheet programs, as well as any and all management styles.

Five years of nose to the keyboard, carpal tunnel, and being sequestered in a ten-by-twelve-foot office. Some might call it economic slavery. Suada Sivac, however, saw it as a sacrifice that would one day be well worth the prize.

Kaloostian finished twiddling with his glasses. He glanced at Toner and shrugged a second time. "Beats me. I don't have a clue what would cause brain waves to act like that," he said.

Angela eyed her friend. "So humor me. Aren't you the guy with all the answers?"

"What's the big deal? I'm a technician, not a doctor."

"You're *so* full of shit. You know that. Come on, give it your best shot."

"Okay. If I had to venture a guess, I'd say from the location of the readings that her brain might be trying to bypass the damage she suffered in the accident. For all I know, she might be regenerating new neurons. But what's the point? Neurons don't work that way. Sorry to disappoint you, Angie, but I switched majors. This is *way* beyond me."

Greg closed the video-clip box on the screen and leaned back in his chair.

"Giving up already?" said Toner.

"I know my limitations," Kaloostian concluded.

"Well, I'm sure the heck not done," Toner said, taking control of the investigation. "C'mon, let's see what the Revkins are made of." She reached past her friend and hit control-F on the keyboard. When the find box appeared, she tapped "DNA" and hit the enter key.

An endless stream of DNA data quickly replaced the medical information. The left half of the screen showed a computerized, colorized printout of the girl's genetic code, with notations, labels, and notes on the right.

Kaloostian whistled, his amazement overwhelming his indecision. "This is impossible. Somebody's trying to analyze this kid's genetic code. My god, people have tens of thousands of genes in each pair of twenty-three chromosomes. It'll take months to decipher this much data. Even if we concentrate only on the ones known to be active in brain and cranial development, that leaves more than three thousand genes to interpret. Guess it's pretty obvious what most of the two hundred megs of data contain."

Kaloostian sat straight up in his wheelchair while Toner paged down for fifteen seconds, finding nothing but more genetic readouts.

"Do you have any idea how valuable this information is?" he said, turning to Toner. "I'll bet this disk contains a complete, prototypal genetic readout!"

"Wait a minute," she finally demanded. "The Human Genome Project finished cataloging genetic codes almost ten years. How can this be valuable? It's common information."

"That's a misconception. Reading more than three billion letters of the DNA code is one thing. Trying to gain an understanding of what each one means is something entirely different. The cost of deciphering and testing that much data is astronomical. No one country or university could afford to do it all. So it was done piecemeal."

"Hold everything—*time out*. Since when did you become such an expert on genetics? Four minutes ago, you were hemming and hawing about brain waves. Now suddenly you're Alex Trebek."

Greg tried to answer, but Toner pressed her point, unable to shake the feeling he was holding something back.

"I've looked through some of the books you keep on your shelves," she said, eyeing her friend with doubt. "I know you do a lot of reading, but didn't you just tell me you skipped physiology in college?"

"You misunderstood. I know only the basics about anatomy, but I did take a genetics course…got an A, too. It's a subject I've always been fascinated with."

The logic was convincing, but Toner's disbelief was written all over her face.

"Come on, Angie, what's the deal?" Greg argued. "Even I admit there's more to life than sex, drugs, and rock 'n' roll. How about giving me a little credit for having outside interests? And aren't you the one who gave me the subscription to *Discover* magazine?"

Angela slowly nodded. She gave her friend the benefit of the doubt, as she had never known him to lie. In fact, her own compulsion for the truth was due in part to his lectures on ethics and social responsibility.

"So you've been studying genetics for years. Prove to me it wasn't a waste of time…and money."

"Okay…I'll tell you what I know, under one condition."

"Which is?"

"You admit up front that I don't have all the answers. What I tell you is information anyone could get from the library or online. You buy that?"

"Whatever you say, Greg."

"Don't sound too convinced," Kaloostian said, shaking his head at his friend's continuing mistrust. "What do you want to know?"

"I don't have all day."

"How about some specifics?"

Toner scratched her chin. "Okay. What's the big deal about Melissa's genetic readout?"

Kaloostian nodded his head. "That's as good a place as any to start. Fifteen years ago, scientists knew there were about 3,500 genetic disorders caused by genes that botched their protein-assembly jobs. The goal in the 1990s was to isolate *only* those disorders. Locating genes for creativity, risk-taking, obesity, and so on was a bonus, not the original intent."

"Like when Francis Collins and his team isolated the gene for cystic fibrosis."

"Exactly. The French tackled some of the disorders, the Japanese some, the United States, Swiss, Russians, Swedes, Germans, and so on, charted others. Each county has access to its own information, but there's not been much of an urge to share all the data with the rest of the scientific community. Keeping everything more or less to themselves is the only way to protect their investment."

Toner bit her lower lip and looked away. After a moment, she pointed a finger in Greg's direction. "All right. So if everyone needs to protect their investment, why don't they just patent their data?"

"They can't."

"Say *what*?"

"Human genetic information cannot be patented. The U.S. Patent Office made a ruling in 1992 that's withstood every lawsuit since."

"You sure? I could swear I read about a company in Palo Alto that received a patent on some of its genetic work last month," Angela argued.

"Probably a bacterial strain—E.coli maybe. If a researcher melds a continuous cell line, you can patent that. On the other hand, somebody would have a hard time trying to corner the market on a new liver that's immune to the ravages of alcoholism."

"What's the difference? Genes are genes, right?"

"Fraid not—the difference is human versus nonhuman. Bacteria's one thing, but trying to patent anything vaguely Homo sapiens is verboten."

"Really?" Toner said with surprise. "I'd never heard that."

"What do you expect? The government prohibits human genetic experimentation. They also run the U. S. Patent Office—kind of a monopoly, you know. Don't look so surprised. It's actually a pretty logical ruling. The very nature of genetic research means that scientists are working with material that's been 'published before.' With such a strict interpretation, it's next to impossible to copyright your work."

"But what about E.coli? Bacteria's been around a lot longer than we have."

"True, but there's also the matter of ethics. Screw up a batch of bacteria and *whoosh*, down the drain. Screw up a human embryo, and some serious shit will hit the fan."

"But does that also mean this entire disk is nothing but genetic code?" Toner argued. "And if that's the case, why would the NSA have it in the first place. Urrrr, that damned Hatton. What am I gonna tell him? He wants me out of the building in less than four hours."

"We've seen less than 5 percent of the entire file. Maybe…"

Toner clenched her fist and pumped her arm. "Like that question in second folder…genetic engineering! Maybe Melissa Revkin's the product of genetic engineering."

"Get real. Not only is human genetic engineering illegal, there's something else you should know about Melissa." Kaloostian reached for the pile of papers. He found what wanted, reviewed it, and handed it to his friend. "This is that article about Olga Revkin."

Toner began to read while Kaloostian talked.

"Your file disk reports that Melissa Revkin's a somewhat *unusual* child. She's genetically alien to anyone in her immediate family, she has brain waves that defy explanation, and according to this, she's a seven-year-old genius with a mathematical IQ above 200. But she also can't tie her own shoes, walk in a straight line, or carry on a normal conversation. I mean, look at this," he said, taking the article back. "'Melissa will spend hours tearing sheets of paper into long, thin strips. She flaps her arms like a bird…She sits at the computer attempting to get on line, typing the same access number over and over for hours on end.' Does that sound like the result of genetic engineering? Unless it was a government job, Melissa Revkin's just an extremely unfortunate kid."

Angela grabbed the article and gave Greg a dirty look. "Let me see, dammit…She's an autistic savant! She can mentally multiply ten-digit numbers by ten-digit numbers in less than seven seconds.'"

Kaloostian nodded in agreement. "She's also delusional, withdrawn, and hears voices."

"That's quite a résumé for a seven-year-old." Toner huffed and shook her head. "But I still need something concrete to go on, Greg, something…logical."

"Good luck, Spud. You work for Uncle Sam. But I just happen to know that the gene for autism was charted over nine years ago. Its appearance in her genetic readout might be just what we're looking for."

Kaloostian typed "autism" and pressed the enter button. Again, success. Though her knowledge of genetics was limited, Toner could see that whoever created the file had reached a similar conclusion. The gene for autism was labeled and highlighted.

Kaloostian quietly scanned the information. Though he said nothing, his nodding head showed he'd found what he was looking for. As Angela watched, he scrolled through page after page of base pairings.

"Greg, who the hell are you trying to kid? Just look at all this crap! There's got to be ten thousand pairings here. How're you gonna know if even one of them's wrong?" Undeterred, Kaloostian kept tapping the page-down key. The encoded information continued to flow—page after page after page.

Soon, even Kaloostian had had enough. He simultaneously fingered the control/end keys to find the last page. The protein encoding stopped, leaving a single-sentence conclusion: "Genes 1044-1070 on Chromosome 7 *normal*—Autism possibility *negative*—see sect. 12MR."

The two friends sat in the silence of their own thoughts, the faint hum of the computer's cooling fan the only sound. Finally, Toner turned to Kaloostian and shook her head.

"I don't like the way this is going, Greg. If she's not autistic, then what the hell is she? I need answers, not more questions."

"I don't know. Maybe it's something else—some other simple diagnosis. But there's only one way to find out." Kaloostian typed "12MR" and pressed the enter key. The computer retrieved the data.

"My guess was the '12MR' stood for Melissa Revkin," Greg said when more information filled the screen. "But medical report's a close second..." he added, as the absence of an index led him to page through the data at a snail's pace. The information in Section 12MR, however, provided only supplementary details regarding Melissa Revkin's accident, injuries, and prognosis.

Suddenly Toner pointed to the screen. "She wasn't in an accident. She ran into the traffic: 'Child left mother's side after church and proceeded directly towards Lakewood Boulevard…'"

"Must've been one hell of a sermon," Greg added. "According to her parents, she'd never run that far before without falling."

"Never will again, either. Talk about bad timing. Let's see what else it says."

Toner and Kaloostian moved through several pages of redundant data. Then Greg stopped the scrolling and began to read about the child's damaged kidney and potential for a transplant. He pointed to the screen and gave Toner a poke with his right elbow.

"Look at this. She's on a steady diet of ALG."

Toner didn't understand. "What's ALG?"

"Anti-lymphocyte globulin. It's an experimental anti-rejection drug used to treat patients after organ transplants. The FDA pulled it from the market after several people died…hasn't been available in the United States since the 1990s. I didn't think it was obtainable overseas either."

"How in the *hell* do you know all this?" Angela demanded, her suspicions again aroused. "I thought you only fixed computers. Oh, and read science journals."

"What's with you today? You're second-guessing damn near everything I say. Have you forgotten how I got here? Have you forgotten where I lost my leg? The University of Minnesota was one of the facilities using ALG. I was a patient there for over a year. Remember?"

Kaloostian was angry. The tension between the two friends was palpable as they sat in awkward silence. Angela sighed and reached out, touching him on the arm.

"I'm sorry? I guess I'm a little jittery…confused about all this. I know how hard that must've been for you. It's been a long day. I'm sorry…okay?"

Kaloostian lapsed into an icy silence, but Toner wouldn't stop.

"Maybe they started administering it to her after the accident?" she speculated "Maybe they're prepping her for surgery."

"No. ALG's illegal. Too many side-effects."

"Well, if it's so illegal, where are they getting it?"

"I don't know."

"Okay. If it's illegal and unobtainable, why is Melissa Revkin on it? Why would somebody do that? What else could ALG be used for?"

The Armenian shrugged. Again they were silent. Finally Toner pounded the desk.

"Dammit, Greg, what other pharmaceutical intent could the administration of ALG have? I'm sorry you lost a leg and got paralyzed. I'm sorry, but *come on*, what aren't you telling me?"

Kaloostian sighed and fidgeted with his beard. He straightened his glasses, ran his hand through his hair, and looked directly into Toner's eyes: "It was never proven, but there are theories it might stabilize the immune system…and reinforce replicated cellular tissue after intensive gene therapy. But it's pure speculation. No one ever attempted to use it for…"

"You don't mean gene therapy, Kaloostian. C'mon, say it—*say it*."

"FINE. Genetic engineering…There, you happy? What's your point, anyway? It never happened. No one's ever done it."

"How do you know? How can you possibly know? If all that's preventing science fiction from becoming reality is ethics, how can you sit there and deny the possibility of Melissa Revkin being the product of genetic experimentation?"

"I know because I know. I know because I've never seen a word about human genetic engineering in the press—or anywhere else, for that matter. Trust me, Angie, I'd know."

"Give me a break," she said, shaking her head.

"Now *you're* the expert," Kaloostian declared. "So answer me this: If someone has reengineered a human, why hasn't anyone read about it in the paper or seen it on the news? Everybody was chomping at the bit to be the first one on the block with a rough draft of the human genome sequence back in 2000. Reengineering a human is also a pretty significant development."

"Maybe she's a clone," Toner said with a shrug. "Maybe that's what the ALG is used for."

"Now *that* makes a lot of sense."

"Hey, it could happen…And something else, Greg. I happen to know it's pretty easy to get published if your work conforms to the prevailing political agenda…and in terms of genetics, that's fairly conservative. But if your work is on the cutting edge, and I mean cutting edge, it's just as easy to stay unpublished." Toner paused, then laughed. "Heck, you do something like this, you'd *want* to stay unpublished."

"So you're saying someone would spend millions…*billions* of dollars, waste a career working in total obscurity, just for the thrill of it?"

"Diet coke…"

"What?"

"Never mind."

"Damn straight, never mind. Look, Toner, cloning a human is not gonna happen anytime soon. Reengineering a human is not gonna happen anytime soon. You remember Dolly, the Scottish sheep. But did you know there were 277 attempted clones, all of which died, before Dolly was finally born. There were also several horribly defective clones that died right after birth. That's a lot of road kill.

"Weren't you listening about the risks involved? Anybody trying to duplicate Wilmut's sheep experiment with human embryos wouldn't earn a Nobel Prize, they'd earn an indictment or excommunication. Trust me…it ain't gonna happen," Kaloostian insisted, folding his arms and looking at the ceiling.

"Oh no, don't you shut me out. We're not done here. I'm certainly not. You keep denying the possibility of human genetic engineering, but if there was...Humor me, Greg—I've got to know. If someone *were* into full-scale genetic replication, who would have...who could have done it?"

Kaloostian refused to answer.

"Fine...maybe you don't know. Even Gregory H. Kaloostian isn't infallible. I'll try another question. *Where* would it have happened? Where's the likeliest place for secret genetic testing—which country, which university, which lab? You know. I know you do. Why won't you tell me?"

Kaloostian exhaled sharply, glared at his friend, and accessed the autofind command. He quickly typed "Monogovody," touched the enter key, then waited. His wait was unnervingly brief.

"Greg, what's going on?" Toner begged. She was running out of time. Instead of finding answers, their search only generated more questions, none offering easy solutions. She knew of Monogovody—who didn't? She'd heard the stories, the rumors—who hadn't? She'd always hoped they weren't true—who wouldn't?

Staring at the information retrieved by Kaloostian search, Angela Toner finally began to grasp the significance of the question asked by the yet-anonymous author of the Revkin file: "Priority—verify or refute genetic engineering. Is this *NYENTZI?*"

It could very well be.

6

Genes 'R' Us

Still no word on their sister's condition, but that was to be expected. The nurses in critical care wouldn't update the medical files until after the 3:00 P.M. change of shift. Then it would simply be a matter of the girls hacking their way into the hospital's databank to make certain everything was being done to make Melissa comfortable. No matter what people might one day say about them, the sisters did take care of their own.

Bedtime approached in their time zone. Soon, their father would knock on the door, poke his head in, and remind them for the thousandth time to take their pills and brush their teeth. Then he would close the hermetically sealed door to their bedroom.

And for the thousandth time, the children would do exactly as he said, wait thirty minutes until both parents were sleeping, then get up again. It was early afternoon in the United States, and events throughout the world were moving too swiftly for them to enjoy the luxury of a full night's rest.

Each girl opened a packet of multicolored pills, which they'd dubbed "the haywire highball." One by one each popped the capsules into her mouth—phosphatidylserine, ginko biloba, acetyl L-carnitine, and vitamin E—washing them down with a strawberry and banana malt. Like much of their lives, the girls' drug regimen was frustratingly routine. Pills in the morning, pills at lunch, pills again at bedtime. Their treadmill existence was tolerable only because they knew that all routines are finite—nothing goes on forever. For the girls, change couldn't come soon enough.

She'd heard her father say it a thousand times: "Quit complaining, Angie. Ten percent of something is better than 100 percent of nothing." Of course, with philosophy his chosen province, he could afford to sit around debating the merits of that laudable 10 percent and still get paid. Kaloostian and Toner did not have that luxury.

Though the Monogovody data search generated a positive response, it did not bring them closer to the truth—whatever the truth might be. The information produced only another series of questions, none of them easy to answer.

On the computer screen was the travel itinerary for one James Paul Revkin, dating from November 3, 1999, to January 25, 2000. The report had been compiled from passport stampings, custom's declarations, and credit-card receipts.

Revkin had left Boston for London, traveling first-class on British Air. He'd spent three nights at the Kingston Hotel in Harlington. On his fourth day in London, he'd rented a car, chunneled to France, and driven to Paris, arriving on November 7.

In Paris, according to American Express, his choice of room changed from economy to first class—and from single to double occupancy. Revkin, and apparently a companion, spent the next six nights at the recently renovated Prince de Galles Hotel on Avenue George V. Receipts from Parisian sites such as the Moulin Rouge, Versailles, the Louvre,

Café de Flore, as well as restaurants and shops, attested to an enjoyable and expensive stay.

From Aeroport Charles de Gaulle, Revkin had flown to Moscow, arriving on Saturday, November 13. He stayed one night at the Reutov Holiday Inn—double occupancy. He checked out the next day.

At that point, the record of Revkin's excursion ended—until he passed customs at the San Francisco International Airport on January 25. For a period of forty-five days, James P. Revkin ate, drank, and slept somewhere in Russia. He went on no tours, purchased no souvenirs, and never used a credit or ATM card for the withdrawal of cash. A month and a half in an expensive country—and it cost him nothing? Travelers everywhere should know such gracious hosts.

The report ended with reference to an exhaustive but fruitless search for information on the missing forty-five days. Near the bottom of the screen was a subheading in bold letters: "Recommendation." Below it was a single word: "Interview."

At the bottom of the report came a second subheading: "Result." It also contained a concise conclusion: "Questionable cooperation."

Kaloostian was about to toggle to the next screen when Toner touched his hand.

"*Now* do you see what I'm talking about? You queried 'Monogovody' because I wanted to know where genetic engineering could've taken place...and this is what we got, a travel plan for Melissa Revkin's father."

"Yah, so?"

"Oh come on, don't be a bad sport. You and I both know that whoever put this file together did so for a reason. Trust me, Greg, we're on the right track. C'mon, page down."

The reluctant Armenian acquiesced. At the top of the next page was a third bold title: "Available Data." Below it was a date: "03/18/01—accident." Next came a single assertion: "Survivors—several—unable to locate." The final portion of the paragraph was equally concise: "Inspection of site—unnecessary—Monogovody total loss."

"There, satisfied? That's what you wanted, isn't it? Monogovody."

"What's this, though?" Toner asked, pointing to a second, single word paragraph. "Samanov?'

Kaloostian hesitated. "Beats me. I've heard the name, but I can't place it."

"Dammit, I'm right back where I started—more questions than answers. Come on, Greg, fill me in. Why Monogovody? What happened there? I've heard as many rumors as the next guy, but they're too ridiculous to believe. And the only publications that mention genetics on a regular basis are sold at supermarket checkouts. Not exactly reliable sources."

"There's not a lot to report," Kaloostian said. "No one knows what happened. There was an explosion in March 2000 that took out the entire complex. The few survivors were burned so badly that most of them died before they could be medivacked to the nearest hospital in Salekhard, Siberia."

"That's what I never understood—how could an entire research facility go up in smoke? I've seen reports describing a military strike. Some people blamed religious fundamentalists, and of course the tabloids stuck with the aliens from outer space. To which theory do you prescribe, Einstein?"

"They all sound so compelling. Okay...fine...you're looking for answers. What version do you want—'Cliff Notes' or Tolstoy?"

Tone sighed. "You know I don't have all day."

"'Cliff Notes' it is. What do you know about Tyrellovich?"

"Not much. From what I've read, his name's synonymous with Monogovody, he was into genetics early on, was a successful Russian businessman, devoted father, doting husband, mad scientist. Take your pick."

"Some of the above or all of the above," Greg added. "In a sound byte, Yuri Anatoliovich Tyrellovich was a relatively unknown academician from St. Petersburg. The Communists granted him a visa to leave the

Soviet Union in 1987 to work with the French, probably as an industrial spy. He showed remarkable promise as a software designer—some of the first multimedia computer games were his—and as a pioneer of artificial intelligence paradigms.

"In the mid-1990s, he branched out and became a system programmer in the drive to map out the human genome. With his background in computer-aided quantitative analysis and some software enhancements he devised, his team was one of the first to decipher as much genetic coding in eight hours as previously took a year."

"I remember that from college," Toner interjected. "Everyone thought it would take forty years to generate a simple map of the human genome."

"Yep—and with the aid of computers, they completed the genome project in less than ten years. He got a big bonus for that software innovation, by the way. In 1996, he returned to Russia. Through some of his political connections, he bought up land around the old Monogovody gulag—a relic from Stalin's reign of terror.

"The way he saw it, artificial intelligence wouldn't work. Computation was the future of biology, and he wanted to be the first kid on the block with the latest toy. I mean it, Angie—the guy was brilliant. He put together an alliance of some of the biggest names in the computer, genetics, and software industries. He called it Empyrean Technologies International, ETI for short."

"What does the *Empyrean* stand for? Is it Russian?"

"No. If I remember right, it's a medieval cosmology term meaning *true* and *ultimate heavenly paradise*. Lots of fire-and-light symbolism."

"Quite a mouthful. I suppose *Genes 'R' Us* was taken."

Kaloostian chuckled. "Must've been. Funny thing, though, the companies that *publicly* worked with Tyrellovich were limited, but he built a substantial network of backroom corporate affiliations, partnerships, obligations—you name it."

"I suppose all those companies were adverse to publicity?"

"Can't say I blame 'em. You remember the flak the South Koreans got for cloning a human embryo in 1998. To put it mildly, that upset a lot of people. Not only that, but the work at Monogovody was experimental. If ETI screwed up, the other companies didn't want their names dragged into the mud. Tyrellovich, on the other hand, made out like a bandit. His startup costs must have been horrendous, so by piecing together all those mutual research and technical cooperation schemes, he saved himself—and ETI—billions of dollars."

Toner shifted and crossed her arms. "What I don't understand is this: ETI wasn't the only gene-splicing outfit in town. From what you've told me, Tyrellovich was just another businessman. What made him so special? Why would any blue-chip company be willing to share its R & D—and who knows what else—with a rookie?"

"Don't know for sure, but I can think of a couple possible reasons. One, with the collapse of Communism, there was a surplus of highly trained technicians. Tyrellovich snapped up hundreds of those people. Another reason might be Monogovody itself. Solitude and isolation like that can't be found every day...even in Siberia. And then there are the reasons we've already discussed—ethics—and the inability to patent one's work."

"Look, Greg, I understand the need for confidentiality and all that," Toner countered, "but you gotta admit, building a research facility in the middle of a Siberian wilderness goes beyond paranoid. We're talking a whole new realm of psychosis. What was he thinking?"

"Can't answer that."

"So speculate—I wanna know."

"Fine, but this is straight out of the tabloids. The rumor was that Tyrellovich and ETI were willing, eager even, to move beyond fruit flies, rodents, livestock."

"We're talking *Homo sapiens*, right?"

"I don't know. I doubt it. Scientists perfected embryo splitting when they duplicated Rhesus monkeys back in 2000. And they haven't been too keen to move beyond that. Maybe—and this is a big damn maybe—maybe chimpanzees, since their genetic code is almost the same as ours. But I doubt it. The ethical considerations for experimenting even with chimps would be almost insurmountable."

"I thought they *cloned* Rhesus monkeys?"

"They cloned Dolly. She was the genetic duplicate of an adult sheep. With embryo splitting, you start with a single embryo and just make a bunch of copies."

"Kinko's for the masses...So you think this is what Tyrellovich was doing at Monogovody?" Angela asked, looking at Greg for an answer.

Finally, Kaloostian shrugged. "What can I say? There's always been gossip that ETI went beyond basic experimentation. Personally, I'm not convinced. Even for someone as technologically aggressive as Yuri Tyrellovich, it'd be too risky. Right up to 1996, when they broke ground at Monogovody, genetics was more wing-and-a-prayer than categorical theory. Trying to find gene-based birth defects, even with a genetic blueprint, is like trying to find a single typo in a volume 180 times the size of the *World Book Encyclopedia* in five hours."

"That's small."

"That's fuckin' microscopic, Spud. You mentioned Collins, Tsui, and Riordan's work on cracking the cystic fibrosis gene. Well, they found not one, not twenty, but 350 different sites where the CF gene mutates. The kind of precision you're talking about makes the moon landing look Neanderthal. I love genetics, but one thing I've learned is that nothing's obvious. Sheep and monkeys are pretty cut and dried. Humans are a bit more complex. We're decades away from understanding even the most fundamental interrelationship between DNA and consciousness. Until all the bugs are ironed out, cloning people is too damned iffy."

Angela threw up her arms in defeat. "This is unbelievable. I watch the news, I hear about all these scientific advances. One minute I'm thinking Tyrellovich ran some sort of frostbitten version of *The Island of Dr. Moreau.* Then you give me the odds and I've got to tell you, it all sounds impossible."

"Ahh, but you have to understand the first rule of science—*impossible* is a word to be used infrequently and with maximum prejudice."

"I'm supposed to assume that nothing's impossible?"

"No, just avoid the extremes," Kaloostian said, wincing as he took a drink of cold coffee. "And be careful what you base your conclusions on."

Toner looked at the computer screen for a moment before turning back with another question. "What happened, Greg? What…who destroyed Monogovody?"

"No one knows for sure. Officially, the explosion went down as an accident. The Russian government ran the investigation, and from what I've heard, they were remarkably thorough. Nothing was left to speculation—from eye witness accounts, to maintenance logs, to forensic work on the bodies."

"And…?"

"And they found nothing."

Toner leaned back and frowned. "Nothing? Come on."

"I mean they found nothing that would indicate an outside source. ETI's obsession for secrecy was also their Achilles' heel. There wasn't much left after the dust had settled."

"Any survivors?"

Greg shrugged, holding his hands out for emphasis. "The numbers were never published, but I heard they pulled less than ten people still breathing out of the wreckage."

"That's one big-ass explosion. Those companies Tyrellovich worked with must've taken a huge loss."

Kaloostian nodded his head and reached for the keyboard. Without explaining, he exited the Revkin file and toggled to the bureau's mainframe data center. As Toner watched, the Armenian typed "Monogovody" and waited. Due to the constant requests for information from in-house and network users, data from the bureau's mainframe flowed like molasses. After a five-second wait, Greg leaned forward and prepared to repeat his request when acknowledgment finally arrived.

"Access denied—authorization unavailable."

For several seconds, neither spoke. Finally they looked at each other.

"It's not even dated," Toner spoke first. "What the hell's going on, Kaloostian?"

"I wish I knew. It's one thing to be told to mind my own business, but to deny authorization before we even ask…"

Biting her lower lip, Angela ejected the Revkin file disk from the drive. She shook her head, pushed her chair back, and stood up, her frustration evident. "That's it. Enough's enough. I've *had it* with being pushed around."

Kaloostian was surprised at Toner's sudden tirade. "What're you doing?"

"What am I doing? I'm taking this damn file back to Hatton and telling him to stick it."

"Oh, no you're not."

"What do you mean I'm not? Since when do you have a say in this? I came to you for technical advice. Thanks for the help and have a nice day."

"Sit down, Angie. I'm not gonna let you tease me like this. You can't come in here with information of this magnitude and then just up and walk away."

"What's it to you? You've been pooh-poohing everything I've said from the get-go."

"But if I'm wrong…what then? If this is what you think it is, it'll be better than finding an autographed first-edition Bible at a garage sale. Think about it, Toner. *Think!*"

Angela could see that Kaloostian was adamant, but she wasn't convinced. "I don't know, Greg," she said, setting down the disk.

"I was a bit hasty, but there's something going on here. This smells of conspiracy."

"Conspiracy, smiracy. Sure, there's probably some sort of cover-up, but I'm not about to put my career on the line over some big, fat unknown. I don't care if that's Adolf Hitler's DNA in there. Hey, now there's a possibility." Toner said with a laugh. "Maybe Tyrellovich was a Nazi, and he replicated a bunch of little goose-stepping clones of der Führer."

Kaloostian's expression became more serious. Angela wiped the smile from her face. "So big deal. Something smells fishy. I'm not the one who's gonna clean the pool," she said.

"Dammit Angie, you know and I know—we both know of no other pigheaded, obstinate, headstrong, gutsy, pigheaded..."

"You already said *pigheaded*."

"Yeah, well, you're more pigheaded than anyone I've ever met, so it needed to be said twice. No one else can do this. *You're it*. Hatton gave you carte blanche on this case. Let's do a little digging and find what's going on. The truth is out there!"

"This isn't an X-file, dammit. I've got nothin' to go on. It's almost two o'clock, and I've got zilch, zero, zip. Even Hatton's not desperate enough to send me on a case where I can't even define the objective. What am I suppose to tell *him*?"

"That's the beauty. Knowing you, he'll believe anything."

"You're forgetting that even Hatton answers to a higher authority. What if NSA wants the file back?"

"That's their problem. You just need a reason to be out of the building by 1700, right? So maybe you could ask the Russians for information on Olga Revkin or Monogovody. What the heck, it was their facility, sort of."

"You expect me to go pick up the phone, call the Russian embassy, and ask about something our own computer system won't give us."

"I'm only saying their information is probably more complete. It's worth a try. Call their consulate in Frisco."

"Are you serious?"

"Of course I am. The Cold War is long over. The Russians are our allies now. Call 'em. Be brave, take the road less traveled."

"Did you ever stop to think there's a reason that road is less traveled?"

Kaloostian shook his head. "Just one phone call on a secure line. Just one."

"This is stupid. Like being in hell and calling for the time and temperature. No matter how often you dial, the message is always the same: 'It's hot...and it's forever.'"

"Stop being a baby," Kaloostian said. He shrugged and waited.

The room was silent. Toner finally sighed and looked at her grinning friend. Shaking her head, she stood up and reached for the file disk. Before she could pick it up, Kaloostian covered it with his right hand.

"Leave it. I want to take a closer look, see if I can dig up any other information."

"And burn a bootleg copy, too, I suppose?"

"Who, me? Never. I just wanna check out a few things."

"Why do I ever listen to you?" Toner muttered. She turned and walked towards the door.

As she reached for the doorknob, Kaloostian called out. "Say Angie— one more thing. Don't tell anybody about this, okay? I mean it. There're too many unanswered questions. Keep a low profile."

"Yeah, loose lips sink ships."

"And bring me some hot coffee when you come back," Kaloostian added.

Toner gave him a dirty look and extended the middle finger of her left hand. Then she opened the door and, without looking back, headed for the elevator.

After she was gone, Kaloostian sat quietly in his wheelchair. Two minutes ticked by. He idly picked up a pencil and glanced at the computer screen, at the unmistakable message taunting him—"Access denied—authorization unavailable."

He knew full well the meaning of the message. His right hand, clutching the pencil, began to tremble. He looked at the Revkin file disk and massaged his forehead with his left hand, elbow resting on the desk.

Mindful of his rapid, tremulous breathing, Kaloostian tried to regain control of his emotions. At the peak of his agitation, the pencil shattered, broken into several jagged pieces by the force of his grip. Stifling a heavy sigh, he threw the pieces at the computer.

"Seven years," he moaned. "Seven goddamned years."

Kaloostian removed his glasses and tossed them on the desk. He brushed the fragments of pencil from his right hand, then wiped his eyes. Fighting tears, his mind raced between the responsibilities of his duty and his love for his friend.

"What am I going to do? Seven years, oh God. I've looked for this…for *Nyentzi*, for seven years. What am I going to tell them, now? Why did it have to be her? Why did she have to bring it to me on a plastic platter? *Damn you*, Angela Toner. What am I going to do?"

7

GEORGIE PORGIE

"This is ridiculous," Angela Toner thought to herself. She sat in her cubicle, staring at a blank computer screen, mustering the courage to accept Kaloostian's suggestion. "Hell, I don't even know where Monogovody is."

Frustrated, arms crossed, Angela sighed and reached for her coffee, only to realize that caffeine was the last thing she needed. With a resolute sigh, she reached for her keyboard and initiated a data search, topic "Russia." A localized map of Western Russia filled her screen. According to Kaloostian, Monogovody was approximately 1,200 miles north, northeast of Moscow. She soon discovered, however, that the approximated parameters left a great deal of ground to cover.

She double-toggled to the autofind menu and typed "Salekhard," the name of the city nearest to Monogovody. In a millisecond, the computerized map shifted to the north central Russian district of Yamal Nenets. Her target, highlighted in red on the Ob River, rested directly on the Arctic Circle, longitude 66.5 degrees.

Zooming out from the district map, Angela got a sense of Salekhard's position, closer to the northern border of Kazakhstan—or the North Pole—than to Moscow. Afghanistan was farther to the south. She zeroed to within a hundred kilometers of her target, but the situation did not improve. While there were nearby cities, they were the kind that appear on a map only because there is room to print the name. Aksarka, Pitlyar, and several other dots were probably no bigger than large villages or small towns—the inhabitants could take their pick.

Stalin and Tyrellovich knew how to pick them. The isolation they sought, the one for punishment, the other for alleged illegal genetic research, was generously available in that cold, remote region. Technology made the world a smaller place, but cities like Salekhard still seemed as distant as the moon.

Leaving the map on screen, Angela prompted her computer to retrieve the telephone number of the Russian consulate. Unlike Hatton, a reputed technophobe, Toner enjoyed the latest electronic toys. Her computer had a miniature digital video camera for face-to-face communication, and she preferred the intimacy of direct visual linkage to sound-only transmission. She donned a headset with earphone and mike for privacy, pressed *enter*, and the laptop's software made the connection.

An attractive but unsmiling receptionist came onto her screen. "Good afternoon. Russian consulate. Lena Yastrzhembsky. May I help you?" Lena, who spoke with a slight accent, had dark hair, a broad face, and an enormous chest.

"Hello. My name is Angela Toner. I'm a special agent with the Federal Bureau of Investigation in Los Angeles."

Toner deduced by the no-nonsense look on the receptionist's face that her next few sentences would be crucial. With nothing better to do on a Monday afternoon, Lena might cut her off in a heartbeat. Toner's best bet was to ask vague, hard-to-answer questions—with the utmost courtesy.

"It's Ms. Yastrzhembsky, isn't it? I'll take only a minute of your time. The FBI is seeking any assistance the Russian consulate might be able to offer concerning Olga Lyubimova-Revkin. As you might know, before her marriage, Olga was a Russian citizen. Sadly, she is hospitalized with depression, and the bureau feels her family—her Russian family—might be of clinical assistance. Olga seems to be exhibiting significant unresponsiveness to her current treatment and medication. Perhaps with the involvement of old friends and family in her therapy, she might respond."

"Ms. Toner, I do not know if I understand exactly what it is you are asking or how we might help. If you care to hold, I will confer with someone else on the consulate staff."

"That would be fine. Thank you very much."

"One moment please," the receptionist said, placing the American on hold. An image of the Russian flag remained.

Angela exhaled. The initial conversation with the receptionist—indeed the entire case—was so confusing, even Toner didn't know what she'd asked for.

After half a minute, the receptionist returned. "Ms. Toner, I have spoken with our consular representative. However, he is on another call. Would you care to wait?"

"That'll be fine. Thank you for your assistance."

The receptionist smiled and switched off. Toner leaned back in her chair, closed her eyes and enjoyed the down time. In the age of multimedia technology, hold music was at least in stereo.

"Crazy Armenian," Toner thought to herself while she waited. "I can't believe I'm going along with one of his lame-brained ideas." Six years she'd known Gregory Kaloostian, but calling the Russian consulate for help with a bureau file was one for the record book. Still, the Armenian knew firsthand the Russians' reputation for hoarding information, and their archives were likely better than what she had at her disposal.

On hold for more than a minute, Angela considered her friend's recent behavior. She couldn't put her finger on it, but he was definitely acting strange and out of sorts. Of course, much of his behavior since she'd met him could be called strange and out of sorts.

"And what a coincidence…he just happens to be an expert on genetics," Angela mused. "What are the odds of that? Somewhere between ridiculous and astronomical. And why's he acting so weird? And why do I have these nasty suspicions? Maybe it's nothing. Maybe it's the Guerrero drug bust. Maybe that's bugging him."

Kaloostian hated to see his tax dollars wasted on the war against illegal drug use. "Legalize and tax" was his motto. Toner, on the other hand, felt that someone who self-administered a rather hefty marijuana prescription for his own medical conditions might have clouded judgment—literally. But Greg had his reasons. His left leg, shredded by a land mine more than fifteens years earlier, had been amputated, leaving him with the torment called "phantom-limb pain."

Due to the limited medical resources in Armenia at the time of his injury, Kaloostian's leg had not been amputated until after he'd reached the States. During those horrible weeks, the only sensations he'd felt in the torn limb were of continuing agony. After the surgical removal of his leg slightly above the knee, the knives of chronic, shooting pain emanating from the now-missing appendage were as intense as before the operation.

For Greg Kaloostian and thousands like him, marijuana was an inexpensive, easy-to-control way to deal with pain. The drug went directly to the sensory cortex, where all sensations, from extreme pleasure to extreme pain, were processed. Once he was able to treat his condition, the symptoms became manageable. Greg returned to school, received a master's degree in computer science, and moved to Los Angeles. Of course, one does not administer a mind-altering substance to someone like Kaloostian without expecting a few interesting "side effects," like the time he…

"Ms. Toner? Excuse me…"

Angela came out of her daydream with a jolt. Staring at her with a curious expression was a distinguished-looking man with striking Slavic features, neatly trimmed mustache, and graying hair. Impeccably dressed in diplomatic uniform, he wore a deep blue suit, overly starched white shirt, and crimson tie.

Toner smiled as he continued to speak.

"My name is Alexander Samanov. Our receptionist informed me that the bureau has need of some assistance—about Olga Lyubimova-Revkin."

"Samanov!" Angela realized to herself. "The name from the Revkin file!" She took a deep breath and began the interview.

"Yes, Mr. Samanov, thank you for your time. Ms. Yastrzhembsky said you were familiar with the Revkin case," Toner said, glancing at the piece of paper where she'd written the receptionist's name. "Did she explain the nature of my call?"

The Russian answered with a smile. "Ms. Yastrzhembsky did not explain the details, but I am familiar with the situation. Anyone with compassion for a mother losing her only daughter…One does not need to repeat such painful news. I understand Mrs. Revkin is hospitalized—depression, I am told. At what hospital might that be, Ms. Toner?"

"I'm afraid I'm not at liberty to say, sir."

"But of course. I was only thinking how refreshing a bouquet of flowers from an old friend might be. It's not important. Helping you help her—that is what we must do. How may I be of assistance?"

"My first question, Mr. Samanov…"

"Please. My name is Alexander. No need for such formality. And you?"

"Yes sir, my name is Angela."

Samanov nodded his head, his smile glued in place like a cheap pen at a teller's window. "Did your mother name you after an angel?"

"After an aunt, actually."

"And look at you now. She must be proud. So, what is your first question, Angela?"

"I wanted to ask you how much you are already aware of Olga Revkin's situation. If you would fill me in on what you know, I won't be repeating unnecessary information and taking up so much of your time. You look to be such a busy man."

The smile on Samanov's face never wavered, but Toner detected a slight change in his eyes. "Yes, Consul Samanov," she thought, "I am good at my job."

"How considerate. Yes, that is a good place to begin. I am afraid, however, that my information is incomplete. What I have read and seen on the television. Very inadequate. Poor Olga…and her daughter so young. How old is she, Angela?"

"You sly old fox," Angels thought, then answered, "She's seven. Her birthday's in August. And unless we locate a donor, Melissa Revkin won't live to see her eighth birthday."

Samanov was silent for a moment, evaluating Toner's statement. He leaned back in his chair and rubbed his chin. "And the doctors are certain there is not a match among her family? They have performed all necessary tissue analyses?"

"There is no doubt. Unless we can find a donor, this girl will die."

"Do you not consider it odd that there is such an incompatibility within her family?"

"Not at all. Please understand—I don't have a medical background, but even among immediate family members, significant tissue variations can exist."

"And you believe relatives of Olga in Russia might offer hope."

"It's a chance worth considering, don't you agree?"

"I am not so sure," Samanov concluded. "As a matter of fact, Angela Toner, I am confused. Why would the United States Federal Bureau of Investigation contact the Russian consulate if that were the only purpose of the call? Would not your Red Cross be more interested in such an inquiry? Pardon my candidness, but am I missing something?"

"Oh, what the hell," Angela reckoned to herself, "might as well go for the gusto." She cleared her throat and launched her spiel. "Mr. Samanov—I'm sorry, *Alexander*—James Revkin and Olga Lyubimova were married in January 2000, shortly after James returned to the United States from his trip to Russia. Did he meet Olga while he was on the trip, or were they acquainted before that? I'm sorry, but this is a delicate question. Do you personally know the Revkins?"

"Yes, actually I do. As one who is interested in technology, I make it my business to become acquainted with noteworthy scientists, especially when one of them is Russian. Does that not make sense? And I understand your next question. No, Olga Revkin was not pregnant before they met."

"I'm sorry to have to ask such a *delicate* question."

Samanov's smile wouldn't quit. "In circumstances such as ours, Angela, all questions are delicate. Do you not agree?"

When Toner nodded in agreement, the Russian asked a question of his own. "What other delicacies do you have written down on that paper in front of you, Angela?"

Toner looked directly into his eyes. "Do you know where they met, Alexander?"

"This conversation seems fixated on the parents rather than the child…Where they met, mmm? At some conference, a blind date, on the Internet? Does it matter?"

Angela shook her head. "Not at all. It's just that I remember seeing a reference to one particular symposium they both attended that was held at…ah, the name escapes me."

"Monogovody…is that the name you were thinking of?" Samanov asked quietly.

"Yes, that's the one."

"I do not know if that is where they first met. Still, I suspect that is where they put the cart before the horse. In the old days, Angela, the honeymoon came after the marriage."

"But why Monogovody?" Toner asked.

"The symposium. Tyrellovich—I suspect you have heard that name, as well. Yuri Tyrellovich sponsored the 1999 symposium on genetics at Monogovody. The Revkins and a great many others were in attendance. It seems they did more than merely *discuss* reproduction."

Angela smiled at Samanov's joke. She sensed he knew more than he was willing to say. Facing an ever-nearer deadline, she had no choice but to play her trump card.

"Is that where it began, sir?" Angela finally said.

"Where what began?"

"*Nyentzi…*"

The smile on Samanov's face faded. Though he said nothing, his eyes spoke volumes. Toner noted he did not seem surprised to hear the word. Indeed, his lack of reaction allowed Angela to conclude she had asked the right question.

"This conversation has taken an interesting turn, yes?" Samanov finally responded.

Toner hesitated, then threw caution to the wind. "You know of the experiments?"

"Yes…Yuri Tyrellovich and his experiments." Another pause, a hardening of the eyes. "His dallying with nature was an affront to God—pathetic and grandiose indecency, perversion."

Samanov's face reddened. The diplomat obviously had a strong opinion on the subject of genetic engineering. Toner remained silent and wary. She was certain he would continue, arguing his convictions, providing her with the information she needed.

"I am sorry," said Samanov, trying to control his emotions. "I am a deeply religious man. I do not agree with Tyrellovich and others of that kind—those who believe they can transcend the abyss between technology and religion with impunity.

"Such people do not understand that creation must be allowed to proceed slowly, naturally. They forget the time when God wielded destiny's hand, not the whims of science and commerce. No, Ms. Toner, I do not grieve for Yuri Tyrellovich. I only fear he is not buried deep enough."

The implications of Samanov's tirade disconcerted Toner. The conversation was moving in a direction she had not expected.

"Alexander, I understand your aversion to what Tyrellovich stood for, but that is precisely my point. Nyentzi has been kept secret for too long. We must work together, openly discuss our mutual objectives."

"What is there to discuss? Did you know Tyrellovich? Do you understand what Nyentzi truly is? Do you know the scope of his experimentation? He called himself a scientist, but I know what he was…oh, that I do. 'Woe to those who call evil good and good evil, who pretend the darkness is light and the light is darkness.' "

"I need your help, sir. *Melissa* needs your help."

"I have no information of benefit to you or the Revkin girl," Samanov asserted, stone-faced. "She is beyond help if you are calling us."

"Please, sir. I need to see you. Is there no one who might be of assistance?"

"This conversation continues to puzzle me. How can it be your files are incomplete? What purpose could I serve, other than to verify what you should already know?"

"You've got a good point there, mister," Angela thought, before saying, "Alexander, I'll be candid. The information I require with regard to Nyentzi must not be tainted by ideology or political pretension. I need to know what happened at Monogovody—what happened to

Melissa Revkin. I agree with you. The evils of genetic manipulation must be stopped."

Samanov sat quietly for more than fifteen seconds, looking intently at Angela. She met his gaze in silence, refusing to admit defeat. At last the Russian spoke.

"As I said, there is nothing I can do to help you. But…others may be able to assist you in your efforts to save the child."

Toner breathed deeply. "Thank you. Do you have a name or number in mind? Is there someone I can call?"

"It would be better for you to talk to our people personally. Do you have authorization for a little trip?"

A flight to San Francisco would be perfect. "Yes, Alexander. That'll work just fine."

Samanov's smile crept back. "Will you be traveling alone?" he asked.

"Yes," Angela said, nodding.

"Is an evening flight today satisfactory?"

"Yes. I think I can be ready by seven."

"Very good. One final item: I am thinking of a very important word in your language—a word most pertinent to our conversation. Do you know the word to which I am referring?"

Toner considered Samanov's question. She then remembered Kaloostian's comment to her thirty minutes earlier. "I believe the word is *mum*."

"*Mum?* I do not think so."

"I assure you, Alexander, mum's the word, though you might be thinking of words like *discretion* or *low-profile*."

Samanov laughed. "Yes, I see. I was thinking of a word in English and you, of course, were thinking of a word in American. But they mean the same thing. Excellent, young lady. I will have Ms. Yastrzhembsky finalize the paperwork and transmit the necessary documents. Leave it all to me. It was a pleasure speaking with you, Angela Toner. We will talk again, perhaps. Please, have a nice day."

"Yes…you, too. Oh, excuse me…one moment, Mr. Samanov…sir…*damn.*" The screen blanked. Samanov had not heard her.

"Transmit documents?" Toner thought. "Last I heard, San Francisco was still part of the United States, not Russia. Maybe he's arranging airfare. Wouldn't that be nice?"

Angela leaned back and sighed with relief. She'd found her ticket out of the building and away from Deputy Assistant Director Hatton. She had not yet determined the nature of her investigation, nor what fabrication she would give her boss. She had no defined strategy, objective, or agenda. Worse, she would be leaving for San Francisco in less than five hours and hadn't begun to pack.

"Angie Toner—on target again…" she silently smirked.

She spun about in her chair, but her carefree moment of triumph was cut short. Walking toward her cubicle was Marcus Heiple, her SWAT team's weak link. Heiple was a blond-haired, blue-eyed, six-foot, former beach bum from Long Beach. He was twenty-six years old, going on nineteen, with a testosterone level to match.

Marcus Heiple fancied himself a smooth operator. Permed hair, tanned skin, unnaturally straight white teeth—a regular Ken doll. To Toner, his phony friendliness and excessive fawning gave him the air of a plaid-on-plaid insurance agent, a person who would say or do anything to make a buck, who saw people as means to meet a quota, who could clear a room in five minutes. The type of person everyone loves to hate.

"Hey, hey *AnGeLa.* Nice to see you sittin' down. I thought by now they'd have taken you out back and paddled that pretty behind of yours. What a naughty girl. I heard Scriff and Hatton were gonna reassign you, demote you, or somethin'. Man, this bullshit we grunts have to deal with—you know what I mean. We're in the trenches here. And what do we get? A bunch of shit. Am I right—uh, am I right?"

Toner grabbed a pile of paperwork kept nearby for such emergencies and began paging through it. "Whatever you say, Marc. Look, I'm buried under all this paperwork here. Gotta metro. Thanks for stopping by."

"You know, Angie, I've been doin' some thinking."

"That explains the smoke pouring out your ears," she quipped to herself.

"Since the bust really was a success, no matter what those dickheads say, we ought to celebrate—you and me. You need to get out more, catch a couple of brewskis."

Before she could respond, Heiple straddled a chair, its back facing Toner. He wheeled closer and crossed his arms, leering with cocky arrogance.

Angela held her breath. Heiple had been a casual acquaintance of her husband. Since Jake's death, he'd assumed an intimacy that had not existed then and certainly did not now.

"No can do, Marc. Those rumors were radically correct. I've been reassigned, and I've gotta be out of the building by 1700."

"See, that's just what I mean. You bust your ass for the man, and ya get it kicked instead. We gotta stick together, Angie. People like us gotta stick together. Hey, you need some backup, just come to me. They give you shit because you're a minority, but that's never bothered me."

"I'm not a minority, Heiple."

"Like I can't tell you're black…duuuh. But hey, what can I do? You just happen to be the way I like my coffee—dark and sweet." Before Toner could react to Heiple's ignorant, self-serving remark, he reached over and patted her on the butt.

Toner's pretended busyness came to a screeching halt. She set the papers on the desk and turned towards him, pushing her chair closer to his. Returning Heiple's hormone-injected smile with one of her own, Angela looked directly into his eyes.

"Marc, when you were a little boy—not last week—I'm talking, oh, age three or four, did your mom or dad read you nursery rhymes?"

"Sure…probably. Why?"

"There's this one nursery rhyme that's always been a favorite of mine. Maybe you know it—Georgie Porgie? Can't remember how it goes…something like: 'Georgie Porgie, what a guy. Kissed the girls and made them cry.' You ever hear that one, Marc?"

Heiple shrugged. Still smiling, Toner reached out, lightly touching his left hand.

"You may not know this, but there's a politically correct addendum to that little rhyme, and I'll bet it's one you've never heard. It's about Georgie Porgie's little female friend, Angie Pangie. Seems he kissed her, too, but she didn't cry."

"She didn't, huh? She must've liked Georgie Porgie. Am I right?"

"Well, I wouldn't go quite that far…She didn't cry, but you know what she did do?" Heiple was silent—the stupid grin on his face conveying the only message he was capable of sending. Toner slid to the end of her chair, stroked his hand a second time, and winked.

"Well, Marc, I'll tell you what she did…she *kneed* Georgie Porgie, right in the balls."

Angela's smile disappeared. She kicked Heiple's chair with her left foot and tightened her grip on his right hand like a vise. Launching from her chair, she twisted his left arm behind his back, the momentum of his spinning chair bending the arm faster and farther.

So sudden was the attack, Heiple could only grunt in pain. Maintaining her grip on his backward extended limb, she leaned forward, her mouth inches from his trembling ear.

"Poor Georgie," she whispered. "He doesn't kiss the girls anymore. Little Angie Pangie gave him such a chop between the legs, his doctor thinks his testicles are his tonsils.

"Understand one thing, Heiple—don't *ever* do that again. And for the record, I'm not black, red, yellow, or any other label. I'm an

American. Not some of the above—all of the above. You got that, cool dude?"

Pushing Heiple's chair away, Toner released her grip and stepped back. She was ready if he came up swinging, but all he could do was stumble away. After several steps, he stopped and turned.

"You're screwing up big time," he hissed. "You can deny it, but I know you want me."

"Oh, I want you all right—*out of* my life."

"You think you're so funny and clever. I've been watching you, Toner, covering your back. You push me away, who's gonna protect you then? Huh, smart ass?"

"I think you're missing the point, bubba. You—protect me? Aren't you the kind of nut case I should be worried about in the first place?"

Heiple said nothing, so pronounced his scowl his eyebrows seemed to touch his chin. His lips were so tense they'd turned white. His body, from clenched fists to hunched shoulders, shook with frustration and embarrassment. He seemed ready to pounce.

Angela was taking no chances. She moved closer to her desk and her service pistol in the drawer. To her surprise, he grunted once, turned, and stormed away. She was certain she'd not heard the last of him.

If the pat on the butt had been the first such incident of sexual harassment on Heiple's part, Angela's reaction might be deemed "excessive force." But his machismo—prolonged stares, rude comments, inappropriate jokes and flirtations, and the constant bump and grind of bodily contact—had escalated for months. He was always maneuvering for position to brush up against her, to prod her, to touch.

Angela didn't consider herself a damsel in distress, but no one, male or female, should have to put up with loutish behavior. After the kind of day she'd had, Heiple was lucky she hadn't gone ballistic. Of course, having to explain the disemboweling of a fellow agent to the Hatton along with why she had to take a trip to San Francisco, would simply be too time-consuming. She would just have to deal with the Boy Wonder when she returned.

How the battle of the sexes had changed over time! A hundred years ago, her reaction to Heiple's advances would have been indignant silence. Fifty years before, she could only have said: "Please, Mr. Heiple, don't." Twenty-five years ago, she'd have slapped his face. Next month, next week, if it happened again, she'd break his arm.

Toner sat down at her desk and breathed heavily. Heiple's behavior got her adrenaline pumping, but she pushed it from her mind. Time was running out and she still had to see Hatton, get his authorization on a travel voucher, head back down to Kaloostian's office with a hot cup of coffee, grab the Revkin file, arrange a flight to Frisco, and pack. She hated being rushed, but the thought of two weeks up the coast was all the incentive she needed.

Operating on practiced instinct, Angela shut off the power, disconnected the external monitor from her laptop, closed the lid, unplugged the power supply, and stowed everything into a padded carrying case. The computer, which weighed less than five pounds and measured eleven inches in width, was as rugged as it was portable.

Angela next took out her Beretta 9mm semiautomatic service pistol and slipped it into a side pouch of the computer case. She usually wore the weapon in a shoulder holster, but she thought it best not to show up at the deputy assistant director's office packing heat.

For most journeys to Hatton's office, Angela took the stairs, which provided convenient exercise. But an open elevator door beckoned her with its tempting solitude. She jumped in, punched the top-floor button, and leaned against the side. After a moment, Angela realized the piped-in music was the same song she'd heard early that morning on her car radio. She recognized the tune, an old favorite she hadn't heard in years.

"It's…it's…oh, I know this one—it's right on the tip of my tongue. I know, it's…!"

The elevator stopped. The door opened and Toner's heart sank. She forgot the song, forgot about Frisco, forgot about everything except which pocket of her bag held the Beretta.

8

Foreign Affairs

It was an encounter impossible to prepare for. Felicia Scriff never expected Toner to be on the elevator. She knew the younger agent was an exercise buff who habitually used the stairs. When the third floor elevator door opened, Scriff charged right in, sideswiping Toner, who was too surprised to get out of the way.

Scriff never liked Angela Toner, nor did she care for Toner's attitude, which she considered disrespectful, irresponsible, and unprofessional. The Guerrero drug bust had been a near-fiasco, and for someone like Toner to receive credit for saving the day was too much to bear.

There was nothing humorous about law enforcement. Protecting God-fearing, honest citizens from the drug addicts, gutter punks, and other riffraff prowling the alleys of America was no laughing matter. Toner's unflagging smile and vivacity was, to Felicia Mildred Scriff, ample indication of the younger agent's contempt for her job, her coworkers, her superiors, her country, and her badge.

The two antagonists were about to reach terminal velocity when a messenger from the communication center came upon them with a cartload of interoffice communiqués and priority packages. If the messenger, who had an envelope for Toner, had awaited the end of the verbal kung fu, he might have stood there the rest of the afternoon.

The young man tried to be inconspicuous, tried to avoid laughing at the nature of the altercation, which had to do with the etiquette of entering and exiting an elevator. By the time he'd arrived, however, Toner and Scriff's language had degenerated from mere insult to uncontrollable farce.

Scriff leaned close to Toner, shaking her right index finger in the younger agent's face. To prevent an escalation of hostilities, the messenger interrupted. "Excuse me, *ladies*. I hate to be rude, but I have a packet for Agent Toner."

The young man carefully stepped between the two adversaries and turned his back on Scriff. He gave a manila envelope, along with an electronic clipboard, to Toner. Toner took the packet and pressed her right index finger on the black square at the top of the clipboard. In an instant, a digitized indicator verified her name and badge number.

"Yep, it's you, all right. Thanks a bunch. Be seeing you around, Agent Toner. You too, Scriff…I guess."

The messenger sauntered to the elevator and pushed the down button. Not a word was spoken while he waited. After fifteen tense seconds, the elevator stopped, the door opened, and the young man got in. Just before the doors closed, he waved and announced in an unusually loud voice: "By the way, Toner, I heard you kicked some serious butt this morning. Bravo Zulu."

The elevator door closed, leaving the two combatants to continue the standoff. The messenger's obviously biased remark was the last straw for Scriff. As things currently stood at the bureau, she could do little to exact revenge against Toner. But if Scriff had one positive attribute, it was patience. She could wait. What's a year?

"I'll have to be sure you're on the party committee next December. We can tie all three events together—the holidays, Hatton's retirement, my promotion. That sound like a good idea, *Angela*?"

"Whatever you say, Scriff," Toner replied. She opened the packet, hoping the supervisor had enough tact to walk away.

"Is that official business—or reward money from the Guerreros for screwing up this morning?"

"Be nice, Felicia. Wittiness does not become you. If you must know, and I sure would hate to disappoint, it probably has to do with that wonderfully interesting case you and Hatton stuck me with."

Toner removed the contents of the envelope. Holding the packet at an angle to prevent her antagonist from seeing what it was, Angela scanned the material. As shock washed over her, she did her best to suppress her disbelief. Scriff was the last person she wanted in on her little secret.

Several seconds elapsed. Toner clenched the documents and forced a smile. "You'll be glad to know I found that hole Hatton wanted me to crawl in. Do you know anything about the case, Supervisor Scriff, or were you just along for the ride?"

"That was all Hatton's doing. Knowing him, it's probably another chance for you to prove your dedication."

"*Felicia*, such an attitude—I'll just have to fill you in." Angela had to think fast. In most clutches her primary weapon was sarcasm. Scriff, as Toner had discovered shortly after they met, was devoid of humor. She was not funny, she seldom laughed, and she resented Toner for both.

"Big counterfeit ring," Angela began, waving her arms for emphasis. "We're talking billions. Run out of the Cayman Islands. NSA's handling the stateside sting, but they need an undercover operative—someone with a tan. I, of course, got right on it. Made some calls, established the contacts—typical boffo performance. Oh well, I'd love to chat but gotta pack. Off to the Cayman Islands. Little sun…little rum…you know the routine. Gee, hope my silk bikini's back from the cleaners. I'll need new shoes, too. Have to look the part. I'd better go powder my nose before I see Hatton. Gotta get that travel voucher signed."

Toner slid the documents back into the envelope. She started to walk past Scriff, but the supervisor blocked her way. They made eye contact, the chilly animosity unmistakable.

"You think you're so special, don't you, Toner?" Scriff seethed.

"That depends on your definition of *special*. Look Scriff, I've really gotta hustle. I don't know 'bout you, but there are things more important than standing around yakkin.'"

"*You just wait.* When Hatton's gone, I'm gonna hound you morning to night. When the big boy's no longer protecting your smart ass, your days'll be numbered."

Toner bit her lower lip and looked her adversary in the eye. "You want to know something, Scriff? My mother warned me about people like you—people who show up for management meetings with a toothbrush, a bottle of Scope, and kneepads. Isn't that right, Fellatio, or Felicia, or whateverthehell your name is."

"You contemptuous, foul-mouthed *bitch*. You'd better to stay out of my way. I'll fix you and your attitude for good."

"As long as I avoid getting between you and a pastry cart, I oughta do just fine. Now, if you'll please get out of the way, it's a busy day."

Toner hurried down the hall. After making certain Scriff hadn't followed, she headed for the women's room. Finding it empty, she went to the last stall, entered, and closed the door. She plopped down on the stool, put her head into her hands, and moaned.

"Damn, damn, damn. What have I gotten myself into this time?" Suppressing an urge to scream, Toner reopened the envelope, withdrew the documents, read them a second time, hoping somehow they had changed. Her ticket out of town wasn't to San Francisco at all. Her destination was, in fact, quite a bit farther.

The envelope contained several pages of digitally transmitted documents, including first-class airfare on Aeroflot—Los Angeles to eastern Russia. The top page was a handwritten note from Samanov, wishing her a pleasant trip and reminding her to bring a heavy coat. After that a slew of credentials, including a liberally worded and prestamped visa. It gave her up to thirty days in Russia, with instructions should her work require an extension. Then a concealed-weapons permit and a memorandum signed by the consul, instructing the Russian border authorities to grant Angela Carmen Toner full diplomatic courtesy.

Samanov was a man of his word. He was also a man with an audacious style of doing business. Not only did each document list her full name, which she had not told him, but also her social security number, address, and most alarming, her height, weight, and hair and eye colors. All unnervingly accurate—except for her weight, which was five pounds too heavy.

"Wouldn't you know he'd get that wrong!" Toner huffed. She slid the papers into the envelope and realized how disturbingly easy it was to access someone's personal data. But Toner knew the Russian diplomat was not the type to do something without reason. The sending of the documents, complete with her vital statistics, was not, in her opinion, an example of one-upmanship. Alexander Samanov moved in a world of subtlety and intrigue, despite the so-called 'New World Order.' In such an arena, calculated reasoning hid behind the firmness of a handshake, the time a politician kept a guest waiting, or here, in the acknowledgment of the importance of Toner's job.

Relations between the superpowers were forever changing. Despite the FBI's behind-the-scenes assistance in Russia's Federal Security Bureau crackdown on organized crime, the two agencies still viewed one another with suspicion. Samanov's message thus was clear. While in Russia, she would be under a microscope. No matter where she went, she might be followed, monitored, or videotaped. Discretion in her words and actions was paramount. In other words, she had to be a good girl.

Toner placed the documents back in the envelope and left the women's room.

"Sneaking out already, Mrs. M. Bwana give you the rest of the day off?" Toner asked, approaching Checkpoint Charlie.

Mrs. Malone put on her coat and reached for her purse. "Neither, honey. I've got a doctor's appointment at 4:30. If I don't leave now, I'll be late. Be a dear, and take these papers into his office. Tell him not to lose anything...and to please *read* it. There's a memo marked urgent that he'd better take care of immediately."

Toner took the stack of papers from the secretary. "No problem—hope it's nothing serious—the doctor's appointment, that is."

"I'm healthy as a thoroughbred. Just a physical. Thanks Angie, you're a peach." Malone waved and walked down the hall.

Angela knocked lightly on the deputy assistant director's door, entering before he could respond. "Mrs. Malone's off to her doctor's appointment. You want these on your desk, or should I just throw them in the garbage and save you the effort?"

Hatton pointed to a small portion of the desk relatively free of debris. "Right here, Toner. Set 'em right here." With exaggerated movement, Angela stacked the paperwork on the desk, brushed away some imaginary dirt, and smiled.

"You'll be glad to know the Guerreros are grabbing all the evening headlines," Hatton continued. "Even the national news picked up on this one. I just got off the horn with the DA's office and everything's going as planned. How about you and your disappearing act?"

"As a matter of fact, that's what I came to see you about. Did you review that file before you dumped it on me? Man, talk about disorganized."

"Didn't have time—read a summary page that came with the disk. What'd you find?"

"Well," Toner began, taking a deep breath. "Apparently some top-gun scientist went off the deep end after her daughter was severely injured in a car accident and since she's not responding to any of the treatment—the daughter needs a kidney transplant—the bureau was called in to see if we could locate a suitable donor for the child from the mother's extended Russian family though why the bureau's involved is anyone's guess. You following this?"

Hatton sat motionless, his mouth open, eyes glazed above the top of his glasses. If she could keep him going a little longer, she was sure he'd drool.

"So, with nothing to go on I called the Russian consulate in San Francisco and talked to the consul who's some guy named Samanov and he was really quite cooperative and friendly and it's his opinion that the only way Olga Revkin could possibly regain full use of her mental capacities would be to spend two weeks in Aruba and being a nice guy he sent me the paperwork including first-class airfare—who says the Russians are cold and aloof—so if you'll just sign my travel voucher I'll be out of your hair taking Olga Revkin to the Caribbean and saving the world from impending doom. Okay?"

There was a long pause. Al Hatton emerged from his stupor. He took a deep breath, shook the cobwebs from his head, and gritted his teeth. No matter how hard he tried, he could never get used to Toner's disarming and puckish behavior.

"I hope—I hope very, very much, Angela Carmen Toner, that someday soon, you meet a new man, fall in love again, and have ten children. I hope that any boys you have get crewcuts, walk around in baggy jeans, looking like Wally, Beaver, Lumpy, and Eddie. On my knees, *I pray to God* your kids grow up and torment you the way you torment me. Now let me see that goddamned paperwork."

Angela handed the envelope to the deputy assistant director. He opened it, pulled everything out on his desk, and began to review it. After scrutinizing every page, he glanced up, took a good hard look at his star pupil, and went back through them a second time. He checked the print and the quality of the paper, looked for ink smudges or any other indication of forgery. Alfred E. Hatton was taking no chances.

"All right Toner, what's this all about? Where *the hell* did you get these? And cut the crap—I want real answers."

"I do entreat your grace to pardon me. I know not by what power I am made bold, nor how it may concern my modesty in such a presence here to plead my thoughts: but I beseech your grace that I may know the worst that may befall me in this case."

"*Stop.* Haven't I told you no more fuckin' Shakespeare. I thought we'd agreed on that?"

Toner grinned. "Sorry, sir, couldn't resist. So...what don't you understand? Seems crystal to me."

"Crystal clear, my ass. I don't understand any of it. You trying to tell me you called the Russian consulate, talked to Alexander Samanov—a man who has a reputation of non-cooperation a mile wide? And because he got lucky last night, he transmitted you a visa, a plane ticket..."

"*First-class* plane ticket."

"Toner, I'm shocked he even took your call. What the hell did you say to him?"

In keeping with Kaloostian's and Samanov's advice about secrecy, Angela could not fully explain the circumstances involving the Russian diplomat's cooperation. This left her one course of action—innuendo, tinged with sarcasm.

"I sure as *heck* didn't tell him I was hot-to-trot for a vacation in Siberia. Look, *sir*, wintering at the North Pole is not my idea of a good time. All I said was Olga Revkin's relatives in Russia might be able to provide us with a means to pull her out of her depressive state.

Samanov happens to be a friend of theirs and seemed honestly pleased he could help."

"That's it?"

"Other than the fact he thought I was cute."

"He obviously doesn't know you very well," Hatton rebutted.

"Be nice. You know I'm adorable."

"I didn't know you weighed 137 pounds."

"Shut up! You're not supposed to read that part. And I don't—I weigh a *lot* less."

Hatton laughed and held up Toner's paperwork, shaking it like a baby's rattle. "I don't trust you, Angela Toner. Not as far as I can spit. If this involved the Jamaican embassy, or anywhere else in the tropics, I'd know it was another one of your goddamned stunts, and I'd personally kick your tush out of my office and down the hall. But this—oh boy—this is good. A free trip to Siberia in the dead of winter…My God, even I couldn't have dreamt this one up. I've gotta call Samanov and thank him. This is *so* perfect."

"And I'm *so* glad you're enjoying yourself."

"Toner, I don't think you know how rare it is for anyone to get one over on you. This here's a red-letter day. I'm very excited about this. By the way, how's your Russian?"

"Better than your English. Come on, sir, you know foreign affairs aren't my specialty."

"Neither is protocol."

Toner shrugged and waited in silence. "So, what do you want me to do about this, sir?" she asked after a moment.

"Get outta here."

"Seriously, what do you want me to do?"

"I just told you—get outta here—amscray. Have a wonderful trip and don't forget to write." With a wide grin, Hatton signed Toner's travel authorization and handed it back. Despite every effort, Angela could not be angry with her boss's exaggerated glee. In all her years of dealing with the deputy assistant director, this was the first time each of them got what they wanted.

She slipped the paperwork into the envelope and headed for the door, turning around at the last moment. "By the way, Mrs. M said I was supposed to tell you to be sure to go through that stack of papers I brought in. Don't forget! She said some of it's actually important."

"Nag, nag, nag…you're worse than my ex-wife. Oh, one final word of advice. *Don't* lose that visa." Ignoring Hatton's laughter, Toner opened the door and stepped out. She waved to him with her fingers and closed the door.

After Toner was gone, Hatton continued to laugh at how perfectly his day had gone. A major drug bust was a total success—well, almost a total success. The only loose end was Toner, and she was on her way to Siberia, of all places. Never in a million years could he have expected a day like this.

Exhilarated, he decided to call his son, maybe arrange a get-together for dinner—patch up old differences. Then, with finger inches away from the autodial button, he saw the pile of paperwork Toner had brought in. He sighed, opened a desk drawer, and shoved in the papers.

"To hell with it. Tomorrow's another day," he thought. As he closed the drawer, a memorandum marked urgent jammed between the drawer and the desk. Without seeing that it was from the NSA, Hatton opened the drawer again, forced everything down, and closed it with a bang.

After stopping for coffee, Toner hurried to Kaloostian's office. It was almost 4:00. Considering the evening rush-hour traffic, Angela knew she'd be lucky to make it home, pack, and get to the airport before her flight departed for Siberia.

She knocked on Kaloostian's office door and immediately went in. The Armenian sat at his computer terminal.

"Here's your coffee," she said with a grin.

"Thanks," Greg replied. "How'd everything go? Any luck with the Russians?"

"You could say that. If you're into fifty-below wind-chills, the Russians were beyond helpful. They were downright accommodating." Toner briefly described her conversation with Samanov.

After hearing her description of the consul, Kaloostian remembered where he'd heard the name before. "I've got to admit," he said with a nod of his head, "you did a great job. When do you leave?"

"My flight takes off at 7:45 P.M. from LA International, flight 5440. There's a layover in Anchorage, then on to Petropavlovsk."

"Where the hell's Petropavlovsk?"

"I looked it up. On the southeastern coast of the Kamchatka Peninsula."

"Why Petropavlovsk? What's there?"

"An airport, I hope. I'm supposed to meet a representative from the Russian Federal Security Bureau—why don't they just call themselves the KGB? I mean, that's what they are. Same product, new package."

"You'll have to ask them. Any indication where you're headed from Petropavlovsk?"

"Nope. Guess I'll find out once I get there."

"That's right. The Russians don't like announcing their travel plans too far in advance."

"Why's that?" Toner asked.

"It invites the 'evil eye.' You've gotta remember, Russia's a remarkably superstitious country. And be prepared for the silent treatment. Russian people, especially Muscovites, are gruff, impersonal, and cold as hell—and I'm not talking temperature."

"Wow. You're making this sound like so much fun."

Greg laughed. "It's not that bad. Once they get to know you, they're charitable to a fault."

"Can't wait," Toner said halfheartedly. "Guess I'd better get going."

"Before you do—I know you're strapped for time—but I've got a couple of things. You know how in all those 007 movies, Q provided James Bond with a bunch of secret weapons and gadgets? Sorry I can't offer much, but maybe this'll help." Kaloostian handed Toner a small box wrapped in tissue paper.

She smiled and opened it. "Oh Greg, you shouldn't have—a Swiss Army knife."

"And not some cheap imitation, either. Even has a corkscrew. Here's something else that'll come in handy." Kaloostian handed Toner a black object the size of a cigarette pack.

"What's this?"

"It's a Russian-English electronic translator."

"Thanks, but I was going to pick one up at the airport," Toner said.

"Not like this, you weren't. You can't buy this brand in the States—it's Russian manufacture and more accurate than those airport models. Over 50,000 words and phrases, and it'll translate either language."

"Where'd you get it—Kaloostian's Electronic Import Emporium?"

"An Armenian friend sent it to me."

"I don't know, Greg. I'd hate to lose it. A cheap one'll work just fine."

"Take it. I can always get another. A little Russian will help you avoid paying forty bucks for a plate of macaroni or a shot of vodka."

"Okay, if you say so…Do these things really work?" Toner wondered aloud.

"None of them are perfect. I read somewhere that asking an early model to translate *the spirit is willing, but the flesh is weak,* ended up as *the vodka is eager, but the meat stinks.* Keep it simple and they work fine…and *no* Shakespeare. You'll burn out the circuits."

"Yeah, I just got another warning from Hatton. That man has no taste for the classics. What's the harm in a little *Midsummer Night's Dream* on a Monday afternoon? *El bossman esta muy friquiado.*"

"Freaked him out, eh? What is it with you two? Hatton's not such a bad guy. Why do you torment him? Cut him some slack."

"So I complain once in a while. What's the big deal?"

"Once in a while," Greg exclaimed. "There's an understatement if I ever heard one. If you were sentenced to hang by the neck, you'd bitch about getting rope burns."

Angela started to laugh, then realized the truth in his joke.

"Fine." She slipped the knife and translator into her computer case.

As she got up to leave, Kaloostian reached out and touched her arm. "Like I said, I know you're pressed for time, but this is important. You're really going to have to keep your eyes and ears open. I have no idea what kind of reception you'll get, other than it'll be based on pure mistrust. Overcoming that is job-one. Got it?"

"Got it. What else should I know?"

"Pay attention to the little stuff. You'll be on your own and far from home; ruby slippers won't work. *So*, to keep you on your toes, I want you to try a little game."

Toner frowned. "Game? I don't have time for games."

"It's not so much a game as a theory, one I developed a few years ago. You see, I believe that at some point in every movie, whether it's a main character, an extra, a prop, whatever—there's a *sailor*."

"*What?* Greg, what in the hell are you talking about? That's the dumbest thing I ever heard."

"Precisely—and that's because you weren't paying attention. Listen, you might think I'm nuts, that I've smoked too much dope, but I'm telling ya, there's absolutely, positively a sailor in every movie ever made. On my mother's grave…"

"And you said pot wasn't habit-forming," Toner countered.

"It isn't—I've smoked it for years. Come on, think about this."

"You're insane, you know that."

"Who isn't? Look, Angie, all I'm asking you to do is give it a try. It'll only take a minute—I'll start. It's an all-time classic, one of the greatest movies eve—*Gone with the Wind*. Definitely a sailor in that one."

"No way. Tara was near Atlanta—not the coast of Georgia. Not a boat in sight."

Kaloostian pointed a finger in Toner's face. "See, there you go, jumping to conclusions, not investigating the possibilities. *Think.* What did Rhett Butler do to serve the Confederacy, huh? He was a gunrunner, slipping past the Union navy with arms, food, medicine. He was a sailor, Angie—a girl in every port. Satisfied? Now it's your turn. Name a movie."

"This is ridiculous…oh all right." Toner considered Kaloostian's question for several moments. Then her face lit up with a smile. "*Lawrence of Arabia.* Ha, you don't find too many swabbies in the Sahara."

"Oh Spudmeister, the walking thesaurus. Have you forgotten another name for camels? *Ship of the desert.* And who rides these ships of the Sahara? Peter O'Toole, Omar Sharif, and a cast of thousands—all of 'em sailors. That's an easy one. Most of them are hidden, tucked away, standing off to the side—in doorways, under bridges. Pay attention, and you'll find them. Trust me, they're there."

"You seem pretty sure of this," Toner said. "Okay, give me three not-so-obvious examples, and I'll give your theory a try."

"*Working Girl*: there's a sailor standing over to the side outside a bar in one scene with Alec Baldwin and Melanie Griffith. *2001—A Space Odyssey*: the astronauts are naval officers. Or how about *Addams Family Values*? There's a scene where Fester's wife is prematurely celebrating his demise at a bar with, can you guess, a bunch of sailors! Three examples—I rest my case."

"Now I know what you do alone late at night—that is, besides medicate yourself. Man, your cable bill must be horrendous."

"Just remember, life is about finding clues. *Comprendé?*"

"Si señor."

"You're sure you've got everything?"

"Hope so. Oh, yeah, the Revkin file." Toner laughed when Kaloostian handed her the disk. "Thanks again for all your help. I'll call you later, okay." She leaned down to give Kaloostian a hug and was surprised to see how red his eyes were.

"Be careful, Angie. And remember—sailors—they're everywhere."

"So you say. Gotta run. I'll talk to you later."

Toner waved to Kaloostian from the door. In an instant, she was gone. All Greg heard were her hurried footsteps. He sat still, looking at the door in contemplation. After several minutes, he pivoted in the wheelchair, pulling himself closer to the computer. Reaching for the keyboard, he clicked the redial prompt.

The monitor instantly displayed the number and destination. Without looking at the screen, Kaloostian leaned back and waited for the connection. After a moment, he heard a female voice: "Good afternoon—Russian consulate. How may I help you?"

9
Two Heartbeats

"Not bad. Not bad at all," thought Angela. Having never flown first-class, she found the accommodations a pleasant change of pace. And on her income, she might never again have such an opportunity. Fitting consolation for having to fly to within a snowball's throw of the North Pole instead of to San Francisco.

A Russian flight attendant had greeted Angela by name when she boarded the Aeroflot 757 wide-body jet. The attendant took her jacket and garment bag, stowed her suitcase, and presented her with a complimentary amenity kit—toothbrush, toothpaste, earplugs, eye-shade, skin lotion, and facial mist to minimize the dryness of the cabin air. After being escorted to her seat, Angela was served a sparkling glass of champagne,

The increasingly relaxed Toner glanced around the spacious compartment. "So this is what the French Revolution was all about," she thought. Her seat was more a mini-cubicle than the sardine chair she was used to. It came with the necessities of business-class travel but unfolded to a six-foot, four-inch lounge for sleep or relaxation, complete with down pillows and wool blanket. With accommodations like this, Toner wondered whether she would ever be able to fly coach again.

At 7:45 P.M., Aeroflot flight 4550 departed Los Angeles International Airport. As the plane rose above the lights of the city, Angela Toner reclined in her chair, sipping a second glass of champagne. Good thing Hatton couldn't see her now. He might have second thoughts if he suspected she was having a good time. Her Siberian exile had made his day, and Toner wouldn't want to ruin that...

It was almost ten o'clock. After a sumptuous dinner of sevruga molossol caviar, fresh mixed greens, pan-seared salmon with dill and lemon, a buttery wild-rice dish, fresh cheeses and bread, and a sampling of desserts, Angela visited the powder room. When she returned, her seat and table had been transformed into a bed, and she stretched out against two pillows.

Basking in the soft glow of her reading light and a goblet of cognac, Angela knew she should get some sleep. The excitement of the day, however, combined with her fear of the morrow, kept her awake. She had that irrational feeling that sometimes occurs on the first day of a trip. It had nothing to do with leaving the oven on, the water running, or her apartment unlocked. Instead, it involved a six-foot-four, three-hundred-pound Russian behemoth named Bruno, likely waiting for her in Petropavlovsk.

Dealing with a socially retarded poster child like Marc Heiple was one thing. Trying to tell a descendent of Attila the Hun to keep his grimy paws to himself was a different story. "No" was likely a word absent from his vocabulary. "Nyet" was a word he probably knew well but had learned to ignore. To make matters worse, Kaloostian's translator refused to tell her how to say, "Fornicate thyself, borscht breath" in Russian. What was a girl to do?

Knowing sleep was impossible, Toner set up her computer and accessed the Revkin file. She'd been so busy earlier, much of the disk remained a mystery. When a new icon appeared with the opening of the screen, Angela knew her coconspirator had been at work. With a quick double-click, she discovered that Greg had loaded a copy of the *AbsoluteAccess* word-processing assimilator, a menu-and file-retrieval program, as well as a video clip.

Toner slipped on a pair of headphones and started the clip. Kaloostian's voice-over filtered through.

"How ya doing, Spud? Hope your trip is going well. Since we didn't have time earlier, I thought I'd provide you with some additional information on genetics, just enough to make you dangerous. Let's begin with the basics. I know you know what genes are, that each cell in our bodies contain 46 chromosomes, and that each of these chromosomes is a DNA molecule. You also probably know that the information within each gene determines an organism's hereditary properties."

A hologram filled the screen. "Here's a 3-D of the double helix. Two extraordinary strands of nucleotides twined together like a twisted ladder that, if stretched end-to-end, would total over six feet. Mm, looks kinda like a spiraled yellow brick road, doesn't it? Well, Dorothy, you ain't in Kansas anymore," Greg said with a soft chuckle.

"Anyway, the rungs of the ladder, or bricks of the road, are composed of four chemical compounds called bases: thymine, adenine, guanine, and cytosine, with a matching pair on each rung. The sides of the ladder consist of sugar and phosphate. DNA's nothing more than a long chain of double-based building blocks, with each gene comprising a section of the ladder. Very basic.

"What gives life its variety is the order of the billions of pairs; and within the thread of a DNA molecule, the possibilities are literally endless. How they match up provides the data necessary for a cell to manufacture a specific protein.

"Here's what most people don't understand: The specific protein a cell produces determines the form and function of that cell. In other words, the infinite base sequencing of the DNA makes any organism unique and identifiable. Each cell in your body contains the codes for you and you alone. But the cells in your stomach, for instance, are programmed to digest food, while the cells in your brain are programmed for the storage and transfer of electromagnetic information impulses…all because of the proteins within the cells. Hope you're following this. If not, rewind and start again."

Toner kept going. Until Kaloostian had lost his leg and became paralyzed from the waist down, he'd taught computer classes in an Armenian elementary school. His explanations, while occasionally long, were always thorough.

"Angie, I know your undies are in a bundle about this Nyentzi thing. I still don't know what it means, but it's my guess that if we had the time to dig through this file, we'd find that someone's been trying to identify certain genetic disorders in Melissa Revkin's DNA. Identifying what abnormalities this kid carries might be the key we're looking for."

Toner bit her lower lip and shook her head.

"I also know what you're thinking," Greg countered. "That you don't think Nyentzi has anything to do with genetic disorders. And I know it's easy to argue that this is old news, which would mean this file isn't worth the plastic it's encoded on. But consider this…"

The image on the screen changed to a blurred black-and-white photograph of a single organic cell, and Greg continued: "Back in the 1980s, it took 147 biologists working in 35 labs in 17 countries several years to map out the exact DNA sequences in chromosome number three of a common yeast cell, which is what you're looking at now. While you may not be impressed, bear in mind that YCHR#3 is the smallest chromosome in yeast, and yeast is about as simple an organism as you can find. This is a cell with only 300,000 base pairs, each a single rung of the DNA ladder—and in humans, there are billions of pairs.

"Think about the effort and money expended to map out a yeast cell. When they started, the scientists thought they were dealing with 34 genes in YCHR#3…but they ended up with 182. They weren't even close. You've got to understand, Angie, how recent, how inexact a science we're dealing with here. The genetic atlas on this one file disk is the culmination of billions of dollars of research over the past twenty years. And we've only had a chance to look at a small percentage of it. Hell, for all I know, it's not even a complete…

"So, what's yeast got to do with Melissa Revkin? For starters, DNA's an incredibly ancient substance—almost as old as the earth herself. Despite its age, deoxyribonucleic acid's evolution was pretty much concluded two billion years ago. When you compare the DNA of man to a yeast cell, only 10 percent of the strands are different—and those differences are recent recombinations of the same old genes. Scientists may have gotten proficient at reengineering lizards, frogs, and chickens, but genetics is still a risky affair.

"Another thing to remember about genetics. One copy is never enough. You need a lot of samples to test a theory, to make sure the programmed change actually works. That means cloning or replicating, and the attrition rate for any cloned organism is still way over 60 percent—not counting unpublished research, which goes straight down the toilet. With odds like that, Angie, messing around with humans is less of a technical hang-up and more a matter of ethics. The tabloids and cheap novels make it sound easy, but for fear of persecution or prosecution by every religion and government in the world, no one's ever tried to clone a human beyond a four-cell embryo—at least not that anyone knows about. Those headlines you're so eager to believe are pure fantasy."

Toner paused the program and sat in silence, contemplating the ramifications of Kaloostian's analysis. After many seconds, she continued.

"Do you see the problem?" Greg asked. "We don't know enough about God's little secrets to do much more than retrovirus defective genes, grow juicy tomatoes, or mass produce some low-grade livestock, much less replicate a sentient being. Throw in the chance of an abnormal imprinting, and you can see why people have gotten so skittish about messin' with our genetic destiny."

Kaloostian's commentary ended. Toner set the computer down and leaned against her pillow. She stared at the ceiling, troubled not only by what she had just learned but also by her inability to better understand the case.

"What am I missing?" she thought. "Why don't I have a feeling for this? I've got nothing. Nothing about the Revkins, nothing about Nyentzi, nothing about Melissa…Melissa…my God."

A supernova of awareness exploded inside Angela's brain, enlightening her like a just-understood Zen koan. She sat up in bed, grabbed her computer, and began a data search within the Revkin file. It had to be there—she was embarrassed and ashamed to admit it had taken her this long to think of it. What she needed wasn't in the medical file—that area had already been explored. A second run through the Revkin family file confirmed her suspicion that it wasn't there, either.

"Think! Come on, Toner, *think*. Where would it be? Somebody put this file together. Could they be so damned clinical that in two hundred megs of data, there's not a single one?"

After another moment, she finally typed her request in the autofind box. "This might not work either, but even autistic kids go to school," she reasoned. In less than two heartbeats, she had her answer.

Melissa Revkin had indeed attended school, though not one catering to disabled children. Even then, she'd gone only half a year. But there it was, what Angela had been looking for—a school picture of the child.

Melissa looked older than seven, though pale and willowy. Her gaze seemed vacant. Not empty, but rather as if she were too deep in thought to pay attention to something as mundane as a picture-taking session. She had short dark hair, cut just below the ears and straight across her forehead. Though Angela suspected that James and Olga

Revkin were not her biological parents, she thought their daughter looked part Russian.

And that smile...

A tear formed before she could stop it. Angela wasn't looking at a hellish experiment, but at a person. The smile is what did it. Not the witless, toothy grin one might expect, but a haunting Mona-Lisa smirk—all lips, no teeth—revealing the uniqueness of her exquisite beauty. Angela smiled in return, imagining what the child might be thinking: "Neener neener. I know something you don't—and I'm not gonna tell."

She wiped away the tear, turned her computer off, and lay back. "What did I expect?" Angela whispered. "Some kind of monster? She's so young, so pretty, so *perfect*...My God, Melissa, what have they done to you?"

The room was dark and silent. Angela Toner was scared and confused. Where was Jake? He was here a minute ago. She listened carefully but heard only the sound of her own breathing, felt only the beat of her own heart.

Her surroundings seemed familiar, but that wasn't possible. She'd never been here before, had she? As she looked around for anything recognizable, her eyes grew accustomed to the gloom. When she tried to raise herself up from the hardness of what felt like a cheap bed in a budget motel, the room suddenly flooded with light and the sound of a woman screaming in pain, bewilderment, and anger.

Toner instinctively shut her eyes, then opened them slowly to discern people around her, dressed in white and wearing surgical masks. And that woman...She tried to tell someone to please shut her up, but she couldn't speak. Just her luck—she needed rest and all she could hear was screaming.

"This is a hell of a poor way to treat a pregnant woman!"

Toner looked around the room a second time and noticed that the crisp white uniforms of the people encircling her bed were spotted with red. Their hands were red, too. Wires and tubes and cords and lines stretched everywhere—in every direction. She didn't know what to make of it, but she was glad she wouldn't have to clean up the mess.

"Room service. I want to speak to the manager." She'd found her voice. "Scottie, beam me the hell out of here. McCoy, prepare a tranquilizer. No, not for that crazy Vulcan—for me, dammit. Wait, hold on there...you can't come in here. Back! Back to the reservation. You'll get no rifles from Kincaid."

The screaming..."Shut that woman up. A shot...That would be great, doctor. Knock her into next week. You've got my permission. What? You can't be serious?"

Toner looked up and saw two eyes staring at her over the top of a surgical mask. The person was shining a light, of all things, directly into her eyes.

"That does it! Now I'm really pissed. What? It's who? It's me? Are you trying to tell me I'm the one screaming? I don't *think* so. And I suppose that's my blood too?...The blood—Jake—the intersection. Look out, Jake. That crazy bastard's not going to stop. *Jake.*

"Nooooo. I'm five-months pregnant. Jake, where the hell are you? You can't die. You can't, you big lug. Don't go, don't leave me. Please don't leave me.

"No, Jake, not both of you. Not our baby. No...take me...please...please take me."

A hand, dripping with blood, reached up and removed the mask from the face above her.

"Melissa? Boy, am I glad to see you. Wait a minute, what are you doing here? How the hell did you get credentialed? What kind of hospital is this?

"I can't hear you—speak up. They're dead? *What?* You, too? You're all dead? Well, that's just great. That's just frickin' great. Now I've gotta clean this mess up myself."

Angela woke as the plane bounced and braked down the runway. She opened her eyes, removed her earplugs, and looked out the window at the bright lights of Anchorage International Airport. Her watch was still set for Pacific Standard Time, and it read Tuesday, January 15, 12:42 A.M.

From what the flight attendant had told her, Tuesday would be the shortest day of her life. After picking up more passengers and continuing west, Aeroflot flight 4550 would cross the International Date Line in less than three hours, which would make Wednesday the day of her arrival in eastern Siberia. Too tired to get up, Angela pulled the blanket over her head, trying to make sense of the dream. She'd had it before, though this was the first time anyone in the operating room had removed their masks.

"How did that fit into the scheme of things?" she wondered. "Kaloostian—he'd know. He could explain all the Freudian nuances."

Gregory H. Kaloostian—now there was a man with dreams. She had seen him on many a morning, red-eyed from another sleepless night battling the specters who took his leg and destroyed his life. Compared to him, she had it easy. The drunk who'd careened through the intersection, killing himself, her husband, and their unborn child, was at least a culpable apparition.

In Kaloostian's dreams, he was the one to blame. He was the perpetrator. He did the killing. And he was the only one left alive…left to relive the terrible moment—night after sleepless night. Toner had tried to convince him it wasn't his fault. In a war, any war, people die—a fact of life Kaloostian still had to accept. But the phantoms had other ideas. They would not release Gregory from their nocturnal visitations under any terms but their own.

The plane came to a halt. Angela rolled over, covered up with the blanket, and closed her eyes.

Kaloostian couldn't sleep. Nyentzi kept him awake and melancholy. With only two hours to go before his 5:30 A.M. wakeup, he decided to make a day of it and try to forget what he must do. He'd sent her a voicemail message more than four hours ago and wondered where she was at that moment.

The euphoria and mania brought by the marijuana he'd smoked earlier had faded to a delicate buzz. He wheeled to his record collection to find music appropriate to his mood. In choosing musical catharsis, Gregory Kaloostian employed various methods—from random searches among his computerized album list, to blind grabs from the shelf, to instant recognition of exactly what he needed.

Tonight, reaching into the Cs, he retrieved an LP whose cover was slightly marred but whose disk was near-mint condition. He knew the album didn't belong under C, but it was easier to find when filed with the rest of his Clapton. With the album on his lap, he maneuvered the wheelchair to his stereo, then put the vinyl disc on the turntable, set it in motion, and donned his headphones. In a moment, the music soothed his troubled mind.

While he listened and relaxed, Kaloostian opened a small wooden box next to the stereo where he kept a spare stylus, album cleaner, and other paraphernalia. Then he saw it, a photograph hidden under a pack of rolling papers. He picked up the faded photo and held it tenderly. He had been a whole person in 1989, standing with his best friend, Krikor Hovsepian, and Krikor's fiancée, Sossi—Sossi Kaloostian—his younger sister.

As if on cue, the tears formed. "Why?" he wondered. "Why did they trust me? Why does anyone trust me? How is an elementary school teacher supposed to know how to traverse a minefield in the moonlight?"

Kaloostian shut his eyes. Even now, almost twenty years later, he could hear the explosion, followed by a moment of silence. Then came the screams that never seemed to end. He frantically manipulated the volume control on his headphones to a thunderous level, letting the music drown the demons that tormented his soul:

> You are the reason I've been waiting all these years.
> Somebody holds the key.
> I'm near the end and I just ain't got the time
> And I'm wasted and I can't find my way home.

The first leg of the journey was over. Disembarking from the Aeroflot jet, Angela Toner stumbled through the Petropavlovsk terminal with her luggage. Searching the crowd for anyone who might be looking for her, she felt a tap on her shoulder. "FBI Agent Toner."

She turned and saw someone presenting a Federal Security Bureau badge. "Oh my God," Toner thought. "Ivan the Terrible on steroids I could handle, but not this, not now. Just when I thought it couldn't get any worse."

10

Lucky Day

First impressions…with that thought, Angela Toner took a good look at the Russian who'd just addressed her. If what the experts say is true about the importance of first impressions, she had better get used to spending time with a Precious Moments doll toting a badge.

Her contact was no more than five-feet-two. Though she wore a heavy gray wool topcoat, Toner was sure she weighed no more than 105 pounds, with the figure of a ballerina to boot. Twenty-five, maybe twenty-six, years old.

The Russian woman's auburn hair cascaded to her shoulders—obviously a head that had never seen the inside of a sweaty SWAT helmet. The hair framed a perfect oval face, milky white and clear of blemish, even with little makeup. Green eyes, long lashes, delicate nose, apparently sculpted from alabaster. Perfect lips, lightly shaded with rose lipstick. Drop-dead good looks—a real killer. Toner hated her already.

"FBI Agent Angela Toner, my name is Nadezhda Andrevna Molotova. I am field agent on special assignment from Federal Security

Bureau. I am being your liaison during your visit to my country. Is this all that is to come of your luggage?"

"Ahh, yes, I tried to pack light. Nice to meet you. Say, I have a couple of questions…"

Molotova turned and walked away. "Come, we have plane to catch. Follow me."

"Now? At this hour?" Toner said, trying to catch up. Struggling with a garment bag, a suitcase on a strap, and her computer case, the frustrated and jetlagged American bumped and bobbed through the surprisingly busy Petropavlovsk terminal.

"Hey, Molotova, I need to stop in one of these shops and buy a warm coat. In LA we don't get more than thirty inches of snow a year, maybe it's only twenty. Who knows? Point is—there's more snow outside than I've seen in years. Would you please *stop*?"

The Russian came to a grudging halt, nodded, and pointed to a duty-free shop fifty meters away. As Molotova walked in that direction, Toner again picked up her luggage and followed like a lost dog.

Once in the shop, the American set her bags down and sighed, her face red from overexertion and exasperation. With her newfound traveling companion standing idly by, Toner scanned the row of coats, wrinkling her face in disgust at the dismal selection. On seeing her hesitate, Molotova stepped forward, took a good look at Angela's figure, and pulled a nondescript brown coat off the hanger.

"Russian coats are very warm. You will find what you need here. This is your size, yes?"

"Yeah. Not much of a selection, though. Is this the only store in the airport?"

"You are in Siberia not Beverly Hills. You also must understand of the time. It is 1:00 A.M., Petropavlovsk time. Be contented for that this store opened the doors for your plane at such lateness of hour. Look around. You do have excellent selection here. In your size, we have this brown coat."

Molotova handed the coat to Toner. Finding another in Angela's size, she pulled it off the hanger. "There is also this brown coat. Ah, look, another of your size. Your lucky day; it is brown, too."

Toner put the coat on. "Praise the Lord, I've won the lottery," she deadpanned.

"It fits. You buy. We go. There is plane to catch." Molotova walked towards the door.

"Whoa—reboot your computer, little lady. I'm glad you approve, but I'd like to look at this one, too." Angela took the coat off and began to examine another, though she'd already decided to buy the first. It fit well, seemed warm and well made, looked good on her, and was half the price she'd pay in the States for one of similar quality. But Molotova didn't need to know that.

"When does this flight leave? My butt's barely awake as it is. And where the *heck* are we going?"

"Our plane departs for Salekhard, Western Siberia, not far from thirty minutes. Despite what opinions you might be having, planes in Russia depart on time."

"You don't have to get defensive. I've never had better travel accommodations than my flight over. I just don't like being given the runaround."

"We will have comfortable time to discuss your trip on the plane. Come."

With a shrug, Angela opened her purse and approached the cashier. After handing over a credit card, she continued to eye her Russian traveling companion. Once the transaction was complete, she cut the price tag off the coat, put it on, and hoisted her baggage for another round of follow-the-leader.

Struggling with her load, now aggravated by a heavy wool coat, Angela tried to keep up with the Russian as they hurried through the busy terminal. After several minutes at a brisk pace, the American had

had enough. She dropped her bags and called after Molotova, who hadn't noticed her standstill.

"Hey, Molotova—stop already."

The Russian slowed, looked back in disgust, and stopped. After a moment, she walked back.

"Okay, Ice Queen, what's going on?" Toner demanded. "All I wanted from the Russian consulate was a little information. Now I find myself competing against you in the thousand-meter track-and-terminal event. Heck, I wouldn't treat the French this badly."

Seeing the incredulity on Molotova's face, Angela hesitated. "Look, I'm sorry I sound bad-tempered, but I'm tired, irritable, and hungry. Comprendé?"

"Ya ponimayu—I understand." After considering Toner's statement for a moment, Molotova continued. "As long as we are to be stopping, answer this to me. Why for are you and FBI interested suddenly in Olga Lyubimova and Monogovody? Why are *you* to come here?"

"Why am *I* here? Why did Alexander Samanov, *your* hotshot diplomat, arrange my flight all the way to Siberia? And why was I met by Federal Security instead of someone with a personality?"

"Why did you contact our consulate? To what interest are events of seven years ago?"

"What is your *problem*? I'm just trying to do my job."

"You Americans think you are number-one big shots."

"Okay, okay—time out." Toner held her left hand in front of her—palm opened and towards Molotova—tapping it with her right hand on a downward motion.

"What is this?" Molotova mimicked Toner's gesture.

"Oh, football, American football signal. Means time out, take a break."

"I do not watch football."

"I'll try not to hold that against you. You've got enough other personality traits that bug the heck out of me. Look, Molotova, I'll give you the benefit of the doubt here. In this business, we're both used to asking all the questions and not very good about answering them. Since we're obviously going to be spending some time together, let's start over. Tell you what: you ask a question, I'll answer. Then I'll ask, you answer. Simple—we take turns."

"Yes, that seems okay. *I go first*. Why was your call made to our consulate in San Francisco?"

Toner thought about the question for a several seconds. "Three weeks ago, Melissa Revkin, the daughter of James and Olga Lyubimova Revkin, was seriously injured in an auto accident and…"

"We know all about the accident. It has nothing to do with Monogovody. What is your interest in Monogovody?"

Toner looked intently at Molotova and then around her, at the bustle of the terminal. The sound of announcements in Russian, combined with the noise of the airport made whispering impractical, and she did not want anyone to overhear. She picked up her luggage, walked to the corner of the empty boarding area, and motioned Molotova to follow her. At a slow pace, the Russian followed.

"Fine," Angela continued. "Melissa Revkin needs a kidney transplant. During preliminary screening for blood type and cross-matching, the hospital discovered that no one in her immediate family was a compatible donor."

Molotova was silent for a moment, looking intently at the American.

"What else? What other reasons do you have for calling us?" Molotova asked.

"Isn't it obvious? We're hoping to locate other relatives of Olga's who might be willing to undergo the compatibility tests."

"Why not to use cloned animal kidney? What of other means? Why does it have to be relative of the child? And what about the Monogovody business, Toner?"

"You're way over your one-question limit, comrade. Answer *one* question for me: Have you been in contact with Alexander Samanov or any other member of the Russian consulate in San Francisco?"

Again, Molotova hesitated. She looked at her watch and at the number of the boarding area. "We need to go. They will be embarking soon."

"Fine, you don't want to answer that question. How about this—why are you being such a *bitch*? And why is Federal Security involved?"

"That is more than one question also," Molotova replied. "Federal Security has been of interest in Monogovody since it was built. Our interest remained after the destruction. I suspect that interest is of yours also. As to being a bitch as you directly conclude, I volunteer my apology. I had recent encounter with American from your Moscow embassy. He was very arrogant and…I do not know what words to use in your language that are not of sexual kind. A jerk—he was a jerk. Perhaps I was to take it out with you. Again, my apology."

"Apology accepted. Please accept *my* apology for his behavior. Who knows, maybe I work with his brother. Let's go catch that plane."

Angela reached down to pick up her suitcase, but Molotova was quicker. Their eyes met. For the first time, they exchanged smiles. The Russian hoisted the suitcase. Walking briskly, they continued down the airport terminal towards their gate.

"Do people in the FSB always cruise first-class? My compliments to whoever makes your travel arrangements. Maybe I'm working for the wrong government."

Molotova smiled but said nothing. The two women sat opposite each other in a cubicle not unlike Toner's earlier accommodations. When not unfolded for sleeping, the first-class pod offered armchair comfort for two for meals and business. They had just finished a delicious breakfast and were comfortably sipping coffee.

"Back to my last question. Have you been in contact with anyone at the Russian consulate?"

"As I informed you, I am on assignment from FSB. I work for small group assigned to investigate Monogovody things or of the research conducted there by Dr. Yuri Anatoliovich Tyrellovich. Alexander

Samanov was conforming to instructions when he arranged for you to come to Russia."

"I just wanted some information. Why would Federal Security care about that?"

"And I could very well ask why FBI and not Red Cross contacted the consulate?"

"Maybe the big bosses gave us girls the stupid assignments while they're catching rays in Tahiti. Heck, Molotova, I don't know. I'm like you. I just follow orders. It's not the first time someone's been given an assignment that made no sense."

"In Federal Security, we do not send agents on assignments making of no sense. We work hard. We do a good job. Very professional."

"I'm glad you people are so perfect, though I happen to know the FSB and your predecessor, the KGB, have a reputation for a screw up or two. Like sending Russian soldiers into Grozny without street maps, or how about the time in 2004 when…"

"You talk of army's mistake, not Federal Security's. You complain of us? Ha! That Edgar Hoover fellow was super-duper boss man at your FBI for many years. He wore women's underwear."

"Only after hours…The man was a fruitcake, Molotova, but that's ancient history. This is now—this is you and me. I'm not looking for a pen pal, and we don't have to be bosom buddies. So here's what we do. Let's pretend this is a movie, and we're the stars. We don't need to be reading from the same page of the script. We don't need to finish each other's sentences. We don't even need to be in every scene together, but let's at least agree on the plot."

"That is a funny way for requesting cooperation, Toner. Okay, let us find common ground or plot, as you say. You should know I did speak to Alexander Samanov. He told me of your conversation. He was impressed by you, and he said that mum's the word. I think that is what you said, is it not."

"Yep, guess I did. So you know about Tyrellovich and Nyentzi?"

"Our information about his research is limited. That is why I was excited when Samanov became contacted with my supervisor. It is she who told me you had called. While you were flying west, I was to meet you flying east. I assure you, Angela Toner, I am no less fatigued than you. It is rare that someone with my experience or rank be allowed to fly first-class. I am only with FSB for two years. With the occasion, we thought it would be better."

"In that regard, you'll get no complaints from me. What I find hard to believe is that you don't have a more extensive file on Tyrellovich. I mean, come on, he operated in your backyard. You trying to tell me the Russian government wasn't involved in what went on there?"

"Are you being quite serious? For your information, Federal Security made mistake of going to ETI and Tyrellovich when we needed advanced computer capability. His people were our *consultants*, but they were always a step down the road. Every attempt to infiltrate at Monogovody was fruitless. He used so much hiddenness that only now have we located survivors of the explosion that destroyed the complex. And do not forget American secrets: Area 51, in your western desert? Even in this year, your citizens are not to be told of those hush-hush secrets there."

"Okay, no more comments about politics. You did mention survivors, though."

"Yes, that is who we are going see. To hospital in Salekhard to meet only member of the number-one genetics research team still alive. Toner, believe me now when I tell you, we knew nothing about any experiments. All your distrust is the same for us."

"How about Nyentzi? What do you know about that?"

"Again, virtually a nothing. In our look for survivors, we found ourselves totally dark."

"How long has your group been investigating Monogovody?"

"My group has been formed only two months. However, there are always questions. In November, during routine update of old computer records, a technician began to suspect some tampering with the files already. It is not unusual to find incomplete records after several years—digital computer files break down over time, as you know. In this case, the technician was attracted to the surgical correctness for which the files were erased. It was evidently intended."

"What files were they?"

"Travel records in and out of Russia. That is why, of course, Federal Security was contacted. When we analyzed nearby data, we realized what was missing were visa registrations, flight information, and destinations for many people. Our own computer experts created a copulation of the various missing datas. From that we also to determine what month and years were involved."

"I think you mean *compilation*—unless your computer people are more than just good friends."

"What? I do not understand."

"Sorry, never mind. Those dates—let me guess: November of 1999 to January 2000—during Tyrellovich's Scientific Symposium."

"That is exactly correct."

"But why Tyrellovich and Monogovody? There were more people traveling during those months than any time in recent history."

"Because Tyrellovich was only one with the skill to do something as unlegal as erase official files."

Toner contemplated the Russian's logic. "That sounds all dark and sinister, but I don't buy it. Your conclusions are circumstantial at best and, if you don't mind my saying so, slightly paranoid."

Molotova frowned. "Toner, I realize you, as American, might throw this up because of old cliché of Russian paranoia. I remind you, after all, that our suspicions are not without good excuse. Our land—our country—has been run over by Huns, Mongols, Nazis. What have you concerned in America? Young Republicans? Too many MacDonald restaurants? Not enough MTV?"

"Sorry. Sorry I brought it up. You're probably right; especially about those Young Republicans—scariest bunch of nonconformists I've ever seen."

"Please to understand, Tyrellovich was huge—a larger-than-life type of figure. He is considered one of Russia's greatest scientist minds. But always the rumors, the experiments in secret at Monogovody. Now he is dead, the facility destroyed. Something happened there. A threat not to Russia only but all over the world. What do you expect? To ignore such evidence, even rumor?"

"So, you discovered the missing data and began looking for survivors. How did you manage to find the person in Salekhard if everything was so secret?"

"In Moscow nursing home was man named Dmitri Sergeiovich Rancich. He had worked at Monogovody. He was in very bad condition and could not speak from burns of explosion. Last month, he was found dead by his nurse. When they go through his personals, they discover a journal, a diary. It was, of course, not current. It was from his time at Monogovody."

"This is getting better every minute. What'd the journal say?" Angela asked. Contrary to her initial prejudices, she was beginning to enjoy working with the spunky Russian.

"It was not electronic journal, Toner, just notebook. So it said nothing. But written were mentions of genetic experimentations Dmitri was to work on. He had notes of making changes in embryos for to implant. Not animal type, but *human*—these were human embryos with this project. They were not messing around with sheep this time, not even chimpanzees. He was also writing the names of other people with the project. That was how we were allowed to find the person in Salekhard."

Toner thought back to Kaloostian's denial that Tyrellovich had worked on human embryos. After a moment, she continued. "This project Dmitri referred to, did it have a name?"

"In his notes, it was only called 'the project.' Ah, like what you said to Samanov—Nyentzi. Do you think of this as that?"

"Could be. Trouble is, I don't have a clue what Nyentzi means. Do you?"

"Nyet. It is not a Russian word, maybe a dialect. I did language search but found nothing."

"And you say Dmitri's dead. What happened?"

"That is a very strange thing to have happened. For seven years he has been invalid in bed. No talk, not getting around for nothing. The nurse said he understood, but he himself never to talk. Then one night there is program on his television in room. He goes crazy. The nurse never see him like this, so he gets shot."

"The nurse shot him!" Angela couldn't resist. Molotova's English was amazingly good, but Toner felt that as a fellow member of the intelligence community, she had a duty to keep the diminutive Russian on her toes. After all, she had that ballerina figure.

"*Of sedation*. She shot him full of sedation. So, later in the night, he somehow to manage strangling his neck on side-rail of bed. Lights out for him, okay."

"No kidding. Did the nurse remember what they'd been watching on television?"

"Aha. That is also my question to her. Yes, she remembered it to be news program—an announcement of Olga Lyubimova. During broadcast, Dmitri began shaking his bed, making strange sounds without his voice. I asked the nurse what did the newsman say about Olga? What could it be?"

"Hold it. I know Olga Revkin was Olga Lyubimova before she got married, but is she still news in Russia, or was it a slow day?"

"What? She is big American scientist, also big Russian scientist. Her daughter injured in car accident. I think that is news!"

"So Dmitri goes buggin' because Olga's daughter was in an accident?"

"No. I asked about that to nurse. He only became *bugging*, as you say, when photograph of the daughter is shown on news—only then. The nurse said it was as if he had seen her before. But that was not possible, no."

"No it's not. One thing bothers me, though: after the explosion, Dmitri and the other survivor in Salekhard, they both get medivacked to different hospitals. Are you telling me no one kept a record of them, no one documented who was admitted? I mean, who's been paying for their room and board all these years? That's one of the questions I'd be asking if I were you."

"I understand what you are saying. I did ask those questions, but I did not find any documents, any lists. I did check to see the payment of Dmitri's hospital bill, but I find that it was an Orthodox nursing home. Your American word—a charity?"

"Yeah, that would make sense," Angela said. After a moment, she continued. "That's quite a bit of research for one person. You're not working alone on this, are you?"

"No, but of course not. There is a small team of us."

"Small team? You surprise me. With Tyrellovich being a national obsession, I would have thought Federal Security would have a small *army* handling the case."

"Like America, we also have not enough funds for larger peoples. But I am of opinion that small team is better. Secrecy is good—it is hard to trust no one. I am of preference for a small team in the field, then to report to single supervisor in Moscow. Of course, we do not have trust for her, either."

"Sounds like your supervisor went to Star Fleet Academy with mine." Toner paused and collected her thoughts. "You mentioned chimpanzees a minute ago. I know that scientists have cloned primates. I also know that our DNA's only 10 percent different from a yeast cell. If that's the case, how different can it be from chimpanzees?"

"Less than two percentages of difference. By cloning monkeys, those scientists proved they could clone people as well."

"Well. There you have it. Now all those tabloid stories are starting to make sense." Toner was silent. She leaned back, rubbed her eyes, and yawned. "I don't know about you, Molotova, but I'm tired. How 'bout we take a break—catch up on some sleep?"

"Yes, that would be very good."

"One final question. Is there anyone else, any other agency, any other organization guarding Nyentzi? Or are all the secrets buried in the ashes at Monogovody?"

"We do not know. I do think we will find out."

"That's what I'm afraid of."

Deputy assistant director Alfred E. Hatton sat anesthetized in his chair. Even his barber, who had an easier job every time Hatton came into his shop, could not keep him so still. The call from Washington had ended more than two minutes ago, and he had yet to shut off the speakerphone. Finally, in slow motion, he reached out, hit the button, and glanced at the time—8:03 A.M., Tuesday, January 15, 2007.

The memo marked *Urgent*, the memo he had not read yesterday, the memo that was wrinkled from being shoved into his desk drawer, was deliberately situated on the desk in front of him. Hatton had read it just several minutes ago during the call from the director in Washington, D.C.

The memo, for all its significance, contained fewer than twenty words: "Revkin File: Removal from NSA vault unauthorized. Return immediately. DO NOT access. DO NOT read. DO NOT duplicate." There was no signature—none was needed. Hatton knew who had sent it, knew the NSA was not to be taken lightly.

He hated them—hated and distrusted their arrogance. They'd tried to muscle in on the Guerrero drug bust, citing the "international nature" of the case as grounds for their involvement. Hatton's pilfering the Revkin disk was just his way of saying "in your face."

The director of the FBI himself had called. He'd demanded an explanation, and in no uncertain terms he told Alfred E. Hatton to get that disk back to the NSA or face immediate retirement. The retirement threat was not a concern. Hatton could be out of his office and fishing in less time than it once took him to spend his army paycheck on R & R in Saigon. But he did have certain concerns, chief among them Angela Carmen Toner. He regretted getting her involved. With luck, she'd be all too eager to depart Siberia's winter wonderland and head back home.

His second concern was the call from Washington. Not so much what the director said, but what he didn't say. He should have been furious, pounding his fists on the table, jumping up and down, and swearing like a longshoreman. But he'd maintained a level voice, completely out of character.

"What the hell's going on?" Alfred Hatton wondered.

Toner awoke in less than three hours. It was 4:00 A.M. Wednesday morning, Siberia time, though her biological clock told her it was time for work. At the rate they were traveling, she would be jetlagged to stupefaction by the time they reached Salekhard.

Angela glanced around the quiet darkness of the first-class cabin and saw a mass of reddish-brown hair sticking out from under a blanket in the cubicle next to hers. She wasn't sure about Nadezhda Andrevna Molotova. The spindly Russian seemed professional enough, though too young and inexperienced to be in charge of a major investigation. At least Toner had a good reason for being on the case—somebody had screwed up.

Angela was trying to get along with her traveling companion. She had kept her sarcasm to a minimum, she was polite and helpful, she laughed at Molotova's jokes…and she was going crazy. She hoped the pace of the investigation would pick up soon.

Kaloostian had told her that Russians could be aloof and standoffish to outsiders. But once they got to know a person, they make them one of the family. For the time being, she would just have to be patient with her Kewpie-doll comrade and hope for a thawing of their relationship.

Unable to get back to sleep, Angela reached down and brought her computer under the blanket. Turning it on, she saw the flashing light on her menu screen. "Voice mail," she whispered. She put on the headphones and began to listen.

Kaloostian apparently had pulled another of his all-nighters. Several times a month, he avoided sleep to exhaust himself for the following few days and keep his nightmares at bay. Toner could tell from the sound and timbre of his voice that he had taken a double dose of his bedtime prescription.

"Highty hi, Spudmeister. I've been doing a little data-mining tonight, trying to figure out this Revkin file. Oops, there I go, blowin' my cover. All right, I confess—I made a copy of your *precious* disk. Can't be too careful. What if yours gets damaged or stolen? Where would you be then? Up the crick without a paddle.

"Hope you've taken the time to review the genetics material I put together. Anyway, like I said, I've been giving this Revkin thing a little thought. Well, actually, a lot of thought. I know I should be writing this down, translate it tomorrow when I'm normal, but there's no time. I checked the kid's medical file for any other medications or special diets she might be on. Thought it might give us some answers, and I guess I hit some pretty serious pay dirt."

There was a pause and Toner heard the sound of Kaloostian taking a drink. One of the side effects of marijuana, besides the caloric cravings, was a dry mouth.

"Remember ALG and how weird that Melissa was on it? Well, there's more. When we were talking earlier, tying to figure out if Melissa Revkin, or the entire Nyentzi Project, for that matter, had anything to do with genetic design—or should we say *redesign* since we're already billions of years down the evolutionary trail, and look where *that* got us. I mean...*oops...Warning! Warning!* Kaloostian's off on a tangent. Danger, Will Robinson, *danger.*"

Toner laughed. After several seconds, Kaloostian was back on track.

"Whew, that was close," he continued. "Almost lost my fragile log-on with reality. Anyway, screw all this conjecture crap. No more talk about Hitler sperm and Nazis. For argument's sake, let's say Nyentzi *did* involve genetic engineering and that Melissa was, or *is* part of it. That being the case, what was the goal of the experiment—what did they change? I mean, she's a minimally functioning human being. You really have to wonder what they were trying to accomplish. So I was more than a little surprised when I checked her dietary report and found the nastiest combination of drugs I've ever heard of.

"Angie, they've got this poor kid on everything from fluvoxamine to melatonin. Now, fluvoxamine makes no sense whatsoever. It's supposed to reduce violent behavior in autistic children, but if you remember the DNA analysis, Melissa's not a true autistic. Melatonin—come on, gimme a break. All the physiological studies I've ever seen were inconclusive about it being the new wonder drug. Does it really boost the immune system or promote sleep? Who the hell knows? Not only that, it's naturally produced in our own pineal glands. So why's this kid on two milligrams a day?"

Kaloostian took another sip of liquid and continued.

"She's on steroids! Can you believe that? Something called methylprednisolone, developed in the 1990s. Remember when I said Melissa's brain cells looked like they might be regenerating? That's what methylprednisolone does—it regenerates damaged nerve cells. Only it's never been used for anything other than spinal-cord injuries. And Melissa's been on it since birth.

"Let's see, what else have we got here? Vitamin E and C in mass quantities, plus double doses of the typical one-a-day crap, calcium, and various extraneous supplements. *Prozac*—they've got her on

Prozac! Maybe because it's a proven beta-blocker...and when coupled with a low dose of fluvoxamine, it somehow tranquilizes an overactive nervous system. I don't know. Oh, here's a good one, methotrexate, normally prescribed for leukemia, cancer, and rheumatoid arthritis. Also Retin-A, aspirin, and the scariest one of all, L-tryptophan.

"Now, I'm not sure how much you know about L-tryptophan, but it's not available in the States—sorta like ALG. What worries me is Melissa's on a dose that oughta be lethal. We need to know why and the best way to do that is to know what the drug does.

"I checked with a pharmacist buddy of mine; that's where I got most of this information, by the way, so don't get all paranoid on me, again. At any rate, he told me that L-tryp was a miracle drug in the 1980s. Perked you up, helped you sleep like a baby, calmed you down when you were nervous. Plus, it's a mind-bending dream-enhancer. The interesting thing about L-tryp is that it's a naturally occurring amino acid—again melatonin."

Kaloostian paused, taking another drink. Toner hoped it was only water but knew it could be anything from Bacardi to Jack Daniel's.

"Like I was saying, tryptophan is something we all get from digesting milk, bananas, pineapple, and whatnot. It's one of twenty or so amino acids our bodies need as the building blocks of proteins. Man, I sound like Dr. Science tonight...What's interesting is what tryptophan does once it's ingested. And *that* might be the clue we're looking for. You see, Spud, tryptophan is converted into that darling of darlings, serotonin—the brain chemical that allows nerves to communicate, regulates moods, sleep, pain, appetite. Hell, they're discovering more every year.

"With all that, you'd think they'd put it in the water supply, like fluoride. But, and this is a big *but*, the man-made, genetically engineered amino acid L-tryptophan was banned after more than five thousand people got sick, some died, and more than a thousand were disabled. They traced the problem to a bad batch that was cooked up in an unsterile vat. Anyway, no one's made it since. Wonder why. Oh well, not our concern. What is our concern is where they are getting it now, and why Melissa Revkin is on such a heavy dose.

"We need to find out, Angie, but be careful what you ask the Russians. *Do not* mention the Revkin disk. That's your trump card. Get some information from *them* first, force them to cooperate with you, or else we're, or else *you're,* screwed.

"Man, look at the time. Guess my ten minutes are almost up. Before I go, I've got a little story to share. This is one of my swear-on-a-Bible-it's-true stories, so sit back and enjoy. While I was recuperating at the University of Minnesota Hospital, I shared a room for a couple of days with a professor with gall-bladder problems. Don, that's his name, was from the mechanical engineering department. He told me about this one student who never should've been admitted to college. The kid was late to class all the time, asked all these ridiculous questions…hey Spud, sounds like you.

"Anyway, Don—that's the professor—told the class to measure the height of the mechanical engineering building using any method they could validate. The only tools they were allowed, though, were a twelve-inch ruler, string, and some Popsicle sticks. You following this—string, ruler, sticks?

"At the end of the week, everybody turned in their reports. Don, was amazed that this kid had the right answer. As a matter of fact, he was the only one in the entire class with the exact—and I mean *exact*—height of the building.

"So Don opened the kid's report to find out what method he'd used, and this is what he found: 'Lost my string, ruler, and Popsicle sticks. Went to the grocery store to buy more. Took supplies back to school. Janitor saw me eating a Popsicle. I gave him one and then asked him the height of the building. He told me.'

"As crazy as that sounds, I'll bet that little sonofabitch is worth $80 billion today. It's *fucking* brilliant, Toner. The kid's a genius. Here's my point—and yes, I'm toasted—let's not psyche ourselves out by trying to be too clever here. Let's stick to the basics. The Revkin file is your Popsicle. What you need to do is find a friendly janitor. On that note, I'm gonna sign off. Time to put on my headphones and crank up the volume. Have a nice trip. I'll talk to you soon. Oh, and one other thing—lay off the Internet. No dialing for dollars or shopping sprees. I don't care what pseudonym or program you're using, it could be intercepted and traced. Can't have that."

Toner shook her head and sighed. She saved the message, turned the computer off, laid her head on her pillow, and closed her eyes. Time to count digital sheep.

After completing the year-end report, Suada Sivac had begun a new assignment. It was now nearly 7:00 P.M., and she was ready to log off the system. Of all the actions required by the rules and regulations of her work, this was the most tedious. Her new computer ran like a rocket, but the log-on/log-off procedures slowed it to a snail's pace.

She understood the concern. The unauthorized accessing of data, together with electronic eavesdropping, virus attacks and other malicious acts, was a major problem in the new millennium. Erecting electronic barricades was the only way to prevent cyber-anarchy. As a security precaution, most of the companies ETI contracted with used a sequence of firewalls, or gateways, through which all connections were made. The deeper into the system users went, the more hoops they had to jump through to reach their goals.

Suada's most recent work with a local HMO was no exception. Though she was only typing a series of reports for the human resources department, once she'd successfully logged on, she could access almost any file or record in the database. Online temps often worked for several departments over the course of a day or week, and widespread access to the host system was the only way that could be accomplished.

Such extensive right of entry necessitated a high degree of trust on the part of the companies that hired Exemplary workers. Suada knew, however, that in the five years ETI had been in business that trust had never been broken—at least not that she was aware of.

11

▼

Nyentzi

"You never did tell me how it happened," Toner said, breaking the silence. The Aeroflot jet had been circling Salekhard Airport for more than twenty minutes, waiting to land. The plows were out in force, but even the Siberians found it difficult to keep the runways clear from the relentless snowfall of a winter storm.

Flying across nine time zones—east to west—Toner and Molotova had kept their interaction to bare civility. Even during a stop in Yakutsk six hours earlier, each had remained wrapped in her own thoughts. Molotova turned toward the American.

"How what happened?"

"Monogovody, the big blast. How did it happen?"

"What I know is this," Molotova offered. "Monogovody was heated and air-conditioned from one power plant. All buildings were attached by underground pipes. The investigators concluded that the computer monitoring the heating system disrupted at the same time a natural gas leak occurred. That connection of highly unfortunate circumstances submerged Monogovody with flammable gas."

"And nobody smelled anything? Why didn't the combustible gas detectors alarm?"

"All detectors were wired through that computer. Without a computer, they could not identify the problem. Several survivors told of an announcement about a mainframe failure just before the explosion. As to smelling anything, Tyrellovich attained a deal with the Trans-Siberian Gas Company. He was able to tap one of the natural-gas lines before the fuel was perfumed at a pumping station. Without perfume, natural gas is without smell."

"Whew, I'm not sure I'd be so eager to buy into that string of coincidences. Man, if you buy that, I'd like to show you some real estate in south Florida." Angela's eyes narrowed with suspicion.

"I will admit, Toner, it does sound preposterous."

The American was silent for a moment. "How many casualties?" she finally asked.

"Between 200 and 220—perhaps. ETI's personnel records were also destroyed. No one knows how many people were there that day, and many bodies were unidentifying."

Just then, the pilot came over the intercom, announcing in Russian that their flight had received permission to land. By her companion's reaction, Angela guessed what was said. She glanced at her watch and leaned back in her seat. It was 8.30 A.M., Salekhard time. Jetlagged beyond comprehension, she had no idea what time it was or even what day it was in Los Angles. Staring out the window, she watched the snow swirl as the plane made its final descent.

The Russian and American agents sat next to each other in a small conference room at the St. Vladimir Russian Orthodox Hospital in Salekhard after a forty-minute drive in an old taxi from the airport to the hospital through the snowstorm. The weather reports were not good. There was even talk the airport might shut down unless the snow abated.

The hospital's director had been expecting them. Once Molotova displayed her Federal Security badge, a unit secretary showed them to a tiny conference room and gave them a thick medical file. Molotova read the patient summary, translating for Toner.

"Her name is Elena Tagi-Zade. She is thirty-eight years old—a member of an Asiatic tribe that settled this part of Siberia thousands of years ago. Of no small importance, but interesting—her people are more like the Eskimo than Russian. Very ancient people. Tagi-Zade received her advanced degree in biogenetics from Moscow University in 1992 with high distinction. She began working at Monogovody a short date after the facility was built."

"When was that?" Toner asked.

"Tyrellovich bought the land in 1996. He began to build the facility later after."

"How bad are her injuries? Will she be able to communicate with us?"

"She was severely burned over 60 percent of her body. She is paralyzed from below the waist from breaking of her back. And…this does not make sense. There are no medical reportings of…I do not understand…there has been never a correcting surgery of her burns. She has been in the hospital for seven years, but they not fix her up."

"Are you sure? What does it say?"

"Nothing—it says nothing. There are no surgical notes, no therapies. Strange…"

"Anything else in her file worth knowing before we go meet her?"

"Well, there is a recent discovery concerning *lympho*…what is this word in English, *lympho-sar-coma*? She has the cancer. But again, there are no plans for the treatment."

Toner touched Molotova on the arm. "Didn't you tell me that she was here on a charity basis? Maybe that's why they're not doing these other procedures?"

"Now I understand. There is not enough money for someone so injured. The hospital cannot afford to do it. Not the government, either. Perhaps she has no family, no money."

"Health-care rationing, up close and personal."

"Not much of other importance in her file. Look at her picture—once very pretty," Molotova said, a grim look on her face. "But that was before the fire that burned her so poorly. Very sad."

"Yeah," Toner agreed, unable to suppress a shiver.

Molotova closed the file and tucked it under her arm. With Toner at her side, she left the conference room and began walking down the hall.

"Are you able to speak any Russian?" Molotova asked.

"I take it she doesn't speak English."

"She is not perfectly fluent but speaks some. We will try English, but if she has difficulties with the understanding, you will have to trust my translation, yes?"

"I guess I will. Let's do it."

They entered the patient's room. It contained an old mechanical hospital bed, two wooden chairs, and a green bedstand with a vase of freshly cut flowers. Toner noted that the furniture, though ancient and well used, was clean and in good repair. The walls had been painted white long ago and were remarkably unblemished. Opposite the bed was a Russian icon of Jesus.

Lying in bed, eyeing them with suspicion, was what remained of Elena Tagi-Zade. Her once-black hair was spotted with gray and patchy with scars. Her left ear was a mass of gnarled flesh. So too her face, pitted and scarred beyond recognition of anything human. Half her nose was gone, as were her left eye, eyelashes, and much of her cheek. A brief survey of the wounds on the left side of her body showed in which direction of the explosion Elena stood on the day Monogovody ceased to exist. How she survived seven years in such a state one could only imagine. Why she would want to stay alive was another questions altogether.

"Good morning. Elena Tagi-Zade. My name is Nadezhda Andrevna Molotova. I am with internal administration of Federal Security Bureau. This is Agent Angela Toner of the American FBI. We would like to ask you a few questions about the Monogovody research facility. May we sit down?"

"Yes," Tagi-Zade answered hoarsely through a mouth devoid of lips. "You may speak English. I understand."

"That would be most helpful. Do you like the flowers?" Molotova asked.

"Was it you that sent them? They are very nice. It has been a long while since I saw real flowers."

"It was the least I could do. Thank you for seeing us."

"I had nowhere else to go."

Molotova sat in the chair nearest the bed. "That is true," she said. "Before we begin to discuss, do you have any questions for me?"

"I have no questions. I have been waiting. I knew someday someone would come."

"Yes, I believe you have." Molotova opened a small notebook and placed it in her lap before continuing. "According to our files, Elena, you were one of the members of Dr. Yuri Tyrellovich's number-one genetics research team at Monogovody. Is that correct?"

Tagi-Zade nodded, her eyes fixed on the wall opposite the bed.

"During your time at Monogovody, did you work with Dmitri Rancich?"

Again, she answered with a nod.

Toner sat quietly, watching the two Russians. She noticed the Russian agent's style—brisk, all business—like stereotyped television detectives of the 1960s.

"I am sorry to tell you that Dmitri recently passed away," Nadezhda said.

"I did not know he survived the explosion. Not many did."

"Have you had contacts with other survivors of the explosion? Any old friends or colleagues?"

"No. I am alone in this world."

"Is your care here enough? Do you require of anything, Elena?" The patient shook her head. "If there is, you may let us know of it, okay? I am not telling you to be merely nice. Now, in Dmitri's personals, we discovered a journal—a notebook—that makes referring to genetically engineered human embryos. Were you aware of such things?"

"It was forbidden. We were not allowed to do that."

"What was forbidden? The genetic works? Such experiments are forbidden by international law."

"No—the journal. We were not allowed to keep notes. Dmitri was wrong to do it."

"And what you did was not wrong?" Molotova countered. Turning to Toner, she whispered, "I think we will find her to be very protection of their work."

"Can't say I blame her. She's been lying in that bed for seven years with only her memories."

After reflecting on the American's insight, Molotova continued, keeping her voice soothing and nonconfrontational. "You knew of the project Dmitri refers to in those notes. Please understand, Elena, there is no danger to you for the answering of questions. We are only seeking information."

"Why is your questioning of such importance now? What do you want from me?"

"We need to know with exactness what was done at Monogovody. Dmitri talked of genetic experimentation in embryos. How many eggs were used? How many eggs were there at Monogovody?"

"There were thousands—thousands and thousands of eggs."

"My God—all implanted?"

"No—of course not all. Some were in embryonic state. Others were not. Different genetic markers, different changes in some. You say experimentation. We did not experiment. We knew exactly what was needed. We knew all the codes, even before completion of the Genome Project was announced. We made only the changes for..." Tagi-Zade did not complete the sentence. Despite Molotova's reassurance, she was fearful of the consequences.

"Needed for what? What was Tyrellovich attempting to do?" Molotova insisted.

"Evolution."

"Evolution? I do not understand."

"Natural selection—Dr. Tyrellovich said it is not working. It is not surviving of the fittest. How can we say that we humans are fittest? Have we made best use of our tools, of our world? No! We need change. Dr. Tyrellovich made that change. The project *is* change."

"What project? What did you do at Monogovody? What did you work on?"

"I worked on the project. We all worked on the project. Number-one goal was to complete the project. Nothing else was to be of significance."

"Elena, what was it called?" Toner asked in a slow, calm voice. As she did, she held up her right hand to Molotova, indicating caution. "The project, Elena—did it have a name?"

Tagi-Zade eyed the American with suspicion. After a moment, Toner asked again. "The project—please—what we have been discussing. Was it called something else? Did it have an official name?"

"Name? It was called 'the project,'" Tagi-Zade responded at last.

"That is what Dmitri wrote," Molotova said, stabbing her notebook with the tip of her pencil. "It also had a name, Elena. We know you know the answer. We know, but we want to hear you say it. What was the name of Dr. Yuri Anatoliovich Tyrellovich's genetic engineering project?"

Tagi-Zade glared at her visitors. "You know, so why you ask of me? For the proof? You want me to prove that I did such work? Do you not believe what I tell you?"

"We need the verification," Molotova insisted. "You must understand, we do not want to doubt you. We are only too concerned with lack of testimony and credentials."

"I am no phony. I do this work," Tagi-Zade said. Her anger grew, and she began to rise from the bed. "I am filled with pride of my work. I gave my life for *Nyentzi*. I am not to be ashamed of it. I am not with remorse. I am not…"

Her bravado was short-lived. She took a deep breath and lay back down on her pillow, gasping with shallow, coarse breaths. Nadezhda reached to the nightstand, picked up a glass of water with a straw, and offered it to the invalid. Tagi-Zade took several small sips and regained her composure.

"The project's true name was Nyentzi," the Russian agent said after placing the glass back on the nightstand. "Is that correct?"

"Yes, Nyentzi. It was all Nyentzi."

"What does Nyentzi mean? It is not a Russian word."

"It is a word in the language of my people. I was very honored by Dr. Tyrellovich. My people were of honor for to use that word."

"Yes, but what does it mean? It is of evidence important."

"We changed the genes. Nyentzi is the project. It is *what* we made. It is *who* we made."

"What does it mean, Elena? What does *Nyentzi* mean?" Angela requested.

"It means…it means he who comes, he who will save our people, all people. It could…I do not know the exact word in your language," Tagi-Zade hesitated. Her right eye closed for a moment. "In my language," she said, opening her eye and staring at the icon on the wall, "Nyentzi means great czar, great king, the czar of the prophecy. It means a new coming, the coming of the one who is awaited."

Toner followed Elena's line of vision. She looked at the wall and hesitantly ventured a guess. "*Messiah*? Is that the word?"

"*Messiah*? Perhaps *messiah*? The Messiah Project...Yes, that is it. That is the word. But Dr. Tyrellovich did not like using that word. We were to call it Nyentzi, only Nyentzi."

Molotova stared at Tagi-Zade with horror. "Are you being serious? Why would he call it that? What was he trying to do?"

"Tyrellovich was wanting to change the world," Elena said, her voice tinged with religious fervor. "He called it Nyentzi...Messiah...because that is who we made."

"*Who* you made? What is that supposed to be meaning?" Molotova demanded.

Elena smiled as she continued to stare at the icon. "Nyentzi are the ones who will teach us, lead us. We made these messiahs—these kings. Oh yes, we made many kings."

"Jesus H. Christ, that's just great," Toner muttered.

"*Da*, Jesus Christ—like that."

The tension in the room was palpable. Elena Tagi-Zade retreated into a shell of denial and faith. Despite repeated questioning, she refused to provide details about the genetic work of the Nyentzi Project. She would not provide information concerning the genetic changes made, what the objective of the project was, nor what had become of the project since the explosion.

"What good can come of your denials of cooperation?" Molotova demanded. "How can you be of help to these Nyentzi if you do not answer our questionings? Already one child, one of your *messiahs* is near death from automobile accident. The child is needing new kidney, but the family is not of suitable donor. And *you* know why. Now the Revkin child will surely die."

Elena finally spoke. "Olga Lyubimova's child? Is it one of Olga's children?"

"Yes, but she has only the one child from your Nyentzi Project…Melissa. Can't you see we are only trying to help her?" said Molotova.

"One? Her? What are you saying?" Tagi-Zade asked in alarm.

"What is wrong? Did you know Olga? Is that why you are upset?"

"Her! You said *her*. Olga had sons. She had two *sons*."

"No. She had one child—a daughter."

"Aaiii," Tagi-Zade screamed. Her fisted hands beat the air in rage. She began to thrash about in bed, spurning all attempts to soothe her. Her language reverted to a jumble of Russian and her native tongue. Watching and listening for half a minute, Nadezhda began to understand the source of Tagi-Zade's agitation.

"It is the project. She is screaming about the project—that it was sabotaged. I am thinking something has gone wrong with Nyentzi."

"Why does she think the project was sabotaged?" Toner asked, her eyes wide in disbelief.

"Very hard to understand. Back to forth in one language, then other. They should be boys—the children should all be boys. That is what she is repeating. Olga Revkin should not have had a girl seven years ago."

"We've got to settle her down. She's gonna have a stroke. Let's call the nurse."

"No, not yet. Elena. Elena, listen to me. How could you possibly know if Nyentzi has gone wrong? What difference would it make if Olga Revkin had a daughter?"

At first there was no response. Finally, the patient groaned. "Olga should not have had a daughter. Only sons. You must show me. You have such a photograph of this single child, this girl?"

Molotova turned to Toner. "Do you have a photo with you?"

Toner took out her laptop and set it up. Leaning over the bed, she showed the computer-generated image to the gasping Tagi-Zade. When the patient looked at the picture of the seven-year-old girl, her one eye went wide in disbelief. A single tear formed and rolled down her scarred cheek. Turning away, the patient trembled with anguish, rattling the bed and swearing in Russian.

"Now what?" Toner asked.

"She is cursing—great numbers of curses. She is saying about 'that bitch Tatiana.'"

"Who the hell is *Tatiana*? This is turning into a bad soap opera."

"Tatiana Mercereau was Tyrellovich's number-one cooperator, his colleague. She was as well a brilliant geneticist. They worked together many years; some have heard they were lovers. There is long story about them—I will tell you later."

"What is she cursing Mercereau for? What could *she* have done?"

"She is saying the child is wrong. The children of Nyentzi should not be female, should not look like Tatiana Mercereau. The babies that were engineered and implanted were all to be males. Not girls, only boys. This is not good. Our interview is done."

"We can't stop now. We've got to find out why she's so convinced Nyentzi was sabotaged by Mercereau and what they were trying to accomplish."

Molotova nodded. "You are right. And who! We need to know who all those surrogate parents are. If we had the travel records, we would know all about Nyentzi. But I agree. We need to know why. What purpose was this Nyentzi to achieve?"

Toner looked over at Tagi-Zade, then back at Molotova. "Could Mercereau have modified the embryos, changed them from male to female? Is that possible?"

"I studied these subjects. It was my college major. It is why I was assigned to this job. Yes, it is possible to do, but how could she pull it over on Tyrellovich?"

"As long as it could be done…Last question—what happened to Mercereau?"

"From what I remember, Tyrellovich removed Mercereau from her job in 1999. She was given a reassigning for reasons unknown. Is that what you are questioning about?"

"That's exactly what I'm questioning about," Angela said. She placed her hands over her mouth and exclaimed. "Oh my God! Is this the wrath of a woman spurned? She could have done it, Molotova. I'm not saying she did, but she could have."

The room was silent except for the sobbing of Elena Tagi-Zade. The two agents exchanged glances of sympathetic understanding.

Toner finally spoke. "You know something, in almost any other situation, I could admire the irony of what Mercereau might've done. But the way it is now, this conversation is giving me the willies."

"Willies? How could that…who are these *willies*?"

"Sorry—bad vibes, goose bumps, that Russian paranoia you keep referring to. It must be contagious."

Molotova nodded and turned back to Tagi-Zade. As distasteful as it was, the FSB agent knew she must continue questioning the former geneticist. "Tagi-Zade, we need more information. We need answers. Why did Tyrellovich start Nyentzi? What was he trying to do? Elena, you must tell us."

"Please Elena, we are only trying to help," Toner interjected. "We can help with your cancer treatment if only you will answer our questions. Cooperation is the only way to save Nyentzi. Can't you see that?"

"You do not know," Tagi-Zade muttered in defiant English. "You cannot know. You cannot understand. I will not help you. I swore oath—my word of honor. I will protect Nyentzi. It is something I must do. It is all I have left."

"You will tell us. You will answer questions for what is good for you. You *will* tell us. Govori! Rasskazivay o Nyentzi, ponyal, Tagi-Zade? Ti u menya zagovorish!"

"Yob tvoyu mat, Molotova!"

Toner recognized Tagi-Zade's angry response to Molotova's demand for information. It was the only vulgarity Kaloostian had told her that she remembered. Realizing she knew some Russian after all, Angela interrupted the argument.

"Elena, please, leave Nadezhda's mother out of this. Please. We're only trying to help."

Both Russians turned towards the American with looks of embarrassed surprise. The tension in the room, which a moment before had risen to a toxic level, now dissipated.

"What does it matter? Tell me that. Of what good is telling you? Things are wrong. The design has been changed. Nyentzi is over. My work, our work, our destiny. It…it…aaaggghh." Tagi-Zade's eye rolled back in its socket, her mouth frothed, her fists clenched, and the entire bed shook.

Toner's reaction was immediate. "She's having a seizure—get the nurse!"

The nurse was not pleased. She rushed into the room, appraised the situation, and hastily administered a heavy dose of intravenous Dilantin to the convulsing Tagi-Zade. She then ordered both agents out of the room.

"Nothing in the chart, eh?" Toner asked. The two agents were sipping brutally strong coffee in the conference room after being chased down the hall by the whirlwind in a white uniform.

"Nothing that I saw. Apparently, she does not have seizures with frequency, so she is not on the medications for regular dosages. It is too expensive for random troubles. The nurse said it was our blame, that we made her over with plentiful stimulation."

"Yes we did, didn't we?"

Molotova sighed and looked away.

"Come on. It's not your fault," Toner offered. "There should have been something in the chart…a red flag…a warning."

"No, it is not that. I was thinking of what Tagi-Zade said. The religion involvement. 'Lo! I shall tell you a mystery.'"

"What are you talking about?"

Molotova turned back towards Toner. "First Corinthians: Chapter 15, verse 51."

"Yeah, nothing like a good mystery. Tagi-Zade said something else back there. Did you catch it? She said it didn't matter anymore. Whatever fancy designs Tyrellovich cooked up, they don't matter. So if Nyentzi was sabotaged by Tatiana Mercereau, it's a whole new ballgame. Back to square one."

"I very much enjoy talking with you, Angela Carmen Toner. Once in the while, however, could you please speak the English?"

"Oh, sorry. Want me to translate that?"

"No, I think I understand what you said, and I agree."

"You also mentioned something else that I think might be worth looking into," Angela said with a grimace after sipping the rancid coffee.

"What is that?"

"Tagi-Zade is a charity case at a religious hospital. Nothing unusual in that, but she's one of only several survivors of a large explosion that, by all accounts, can be directly linked to human error, mechanical malfunction, or both."

"Yes, the gas leakages and computer mishappenings."

"Exactly. This is 2007, Nadezhda. When cars crash, lawyers show up. When planes crash, lawyers show up. When people get blown to pieces, lawyers show up. But what happened at Monogovody?"

"I do not know," Molotova said, tilting her head. "Now that you say it, I am also wondering. Could this be something to look around to?"

"Let's do some digging tomorrow. A quick check of major Siberian personal injury settlements in the past seven years might prove interesting. Countercheck the search with key phrase *Monogovody*. Maybe something will turn up. I find it hard to believe that both Elena Tagi-Zade and Dmitri Rancich are penniless cripples in charity institutions."

"We will do that, do some of this digging you keep talking about. But for now, let us go find hotel and check in. I hope the taximan is not buried under the snow."

They finished their coffee and put on their coats. Toner slung her computer bag over her shoulder and left the conference room, walking with Molotova towards the front exit of the hospital. All they could see through the many windows of the hallway was a panorama of white.

Toner turned to Molotova, who was unusually quiet. "You okay?"

"I was thinking about Tyrellovich. I read of him in school," Molotova said. "His personality type. What was that? Yes, type A—he was a type-A. Very impatient kind of guy that Yuri Tyrellovich."

"That's an understatement. Couldn't wait for the second coming—or first, depending on your point of view—so he took matters into his own hands and…"

"Did what we thought only God could, or should, do. I do not like this. I do not like mankind doing God's work. It is evil. Nothing good can come of it."

"Well, Tyrellovich might've been playing God, but after seeing Tagi-Zade's reaction to the Melissa Revkin revelation, I have to question the entire project. Maybe Melissa is a mistake or a mutation or something else entirely. That would explain her autism."

"Autistic? You did not tell me she is autistic," Molotova said with a trace of irritation in her voice. "But it is of no consequence—Melissa Revkin is not a mutation."

"You seem pretty sure of that."

"Yes. We have located two other children we suspect are Nyentzi. They are not autistic, and they are both unquestionably female."

It was early evening in Los Angeles. In the stillness of a Spartan office, a man effortlessly typed an eight-character password. In doing so, he sidestepped one of the most elaborate security systems in the world. No matter that the password itself was computer-generated, nonsensical, and randomly changed—his ability to penetrate the defenses of the FBI was a foregone conclusion.

With the unauthorized access undetected, as planned, the intruder maneuvered through the menus to his goal—the personnel files. All he had was a name, but that was enough. In a moment, he would know as much about the target as her mother, therapist, or psychographic data collector knew.

After he pecked out the name—he was in no hurry—the information he sought filled the screen. Picture, date of birth, marital status, identification numbers, bank accounts, income, 401(k) investment portfolio, credit-card balances, address, phone numbers—it was all there. Who was this Angela Carmen Toner, he had wondered yesterday. Now he was about to find out.

12

Ninety-nine Bottles

It would not stop. Growing up in Michigan, Angela had been through her share of winter storms but never anything like this. Since leaving St. Vladimir's, all she'd seen of Salekhard was a mantle of white falling from the sky, changing the textures of the city. The snow also changed her priorities, from getting some sleep to finding a store where she could purchase a pair of heavy winter boots to go with her Russian coat.

They drove from the hospital to the Hotel Salekhard in the same taxi that had picked them up at the airport ninety minutes earlier. Angela was surprised at the number of heavily bundled pedestrians and snow-covered vehicles navigating through the blizzard.

"People who live here must sure love snow."

"For many, it was not by their choice," Molotova said without looking out the window.

"Come again?"

"Stalin and the Communists forced thousands of people to Salekhard in 1930s and 1940s. Ethnic Germans, rebelling peasants, dissidents, other troublemakers. Entire families were put on trains and sent to here, told to build homes, factories. Many thousands died their first winter, especially women and children. Stalin and his KGB. It is why that nurse at the hospital gave me the frigid arm."

"Guilt by association, eh? Well, there're parts of the United States I wouldn't flash my badge either. But I thought Salekhard was older than that."

"It is. The Cossacks conquered this territory centuries ago. Then a fishing village was built. Fishing is the number-one industry, but most of the product is to be exported. Even when the people were starving sixty years ago, Stalin insisted that the fish be sold to foreign companies."

"Nice guy, that Joe Stalin."

"May he roast in hell. The political prisoners were even worst for that. They were forced to walk two hundred kilometers to the Monogovody Gulag. It was not a happy place then. But Salekhard is very fast growing now. Much natural gas and oil underground. Life is better today, though cold, always cold."

Loaded down with their luggage, Toner and Molotova entered the lobby of the hotel and approached the front desk.

"Dobry den," the desk clerk said with a wide smile.

"Ah, tak sebe. Pozhaluista govorite po angliyski. Our guest is American," Molotova said, nodding towards Toner.

The clerk, an older man in thick glasses and a faded wool suit, bowed slightly. "I am sorry. So nice to see an American face in the coldness of Siberia."

"You should be having two reservations—Molotova and Toner. The arrangements were wired from Moscow."

"Of course," said the clerk. He nervously looked through his book and saw a note indicating that one of his guests was with Federal Security. Despite the warmer climate of the Russian political scene and the fact that this agent was young and pretty, the clerk remembered all too well his life under the KGB. As the song goes: "Meet the new boss—same as the old boss."

"Both rooms have been made in preparation. Check-in is not normal until the hour of 1:00 P.M., but we have made special arrangements to you," he continued with an exaggerated smile. "Please to sign the registry—and your guest. Nosilschik: Otnesite ih bagazh v nomera."

The porter came quickly and began putting the luggage on a small cart.

The clerk handed Toner and Molotova two envelopes. "Your room keys. And Ms. Toner, there is a message for you. You may access it from the HDTV in your room. If you have no extra questions, the porter will carry your luggages. Have a mostly pleasant stay."

More to herself than anyone else, Angela wondered about the message waiting in her room: "I don't get it. No one knows I'm here. How could I have a message?"

"Our itinerary was to be logged with the Russian consulate in San Francisco. Your people could have checked with there, perhaps," Molotova suggested.

"Of course. Whew, that jet lag is really banging me upside the head. I am so out of it. Hope this place has comfortable beds 'cuz I need a hot bath and a nap in the worst way."

The elevator door opened, and the porter stood aside, allowing the women to get on first. No one spoke as the elevator rose. For Toner, recognition came slowly, but after several seconds, she cocked her head and listened—to the same song she'd heard in the elevator in LA before she'd been interrupted by Felicia Scriff. She was about to ask Molotova whether she recognized the tune when it ended. Angela knew the song was going to haunt her for the rest of the day. But no matter how hard she tried, she could not think of its name.

They reached the third floor, and the weary travelers followed the porter down the hall to their rooms. The porter stood to the side and the women inserted their keys into the locks, opening the doors.

"So, your room is next to mine. That's convenient. If you've got my room bugged, it'll save me the time of telling you what the message was all about."

"Very funny, Toner. Get some sleep. I will see you at six o'clock for dinner."

"Sounds good. Are there any good restaurants in Salekhard?"

"I have one in mind. You will not be disappointed," Molotova said, tipping the porter

"Okay, six o'clock it is."

Toner took her luggage from the cart, entered the room, closed the door, and looked around. Again, she was impressed with the accommodations. Two full-sized beds, quality furniture, satellite television—all the amenities of home. Throwing her luggage on the bed nearest the door, Angela walked to the second bed. She turned around, and with her arms spread wide, fell back with a satisfying *whoosh*.

She stared at the ceiling for a moment, then rolled to her side, from which she spied a refrigerator in the far corner. Crawling across the mattress, she leaned over and opened the door of the small appliance, expecting to find it empty.

"Oh my…"

Molotova waited fifteen minutes before venturing into the hallway. She looked at the door to Toner's room to make certain it was closed. She then walked briskly down the hall towards the emergency exit. Inserting her key, she glanced back a final time, opened the door, and darted down the stairway.

At the bottom of the stairway was a door opening to a small lounge on the first floor, away from the front desk. Seated in a chair and on a couch were two well-dressed men with heavy overcoats, scarves, and gloves draped across their legs. When Molotova approached, they lowered their newspapers and nodded.

Molotova took a place on the couch. "Dobry den, Mikail Ivanovich…Peter Pavelovich…kak dela? Let us whisper in English. Anyone who is noses will think we are tourists, okay? I am sorry to be keeping you waiting. The plane was late, and taxi ride to hotel was slow with all the snow. Is there anything to report?"

The men nodded.

"Good. The American and I have learned a great amount about the project. I will talk to you in greater details later this evening. We meet here again at 11:00 P.M. Now, what do you have for me?"

"I was finally able to repair your GPS pad," said Peter, the younger of the two. He was twenty-three years old, of average height, wiry, with unusually long brown hair for a federal security agent. It suited his cover as a computer and electronics hacker, or at least that was his excuse. His long, slender fingers were made for playing the piano or dabbling in his favorite hobby, electronics.

He handed Molotova a wallet-sized Global Positioning System device. She turned it on and waited a moment until the unit performed its triangulation computation off three orbiting satellites, one of them military. In less than ten seconds, the gadget provided the latitude and longitude of their position on a digital display. Pushing a second button produced the name of the city, and a third button offered the street address of their hotel.

"Amazing technology. Thank you, Peter Pavelovich."

"There was a malfunctioning memory module I was able to make good without much trouble at all. It was my pleasure," Peter said with a smile.

"You certainly do good work. Thank you. Mikail Ivanovich, what of you?" Molotova asked the second man, who looked to be in his late twenties.

"Here are keys for a car. There is a full tank of petrol," Mikail reported. He had short reddish hair and a neatly trimmed mustache. As a former military cadet, he took great care in keeping his six-foot, two-hundred-pound physique trim and athletic. "It is parked in the ramp, level 5C, license plate number 4HG-ZK22. It is a black Ford—a '99 but in top condition. I drove it over myself. The tires are in good shape for the snow."

"What is the forecast?"

"Not good. The storm is moving southwest and will continue through the night."

"I am only planning a short drive to the restaurant," Molotova said, rubbing her neck.

"Are you all right, Nadezhda Andrevna?" Peter said.

"There is nothing wrong. I am just tired and sensitive from the long flight. Before I forget to remember, there is one other item of highest priority. I would like a security detail assigned to Elena Tagi-Zade at St. Vladimir's. We may need to talk to her in greater detail after our trip to Moscow. Do it promptly. I do not wish to take any of the chances. Also to call hospital and find out her condition. I am afraid she did not do well with the questioning. Now, about tomorrow..."

Toner sprawled across the bed, savoring one of the bottles of excellent beer she'd discovered in the refrigerator. No two brands were the same and the variety was global—German, English, Chinese. There was even a bottle from an American microbrewery, the kind Kaloostian loved. She'd once bought him a six-pack of the hard-to-find brew to help celebrate Armenian Independence Day.

Angela leaned back against two pillows and accessed her video message through the television. After she passed the voice-recognition test initiated by the caller that surely meant bureau business, Deputy Assistant Director Hatton's face filled the screen. Toner frowned when she saw him. Not that he was ugly, but she knew his tendencies. He hated video messages and used them only as a last resort or if a message was unpleasant.

"Hello there, Angela Toner. I was hoping to greet you in Russian, but nobody around here has an electronic translator. Kaloostian said he loaned you his. He sends his best, by the way. Too bad you're not in. I'll have to leave a message.

"Well, no use beating round the bush. I've got some *bad* news. Melissa Revkin died last night. According to the report, the cause of death was kidney failure combined with a brain aneurysm. As far as you and I are concerned, that closes the case. But, of equal importance, I want you to stay put for the next two weeks—just until the Guerrero arraignments are complete. No use you stumbling around here getting into more trouble, right?

"Being a nice guy, I've authorized you two weeks of paid vacation. Don't worry 'bout the paperwork. I've already got it processed. We'll reimburse you for your hotel, food, and transportation expenses. Such a deal, eh? I've also lined up an exciting new assignment for you when you get back."

Hatton's expression to that point was all business. Now it changed to one of concern. He glanced to either side before looking directly into the camera.

"Listen, Angie, I don't know what the hell's going on with this Revkin thing. My orders are coming from higher up, so don't blame me. Personally, I don't want to know who or why or where or how. All I know is that the orders were explicit. They want that file disk back ASAP. You can FedEx it from the hotel.

"I know you're spouting steam right about now, but this is not my fault—or my idea. You're not that far into the case anyway, right? Your instructions—and this is a direct order—are to cease all communication and contact with the FSB concerning any aspect of the Revkin file *immediately*. And get that disk out in today's mail. If you've got any questions, contact the office. I'm sorry, Toner. There's nothing I can do. So soak up the sun and we'll see you in a couple of weeks."

The screen blanked, leaving the marooned FBI agent sitting numbly on the bed. Angela took a gulp of beer, her lips tight with frustration. With a heavy sigh, she rose from the bed and opened the refrigerator. Removing two more bottles of beer, she walked towards the bathroom, kicked off her shoes, and went in. As she began to fill the oversized tub with hot water, she muttered angrily between sips of chilled lager.

"Spineless bureaucrat…two weeks of vacation in goddamned Siberia in the dead of winter…I'll get him *and* his little dog."

A half-hour later, stumbling from the bathroom in her robe, hair dripping from the water and steam, Angela answered an incoming call. In her left hand was a damp towel. In her right, a half-empty bottle of beer.

"Greg!" she said to the face on her television. "What the hell are you doin' calling me here? How'd ya track me down? You find the number written on the wall of some bar on the East Side? I thought I was in exile here—incommunicado."

"Wasn't easy. Malone wouldn't tell me, so I've been calling all the hotels in Salekhard. Yours was the third on the list, and they weren't too keen about buzzing your room. Hey, is this line secure?"

"Who cares—talk all you want. This is the vacation of my discontent." Laughing at the confused look on his face, Toner began to sing and sway. "Man, I had a dreadful flight—I'm back in the USSR. You don't know how lucky you are, boy…back in the US—back in the US—back in the USSR."

"How many beers have you had, Spud?" Kaloostian asked when Toner took another sip. "Listen, this is no time for ninety-nine bottles. I need to know what the hell's going on over there. I just found out Melissa Revkin died, but the hospital's not releasing any information. Then Malone told me the shit hit the fan in Hatton's office, that the case is closed, and you're on vacation and best left alone."

"How'd Mrs. M find that out? She must be eavesdropping again. Naughty, naughty. She'll get in mucho-mucho trouble if she's not careful…Yes, Greggy, it's true. I've been banished to Siberia for my sins, driven from the land of sunshine, sand, and smog. But I have good news. There's a silver lining on this sad day, my friend. A streak of sterling, glimmering in the somber winter darkness of the Siberian sky."

"Don't get theatrical, Toner. What's the good news?"

"The room has a refrigerator…the refrigerator has beer…it's good beer…and there's plenty of it. Ha! I may never leave this room." Angela held up a bottle of American beer. "Lookee, lookee."

"Hey! The good stuff. I'm impressed. Nice hotel."

"Where are you calling from, anyway?" Toner asked. "That's not your office."

"My apartment. What time is it there?"

Toner looked at the clock on the wall. "Mm, almost one."

"Well, it's 2:00 A.M. here. I'm working late again."

"How're you gonna make it to work tomorrow? Even the nominally medicated Gregory Kaloostian has to sleep sometime."

"I'm calling in sick—Shanghai flu. Don't worry, though. I'll be better by the weekend."

"Yah bum…So whaddaya want? Lookin' to rub a little salt in the wound?"

"Maybe later. Right now we need to talk. I took the precaution of bouncing this call off a couple of satellites to make sure nobody could trace it. I'm not taking any chances."

"Get real, Greg. Nobody gives a rat's ass if you or anybody else calls."

"I ask again, little buddy, how many of those have you had? I know misery loves company, but this ain't Mardi Gras. Come on, don't leak out on me. I need to know what's going on."

"I am not in the mood for an interrogation," Toner retorted.

Kaloostian hung his head in mock defeat. "Come on, be nice," he whined.

"No way. I'm through with this."

"Please."

Toner shook her head in defeat. "Oh, all right. It's your calling card, and I've got nothing else to do for the next two weeks. Where to begin? Let's see, Federal Security found two survivors from Monogovody. One had just killed himself—I should send flowers—but he left a journal about the project and the genetic work they were doing. The second survivor's bedridden in a hospital here in Salekhard. She'd been on Tyrellovich's top research team."

"Did he confirm what we thought Nyentzi was—the experimentation?"

"Oh yeah, only she didn't see it as experimentation. You know, I cannot believe I let you talk me into this. Just two days ago—*two days*—I was a happily miserable in sunny California. Now I'm miserably miserable in Siberia. You wanna know how cold it is here, Kaloostian?"

"I'll take your word for it. What did the second survivor say?"

"This case is so damned unbelievable. I feel like I'm trapped inside some cheap multimedia game. *2007—Rendezvous to Siberia—The Angela Toner Story.* A sad, but true interactive game, complete with 3-D graphics, sound effects, and no chance of winning."

"Angela."

"Lost your sense of humor, huh? Fine, I'll stick to the facts. First, Melissa Revkin is one of several *thousand* embryos manufactured at Monogovody. And at least a hundred of those were implanted during the 1999 Symposium. Yep, you got it. Revkin's travel itinerary was right on the money. I don't know how the FSB did it, but they've located two other Nyentzi in Moscow they think are from the same batch. Tyrellovich managed to do seven years ago what everyone said couldn't or shouldn't be done. He reengineered and cloned humans."

"Are you serious? This is fucking fantastic. I'm speechless. They did it. They really did it! To hell with the ramifications, this is…man, this is so…scientific."

"Well, before you leap-of-faith outta your wheelchair and shout 'hallelujah,' I suggest you wait 'til I'm finished. You ain't heard *half* my day yet."

"What's the other half?"

"Both Monogovody survivors indicated, in one way or another, that the original genetic design was altered or sabotaged or got somehow screwed up. So not only do we have dozens of unsupervised genetically modified seven-year-olds running around, but the blueprint's been changed."

"They said what?"

"Hold that thought. You haven't heard the best part. Last, but not least—oh, most certainly not least—this project—this fantastic scientific breakthrough—is called the Nyentzi Project. Feature that."

"We already knew it was called Nyentzi, didn't we?"

"Oh yeah. But we learned what Nyentzi *means*." Toner took another sip of beer and checked the fluid level of the bottle. "I am time-zoned and jetlagged beyond belief, Gregory. I need another beer."

"No. In a minute—not now. Sit back and relax. Dry your hair, clip your nails, anything; just leave the beer alone. Like you said, you're not going anywhere. It'll keep cold."

"Party pooper. Anyway, like I was saying, translated to English—Russian too, for that matter—Nyentzi means messiah. Tyrellovich called it the Messiah Project. He was trying to create a messiah."

"No way!"

"Yes way. Capital Y-E-S way."

Kaloostian became very serious. "Angela Carmen, you are drunk."

"Not drunk enough. I don't think there's enough beer in that refrigerator to do the job after the kind of day I've had. My Russian FSB crony almost had a cardiac when Tagi-Zade told us that. It's some Asian dialect apparently—*Nyentzi*, that is."

"You believe him?"

"Her—the survivor's a woman. So's Molotova. So was Tatiana Mercereau, Tyrellovich's *numero-uno* colleague—and according to Tagi-Zade, the one who might've sabotaged the project. Women are taking over, Greg. You better watch that male-chauvinism crapola. When our day comes, and believe me it will, we'll be taking no prisoners."

"That's fine and dandy, Ms. Age-of-Aquarius, but if it's all the same to you, I'd like to stick with the current topic, which happens to be Nyentzi."

"Whatever. What more do you wanna know? I'm tired."

"I just want to be sure I heard you right. You said *messiah*, didn't you? You're sure that's how *Nyentzi* translates?"

"It's as close a translation as we could get. What's the big deal?" Toner asked with a crooked grin. "Oh, I get it: Now you're thinking Shroud of Turin. Sorry, Greg. You may be all fired up about this, but personally I don't give a Clark Gable."

"You damned well better! Didn't you just tell me that a group of possibly insane scientists genetically altered, probably cloned, and subsequently implanted scores of embryos—embryos that may have a strong disposition to world conquest or religious fanaticism? At the very least, aren't you a bit concerned about the world's ability to absorb a hundred more Jewish cynics?"

"Big frickin' deal. And who says they're Jewish?"

"Okay, cynics aside, you've got to be a tad bit appalled. My God, I happen to think this is headline news."

"Who's gonna believe you, huh? Who? The only paper that'll print a story like this tends to feature headlines like 'Howard Stern's Battle with Mental Illness—the Untold Story.' And it doesn't take a genius to figure out which one people'll believe."

"Angela."

"Maybe, maybe if we get lucky, CNN will pick up on it. 'Genetic messiahs cloned—enough for every religion to get its own. Film at ten,'" Toner deadpanned. She paused for breath and took another swallow of beer.

Kaloostian sat quietly, unamused.

"Sorry Greg, but what do you expect? I've been pulled off the case and here I sit, dripping wet, exhausted to imbecility, and stuck in this hotel room for two weeks."

"So you said. Realistically, though, it's only a technicality. You've been authorized two weeks vacation. As long as you're there..."

"Slow down, boy. You're forgetting I also received some pretty explicit instructions from *your* friend, *my* boss, Mr. Alfred E. Hatton, to cease and desist. No more contact with my ballerina buddy from Federal Security. You'd like her—cute as a bug. Nice kid, too...No further contact, Kaloostian. That's what the man said. None. Not on my life. Under no circumstances. *Finito*."

"Pooh. You're not seriously considering following that vague and arbitrary directive, are you? It wasn't even in writing. And as you've so fondly said in the past, 'A verbal order's not worth the paper it's printed on.' Right?"

"Are you nuts? They could really throw the book at me. We could be talking treason here—aiding and abetting a foreign power. Hearing about it secondhand's one thing, but I've never seen Hatton act so trounced."

"Wake up, Toner. Pay attention. Don't you realize what a privilege it is to witness history? Think about the implications of what Tyrellovich did. We're beholding the most significant act of scientific espionage and skullduggery since the Rosenbergs. Oh hell, who am I kidding? Nyentzi makes the Manhattan Project look like origami. This is the big one, Angie. This takes mankind to a whole new plane of existence."

"Uh oh, I feel a speech coming on."

"Damn right it's a speech. You're the one always crying about integrity and doing the right thing, sifting through all the evidence for any kernel of truth. Well, listen up, little lady. In the search for truth, you won't find neon signs, billboards, or fireworks. The truth is always hidden away, buried between the lines. You have to work hard to find it. And when it comes to Nyentzi, there're too many unanswered questions and loose ends for us to close up shop and hand that file over to people who'll bury it forever. We can't walk away now. We can't. What'll you tell your grandchildren?"

"This is so typical...men! You are all alike, you know that. And something else, Kaloostian. I keep hearing the word *we*, but when I look around this hotel room, all I see is lil' ol' *me*."

"My neck's already on the chopping block. When I heard about Melissa's death, I called the hospital to verify she'd been there. They weren't too cooperative, so I went online with a *slightly* illegal program I keep in my arsenal of cyber-tricks. I tapped into their medical records department and located her file, but it had already been encrypted and sealed. And, well, that's not playing fair."

"Nothing's fair in this world. You of all people should know that. Man, they're gonna hang you by your thumbs if they find out. So how does your nifty little program work?"

"PFM, Angie—Pure Fuckin' Magic. It's a modified cracker program that generates security passwords and codes until access is attained. That part's pretty routine. But I went a step further and designed an add-on that delves even farther, automatically locating whatever file I've instructed it to. Once that's done, the file is copied, encryption and all, right into my computer. It's that simple."

"Get over yourself! You've got the complete Revkin autopsy. Boffo job, Greg."

"Before I take a bow, I should tell you I didn't get the entire autopsy, just part of it. Whoever set up the firewall and security parameters down there is good—real good. A sniffer defense isolated my breach after less than sixty seconds and initiated countermeasures on their end. If I hadn't been monitoring the connection, they'd have accessed my computer, identified me, and erased my entire hard drive with a banzai virus. Luckily, I terminated the link before the virus could incubate."

"You're screwed if they trace that transmission back to you. My God, hanging will be too good. That's a Marine Corps facility. Do the words *National Security* mean anything to you? It's not worth it. This case is just not worth it."

"Wrong. This isn't about some screwy bureau file. We've got a body count in the hundreds, and by the looks of things, it's growing every day. Every law of God, nature, and man has been violated. The Russians don't know what's going on, and our own government is trying to shut the investigation down. Nothing makes sense, Angie, and you know it. This smacks of cover-up. If you weren't in the bag right now, you'd be saying the same thing."

Toner vigorously shook her head. "You are nuts. You're nuts, you're nuts, you're nuts—out of your fucking mind. We're not talking about life, liberty, and the pursuit of the minimum wage, dammit. Do you have the slightest comprehension what you're asking me to do? Do you?"

"Of course I do. Look, don't get all panicky. I just want you to stretch Hatton's no-contact directive concerning Federal Security. I've given this a lot of thought. We can create a paper trail from Salekhard to Moscow using your credit cards. It'll look like you're off on a sightseeing excursion. Once you're in Moscow, we can set up a computer link so I can transfer the information I glean from the autopsy."

"Nihon-go o hanashimasen. Nihon-go o hanashimasen."

"Stop it. I don't speak Japanese, either. And closing your eyes, holding your hands over your ears, and singing "Mary Had a Little Lamb" won't make me go away any quicker."

"This is bad, very bad," Toner admonished, taking a long drink of beer from the almost-empty bottle. "You know, if I do this, you won't respect me in the morning."

"That's not true, dear. I don't respect you now. Just kidding. Come on, hey. Can I count on you? We need to learn more about those kids.

We need to know what genetic modifications Tyrellovich made. I'll work on the autopsy. You take a little road trip to Moscow. Piece of cake. And on the way there, you can check into Tyrellovich and Mercereau background. Look for any hints of what they might've been up to.

"Obviously, there's no time for a lot of digging and cross-reference research, though we might find something on the net or in the archives. I just can't believe Melissa Revkin was their goal. She might have been a tragically simple kid, but I think there's a lot more here than meets the eye. There's got to be more, and those kids in Moscow are our only hope. Come on, Angie, just for a couple of days."

There was a long, contemplative pause. "Fine. Anything to get you to shut up and leave me alone. I'll see what I can figure out at this end. If I need you, can I contact you at this number?"

"Absolutely. I've got it rigged so any call to me will be virtually untraceable."

"Well, that sure makes me feel all warm inside."

"Buck up, Toner—it's not a job, it's an adventure. Which reminds me, seen any sailors lately?"

"*Bridges of Madison County*. No sailors. None. Not a one."

"The word *bridges* in the title suggests water. Anytime you've got water, chances are there's a sailor."

"That's cheating. What the heck—you make these rules up as you go?"

"Got 'em all written down. Remind me to email you a copy after I've cracked the Revkin autopsy."

"You better be careful with your snooping around, mister. Monogovody got blown to smithereens seven years ago. It might've been over those kids' genetic codes."

"I'm a guy in a wheelchair. Who's gonna harass a guy in a wheelchair?"

"If I were there right now, I'd be harassing the hell out of you. I can't believe you're talking me into this. Hey, weren't you the one who got me into this mess in the first place?"

"Have a nice day, Angie. Gotta run." Kaloostian concluded.

The screen blanked. "Crazy Armenian," Toner spouted to no one in particular.

Angela rolled over on the bed and lay back against the pillows. Mentally reviewing the Revkin case led her to the immediate conclusion that everything that could go wrong had gone wrong. Such was the story of her life. She humorlessly summarized her Russian trip by rephrasing Caesar's famous passage: "I came, I saw, I froze my butt off."

In less than six hours she was to meet her Russian traveling companion for dinner. She'd need that long to decide the best way to break the news to Molotova about her orders. She'd have to tell her something, maybe even the truth. Her new friend deserved that much. The diminutive Russian had loosened up and was turning into a good-natured partner. Not many people could put up with Angela Toner when she was in "poor, poor me" mode.

For some strange reason—"must be the beer"—Toner thought about Marc Heiple. Not about him personally but about something she had once heard him say, something that actually made sense. She was sure it was a quote, but Heiple had made it his own. A reference about imagination being more important than knowledge. Assuming that was true—and it made a fair amount of sense—then perhaps her situation wasn't as discouraging as it seemed.

What she knew about Melissa Revkin, Monogovody, Yuri Tyrellovich, and the Nyentzi Project might be vague and speculative. And she had virtually no resources at her immediate disposal for researching the subjects in question. But she did have her imagination. Moreover, according to her mother, it was one dandy imagination at that.

Try as she might, however, Angela could not concentrate. She tried to list mentally the known facts of the case, but her mind jumped from fact to fact. Melissa Revkin—not autistic, and certainly not messiah material. Inclined to mathematics. Tons of medications.

Why all the meds? Maybe that's the key. Then again, maybe it was just Melissa? The key is probably the two kids in Moscow. Are they on the same prescription?

Nyentzi—another scary thought. Sabotaged…from what to what? And why?

Messiah—was Tyrellovich thinking biblical, or was it in reference to some mystical idealism advancing a fantastically demented scheme?

Tagi-Zade and Rancich—bedridden survivors still protecting the project that destroyed their lives.

And Monogovody—a mystery in itself. There'd been no apparent legions of lawyers descending on Siberia, despite the loss of property and lives.

Tagi-Zade had mentioned Darwin—complained that natural selection wasn't working. Then she'd gone ballistic when learning the embryos were changed from male to female. Why again? Why would the change matter? Why make the change at all?

Women live longer, but as one comedian noted, that's because they don't have wives.

None of it made sense, though there had to be a common thread. Something had to make sense. Maybe she should start with that. What made sense?

The file made no sense.

Hatton and Kaloostian's behavior made no sense.

People living as far north as Salekhard, utter madness.

"And that 'Welcome to Siberia' sign at the airport makes about as much sense as those 'Welcome to the Illinois Toll Way' signs I run into every time I drive to Michigan," Angela thought with a hazy laugh. "Who the hell do they think they're kidding?"

She closed her eyes, drifting in and out of wakefulness, reveling in a sensation of floating. At the moment when sleep transcended reality, her brain began to play games with itself. The realization did not come in a streak of charged electricity or the light bulb of comic book lore.

For Angela Toner, who had faded into an oblivion of beer and exhaustion, it began with an inane white cap on a dark background. As the image lazily spun in her head, it grew larger and more defined. A man with a deeply jowled face, smoking a pipe at a cocky angle, wearing a deep blue uniform with lots of buttons and bell-bottomed pants…

"I know this guy," she realized in the instant before sleep overtook her. "It's…it's…Popeye?"

Had an alert and motivated human being been keeping track, he or she might have noticed two unauthorized accesses into the bureau personnel files in the past twenty-four hours. The security software that monitored and controlled the files, however, was not programmed to such exact parameters.

It would prevent access without authorization, which both entrants ostensibly did. It would prevent repeat visits by the same source to the same site, yet each "guest" had accessed only a single file on a single occasion. It would prevent attempts to liquidate or extract classified or sensitive files. And it would prevent attempts to alter a file or download additional programs or files.

These invasions met none of the criteria. Each "guest" had accessed only a single file on a single occasion. Unless some alert computer tech detected the encroachment during the next update of the digitized logbook, they could remain unnoticed for months, perhaps years. Even discovery next week would be too late. Time was running out.

The third intrusion was water over the dam. It accessed the bureau's personnel files—cracking through automated defenses with astonishing ease—not even bothering with electronic passwords. It too scanned information about one particular agent. What no one could know was that this time the information was added to an already extensive dossier on a particular thirty-two-year-old female agent with an irreverent disposition.

Angela Carmen Toner could neither have understood nor appreciated the fact that this most recent intrusion into her file might lead to her fifteen minutes of fame. And she certainly would not have appreciated the fact that when her fifteen minutes of fame finally did arrive, she might not be available to share in the festivities.

13

Hang Me in Rags

Kaloostian blinked hard, not fully awake. The window shades made it difficult for him to determine whether it was morning. Cursing the god of nearsightedness, he groped for his glasses, found them on the nightstand, put them on. As the clock came into focus, he saw that it was 6:33 A.M. He'd managed four hours of sleep.

The explosion that took his leg and paralyzed him from the waist down had caused internal injuries making the start of every day a challenge. Knowing this day could prove interesting, however, gave him more motivation than usual. He reached up, grabbed the support bar over the bed, and pulled himself into a sitting position.

Using his powerful arms, Gregory pivoted to the right. With a sharp grunt, he dragged his torso to the edge of the bed, careful not to spill the drainage bags filled with waste during the night. Flexing his shoulder muscles rid of the morning stiffness, he pulled himself up and off the bed. After verifying the position of his wheelchair, he lowered himself onto the padded seat.

Secure with a lap belt, the Armenian wheeled out of his bedroom towards his computer station. Before going to bed, he'd left the computer running in an effort to crack the Revkin autopsy. Deciphering any encrypted file was a time-consuming task that, more often than not, ended in failure. As good as most encryption software was, Kaloostian knew he had one advantage—the federal budget.

Technology advanced so quickly that taxpayer-supported government agencies could hardly afford the latest electronic tools and toys. The FAA had waited until 2003 for a new computer system to support its radar network of regional air-traffic-control centers. Before then, it had been forced to use antiquated computers from the 1960s in its efforts to prevent midair collisions. The same fiscal pressures cost the government more $115 billion in uncollected taxes because of the Internal Revenue Service's aging system. Though partially updated in the late 1990s, it was still unable to sift through a massive backlog of files.

If the Revkin autopsy was encrypted at the Santa Ana Marine Corps Air Facility, chances were good that Kaloostian's software was at least two generations ahead. That edge, slight as it might be, was all he needed to be optimistic.

After taking care of the more pressing matters of personal hygiene, the surprisingly cheerful Armenian came out of the bathroom, wheeled to his computer center, and saw the program was still hard at work. Success was just a matter of time and patience. Satisfied that the computer could continue without his help, Kaloostian spun around and headed for the kitchen.

Having called in sick the night before and with a "free" day ahead of him, Greg was tempted to invite his neighbor over for breakfast. In the three years they had lived next door to each other, they'd exchanged keys, personal secrets, and recipes. A slow day for him, however, did not necessarily mean the same for the rest of America's working population. He knew she was probably involved in a project, and he did not wish to impose.

Deciding to forgo his usual, microwaveable meal, Kaloostian began to gather the ingredients for a vegetarian omelet, freshly ground coffee, multigrain toast, and a fruit salad. With CNN's morning news blaring in the background, he began to prepare the healthiest breakfast he'd had in a week.

The roar of the cannon's salvo nearly caused him to drop his coffee in his lap. Years before, he had programmed the end of the *1812 Overture* into his computer as the default beep for the completion of a task. Unfortunately for Kaloostian—and his neighbors—the computer's multimedia applications were wired through his stereo, and he had forgotten that the external speakers were on at a volume normally reserved for headphones. His logic had been that once it was accessed, he would work on the autopsy immediately—sleep or no sleep. Tchaikovsky's rousing finale was an effective alarm clock.

Propelling his chair from the kitchen table to the computer, Greg saw the message box signaling that the autopsy file had been breached. As eager as he was to see how much information he had gleaned before being forced to terminate the connection, he had another task to complete first.

With a universal remote, he shut off the television in the kitchen. He next flipped several switches on the stereo, dropped one of his personally recorded compact disks into the tray, and filled the apartment with music. No matter what he was doing, Kaloostian could not work in silence. Whatever excuse he gave Toner and others who questioned his loud music was inconsequential to the fact that years of too-high volumes, not to mention the blast of the mine that destroyed his leg, had left him with a pronounced ringing in both ears. Silence was no longer an option. Any sound was better than the chronic buzzing of tinnitis.

Satisfied the music was loud enough, Kaloostian wheeled over to his computer and dove headlong into Melissa Revkin's physiology. The result of ten hours of deciphering made him whoop like a rodeo-bound cowboy. He might not have the entire document, but whoever compiled the autopsy had done him a great service in providing a summary page and index, followed by pathology, lab, and genetic interpretation reports. This was definitely not the work of the author the Revkin file.

Scanning the material, he couldn't tell whether Melissa was one of a hundred clones or simply a one-of-a-kind genetically reengineered embryo. None of his earlier queried sources had uncovered the slightest clue as to what Dr. Yuri Tyrellovich had been trying to achieve. Nor could Greg tell whether the experiment had been a failure or whether Melissa was simply a defective product, and thus quite normal.

But now he read with amazement. The research teams at Monogovody had not merely dabbled in genetics—they'd embraced it with the fervor of true believers. The autopsy was proof at last that man had moved beyond simple gender changes, embryonic protein experimentation, and hereditary gene therapy. Humans had usurped the very throne they claimed to venerate.

Though some were missing, the pieces of the puzzle began to fit together. Gregory Kaloostian finally understood the significance of Melissa Revkin's drug and vitamin regimen, the rationale for secrecy, and perhaps the true meaning of the word *Nyentzi*. The realization made his skin crawl and his face pale. Staring at his monitor, he was thankful he'd never bought the argument that 90 percent of the brain's total mass is unused or that most genetic code is litter.

"Well, there goes the bell curve," he said with morbid seriousness.

Toner and Molotova took their seats at the table near the wall.

"Man, it's cold out there. How do these people stand it?" the American asked.

They had driven from the hotel to a restaurant several kilometers away. Snowplows, many of them relics from the 1970s, were out in force, clearing the streets as best they could in the dim glow of the streetlights.

"I will be admitting when I say the coldness does limitize things to do. We are lucky to have a car to keep in hotel's heated garage. Of otherwise, Chekhov's would be too far of walking. Of course, it is high priority to find you a pair of boots. Maybe we later shop."

Toner glanced around the room with approval. The table Molotova had reserved was the best in the restaurant. It gave its ever-wary occupants a full view of the bar and front entry. Even when off duty, the federal security agent remembered her training.

The restaurant, *ryestahran* in Russian, was a wonderfully old-fashioned eating establishment offering the food and ambiance Toner loved. Oaken bar with marble countertop, waist-high wainscoting topped with faded ceramic tile to the beamed ceiling, antique light fixtures—no two alike.

Shelved books lined the walls. There were pictures and paintings of the restaurant's namesake, Anton Pavlovich Chekhov, the playwright and author, who wrote of the helplessness and pessimism of the Russian people before the Bolshevik Revolution. As Molotova had explained to Angela in the car, his work had taken on new significance during the economic upheavals of the 1990s.

Noting the gusty appetite for food and drink of other patrons, Toner was pleased that they seemed anything but helpless and pessimistic. The storm raging outside did little to dampen the spirits of the Siberian people.

"This is a nice place—nice atmosphere. How's the food?" she said, admiring the decor.

"Very good. I only have eaten here once before, however."

"When was that?"

"November, when our team came to Salekhard to investigate the Monogovody suspicions. We took a helicopter to the place that was once the facility."

"Anything left?"

"Ruins. Some shells of structures, nothing remaining of interest. We only came away with increasing questions. But as we speak of the cold, I should tell you that Siberia's weather was part of the problem with Monogovody's destruction."

"How's that?" Toner asked with interest.

"It gets so cold here that Tyrellovich specially designed the facility. He had the foundation blasted out of the tundra so most of the buildings were in part underground and therefore warmer. Out of doors, in your temperature, it could be minus-seventy degrees. Steel cable can freeze and snap. Scotch® Tape is so cold it breaks like thin ice."

"But how did that contribute to the damage of the blast?"

"With much of buildings below ground and connected, the explosion was compressed. After explosion was done, what goes up came down. Many survivors were crushed."

"You've really done your homework. Your job must keep you busy. Do you have time for anything else? Do you date much? I mean, what are the men like in Russia?"

"My work keeps me overly occupied, but I would like to believe that I am a modern, sexually emaciated woman. What? What is so funny? Did I use a wrong term?"

"Emancipated, emaciated," the American explained. "I could go either way on that one."

"Your language is so difficult, Toner. Twenty-six letters in the English alphabet, more than forty sounds to make from them."

"Blame it on the French. Besides, what good is a word if you can't spell it at least two different ways?"

Molotova looked at Toner with skepticism as a uniformed man approached their table. "Ah, finally—here is coming our waiter. We will order a drink and appetizer before the meal? It is another of our Russian traditions."

"Great. How 'bout a Bloody Mary? Can I get one of those?"

"If it has vodka in it, of course. Ofitsiant! Butilka vodki, dva stakana, zakusku i smes dlya amerikanskoy krovavoy meri."

"Konechno, siyu minutu."

The waiter walked back to the bar to fill their order. "Russians sure love vodka," Angela observed while watching the other patrons. "Does it come with the meal, or is it one of the appetizers?"

"But of course we love vodka! And it always comes before dinner. Not only that, but once a bottle is opened, it must be finished."

"We're going to drink an entire bottle of vodka? Well, that outta send my jet lag into next week."

"It is another custom—what can I say? But you know, I have seen people, foreigners like you, begin to drink vodka and think everything is okay-dokay. But vodka is like Russia. It sneaks up, a delayed reaction. Then, *whack*...it cuts off your head like a guillotine."

"I can't wait. Simple and brutal."

"You must understand, Angela, despite our similar features, the United States is different than here. For example, in your country, there is a chicken in every pot, for what the politics are wanting you to believe. Russia is more simple, more of the earth. We vote for what we need to survive—free vodka and vegetables."

Toner nodded. "I've got a friend in Los Angeles who has all these weird theories. One of them has to do with the influence that drugs and alcohol have had on civilization. See if you can follow his logic: Anthropologists claim that the catalyst for the rise to civilization began with the domestication of grain by the Sumerians thousands of years ago."

"I have heard that also. It makes perfect sense to me."

"Okay—so far, so good. But there's always been this raging controversy as to what prompted early man to raise corn, wheat, potatoes, and so on in the first place. Was it to make bread—or was it to make beer, wine, and liquor? No one's been able to pinpoint which came first. According to my friend, if it was beer, then our entire civilization was founded on the principle of getting high."

"Your friend—he is Russian, no?"

"Not quite. Armenian."

"Ah, wonderful people. He has the good point. Much of Russian history is like that. For examples, did you know that our Prince Vladimir, the patron saint of the hospital Tagi-Zade is living at, choosed Christianity as the religion of the Eastern Slavs because Islam forbids the use of alcohol?"

"Come on, you serious?"

"Yes, it is exactly true. Your friend may be smarter than you think."

"There's a scary thought."

"His theory makes perfect sense," Molotova said with a hearty laugh. "This country could never stay sober. There would be a revolution like the world has never seen. Take away a Russian's vodka, and there can only be trouble. Vodka is the blood of Russia's soul."

"Heck of a religion—more than 35,000 deaths a year from alcohol poisoning."

"That is also true. For good or evil, Vodka is the patron saint of Russian vitality. We buy 320 million cases each year. That is many times more than entire world put all together."

The waiter arrived at their booth with menus, two tall glasses, a bottle of vodka, a small pitcher of tomato juice, and several small tins of seasoning. Surrounding the drinks were dishes containing salted herring, marinated mushrooms, pickled cucumbers, and smoked salmon.

After the waiter left, Toner asked the obvious question.

"What's all this? I thought we only ordered drinks, and mine was supposed to be a Bloody Mary. You mix your own here?"

"Most Russians drink vodka straight up. For the Bloody Mary, however, it is allowable to have customers blend their own. These other treats are appetizers, treats to eat with the vodka. It is not good to drink on an empty stomach, correct? Here, I will do the mixing."

Toner popped a mushroom and watched Molotova add tomato juice to each glass and, with the skill of a chemist, sprinkle just the right blend of spice. After stirring vigorously, she handed one glass to Toner, who took a sip.

"Delicious. My compliments. Whoa, be careful where you set your glass. This table is a little wobbly."

Molotova wiggled the table, then looked around for their attendant. "I will see if the waiter is able to level it up for us."

Angela took another sip of her drink and smiled. "So, what other Russian patron saints should I be aware of?"

"Well, my younger brother is involved in another notable Slavic religion."

"Really, your brother's a priest?"

"No, not of course. He is into the hockey."

"Oh, that religion. Is he a professional?"

"Nyet. He was a player type until he suffered a bad-tempered knee injury when he was nineteen years old. Now he is coach for teenager kids. It does not pay him enough money, but it is something he very much enjoys and is highly good at."

"How old is he now?"

"He is two years my younger—twenty-three. Why you ask?" Molotova asked with a wink. "Would you like to meet him? He is a single kind of guy."

"Heavens, no. I didn't come all this way to meet a man. Thanks but no thanks."

"Yes, I understand from where you come. Men! I have had the boyfriends, but I will never be understanding of them. Will they not ever grow up?"

"Boys and their toys," Toner said. "I think it's some sort of reverse maturation. The older men get, the more childish they become."

Molotova nodded vigorously. "Oh, so true. Big tough guys."

"What about you? You're not married. Are you looking for the right man? Lookin' to fall in love and have your heart ripped to shreds?"

"No thank you. I have learned my lesson. If love is a red dress, hang me in rags."

"Yes! And if love is aces, deal me a jack," Toner said, adding the correct addendum.

Contact was made. Across diverse cultures, different races, and several years in age, the two women had found common ground—their mutual confusion about the opposite sex. Sharing a laugh and heartfelt smiles, Toner and Molotova extended their right hands and high-fived across the table.

"Great song," Angela remarked.

"Yes, I love the rock 'n' roll music," Molotova said. "It is good way to learn English by listening to such songs. A toast, my friend. Let us share a drink to each of us. May your dreams be always precious."

"And may your hard drive never self-format."

The glasses clinked.

They finished their drinks and Molotova mixed another. The conversation turned to small talk as Molotova assisted the American in reading the menu.

"Your name—Nadezhda—how does that translate to English?" Toner asked.

"It means hope. My father, the endless optimist, named me."

"Do you have a nickname? Does everyone call you Nadezhda?"

"No. No one calls me that. There is shorter version—Naddie. Call me Naddie."

"Angela is shortened to Angie," Toner said, extending her hand.

"It is very big pleasure to finally meet you, Angie Toner."

After several minutes explaining the house specialties and ethnic dishes, Molotova noticed a man with a scruffy beard and dark glasses approaching their table. He scrutinized the two women from ten meters, turned, and walked to the front of the restaurant. Donning his coat and fur hat, the man left without looking back.

"Did you notice that guy?" Molotova asked Toner, still trying to decipher her menu.

"Where? Is he cute?"

"No, that is not what I am meaning. The man came toward our table, looked at us most precisely, then left the restaurant."

"You must've glowered."

"That is not it. He was not interested in us as dates. Mmm, highly unusual."

Toner shrugged and turned back to her menu. Molotova, however, was not convinced. Something in the man's demeanor made her uncomfortable. Perhaps his eyes, staring at her over the top of his dark glasses. Though she was sure she'd never seen him before, she'd seen a glimmer of recognition—of identification—on his part. Were they being followed?

"If that is the case," Nadezhda asked herself, "what kind of idiot would allow himself to be seen by his prey? Are Mikail and Peter doing their jobs? I may have to contact them before eleven o'clock."

Several minutes later, as Toner and Molotova waited to order, their conversation reverted to the business that brought them to Salekhard.

"Speaking of hockey and other matters of the spiritual nature," Angela said, "what do you know about Tyrellovich's religious tendencies? Tagi-Zade's messiah reference could shift the entire direction of the Nyentzi investigation."

"I do not know much about his religiousness, other than he was of Orthodox faith. But I agree with your concerns that religion and genetics are a bad mix. Are you yourself a religious person?"

"Not really. I've grown away from the wind-up-God-on-Sunday routine. I don't know. Maybe I'm too cynical."

"I do not know either, Angie. I have strong beliefs, but I agree that we need to learn much more about Tyrellovich and his convictions. Do you yourself have beliefs?"

"Sure. Some are pretty strong, but they're hard to define. Most don't fit into the prevailing religions. Kaloostian, my Armenian friend, and I got tired of all the Madison Avenue pseudo-saintly schemes: Jesus T-shirts, Bible websites, and what not. Anyway, we started our own religion: 'The Los Angeles Chapter of Our Lady of Everlasting Toil and Perpetual Angst.' Basically, we just sit around complaining about our jobs and life in general for an hour with a bottle of wine and some good bread. It's a perfect theology—serves no profound purpose, doesn't try to sell you anything, but you always feel better later on."

"I am not sure I would find that enough. I am believer in God and the Orthodox Church."

Toner shrugged. "I'll be the first to admit my philosophy isn't for everyone. When you get right down to it, if there're five billion people on this planet, there're five billion religions. No two people will ever agree on every aspect of every theism, scripture, or dogma."

"True," Nadezhda said in agreement. "Was that your friend who was leaving you a message at the hotel when we checked in?"

"Actually, it was my boss. I hate to change the subject, Naddie, but I think we should discuss a little business matter that came up in the message."

"About Nyentzi?"

"Definitely Nyentzi."

"Was it not good news?" Molotova asked.

"Not at all."

"So, we have much more to discuss. Before you tell me more, let us order our dinner. It will make the talk better, okay?"

Nadezhda looked around the bar for their waiter. As she did, she saw the headlights of a car come to a sliding stop in the no-parking zone directly outside. A bundled man leapt from the front door. Another figure got out the back. Even in the dim light of the room reflected off the glass, Molotova could tell it was the same man she'd seen moments earlier walking by their table.

Molotova tensed when the man reached into his coat. As if in slow motion, he retrieved a short-barreled automatic rifle. The man and his companion brought their weapons to bear. Using all her strength, the Russian agent forced the heavy, unbalanced table on its side with a desperate push. She then launched herself at the wide-eyed American, knocking her backwards out of her chair. They fell to the floor amidst shattered glasses and spilt vodka. In the next instant, the heavy staccato of automatic weapons erupted, obliterating the huge glass window of the restaurant. The ambiance changed from an evening of indulgence and merriment to pandemonium.

All semblance of order died. The muzzle flashes of the gunfire lit the snowy street like the flicker of candles on an old-fashioned Christmas tree. Patrons and staff alike dove for cover or scattered in every direction. Shards of glass, oak, tile, and china flew every which way while the men raked the room with their lethal wares. Hiding behind their overturned table, Toner and Molotova drew their 9mm service pistols. With bullets flying in their direction, they prepared to defend themselves

The barrage continued, preventing their escape. Surrounded by screams, smoke, and hysteria, the two women exchanged glances and waited for the sound that would signal their only chance of survival.

14

No Big Deal

The operation had been foolproof—until now. Years of planning, preparation, scheming, and financial inducement had gone into making the dream a reality. Overseeing the far-flung enterprise, now in its seventh year of operation, the man realized with frustration that while his watch was waterproof, his laptop computer shockproof, and his office soundproof, no one had ever been able to design anything foolproof. Fools were simply too persistent at their craft.

Dolts, buffoons, slackers—they surrounded him on all sides. Much as he hated to admit it, his father had been right. If you want the job done right, do it yourself...or design someone who can.

Sitting in his office, surrounded by computers and communications equipment, the thirty-four-year-old man was surprised—and, he hated to admit, impressed—by the speed of her progress. In the three days, the annoying FBI agent had procured a restricted file, made contact with a foreign representative, met with an eyewitness, and now, with her new friend, seemed on the brink of learning more than they should about his little endeavor. Such persistence and efficiency simply would not do.

He had contacted a local cleaning service, only to learn it did not have a competent franchise at the location he'd requested. Neither was it able to promise delivery in a timely manner. So much for customer service.

He'd thus been forced to deal with locals through an intermediary, and he was not optimistic. Even if they failed, however, he would be ready at the next rendezvous. He knew her destination. Next time, he would not be the one caught off guard.

In the meantime, he initiated another effort to slow her progress. Logging onto the Internet in a manner preventing anyone from tracing his call—something few thought possible in the third millennium—he began to shut down every credit card listed in her credit report. Let the troublesome American try traveling without money.

The mark of amateurs—both men stopped to reload at the same time. This was the moment Toner and Molotova had been waiting for. The agents popped up from behind their table and shot towards the front of the restaurant, hoping for the best. With no time to aim, their approximated shots were remarkably accurate—especially from the perspective of the two unwelcome guests.

The man who had earlier cased the restaurant took a bullet in the throat that shattered his larynx, severed a major artery, and clipped his spine. His body spun from the impact, blood flying in a misty, red semicircle. His startled colleague dropped to his knees on the snowy pavement. In the dim light of a street lamp, amidst the snow and blood, he tried to reload.

The gunman's pudgy hands, encumbered by heavy gloves, could not pull the extra ammunition clip from his pants pocket. Cursing and trembling with panic, he could not ignore the jerking death spasms of his friend, whose crimson gore pumped into the snow.

Sensing victory, the Russian and American emerged from their cover. Fewer than twenty seconds had elapsed since the first shots shattered the restaurant window. The hysteria of the other patrons momentarily ceased, the respite providing an opportunity for many of the people huddled on the floor to take a collective breath.

The surviving aggressor, watching his companion's life ebb and twitch away, still fought with his pants for the extra ammunition. The biting Russian wind, his consumption of vodka, and his weakening nerve deprived him of even the most fundamental skills. Through the frozen vapor of his panting breath, he could see the glint of gun barrels inside the building—aimed at him. His time was running out.

He cursed his dying friend for getting him involved, cursed his own greed for taking the job, cursed his wife for not insisting he stay home. They had promised no resistance. They had told him it would be an easy job. They had guaranteed a bonus. They had lied.

Seeing two armed customers approach through the haze and wreckage, the man prepared to flee the scene. He dropped his weapon, pivoted in the snow, tried to stand, slipped, then found his footing. But before he could continue, a sports utility vehicle skidded to a halt directly in his path. Not knowing what to do, the man paused, his arms useless at his side. Through the tinted window of the four-by-four, a shotgun blast lifted him off his feet and deposited most of him in a nearby snowbank. The cavalry had arrived.

Witnessing the timely demise of the second attacker, Molotova lowered her pistol and began to walk to the front of the restaurant. Toner hesitated. Despite apparent assistance from the Ivans-come-lately, she sensed something was not right. She could hear Kaloostian's voice in her head, urging caution. In a millisecond, Angela realized that law enforcement personnel from *any* country generally do not shoot through their own car windows. Nothing to do with etiquette or safety—just too many forms to fill out later.

Her intuition overruled her sense of optimism. Toner grabbed her Russian colleague's arm and pulled her back. At that moment, the doors of the second vehicle opened, spilling four individuals in dark clothing—guns drawn—into the snow-filled street. Assessing the situation, Toner realized that if life were a Western movie and this was the cavalry coming to the rescue, she and Molotova most likely were the Indians.

The newcomers wore full-mask stocking caps, similar to the one Toner used on SWAT duty. Displaying none of the bravado that killed the earlier arrivals, they approached with cautious professionalism. The first two crept towards the restaurant, stepping over one body, then the other, while the second pair covered the street in both directions.

Recognizing Toner's trepidation, Molotova retreated towards their overturned table. She fired once, purposely missing her target but slowing the advance. The first of the two sinister intruders dropped to a crouch, while the two guarding the street fired several shots in either direction to scare away potential witnesses.

Covering each side of the smashed window, the first team—like its backup—consisted of one man with a pump shotgun and another with a semiautomatic rifle. From an FBI weapons class she'd taken, Toner recognized the shotgun as a Binelli 12-gauge. Its rate of fire was as high as three rounds per second. Loaded with 00-buck, each round contained the equivalent of nine .32-caliber pellets. The weapons instructor had told the class to do the simple math. Using an extended tube magazine under the barrel, the Binelli could pump out 1,620 rounds per minute.

Angela understood the danger. Now was not the time for heroics. Discretion was the better part of valor, which meant their survival depended on beating a hasty retreat.

The nearest assailants pivoted inward from the sides of the window with precision. They did not behave like the buffoons who lay dead in the snow but like men with extensive training in special forces operations. Working together, they raked the interior of Chekhov's restaurant with a second shower of lead. Loud, sustained blasts of artillery mixed with the steady crack, crack, crack of a Heckler & Koch assault rifle, adding to the destruction.

Amid the roar of the attack, Toner grabbed her bag and coat off the floor. Using the darkness and smoke as her shield, she scrambled towards the kitchen in an awkward crouching lope. She signaled to Molotova to follow. Mirroring the American's example, Nadezhda fired shots in the direction of the street, then in a stooped position inched away from the table, unable to reach her own coat and bag.

The flash of Molotova's pistol was a beacon. The two attackers homed in on the women's position and launched a barrage. The heavy oak table disintegrated in a cloud of wood chips and lead. Anticipating their marksmanship, the Russian agent dove towards the kitchen and out of the path of destruction.

As Angela looked back, her Beretta ready to slow any pursuit, Molotova led the way towards the outside door of the kitchen. They fled through the wreckage of the scullery, careful to avoid spilled food and still-burning stoves. Other patrons and service staff joined their exodus from death. When they reached the door, the agents allowed other panic-stricken customers to run out first. Only in the absence of further shooting did they follow, advancing into the alley blanketed with knee-deep snow.

Molotova and Toner realized their only avenue of flight was down the alley toward the Salekhard shopping district. In heavy boots, the Russian took the lead, pushing forward as fast as she could. After only a few meters, she stopped and waited for Toner, who wore only a pair of loafers on her feet. While she waited, Molotova peered down a narrow passage between the restaurant and the building next door, toward the street in front of the restaurant they had fled. At that moment, a man with a pistol came into view, shouted to the attackers, and fired in their direction. With Molotova looking on in horror, a shotgun blast and a hail of bullets sent the latest arrival flying backwards, where he landed out of her field of vision.

"Nyet," Molotova screamed. She staggered but did not fall.

Following her line of sight, Toner looked towards the street but saw nothing. "Naddie! Come on—we've got to go. Come on."

Toner grabbed her and pulled. Arm in arm, the two agents struggled through the snow towards the mall.

"Molotova, settle down. We're safe, at least for now." Toner had pulled her unwilling companion much of the way.

Inside the mall, the FBI agent recognized the universal symbol for a rest room. Shaking the snow from their heads and clothes, the two fugitives went in. After verifying there was no one else inside, they collapsed on the floor. Their ears ringing from the blasts of the shotgun, the two women contemplated the nearness of death.

The Russian cleared her throat, hyperventilating when she spoke. "You are correct…cannot allow my emotions to dictate action…consider options…think logically."

Sick from the shooting she'd witnessed as well as the reality of their predicament, Molotova pulled herself to her feet, leaned over one of the sinks, then began to retch and cough, scarcely able to function. Toner said nothing, unable to fathom the sudden change in the Russian's behavior—from cool and professional inside the restaurant to a quivering bundle of nerves.

After several moments, Angela spoke. "You all right?"

Molotova stopped. "In training, the instructors tell you: 'Do not allow emotions to force you to make the mistakes.' They say be logical, not be emotional. But I tell you, Toner, my emotion this moment is of being scared shitless, as you Americans say. And that is highly damned logical."

Toner nodded. Breathing heavily, in through her nose and out through her mouth, the SWAT-trained American gradually brought her metabolism to near-normal. Slowly moving to a standing position, she took out her Beretta. With one eye on the rest-room door, she replaced the half-used clip with her fully loaded spare. After making sure the mechanisms were in perfect working order, she slipped the 9mm back into the holster.

Angela turned towards the still-shaken Molotova. "Come on, Naddie. We can't stay here. Let's call the cops and get someplace where we're safe."

"No."

"What? What do you mean, no?"

"That man…that man I saw in Chekhov's. I know now where I have seen him on previous time. He was a police official with regional security—an escort to the site of Monogovody in November. We killed him. We killed a policeman. And Mikail…he is…he was…in the street."

"Naddie. Hey, lose the babbling. What the hell are you trying to say?"

"From the alley when I stopped from running, I saw them shoot Mikail. He was there. He—Mikail—he was member of my team. They shot him! They *shot* Mikail. He was a Federal Security officer. They shot a Federal Security officer. The police shot a Federal Security Bureau officer."

"Shit," Toner muttered, her voice trailing off into the silence of their own breathing.

Nadezhda turned back to the sink, twisted the faucet, and splashed cold water on her face. The silence lingered, neither woman wanting to ask the obvious.

"I don't think that second batch was regular police—in any way, shape, or form," Angela stated at last. "They were a little too good at their jobs. Naddie, Naddie, what's going on? Who knew we were going to Chekhov's? C'mon, what's the story?"

"Now? You want to know all this now? You were right before. We should go."

"No way. Not after what you just told me. I'm not gonna run around blind in the middle of a blizzard. Come on. Talk to me. Who knew we were going to be there?"

With hesitation, Molotova answered Toner's questions. "There were two men from my team here in Salekhard—Mikail and Peter. They knew. They were in a car outside the restaurant, watching."

"Watching for what? Were you expecting someone to take a shot at us? Was this some sort of set up? *Talk to me, Naddie.*"

"No," Molotova asserted, surprised by Toner's anger. "No, I was not expecting this to be happening. We were being…what you say…low keys. We did not expect anything, anyone, to be protecting Nyentzi. Seven years ago Monogovody was destroyed. We understood there was a possibility, always the possible."

Toner didn't press. She could see the toll the evening had taken on the younger agent. Eyes lowered, she reached the apparent conclusion. "Mikail's dead. Probably Peter, too. Oh God, I'm sorry. I truly am. Were they close friends?"

Molotova covered her eyes with a shaky hand, trying to hide a tear. "I am sorry as well. They were associates but friends, too. Good men."

Neither woman spoke for several moments.

"If the first bunch was who you think, then the regional authorities and possibly the city police can't be trusted," Angela surmised. "And we're stuck in a rest room in a mall in the middle of Siberia during a blizzard. Does that pretty much sum up our situation?"

"Yes, that is our precise precipitation."

"Whatever," Toner sighed, leaning against the wall, biting her lower lip. "Situation hopeless—all conditions normal. God, where have I heard that before? Okay, quick inventory. Then we're out of here. We've got my purse, money, computer, and coat. We also have two 9mms and two extra clips of ammo. That won't do. Let's go shopping."

"Are you being mental?" Molotova retorted. "We need to keep going. Right now."

"We can't stay here, but you need a coat, and I need some boots. Priorities, Naddie."

"But to go shopping now? People are trying to kill us badly. Take taxi and go."

"If the local authorities are involved, the first thing they'll be looking for is two women—one without a coat and one without boots."

"Madness—utter madness."

"*Bridge on the River Kwai*, right? Probably a sailor in that one, too."

"Angie, you are acting very crazily. How can we shop after being tried of killed?"

"Just pretend it's the day after Christmas at the local department store. Can it really get any worse than that?"

Molotova did not respond.

"Good, I thought not," Toner concluded.

Still shivering from the cold and the chase, the dispirited Russian stood next to the sink, her arms wrapped around herself. Toner stood up and slowly approached. Not knowing what else to do, she reached out and gave her a hug.

"Hey," Angela whispered, "it's not that bad. Things could be worse."

"Like how could that be?" Molotova answered, her voice high and shaky.

"Well, the first two shooters could've waited until we'd finished the entire bottle of vodka."

"From that perspective, I am guessing things could be the worst."

"Whaddaya know, a smile. Come on, Naddie. I need you," Angela said, looking her friend in the eye. "We need each other. How about it? Time to go, okay?"

"Okay, but first, we should discuss all the critical details of the case, clean the air."

"Such as?" Toner asked.

"Your message in hotel. You said it had to do with Nyentzi."

"Yeah, I see what you mean. Maybe it is time to clean the air. The message at the hotel was not good news. It was from my boss telling me that Melissa Revkin is dead and that I've been taken off the case. He also gave me explicit instructions to terminate all contact with you or any other member of the FSB regarding any aspect of the Nyentzi Project."

"I...I do not know what to say. Were you given reasons? Were there suspicions available? Is it something I did? Was this ending of the case coming from your request?"

"No! I'm as upset as you. Until now, I hadn't decided what to do. Part of me wanted to walk away from this whole thing. I've gotta be honest, Naddie. Nyentzi's got me so confused, I don't know what to do. Should I just walk away; send the file disk back to LA? Oh well, guess that's not an option anymore."

"File disk? What file disk are you referring of?"

"Oops. I was going to tell you. Really I was. I'm sorry. I was playing my cards close to my chest. We both were. That can't be helped now." Toner paused to collect her thoughts. "From what I've been able to figure out, someone, probably a member of one of our intelligence services, put together a file on Melissa Revkin—mostly medical stuff. Since she was in a coma, the hospital was monitoring her brain waves and doing DNA testing. You already know the results of the DNA tests, but the other stuff I didn't tell you about. Part of my hesitation was, well, I don't know anything about brain waves. Kaloostian—I showed him the file—he picked up on it right away. Said there was some weird stuff going on inside her head, like nothing he'd ever seen before."

"What sort of *weird stuff*?"

"Unusual synaptic activity. I think that's what Greg said. Her brain waves were spikes instead of being almost flat. He thought too much going on inside her head considering her condition. As soon as we get the chance, I'll show you. I promise."

"Well, it certainly looks like the plotting has thickened. What else have you hidden and not told? Does it take the killing of my friends to make you accepting of me?"

"Listen, I share information with people I know and trust, and I know you feel the same. Hell, it's what we were taught. It's our job. And you've got to admit, up until a few hours ago, you and I were hardly kibbles-and-bits. That I could even contact your consulate without clearing it first with Washington is one heck of a leap forward from the Cold War—right?"

The Russian did not speak but slowly nodded.

"But not anymore," Angela continued. "There can be no secrets between us. I trust you. I trust you with my life. We're in this together. I've got no one to turn to, so I can't very well walk away from the case now, especially after a bunch of Ruskie hoodlums ruined our dinner."

Molotova nodded again. "Yes, we must both be trusting of the other. So I think it is my turn to go clean. There is also something of importance I did not tell you."

"It's the journal, isn't it. Dmitri's journal"

"Yes. You were wondering about that, eh? Well, I did not tell you what was in it besides the names of other team members—like Tagi-Zade. Yes, there is more."

"Like what?"

"Angie, I am not trying to rockwall you, but there is much information. We do not have time for all the details. We should go—go now."

"Wait a second. I just want to know the basics. It'll give me something to think about while we shop. Come on, one little detail."

"So impatient. Fine, I will tell you that Dmitri made references to Nyentzi like there were three of them—three different types."

"Oh, that's a pretty minor detail," Toner declared, throwing her hands up in the air for added effect. "For the love of God, Naddie! Are we dealing with three genetically altered batches of embryos? What? What did the journal…what did he write in the damn journal?"

"No, not three genetic changes. Only one that was implanted, but three *parts* of Nyentzi. When Tagi-Zade mentioned *messiah*, I began to have thoughts about the journal, which I was not understanding previous. I think I may know what he was writing about."

"So tell me."

"First, Tyrellovich is a Russian. In Russia, there has always been a trinity: Mother Russia, the earth, and the church. Now, because he was also a religious type of guy—of Orthodox faith—it might have the meaning of holy trinity. You know—Father, Son, Holy Spirit."

"I see. Good guess—Tyrellovich would be the Father. The children would be the Son—daughters now, thanks to Mercereau. That leaves the third component of the trinity. Who or what is the Holy Spirit? Any ideas?"

"I am without guesses."

"Oh well, I asked for it. That's definitely something to think about. Okay, let's go."

"Find something you like?" asked Toner.

"Angela, I lost my wallet and my money at the restaurant. I cannot pay for a coat. Even with my paycheck, I cannot afford clothes in this store."

Toner looked past her at racks of women's outerwear. "Staying within our budget is not one of my concerns right now," she said, looking apprehensively over her shoulder. They'd left the rest room and walked the stairs to the top floor of the mall. Avoiding the main concourse as much as possible, the two agents found just what the American was looking for.

"How about this?" Toner said, holding up a multicolored designer ski jacket. "Your size?"

"Yes, but please, no. It is beautiful, and I have always wanted an American ski coat, but let us look for one more simple, less money."

"No time for debate, Naddie. We've gotta keep moving. And whether you care to admit it, you probably saved my life back at Chekhov's. The least I can do is buy you a coat. Besides, I'm loaded for bear." Angela opened her purse and displayed an array of plastic.

"For bear? Oh, I see what you are meaning." Nonetheless, Molotova clicked her tongue and shook her head. "I think you should save your money, Angela. I do not have the need for such a superior garment."

" 'Course you do, and this is one garment someone on a Federal Security agent's salary could never afford. Heck of a nice disguise, don't you agree?"

Nadezhda tried to push the coat back onto the hanger, while Angela held onto it for dear life.

"It's no big deal," Angela continued. "Besides, this way I'll be able to harass you for the rest of your life about the coat *you* picked out for *me*. Not that my coat's not nice, but from my perspective, this is a small price to pay. Trust me on that! And we need to find me a pair of boots, and gloves and hats for us both. Come on."

Quickly filling Toner's needs, the two shoppers approached the service desk. The American offered one of her major credit cards to the sales clerk, a young woman, who gratefully accepted it. The storm, though not strong enough to shut the city down, was keeping many shoppers at home.

While the cashier scanned the card, Molotova found two pairs of gloves, along with warm hats for each of them. Handing the additional items to the clerk, they impatiently waited for the transaction to be completed.

"I am very sorry. They are not approving of the purchase. Your credit has been denied," the saleswoman said apologetically, her eyes lowered in embarrassment.

Molotova and Toner exchanged glances—one of surprise, the other of exasperation.

"That's not possible. There's got to be a mistake." Toner insisted, trying to keep the tinge of annoyance and panic from her voice. "Could you please try again?"

"As you wish," the cashier agreed. With the majority of her pay coming from a commission on the clothing sold in her department, she was more than eager to satisfy the foreign customer.

Ten—twenty—fifty seconds—almost two minutes they waited. "It is taking very unusually long," the clerk observed. "There could be a problem with the line. Please to accept my apology."

"No problem," said Toner, trying to hide her concern. She knew nothing was wrong with any of her credit cards unless…unless someone was purposely shutting down her credit line, stranding her in Siberia. Sneaking a peak at Molotova, she saw her friend was thinking the same thing.

"Here it goes. Success finally!" the clerk declared. "The purchase is now approved. That has never happened before. Perhaps the storm has agitated the circuits. I am very glad to have you ask me to try for a second time. Thank you."

"No problem. And thank *you*."

The two shoppers left the department store carrying their bags. Standing in the hallway near the stairway, Angela pulled on her lined boots. "As long as we're here, let's make one more stop."

"For what purpose?" Nadezhda asked, removing the price tag from her new coat and slipping it on with an air of unaccustomed luxury.

"What were our plans for tomorrow?"

"We were to fly to Moscow in morning for to see the Nyentzi children, but I am thinking that the airport is being observed."

"Probably the railroad, too," Toner added.

"There is no doubt of that. Even as such, the train to Moscow would take two days, many stops from Salekhard to Moscow. You can forget all about buses, too."

"I figured that. Well, that leaves us one option. Where's an ATM?"

"I think one is near the south exit of the mall. What idea do you have, Angie?"

"Let's just say the best way to grandma's house isn't always over the river and through the woods. Here's what we need to do…"

They'd done it—high fives were in order. In the nick of time, they'd lifted the block on the credit card. All their assumptions were correct. Expecting he did the same to her other cards as well as to her companion's, the two young conspirators began accessing the computer systems carrying both Toner and Molotova's financial records.

They would soon need all the credit cards. Within minutes, one or both of the adult women would withdraw the maximum cash advance allowed on each credit card. They would then stop using the cards to prevent the tracing of their path to Moscow. So simple and obvious, even for a child.

In the high-stakes game of life and death, beyond the computer-animated games the girls were used to, there was no margin for error. Then again, they needed none. The Russian and American must succeed. The consequences of failure, calculated and discussed among them, were not acceptable.

Exchanging no words—each knew exactly what must be done—the girls' slender fingers flew over their computer keyboards with lightning speed. While they worked, computer-generated music—a symphony the girls had composed several years earlier—softly played in the background.

15

THELMA AND LOUISE

He could just see her, sipping vodka daiquiris under a plastic palm tree by some heated indoor pool—at government expense. Almost thirteen hours ago, he'd left the message and so far not even the courtesy of a response. That she might have returned the file disk as requested would be asking too much.

Alfred E. Hatton couldn't win. NSA was ready to line him up against the nearest wall. Washington was only hours away from initiating diplomatic inquiry into the status of her Russian-supplied visa. Some bottom-feeding journalist was snooping, looking for the team leader from Monday's Guerrero drug raid. And the Russian consul had failed to return his repeated calls.

At the rate the shit was piling, Hatton was beyond need for a shovel. By noon, he'd be walking on stilts or driving a backhoe.

The deputy assistant director looked at his watch. Almost 8:30. He'd been at his desk three hours. The problems of Wednesday had spilled into his personal life, providing him with another sleepless night. "It's evening over there. Maybe she'll call," he thought. "And maybe Madonna's kid'll grow up to be a good Catholic. Yeah, fat chance."

He should've stayed in bed. Leaning back in his chair, feet propped on the desk, Hatton had watched the sunrise two hours earlier. Once the sun was up, he'd become too relaxed to muster up the energy to move. With a pronounced effort, he shifted in his chair and put his feet on the floor. Now was the time he'd normally be shuffling paperwork, and he was catching a second wind. Then again, it might be the burrito he'd eaten for breakfast.

Opening the lower right-hand drawer of his desk, the deputy assistant director retrieved a roll of antacids and a laptop computer, similar to Toner's latest toy. She'd be shocked to know he owned such a machine. She thought Al Hatton couldn't tell the difference between a laptop and a phone book. The wisecracking agent considered him a total Luddite—technologically inept and computer illiterate.

That was fine with Hatton. He'd learned long ago to have a few surprises up his sleeve, especially for those who thought they knew him best. He might not be as proficient as Kaloostian—or Toner, for that matter—but he knew enough about thingamabobs, gizmos, and other electronic whatnots to make himself dangerous.

After popping two antacids and booting the computer, Hatton decided to check Toner's personnel file, hoping beyond hope for recently entered data that might provide a clue to reaching her. He typed the daily password and waited. He wanted to ask the Armenian whether he knew of Toner's whereabouts, but Kaloostian had called in sick the day before. If the search through her file was unsuccessful, he'd call his friend later in the morning. There had to be a way to contact the free-spirited nemesis.

"Sipping a goddamn daiquiri," he mused again, just as connection was made to the bureau's human resource file system. "Wait a minute. What the hell is this?"

"Enough! There'll be no pouting. You're taking this much too personally," said Toner.

Molotova continued to fidget on the toilet seat. "You have seen too many Russian gangster movies. I do not know if your crazy idea will work."

"Then what's all that you said about chyorniy rinok? I thought that meant the greasing of palms."

"It does, but it is not the guarantee. I can only try. And not so much eyeliner! You are piling it on with a shovel, by the feel of things. Why so much? You yourself said I would look good without all the makeup."

"Shhh, no talking back. You do look great, but we can't take any chances."

"What if he is gay man?"

"Tell him you're Barbra Streisand. I don't know. Just get us a car!"

The two agents had taken refuge in the dimly lit, poorly ventilated rest room of a petrol station several blocks from the mall. The cold, which had made the walk from the shopping district almost intolerable, now kept the stench to a minimum.

After a lively debate over the workability of Toner's strategy, Molotova had agreed to give it a try. Still, she insisted the plan lacked subtlety and was no better than an adolescent prank.

"Exactly, my charming friend, and that's why it's gonna work," Angela insisted. "Psych 101—all men respond to visual stimulation. After that phone call, he can't wait to make your acquaintance."

Unable to use public transportation to get to Moscow and facing the likelihood of credit transactions being traced, the American had devised a simple scheme just short of stealing a rental car. All they needed, Toner insisted, was a bundle of cash and Molotova's womanly magnetism, with several minor modifications.

"Why do you not let me look in the mirror? You are making me up like a sleaze basket or worse."

"Tsk, tsk. You look beautiful. Is this your natural hair color? Very nice."

"I will confess that I have used headlighting for to enhance the blondness."

"Well honey, your secret's safe with me. Now, one last item," Toner said, opening the reluctant Russian's ski jacket and unbuttoning the top two buttons of her blouse. "Look the part, they always say. There—*perfecto*. All set for your audition. Go get 'em, Nadezhda."

"I feel so…inexpensive."

"Remind me to teach you the difference between cheap and economical. Besides, you know that if I spoke Russian, my lady-of-the-evening friend, I'd be the one with the makeover. So lighten up. I'll stand watch in case you need a little support."

They'd chosen the Trans-Siberian Car Rental Agency for four reasons. It was within walking distance; it was not an international chain, with superfluous rules; it had a branch office in Moscow for returning the car; and most important, only one attendant was on duty. Molotova had verified that final item during an inquisitive phone conversation minutes earlier. She located just what they needed—a youngish-sounding male easily captivated by her sultry voice.

Going back out in the cold took as much courage as the women had displayed earlier at Chekhov's. Toner took up her position behind a garbage dumpster. Molotova, shaking her head, trudged through the snow, occasionally looking back at her American friend. But once the beautified pigeon approached the lights of the car lot, her womanly walk became so exaggerated Toner could hardly suppress her laughter.

"My God, it's a good thing she can't see what she looks like," Angela thought with relief. "Mae West meets Nanook of the North."

Nadezhda entered the office and removed her hat. Making sure the attendant was watching, she slowly shook the snow from her reddish-blonde hair. Unbuttoning her stylish new coat, she approached the counter like a breath of spring air and engaged the clerk in an animated discussion. After pouring out her heart over her fabricated story, she casually removed the coat and draped it across the counter, her smile snaring the unwitting target.

Leaning closer to the wide-eyed clerk—a youngish twenty-year-old with black hair and faint mustache—Molotova continued her spiel, complete with batted eyebrows. To Angela Toner, watching from a distance, it was a sight to behold. She'd never before witnessed such an obvious pretense of erotic affection, and its effect amazed her. Not that the boy was gullible, but that he was driven by some primal instinct to protect a damsel in distress. So much so, Toner almost felt sorry for him.

"Must be a bitch to have two brains," she reflected with compassion. "And to have the one in his pants calling the shots. Mm, mm, mm."

Out of habit, the clerk produced a standard rental form. Daintily shaking her head, Molotova presented her own preauthorized form—a wad of Eurodollars. She coyly peeled several bills from the bundle and laid them on the counter. When the man shook his head no, the actress nodded yes. She turned around and pointed to a vehicle in the lot.

Driving the hardest bargain possible, Nadezhda leaned over the counter, exhibiting the possibility of reward for good conduct. The clerk stared down into the milky white of her exposed breasts, his Adam's apple lodged in his throat. He was unable to move or speak. Taking advantage of his plight, Molotova casually dropped more bills on the counter. When the clerk picked them up, she slid her hand over to his, squeezing it softly.

Hypnotized, the boy again fished in the drawer, this time producing a set of keys. He held them in his trembling hand while Molotova cupped his hand in hers. As he almost drowned in her deep green eyes, she withdrew her hand, now holding the keys.

Molotova picked up her coat, pointed to the parking lot, and sauntered to the exit. Like a hungry dog on a short leash, the clerk followed. Helping her into her coat at the door, the youth was delighted with his compensation, a peck on the cheek and a whiff of perfume. Nadezhda allowed him to open the door, and together they stepped into the frigid Siberian night, moving towards the vehicle they had discussed.

Unable to see Molotova's path, Toner moved from her hiding place for a better view. The cold had penetrated her coat and boots, making her wish the scenario would unfold at a faster pace. With a shiver, the American caught sight of her friend as she opened the car door. Taking advantage of the moment, the rental clerk grabbed Molotova from behind and forced her into the front of the automobile.

Before Toner could react, the diminutive agent pivoted slightly to her right and brought her left elbow around behind her, catching her assailant directly in the face with a well-placed *crack*. Stumbling back in pain, both hands cupping his shattered nose, the clerk grunted in pain. Molotova spun in the driver's seat and administered a kick directly to his groin, dropping him like a stone onto the snowy pavement.

Pulling herself upright, Nadezhda grabbed the door, slammed, and locked it. Inserting the key into the ignition, she started the engine. After turning on the lights, she lowered her window, and with a downward glance, made sure the clerk was still breathing. Prostrate on the bloody snow, the lascivious counterman groaned and clutched his groin with his hands. Satisfied he would survive, she put the car in gear and drove out of the parking lot.

A short distance away, Molotova stopped so Toner could jump into the passenger seat. The moment the door closed, the two agents sped away.

Angela howled with glee. "Whoa, it's the kung fu queen. I'd like to sell tickets the next time you rent a car. What happened back there? I was jumping up and down so much to keep warm, I couldn't see a thing."

"That fathermucking lowerlife wanted more than money. All the long, he was demanding favors in return for the car. What did he take me for, some sort of prostitute? I thought he was the gentleman type.

Then he jumped me from the back, and I had no choice but to kick him in his privates with excellent force. I am also thinking I broke his nose."

"Well, under the circumstances, I think he got off pretty easy. I mean, take a look in the mirror, and tell me you don't look like a nun out for a Sunday drive."

Molotova glanced at her laughing friend and then into the rearview mirror. "My God. I do look like a trumpet. Now I am understanding why you would not let me see in the rest room. What have you done to me? Where is the tissue?"

"Just drive. After everything that's happened, let's not get killed in a car wreck. We can clean it off later."

"You are terrible, Angela. You made me take advantage of that poor guy—big time."

"He loved it. Let's just hope he's too embarrassed to call this in as a stolen vehicle. And remember what they taught you in training—when in an emergency, use any weapon at your disposal. How much did this cost us, anyway?"

"The cost was highly fair. I explained carefully that I had lost my credit card after big fight with boyfriend. I told him I needed to be getting home to my good-for-nothing rich husband, who is just happening to be a banker. Then, like we discussed, I told him he could put different credit-card number on his form, fill in the phony name, and I offered four hundred Eurodollars for his troubles. For extra enticement, I promised to bring the car back in the morning when he finished work, with the *big* bonus."

"Sounds fair to me."

"But plainly he wanted bonus right then. He did not seem to be a patient kind of guy, you know. During entire time, he kept looking down my blouse—all because of you, Angela Toner. You cheapened me up, for sure thing. And when he made move to grab my butt, I was forced to chop him. This is not good for Federal Security reputation if

I am discovered. Now we are two outlaws, like in the movie *Thelma and Louise*."

"No way. That's one comparison I'd rather not be associated with."

"Why not? It was very excellent movie!"

"Yeah, but remember, Naddie, they never made a sequel."

"Oh, that is true. Then we will have to write our own script, okay?"

"Sounds good. Let's look for the highway. Wait! I just saw something. Turn here."

"What? What are you seeing?"

"Golden arches—I'm starved. Let's eat."

Despite the growling of her stomach, Angela Toner deferred ordering until after a visit to the women's room. The two travelers stood in front of the mirror, feverishly working with soap, water, and tissues to remove the layers of makeup Toner had applied to her unwitting accomplice.

"You could have told me at earlier time you did not have the makeup remover."

"I said I was sorry," Toner responded with a forced grin. "You can't expect me to carry every necessity known to woman in one little computer bag, can you?"

Her face red from scrubbing, Molotova decided she was again presentable to the world. "And remind me, Ms. *Cosmopolitan* girl, to never again allow you to assist my makeup efforts. My cheeks are raw from the cleansing."

"Oh, pooh. It's just the glow of good health. You're lucky I didn't bring any sandpaper. C'mon, let's go order."

Several minutes later, Toner and Molotova sat in a corner booth, their trays piled high with Big Macs, double fries, chicken nuggets, and liters of coffee.

Her mouth half full of Big Mac, Molotova glanced around the fast-food lounge. "It is very unusual to find a McDonald's not overly crowded here in Russia," she observed.

"I think the snow might have something to do with it."

"Oh, not at all. No matter the weather, Russian people love the Big Mac and fries. Billions sold, and they have still not run out of food. Not many other food-eating establishments could say that in Russia. Plus one other big factor."

"What's that?"

"Always heated. Very warm place in bad weather."

"I'm amazed your comrades here at the North Pole put up with this. It's cold, it's snowing to beat the band, and it won't be any different tomorrow or next week. How do these people do it?"

"You must understand, Angie. Winter is not the bad guy for us. If it was warm here, even like Canada, we would perhaps be speaking German. Russia's savior is the severe winter that keeps the enemy out. I could not imagine life in place that was perfect sunshine all the year. How boring."

"Yeah, I can see how that would work. Live in a place desolate enough, and you don't have to worry about someone trying to take it away from you." Toner paused to take a sip of piping hot coffee "You know, I've been thinking about our plans. If the people responsible for shooting up Chekov's knew we were going to Moscow tomorrow, they might know our whole itinerary. Maybe we should lay low for a couple of days, make them think we've gone somewhere else. That would also give me some time to contact the bureau."

"Do you believe so?" she Molotova asked. "Despite Mikail and Peter's death, there is not the reason to believe that we have been compromised."

"I'm not so sure. Think about who knew the details of our schedule. We must've sprung a leak. If they knew we'd be at the restaurant this evening, we might be walking right into another trap. Where'd you make those reservations from?"

"My hotel room...could it be someone at hotel who informed our whereabouts?"

"Or the phone was tapped, meaning they probably know about my two calls. Did you make any of the travel arrangements from the hotel?"

"No. The arrangements were made earlier. And I kept details to myself. Even my team members were in the shade about the Moscow girls. Mikail and Peter had the tickets to fly, but I did not tell them for what exact purpose. For all they were knowing, it could have been another member of Monogovody genetics team to be interviewed by you and me."

"How about your boss in Moscow?"

"No, not her. She is knowing of altogether mission, but I was given much liberty. She was desiring results, not details. And my boss is not too smart a person. I do not think she is capable of such sneaky guile."

Toner nodded. "I like your boss more and more, but I'm still worried. If our hotel rooms were searched, they'd find plane tickets, but no address, right?"

"Yes. I have the address in memory. Even my computer files were coded. Uh oh."

"What?"

"Peter! He is a notorious computer-hacker guy. It is how we recruited him for Federal Security—from arresting him for cyber-crime."

"You think he could've accessed your personal files? Could he have been carrying the addresses of these girls in Moscow in his wallet or something?"

"No, the more I am thinking of it, the more I am of the mind that he could not have gone into my computer without my perception. I kept the files we shared incomplete, with minimizing information. Peter and Mikail only knew what I wanted them to be knowing."

"That's an interesting way to file your data. Where'd you learn that method?"

"My father was a major in the Russian army. When I was younger, he told me that the KGB, so he had heard, would be having double files. I thought it would be good system."

"How's it work?"

"One file is for the bosses, with the good stuff. But because not all should be seeing it, there are not signatures, dates, reference points, and other identification things. A second file is for everyone else. It looks very perfect, with all the proper identifiers, but certain information is not included. The important stuff is for big honcho's eyes only."

"Sounds like a lot of extra work."

"It is much work, but it is also highly protective of secrets. In old times, secret information was power. If a person could know something over others, they would be at the advantage. There was much stabbing of backs in those days."

"I don't think those days have left us, Naddie, so don't get too nostalgic. Whether you know it or not, you just described the Revkin file I've got loaded on my laptop."

"Seriously?" Molotova asked, her French-fry poised midbite.

"Seriously. Once we hit the road, I'll boot up and show you. Too bad you don't have Dmitri's journal with you. I'd love to see what he wrote in that."

"I have very much of it taken to memory. I will tell you most things in the car."

"Good. What *were* our plans once we got to Moscow?"

"I had appointments with the girls, posing as a school official. In my room are artificial identification cards telling people we are with educational institution concerned with the girls' scholastic progress."

"Scholastic progress—come on, these are seven-year-olds, right? Am I missing something?"

"Well, I did not desire to alarm the parents by saying I was with Federal Security. Be aware that in Russia all children take aptitude tests in preschool. These girls, however, took the tests and achieved very low scores. The parents said they were in a special-education program, but records show that is not true. I convinced the parents we will merely be there to sign off, so they can pursue education at their expense."

"What about me?"

Nadezhda answered with a broad smile. "You are American representative of teaching association coming to Russia to learn more of our highly superior methods of education."

"Had to get the propaganda in, didn't you? One problem, though—we don't have the identification with us. How do you propose getting in to see them now?"

"Perhaps the mother and father will not be demanding to see badges. Hey, you know what? We are renegade agents—we do not need no *stinking* badges. And if there is problem, we use other method."

"What other method?"

"It involves much bluffing," Molotova said with a straight face.

"Sounds like renting the car was practice. I hope you don't mind a little criticism, but that story's got enough holes in it to fly the space shuttle through. Come on, these are kids. Would any school system bother to send a taxpayer-supported employee all the way to someone's house just to collect a signature?"

"Perhaps. Perhaps not. I should be letting you know, however, that the real school system thought the scores were bad enough to retest them. Even when tested apart, they scored identical marks. Even for twins, that is very hard to believe."

"Twins? You said *twins*, didn't you?"

"Yes, the girls are twins. I thought you knew that."

"Never even dawned on me. I just assumed they were a couple of unrelated kids. I know they're replicants, and that explains a lot of the similarity. But raised in the same household—I didn't know."

"I was not trying to hide anything by not announcing they were twins. Honest."

"I know you weren't. It's not a problem, just one of those details that slipped through the cracks." Toner stopped chewing and pointed with her Big Mac. "Actually, now that I think of it, it is a fairly serious development."

Molotova cocked her head. "In what way?"

"Melissa Revkin is...*was* Nyentzi. I don't think there's any doubt of that. We'll know more once we hook up with my friend Kaloostian and get the autopsy results, but she was raised alone, not as a twin. She's got a younger brother, and he's actually James and Olga Revkin's real child, not a surrogate. And Melissa was classified or diagnosed as borderline autistic. Could that have something to do with her not being born as a twin? Or was she born a twin and one died? What's the connection?"

"I do not know. Perhaps we may have to wait until we meet these girls."

"How'd you find them, anyway? Our people stumbled onto Melissa only after the car accident."

"Well, like I was telling you, I have not met this family. The Moscow school system administered all the tests. We also know the parents were at the Monogovody Symposium in year 1999."

"I thought the computer files were erased?"

"Yes, but from what we now have realized, only those files of the foreign-travel type were erased by the shady culprits. Since the parents of the twins are Russian, their travel records were still in the computer databank and, surprisingly, very easy to locate. Many cross-referenced audits did not prove they were precisely at Monogovody, but they were nowhere else in world at that time either."

"How wide was your cross-referencing net?"

"Quite selective. We knew that Tyrellovich invited certain members of the scientific and academic communities. Couples in such a match were crossed with records of Russians having children born between

July and September of 1999. Not a perfect method, but the best I could do."

"And?" Toner asked, wanting a better explanation.

"And what? What is *and*?"

"What else…who else did the search identify?"

"Nothing and no one promising. That is why we were so excited to be contacted by you on Monday. You were the first other agency to possibly identify Nyentzi. It is why we rolled out the red-carpet treatment. I was prepared for eventual contact, and it was you!"

"I'm flattered. Did Samanov know the nature of the investigation?"

"No, he was not told specifics. Several senior members of the overseas diplomatic corps received instructions regarding Nyentzi inquiries but nothing more."

"Don't bet on it. He seemed pretty familiar with Nyentzi. You may not have given him specifics, but I think he put two and two together."

"Why do you feel he knew so much?"

"One, because during our conversation he went nuts about ethics and the evil of genetic engineering. Two, because he knew I'd be going to Siberia to meet you. And if he'd told me that, I probably would've told him no thanks."

Looking at her watch, Molotova cleared the paper scraps from their meal. "I have another question to ask, but I would first like to see this Revkin file. Let us finish up and discuss this further in the car."

"All right. Do you want me to drive first, so you can chart our route on the map?"

"That would be fine. On a night like tonight, be glad, Angie, that you have only the one obstacle of bad snow. In rush hours, there would also be Russian drivers to swerve and veer you around."

"Oh come on. People around here can't be any worse than drivers in California!"

"Please to understand, until several years ago, Russian motorists did not use headlamps for night driving because it was felt the light would blind approaching automobiles."

"Mm, I'll let you know if I have to take back what I said about California drivers."

Suada rubbed her eyes and plodded toward the kitchen. She'd been up until 3:00 A.M. finishing a human resources report. Now refreshed by six hours of sleep, she went to retrieve the morning paper. Looking through the peephole to make sure the hallway was empty, she unlatched several locks, opened the door, and picked up the *LA Times*. With suspicious haste, she closed and relocked the door.

Tossing the paper on the table, Suada went to the counter and filled an oversized mug with fresh coffee. After a quick shower and a light breakfast, she would have another long day at the computer. At least this job was more exciting than updating personnel files.

Delta Psi Computer Technologies had contracted with ETI for the drafting of news releases concerning its latest programming breakthrough. On the verge of unleashing the world's first prototype of an artificial-intelligence operating system—or so it claimed—Delta Psi hoped to convert that segment of society harboring an anti-technologist attitude. Rather than peddle more silicon snake oil, OCT was gambling on a program that adapted to the user, rather than the other way around.

Called Quixote, the new system not only allowed users to charge windmills but to slay a few dragons as well. Each time a user entered the main menu, fully integrated with voice-recognition software, artificial-intelligence modules would gauge the previous aptitude level achieved by the user and adapt itself accordingly.

The logic in such a system was obvious. Rather than defy the urge not to compute, Quixote offered each user, from novice to expert, the opportunity to integrate with computers to any degree desired. Even

Suada, with her profound understanding of advanced electronics, thought it a sure winner. Had ETI not by contract explicitly prohibited personal use of such information, she'd be on the phone with her broker now. Honesty has its costs.

Walking towards her bedroom, Suada glanced at the newspaper. Though she would have a chance to read it later, scanning the front page now allowed her the luxury of knowing whether the world had ended during the night.

From what she could see, the world was still up and running. Lakers winning streak at ten—big deal. Summer road-construction projects expected to cut Interstate 5 to three lanes—not to worry, she didn't own a car. Senior Russian diplomat dead in fiery car crash in San Francisco—she stopped and began to read. While it did not affect her directly, her friend across the hall was always interested in Russian politics. She would have to call him later.

16

Good Fortune

Events were spiraling out of control. What he'd expected to be a routine search for information was turning into a circus. A coded email advised him to visit the web site of the *LA Times*. It also told him to prepare for a quick exit should that prove necessary. His response was not to their liking. As long as his best friend remained immersed in the international intrigue he'd initiated, he would refuse to abandon her.

His visit to the net was disturbing. The timing of the accident might be a matter of unfortunate luck. The more he read, however, the more he knew this was no random crash. An absence of witnesses, a police report from the officer who'd attempted CPR that indicated a smell of alcohol on the victim's breath, the smear of lipstick on a starched white collar—the story did not match the profile of the man Kaloostian had known for years.

Alexander Samanov may've been a bad driver, but as a born-again Christian, he would not have consumed alcohol. Samanov was technically a teetotaler. On the other hand, he was also thoroughly Russian, limiting his "abstinence" to vodka in small amounts. Any drinker worth his salt knows that vodka does not leave a pronounced smell on the breath.

Attempts to reach Toner at her Salekhard hotel room proved unsuccessful. She was out or not answering the phone, both unlikely for such a prolonged period. What was initially a minor concern for her well-being gradually turned to legitimate anxiety. Every instinct told him this string of events could not be considered coincidence.

Someone had swatted a hornet's nest with a broom, and people were getting stung. Kaloostian had a sinking feeling the broom in question had his fingerprints all over it. He knew he should not have involved her. He also knew that given the manner in which events had unfolded, her involvement was unavoidable.

Unable to wait for news—good or bad—he decided to surf. Though his computer was wired for audio/video Internet access, for today's search Kaloostian preferred the slower, more reliable word-processing method. His chances of receiving a response would be greater, since many Russians had yet to upgrade to the more expensive voice option. Of equal importance, the quality of the transmission would be better. There was no room for error.

The first connection was a global link to Russia at the overseas news digest address—*http://www.russiatoday.com*. Once coupled, Kaloostian went deeper and deeper towards the target site, more than a little off the beaten track. Upon contact, he typed a message in Russian and threw the hook into the silicon waters of the planetary net: "Salekhard! Looking for latest enforcer action. What's rocking tonight?"

The wait was short.

"very exciting tonight. reports not yet complete. restaurant named chekhov's site of attack. many dead..."

The more Kaloostian read, the worse it got. "My God...What have I done?" he wondered as the news filled his screen.

Toner and Molotova sat in the 2004 Lada Explorer—the result of a Russian-American cooperative venture. Designed as a luxury sports-utility vehicle, it was also built to tough Russian specifications.

"Are we not going to go? We are just sitting here."

"I just want to check everything out first. I've got this impression of Siberian driving, like 'next exit 500 kilometers.' Being stuck in the middle of nowhere won't do us any good."

"Not to worry. The road from here to Moscow is new. It is even paved."

"I feel so much better knowing that. Are we going to be able to get fuel for this tank along the way?"

Lightly pounding the dashboard, Molotova was anxious to begin the trip. "Not to worry. There will be places for to refuel. Come—let's break like the wind—get this road to show."

With a final sidelong look at the rambunctious Russian, Toner complied. "All right. I guess now's as good a time as any." The American slipped the transmission into gear and the Lada began to move, its heavy snow tires churning through the snow and slush. The all-wheel-drive vehicle accelerated as Toner followed Nadezhda's directions. Within minutes they were on the highway, heading southeast for Moscow.

The heavy snowfall kept traffic to a minimum. The headlights, even augmented by the fog lamps, could scarcely penetrate the thick wall of snow. Toner drove cautiously. After several minutes, she brought the vehicle to 100kilometers per hour, as fast as she was comfortable driving in snow on the interstates back home—about 60 mph. From their earlier calculations, Angela knew the 1,800-kilometer trip would take just over twenty hours. Glancing at the clock on the dash, she estimated their arrival time in Moscow at six o'clock the following evening, Thursday, January 11.

Toner quickly grew accustomed to the feel of the car and road. She looked at her companion, who was digging through the storage compartments. "What are you looking for? I thought you said we wouldn't need a map."

"The book! This dumb car did not come with a recipe book."

"Recipe?"

"You know! How to use—how to operate. The recipe book for owners."

"Oh, the owners' manual. We don't need one, do we? The controls are similar to my van back home. Besides, they make these things pretty idiot-proof."

"There is no such thing. I just do not wish to be pressing all the wrong controls. If light comes on the dash, I want to know what it is for. Unawareness is not gladness."

"We'll do fine. I'll just wait for you to fall asleep before I press every button I can find." Seeing the Russian's horrified look, Toner continued. "Not to worry, Naddie. I'll be good."

"Best behavior. That is all I am asking."

"Girl Scout promise. Not to change the subject, but this is a great car. You did a nice job picking it out, even with all that makeup obstructing your view. It's got every option I'd ever want—except, of course, some CDs to play in the stereo."

"I am not a car person. Even new, I worry about things falling to pieces. I saw that it was all-wheel-drive type and dark green with color."

"Dark green—your favorite color?"

"It blends very well with landscape—in city and on the road. If someone is trying to find us, all things add together, correct?"

Toner nodded. "How 'bout if I drive for three hours—until just before midnight. Then you take over."

"Sounds a-okay."

The conversation trailed off as Molotova turned on the radio. Using the autoscan option, she searched for FM signals. The amber-colored illuminated digital display perused the audio spectrum until it locked on to a weakly received station. She adjusted the controls, and the sounds of Mozart filled the car.

"For now, this will be relaxing. If we get tired, I will find music with cutting edge of harshness. That will keep us awake for sure."

Angela nodded, her attention on driving. After another period of silence, the American spoke. "You know, I don't mind saying that we got pretty lucky back there at Chekhov's."

"Are you meaning our good fortune shooting? Was that your shot that hit that man?"

Toner shrugged. "I don't know. I'm not one to keep score. I'm just glad neither of us got hit. With all the bullets flying, that in itself is a miracle."

Molotova solemnly nodded. "Have you been close to being killed in a shoot-up battle?"

"No. Until a couple of years ago, I never gave death much of a thought. Figured I'd live to be a hundred and end in a nursing home. Then I'd have to Kevork myself to avoid listening to orchestrated Alanis Morrissette music piped into the rec room."

"That is a highly scary thought. I have to wonder, Angie, is nothing sacred?"

"Not anymore," Toner said, falling silent. After a moment, she continued. "You wanna know something, it starts with Santa Claus, when you find out he's a fake. One innocent little lie starts the dominoes tumbling. You start questioning authority, knocking your parents and teachers down a notch or two. Then it's God, religion, the perfect marriage. What the heck's left to believe in?"

"I have no answer, Angela. Is trouble with your man why you are no long married?"

"Oh boy, wish it were that simple. Guess it's time to 'fess up, Naddie. When you asked me yesterday if I was married, and I said that I used to be…Well, it's not that I'm divorced and keep the ring with me for the memory." Toner paused, taking a deep breath. "My husband was killed in a car accident almost three years ago."

"I am so sorry. I had no idea you were hiding sorrow."

"It's okay. Yesterday I wasn't in the mood to talk. It's something I try not to think about…I was sitting where you are now in my husband's sports car. He was going too fast. Yellow light. He roared through. There was no way we could've avoided the accident."

Molotova said nothing when Toner hesitated, her hands tightening on the steering wheel. Choosing each word as if the wrong one would reopen unhealed wounds, she kept talking.

"Some drunk in an old pickup truck came out of nowhere, broadsided our car on Jake's side. He died instantly. I was knocked unconscious. Woke up screaming in the emergency room while they were prepping me for surgery.

"I found out later Jake was dead. As bad as that, I was five months pregnant. Lost the baby, too. Doctors say I might never be able to have kids."

Angela stopped. Since the accident, she'd kept her personal life from every coworker at the FBI but one. Kaloostian knew the story, mainly because he had an unnerving knack for inducing the darkest secrets from the dimmest recesses of other people's pasts. That was probably his part of his own therapy—knowing that others' lives were full of ache and loss, too. Yet here she was, traveling with a woman she hardly knew, pouring out her heart. Angela couldn't say why, but Toner trusted Nadezhda Molotova more than anyone she'd met in years.

"I don't know why I'm telling you this. I…I've never been one to…never had the need to reveal things about myself. You're an easy person to talk to, Naddie. Thanks."

"It is okay. Talk all you are wanting. I am not going anywhere too far."

"Ah, a captive audience…You know what made Jake's death so hard? The silence—the unbearable lack of acknowledgment from people. Oh, they'll look at you, solemnly nod their heads, but that's about it. People sent cards, a few phoned, but for the most part, everyone, even my family, became so distant I could've been on the moon. My friends stopped calling, afraid I wasn't up to talking about anything other than the accident, unwilling even to listen.

"I wasn't wallowing in self-pity. I wasn't walking around with a need-a-hug sign on my forehead. But once in a *damn while*, it would have been nice to see, to feel a tangible demonstration of sympathy. Have we become so immune to suffering that we can't—or won't—share in someone's grief and loss? Do you know what I mean, Naddie?"

Molotova was silent before answering the question. "I do understand what you are saying. People try to hide their own lack of coping, I think." Molotova paused. "Please understand with what I am about to tell you. I am not trying to take away from your loss, but I truly do know what you are saying. My father died in 1994, when I was thirteen years old. I will maybe never know what he died from—the bullets, his depression, the hardship of trying to provide for our family. Take your picks. But you are so right. I was just a young girl and I had no one, no one to help me.

"Russian people are different from Americans, Angie. We have known so much sorrow—so much suffering for so very long—that it is expected for us to be strong. But I was just a child. My father was dead, and I felt like I was all alone."

"Do you want to talk about it now?" Angela asked, her voice tinged with empathy. "I would like to know more about your life, your family, your loss."

"It is going to be a long night, is it not? We can keep each of the other awake with tales of sadness. Okay, I will tell you about my father. After he left the army, he could not find work. He had hardly no pension, very little saved money. So he accepted offer to protect big-shot banker, a capitalist czar. There were many abductions then for the ransom money. So he became the bodyguard of rich man—my father, the loyal Russian officer.

"After only short time on job, an attempt was made on the man he protected. Father could have run away, could have been still alive, but he foolishly and bravely resisted. They killed him." Nadezhda paused, reliving the moment.

"I think he wanted it that way. Mother found out later his military insurance, which paid us some funds, was to expire just after he died. She used the insurance money for our education. If not for that, I would be pushing brooms or changing diapers. He wanted to die. It was the only way Vassily and I could have our education. I am convinced."

"Are you sure that's why? He might've been shot even if he had run away."

"No. I think it was his feeling of his failure as a father, a husband, and as a man. He was very unhappy. The military was his life, and it was gone. Many Russian officers killed themselves out of disgrace because of how bad things for the military became, especially after the fighting in Chechnya. It was so bad around our tiny apartment…And we were lucky. We had two rooms. Many families had only one. We shared toilet and kitchen with another family. With all the soldiers returning from Eastern Europe, there was not sufficient housing. There was no money to build new houses.

"Living like barnyard animals made everyone so uneven. Father was already brief-tempered. Life was not improving. He felt it was his fault. So the smallest problem and he would be mad with rage and frustration. Mother would kick him out of the apartment, and he would go on long walks until he calmed down."

"What did he do in the army?"

"He was a battalion commander for the Russian 27th Guards Motorized Division. They were based in East Germany until 1992, and then he came home. He tried to remain happy and lucky but instead was bitter."

"His death must have been very difficult for your mother. How's she doing now?"

"My mother, too, is dead. She died in the summer of 2004—almost three years ago. It was the cancer. I think it was from Chernobyl, but with the amount of toxic waste in Russia, who is knowing?"

For a moment, Toner was silent. "I can say I'm sorry, Naddie, but to be honest, I'm at a loss for words. I think now I understand why people shut me off after the accident. What does someone say when a friend or relative loses most of their family?"

"As you were saying, just being there is nice. Understanding the loss is good, as well."

"I guess so. Why do you think it was Chernobyl that caused your mother's death?"

"We were visiting relatives in Minsk. I was only a baby, one years old. I stayed with cousins while mother took a drive south to see old friend from school who was administrator assistant in Narodichy district. She was there when the nuclear reactor core exploded. She was under all the fallout but not me. When she became pregnant one year later with my younger brother, she was most concerned he would have deformity."

"But he grew up to be a good hockey player, right? No deformities?" Toner asked.

"No, no signs of radiation poisoning. He is okay. But he is my brother. That by itself is a torture, mostly for me, right? He is okay, but I wonder how he will ever find a girl. Always making the jokes and hanging about with his guy friends, not a very serious fellow."

"Yeah, Jake could be like that, too. He was a lovely man. Jacob James Alvarez—half Puerto Rican, half Irish."

"Do you have a photograph?" Nadezhda asked.

"I've got one on my desk back at the office, but I no longer carry one with me. Too distracting."

"I understand. I too have pictures of my parents, but they are in my lost purse. That is not the same as losing a husband, correct?"

"I don't know. My folks are still alive. Guess I can't relate to that. What were your parents' names?"

"My father was born Andrei Petrovich Molotov. Mother's full name was Vera Mikhalchenko Molotova. Mother was Ukrainian, you see, not Russian."

"The Molotov name, any relation to the cocktail guy?"

"Common question. I understand that he would be a distant cousin, but in Russia, everyone is the cousin, it seems. My family is not fancy—just good peasant stock."

"Now that I can relate to. What else do you remember about your father?"

"He was tall and handsome. Kind, very smart, wrote wonderful poetry."

"You serious? Your father was a poet?"

"Not a published kind. Not famously like Yevtushenko. He loved to write haiku love poems to my mother."

"Love poems? I thought haiku was about nature."

"Some of my father's poems were, but he also wrote romance haiku. Haiku is about depictions of everyday concerns. But it is also for capturing a moment, about awareness of truths. My father was a romantic, Angie. He captured love moments. Do you want me to tell you one? I have some of them in memory."

"Sure, I'd love to hear one."

"Okay, but first I will have to write it down in Russian—and then see if I am able to properly translate it to the English. Do you have any paper?"

"There's a notepad in my bag. Use that."

Nadezhda unbuckled her shoulder restraint, turned around on her knees, and reached into the back seat. After a brief search through the computer case, she located the paper, along with a pen. Sitting back down, she scribbled three lines in the Cyrillic alphabet.

Talking quietly to herself, she began to translate the haiku into the five-seven-five-syllable style from Russian to English. After several false starts and corrections as well as a bit of choice Russian interjection, Nadezhda looked at Angela.

"I think I have it. It is not exactly the same. Like the usual, something is lost in the translating, but it is very close to my father's thought. Here it is…'Your smile, your soft touch/Caress my mind as I stir/First thoughts of the day.'"

Nadezhda's demeanor changed to cautious optimism. "What do you think? Do you like it? Do you think my father captured a moment?"

Toner's eyes were wide, and her mouth was open. "It's beautiful. Your father wrote that for your mother? Wow."

"He would send her little envelopes inside the regular family mail. They were for mother's eyes only. When I was older, after his death, she let me read them. I cried for a week. They were in love, those two."

"May I see it? It just amazes me that your father wrote those for your mother. He must have really loved her. Who said romance was dead?"

"It was those long separatings from mother's warm bed, I am thinking. All his lover energy had to find another escape. What about you? Did your husband write poetry?"

"Jake! That would be the day. I loved him dearly, but a poet he was not."

Molotova handed the haiku to Toner, who sighed and began to reread the verse.

"Angela, when I was getting the paper from your computer bag, I saw your computer. Remember what we said at the McDonald's? We should set the laptop up and review that file. Who is knowing, we might be able to answer important questions."

"Sounds good to me. Boot that puppy up. You can fill me in on Dmitri's diary, too."

"Oh, yes. I am glad you mentioned it," the Russian said, climbing over the back of the seat, digging through the shoulder bag for Toner's laptop. She opened the cover, set up the keyboard, and checked the battery. "I do remember something about the third Nyentzi—the one we thought might be religious reference for Holy Spirit."

"Oh yeah. Anything important?"

"Dmitri did not exactly write what it was, as I said before," Molotova said. "But his writing made some reference for there to be something designed. Not human—this was different. Machines of some type, to be created by the children of Nyentzi."

17

Full House

"I hate that," Angela said, echoing Molotova's sentiments. They'd been driving almost eight hours. With little sleep and enough caffeine to raise the dead, the natives had grown progressively restless.

"You know what else drives me nuts? Numbers, statistics, facts, data, figures—all that crap. Jake could tell you how many RBIs Kirby Puckett had in 1991, the first NFL fullback to run a thousand yards three years in a row, or how many horses his first car had under the hood. A walking encyclopedia of trivia bullshit. But my dress size, his mother's birthday, our anniversary—nothing. A total blank."

"Ugh, how true. My dumb brother could tell you all the useless hockey data for every team in the world, who was Stalin's army chief-of-staff in 1944, or what year what movie star was in what movie. But half the day, he would be too busy looking for his ice skates that he again misplaced. His mind was short-circuited big-time, I can tell you."

"Yep, when you get right down to it, things haven't changed since the hunter-gatherer days. Women still gather up all the dirty laundry, dishes, and empty beer cans. Meanwhile, the brave and stouthearted males hunt for their wallets, car keys, TV remote control."

"You should write a book: *The Seven Habits of Highly Obnoxious Men*."

"I am man; hear me whine. And that ludicrous woo-hah grunt they do. Like they're all these tough macho Marine warriors ready to storm the beaches."

"But in truth the only shooting they ever do is computer game."

"And look what they do to us. We're forced to wear these damn pantyhose, bras, tight shoes, makeup. Then we get home and practically rip our clothes off, can't wait to put on an old pair of sweat pants and T-shirt. The hubby or boyfriend sees us stripping like banshees and thinks 'cuz we're suddenly not wearing body armor, we're hot to trot. Graciously submit, my ass. Bam, you let him have it with both barrels. Clueless."

"Enormously and totally clueless."

The women paused and exchanged knowing glances. As if on cue, they extended their arms and slapped open palms across the front seat of the Explorer.

"Do they not know what a huge difference there is between what they know and what they think they are knowing?" Nadezhda continued, refusing to let the matter rest.

"Yeah, and they can't even admit there's this vast difference between what they don't know and what's either some unfathomable mystery of the universe or completely irrelevant. Trying to get a man to admit he doesn't know something is like trying to get the pope to advocate birth control."

"Or get a man to ask for directions. Of course, men have opinions. Women are bitches."

"Men are assertive. Women are pushy."

"Women retaliate by making comments about another woman's dress. Men start a war."

"And those initials. AWM, NAWM, RAWM. So he's an angry white male. Big hairy deal! You know what else I hate?" Toner asked.

"I can just imagine."

"How men screw us every chance they get—literally, figuratively, financially. Men pay $4.00 to clean and press a shirt. Me, I get to pay $8.50. Why? 'Cuz it's a blouse!"

"I hate that."

"I hate that too. And haircuts."

"Girlfriend, do not get me going on hair," Nadezhda said with a grimace.

"Fifty bucks! A guy can get a haircut for fifteen. 'A little off the sides, Ralph,' the man says. But a woman's hair's gotta be contoured."

"And sculptured and waved and headlighted and dyed. I hate that."

"Amen. One day, my Slavic friend, women are gonna take over all the manufacturing operations of the world. When we do that—when *we* control how tight the lid goes on the jar—watch out. We won't need a man around the house anymore."

"Who needs them? They treat us as if we are cute little girls."

"I hate cute," Toner said through clenched teeth.

"I hate it, too. They think we are little girls with unicorn fantasies, looking for some prince—who is but only a frog."

"Or toad."

"Or toad to come along and rescue us from our virtue and boredom living."

"Can we talk? After awhile, you get sick of hearing the same dumb questions, over and over and over. 'Are you going to eat that? Got a headache tonight, dear?' So you get a little testy, show a little spirit. Whoa, suddenly it's PMS, and they're making these totally asinine generalizations!"

"Yes. That we are helpless damsels in destitution."

"Bimbos! Or worse."

"You are lucky you are brunette. Try the blonde jokes. I am so up to my throat with those, I could yell bloody manslaughter."

"Jake was always complaining about how women squeeze the toothpaste in the middle of the tube instead of the end. Isn't that just about the dumbest thing you've ever heard? I mean, where do you squeeze toothpaste?"

"In the middle. I have always squeezed it in the middle. What about you?"

"Well, in the middle, too. You don't think?" Angela asked.

The momentary silence was deafening.

"Naaaah," they concluded.

"There. Slow down. The exit ramp is ahead."

Looking to where Molotova pointed, Toner spotted their destination, a rest stop just north of the Siberian city of Syktyvkar. Glancing at the digital clock on the dashboard, she saw it was 4:30 A.M., Greenwich Time plus three. Toner estimated it to be early evening in LA. Kaloostian would be home after a day's drudgery in the electronics shop.

They pulled into the parking area. The two travelers had made excellent time. As long as the weather didn't get worse, they'd be able to reach Moscow by evening. A more pressing matter was the accuracy of the Lada's onboard navigation database. According to the readout, the relaxation kiosk they now approached should be equipped not only with functioning toilets but also with computer-compatible phones.

Peering through the windshield, Angela nodded with approval. The building was not the log cabin she'd dreaded, but a modern, well-lit, fully functioning shelter from the storm. Despite the lateness of the hour and severe weather, several cars and larger trucks were parked in the oversized lot.

The two women buttoned their coats, opened their doors, and stepped out. Toner carried the computer bag, Molotova cradled her

9mm pistol lightly in her right hand. Closing and locking both doors, they surveyed the area. Seeing nothing but white, hearing only the wind, they approached the building.

Still holding the weapon, Molotova opened the glass door and entered first. Confirming that the site was safe, she nodded to Toner, who joined her.

"Let's find the phones and call Los Angeles first. Then we can take care of any other business."

"Sounds like the plan."

Looking in either direction, Nadezhda spotted the universal communication symbol and poked her friend. "This way."

Walking down the hall, they saw a row of booths, most equipped with the early-model video communicators Toner had hoped for.

"We're lucky these older models still take Eurodollars instead of only plastic. I'm not sure how long we can go without using a credit card, though"

"If all we are needing is food and fuel, we will make it to Moscow without a problem."

Toner nodded as she looked into each booth. "Hope so. Here, let's try this one." Setting the computer bag on the ledge, she reached into her pants pocket and retrieved a roll of bills. She fed several of the larger denomination Eurodollars into the hungry slot, waited for a dial tone, and dialed Kaloostian.

Both travelers squeezed into the larger-than-normal booth and watched the display of punched numbers as well as the current charges and amount deposited. The message changed as the number routed from their booth to an orbiting satellite. Then, instead of making a connection, the number changed, and the process began anew. A third time, a new number scrolled across the computerized screen.

"What is the problem? The number is recycling. Hang up and try again, Angie."

"Not yet. I think it's Greg. He's bouncing all incoming calls to prevent tracing. I wonder whether he's heard about what happened to us in Salekhard. Let's wait a second."

Five times a number appeared but didn't connect. On the sixth attempt, the shuffling ended, and Kaloostian's apprehensive face appeared on the screen.

"Oh my God, Angie. Am I glad to see you. What the hell's going on over there? The Internet police scanner was talking about a shooting at a restaurant in Salekhard, several fatalities. Was that you?"

"What do you think?"

"I think you've run into some problems."

"Problems? Give us some credit, Kaloostian. Joyce Brothers has problems."

"Well, it's good to see you in one piece. When you didn't call, I thought the worst. I had to rely on the web for news out of Salekhard, and they're as bad as the networks for sensationalizing a story."

"Weren't you at work today?"

"Nope, another sick day. Been waiting here for you."

"That's sweet. Hey, I want you to meet someone. Greg, this is Nadezhda—Naddie—Molotova. Naddie, meet the infamous Gregory Kaloostian."

Nadezhda waved. "Hello Gregory. It is a pleasure to make your acquaintance."

"The pleasure's all mine. Thanks for taking care of my globetrotting friend. Looks like you two are in a phone booth. Where are you calling from?"

"We're about five hundred miles southeast of Salekhard."

"How'd you get *there*?"

"Borrowed a car. It's a long story—tell you later. Where are you?"

"I'm over at UCLA in one of the computer labs, doing a little research, trying to answer some of the questions raised by the autopsy. So I wouldn't miss you, I rerouted all calls made to my home number to here. And to avoid a trace, I've been bouncing them off half-a-dozen satellites. Listen Angie, I know you guys have had it rough, but I've gotta tell ya, the shit's rolling downhill, and it's picking up momentum. I want to apologize for getting you involved in this. We should've walked away from that damned file when we had the chance."

"Gregory H. Kaloostian, I'm surprised to hear you say that. Now that we've been shot at, almost killed, forced to abandon all our luggage."

"All right already! I said I was sorry," Kaloostian confessed with sincere repentance. "It sounds like you're pretty sure that shooting was directed at you."

"There's no doubt. Naddie ID'd one of the shooters as some local law enforcement flunky who cased us at the restaurant. To make matters worse, at least one Federal Security agent from Naddie's team was gunned down. Is that conclusive enough?"

"I'd heard that over the net."

"And now after all that, when we're risking everything, you apologize and want to call it a day. What's gotten into you? Men. You're all alike."

"Oh, please, don't go off on the sexism tangent. Please! I'm not ready to call it a day. I just don't want to debate the wisdom of our earlier decisions. Besides, as you so often say, hindsight isn't always twenty-twenty. I just want you to know it's not too late to extradite yourselves from the case."

"Cut the crap. There's no turning away, and you know it. What am I supposed to do, anyway? Click my heels and wish I were back in LA? Let's get to work. You get that autopsy deciphered?"

"Yes, ma'am. It's ready to download whenever you want it. I figured we'd be pressed for time, so I taped a little introduction to go with it. I also accessed your voice mail. There're two messages."

"Hey, how did you do that? You'd have to have a voice print of me saying...Gregory H. Kaloostian, you sonofabitch. When did you pull that little stunt?"

"I'll tell you about it sometime. Anyway, the first message is from Hatton. He's nervous as hell and offering the earth, wind, and stars in return for that disk."

"I'm sure he would. Why don't you give him your copy?"

"Seriously, he's genuinely concerned about you," Greg said, ignoring Toner's question.

"Nice feint, Cyrano. What else did he say?"

"Not much. Then again, that's the point." Kaloostian paused before he continued, weighing his words. "I've known Al for years. I realize he's not your favorite person, but this case has really gotten to him. It's very uncharacteristic of Alfred E. Hatton to be running scared, and that's the impression he gave me. I spoke to him yesterday, before he left the message for you. He was upset even then. Listening to him plead with you gave me the impression he had his own troubles to worry about."

"Al can take care of himself. The second call? Who or what was it about?"

"Just understand he's on your side, okay? The second message was some guy from human resources. He left his name and number."

"What did he want?"

"I didn't listen all that close. Sorry, Angie, my mind was elsewhere."

"Wonder why," Angela sarcastically concluded. "Speaking of messages, there's a possibility somebody listened in on our call from the phone at the hotel. Which means they might be able to ID you."

"I figured that was a possibility. Anything else?"

"How about the Revkin file?"

"Listen to my report. There's not enough time now. But there is one thing I want to tell you. I've taken a week's vacation. Told them it's a medical emergency."

"What's the emergency?"

"If I don't get you out of there in one piece, you'll find me and kill me."

"That's no emergency. That's business as usual," Toner rebutted.

"For you from Los Angels, it is 011-7-095-5538258. My personal access code is only a number, not voice ID. When necessary, we can leave you a message, and you can find it."

"Great idea. What's the access code?"

"32863."

"Got it. Listen guys, be careful. Don't let your guard down for a minute. And trust no one. Review that autopsy. It's dynamite. Good thing you'll be sitting down."

"Whatever you say, Greg. We'd better go. Thanks again for your help."

"No problem. Hey, Naddie, nice meeting you."

"And you, Greg. Thank you and be careful."

"We're outta here. Talk to you again soon. Bye."

The screen blanked. Toner and Molotova exchanged glances, each wondering what revelations the autopsy might hold.

"Well, that went pretty well," Angela said at last, as she finished packing her computer into its case. "You're being pretty quiet. Anything the matter?"

"I was just thinking. Your friend Gregory is a nice man, but why does he talk so loud?"

"He's kinda hard of hearing. Too much loud music."

"He seems very fond of you. Are the two of you…?"

"Are we what? Oh, that. No, purely platonic. Actually, all of Greg's female relationships are platonic. You see, Naddie, the land mine that blew off his leg also clipped the family jewels."

"Family jewels. I am not familiar with such a term…Oh, *oh!* I see."

"What's next? I saw a coffee dispenser around the corner."

"Just what I am not needing at this minute. I will visit the rest room. All that previous coffee has made me urgent. You wait outside for me. Then we switch turns, okay?"

"Sounds good." Toner slipped the Beretta into her coat pocket as Molotova hastened to the lavatory.

Exhausted, Angela stood on wobbly legs, scarcely able to concentrate, much less stand guard. Just as her head jerked from sleep's relentless pull, she felt the cold draft of an opening door. With a sharp intake of breath, she groped for her Beretta and turned towards the exit. With a sigh of relief, the American exhaled and relaxed.

A darkly dressed woman, heavily bundled against the cold, entered the lobby, carrying an equally bundled child. Using her left hand, she shook the snow from herself and then slowly, with patience and love, unwrapped her baby. The mother whispered words of comfort the keep the infant from crying. Once free of the heavy outer wrappings, the woman walked towards the vending machines.

Her passing sparked an awareness in Toner, so powerful she was unable to stop staring. The mother, seeing the stranger gawking at her like a freak in a sideshow, clutched her baby and hurried by. From a safe distance, the woman looked back over her shoulder, afraid Toner might follow.

Only when Molotova approached was Toner able to rejoin the world. Before the Russian could say a word, the now-alert American began to describe what had happened.

"I've got it, Naddie. I think I finally understand. I mean I think I've found a flaw in Tyrellovich's scheme."

"What are you talking about?"

"I was standing here, when this woman came in carrying her small child. Naddie, it was beautiful, this perfect moment. She whispered words of love. Then she hugged the baby, and I thought what a grand experience life is. This wonderful roll of the dice—part genetic, part environment, nature *and* nurture. Not one or the other but both, working together. So there I was, literally staring at this poor woman, who must've thought I was some kind of lunatic, when it hit me like a ton of bricks."

"Who hit you? The woman?"

"No, a thought. About Nyentzi—Tyrellovich's grandiose project."

"What about that?" Molotova asked.

Toner could barely contain herself. "It's like this: Maybe we've been treating his work with too much reverence, giving him too much credit. He was only human."

"What are you talking about? Give me the point."

"Okay. We've got this scientific venture everyone at Monogovody called 'The Project.' It's got a name, all right, but for these people, it was so big, so important, they simply called it *The Project*. But that's not what it was. It was something else—similar, but with some distinct differences."

Toner stopped and looked directly at Molotova, waiting for her to ask the appropriate question. After several awkward moments of silence, Molotova understood what she was expected to do.

"Fine, if you are insisting for me to ask, I will. Angie, if 'The Project' was not a project, what was it?"

"An experiment! Think about it. These people had no way of knowing for sure whether their genetic changes would work. Nobody's ever cloned or replicated humans before or made alterations in the human genome. They were flying blind, applying all these unconfirmed theories. And you know what? A theory has to be proven."

"I am not sure I follow your argument. Are you saying because Melissa Revkin was autistic, and that is not what they were after? And added together with the twins in Moscow who have the apparent low test scores, that indicates an unsuccessful theory? Are you believing the theory of the genetic changes was a failure?"

"Maybe, maybe not. Take those thoughts a step further. Tyrellovich and Mercereau are scientists, right? As scientists, they conduct themselves using time-honored scientific methodology. Think back to your own science classes. A proper experiment must be conducted with two groups."

"Yes! Group number-one is the control group for which the variable being tested is not changed."

"Exactly. And group two is the experiment group—identical to the control group but with one variable altered. And that's the way the scientist can measure the degree to which that one variable affects the overall hypothesis."

Nadezhda nodded but was still not convinced. "We could review the autopsy to determine what genetic changes Melissa had done to her, but there is no way for to know about the twins. We do not even know what hypothesis Tyrellovich was trying to prove."

"I agree, but let me tell you something else I realized while looking at the mother and child," Toner said. Tyrellovich's research group invites a select group of scientists and scholars to the 1999 Monogovody Symposium. These people are no dummies. The average IQ in that group must have been 175. Even after being briefed about the experiment, they must've understood the risk of not knowing whether they were in the control or experiment group. Is one a failure? Who knows? What about the other? Is it a success? Who knows?"

"I am not following your logical thoughts. They are logical I am assuming, correct?"

"Of course. T and M controlled every aspect of this project. At least they thought they did. But think about all the variables that had to be controlled in both groups—nutrition, parenting styles, stimulus, education, prenatal and postnatal health, you name it. That's a hell of a lot of control, none of it easily achieved. But they ignored or minimized the importance of one other variable, probably the most important one."

"What element is that?" Nadezhda asked.

"The human element—the bonding of parent to child. James and Olga Revkin were nothing more than foster parents to Melissa. But as far as they were concerned, she was their child dying from injuries, needing a kidney transplant, needing them. They're reacting like any parents would. It's like what Kaloostian said to me on Monday. I thought it was another one of his oddball quotes, but now I see what he meant. 'Love hides in molecular structures.' Greg said it's from some song by a group from the 1960s. The Doors I think."

"I have never heard of them."

"Doesn't matter. But don't you understand what it means? Love. It's preprogrammed. It's innate. It can't be factored out of the experiment. It's a biological constant. It's why Olga Revkin's being detained. It's why her husband's agreed to talk to Greg. If there are others like them and they are willing to cooperate, we might be able to identify some of the other Nyentzi parents. Once we do that, we ought to be able to find out who's running the show."

"I do not doubt what you are saying, Angie. Controlling so many of such factors would be impossible. In fact, I do not think it can be done. And that is what has me worried. What if those factors are not important?"

"They have to be," Angela insisted. "The experiment wouldn't be valid without proper controls."

"Should we not also consider the possibility that the genetic changes Tyrellovich achieved are so complete as to make all other variables irrelevant?"

Toner sighed as though a great gust of wind in her sails had just melted away. Biting her lower lip, she weighed Molotova's question, searching for an answer.

"As you consider that," Nadezhda continued, pressing her point, "also remember the meaning of *Nyentzi*. If the project's name is an indication of its purpose, then why so many embryos, so many children? And why would the children of Messiah program be twins?"

"I hadn't thought of that. Damn. On that note, I'm off to the women's room. Back in a flash."

She looked at her twin and as one they looked at the clock on the wall. It was 4:38 A.M. Their parents thought they were sleeping, but sleep would have to wait.

Again their prediction was accurate. The call to Los Angeles had been made from the correct time zone in Russia, its path successfully traced. They'd almost lost the number among the satellite bounces, but with help from the others, they'd verified the point of origin and target.

The girls were impressed. For an adult, the disabled man in the wheelchair was technologically proficient.

By now, the secrets of their martyred sister—their flesh and blood—should have been transmitted to the American's computer. Their plan was proceeding exactly as it should. The two travelers would now have time to review the file and gain an understanding of who and what the twins were. It was not what their stepbrother wished, but sooner or later, he too would have to learn his limitations.

As they prepared to resume their communication with the others, Lara coughed. The spasm was brief, but it was occurring with increasing frequency and severity. Katya knew she was next. In a moment, she too coughed. Displaying a rare instance of autonomous thinking, Lara typed one of the numbers they'd intercepted. The computer quickly made the connection.

Their expected visitors must hurry. They were all running out of time.

18

WUNDERKINDENUNDSOWEITER

The knock was soft and hesitant. If he hadn't been sipping coffee in the kitchen, he would have missed it. Kaloostian knew who it was. Even after he'd wired the door chime through his stereo—to hear it with headphones on—she continued her habit of gentle knocking. It was so like her.

"I heard that, Sivac!" he bellowed, imagining her startle followed by a giggle. "This better be good. I can't have the entire building spreading idle gossip about us." Kaloostian wheeled to the door, undid the lock, opened it, and winked.

"Suada, my dear. We simply must stop meeting like this. Quickly, into my lair before the Widow Johnson becomes suspicious."

Suada Sivac continued to laugh, as Greg intended. They'd been neighbors for more than three years. Both refugees from troubled pasts, Gregory and Suada had gradually become more than just good friends. They now looked after each other like family, replacing what each had lost years ago.

"What brings you out on the dreary January evening?" Kaloostian asked. "Hey, can I get you a cup of decaf? Fresh ground."

"Oh no, there is no need to bother."

"It's already made. C'mon, kiddo, one cup. Stay a bit. Put your feet up. Relax for once."

"You have it already made? It won't be a bother? I'm not interrupting your work, am I?" Suada inquired, not wanting to inconvenience her friend.

"No, I just got off the phone and was having a cup myself. This is fine."

"Well, since it's made. Okay."

"Great. Go sit on the couch and I'll bring it in. No Suada, you're a guest in my house. *Go sit down*. Quit treating me like some old man in a wheelchair."

"You are an old man in a wheelchair. I'm just trying to help."

"I'm not that old, dammit. Now sit!" Kaloostian ordered. He filled one of his special cups full of steaming hot coffee, snapped on a lid, slipped the cup into a holder on the side of his wheelchair, and went into the living room. Wheeling to Suada, sitting on the edge of the couch, he gave her the coffee.

"What's new? You got a few minutes?"

"I'm caught up with my work, but I don't want to be a bother. I just stopped in to see if you'd read today's paper," Suada said, sipping.

Greg knew what she was referring to. "The diplomat in San Francisco, yeah. Pretty unfortunate."

"Drinking and driving—bad combination. It's a good thing you don't do that, Gregory. You'd kill yourself for sure." Kaloostian smiled and shook his head. He'd sat through several lectures by his kindhearted neighbor on a variety of bad habits.

"Did you know that man, Samanov?"

"Never met him. You know, just because Armenia was once part of the Soviet Empire, Suada, doesn't mean I'm on a first-name basis with every Russian in the world."

"Well, I thought because you are such an important person with the government…"

"I fix computers, dear. Beyond that, I'm simply a legend in my own mind. Hey, as long as you're here, I've got a little computer question for you."

"You flatter me. I'm not nearly as proficient as you with electronics."

"This is more of a software problem. I got a call from a guy down at the bureau late this afternoon. He thinks someone's been hacking into our personnel files."

"From what you've told me of the mainframe security measures," Suada said, "that means nothing was altered or downloaded. Correct?"

"Exactly. Somebody was just snooping around. Since the software is government issue, there's not much we can do to enhance the system's safeguards. I did install an add-on utility, though. Doesn't do much, but it does recode the file after each access. The guy at the bureau told me one of our coworker's file has been recoded three times in the past three days. Someone's definitely gaining unauthorized entry. What I'm wondering is this: You work with all sorts of companies. Your access software is supposed to bypass all the security parameters, but does it leave a trail? Is it possible to follow the path of whoever's entered the system back to the source computer?"

"In theory, but I've never tried it," Suada said with a shrug.

"Does your software come with any instructions or read-me files?"

"No. We just log on, and it's programmed to do the rest."

"Damn, you'd think they'd provide some documentation. What's that company you work for?"

"You mean ETI?"

Kaloostian held his breath. His mind raced when he made the connection for the first time. "Yeah, E-T-I. What does it stand for again?"

"Exemplary Temporary, Inc. I've told you that before. You must be getting senile. Why? Are you looking for a new job?" Suada laughed.

"No, I was just thinking about another company—from several years ago—used those same initials. No big deal. They're out of business, anyway. Who owns ETI? It's not a franchise, is it?"

"No, sole proprietorship. It's based here in LA. The owner's a weird guy, Greg, even by *our* standards. Runs the company out of his house in Beverly Hills. I've personally never met him. He's kind of a hermit."

"What's his name? Maybe I've heard of him."

"Eldon…Dr. Eldon Tyrell."

"*Tyrell*?"

"Yes, Eldon Tyrell."

Toner came out of the rest room and spotted Molotova standing next to the same booth they'd used to call Kaloostian. The Russian said nothing when she approached.

"Whatcha doing? Looking for change?" Toner asked.

"Huh? Oh, I did not see you approach. I am sorry. I was deep in thinking."

"Yeah, things are pretty quiet around here. Shall we go?"

"Yes. I am ready." Molotova said as they walked to the door, buttoning their coats along the way. The frigid air gushed into the lobby the moment they opened the front door. Toner hurried ahead. Nadezhda paused, however, looking over her shoulder at the communication center one final time before joining her friend.

Back on the road, the two travelers continued their drive towards Moscow. In the comfort of the Lada Explorer, they took off their coats, turned up the heat, and activated Melissa Revkin's autopsy report.

Kaloostian's face filled the eleven-and-a-half-inch monitor. Instead of his usual grin, his face showed concern and uncertainty. "Hey, Angie. If you're listening to this, it means you're all right. I surfed the net today, got *some* news out of Salekhard about a shooting. Fortunately, none of

enhancing the data-processing capabilities of these children's brains, he literally turned them into walking, talking computers. Remember all of the attempts at producing artificial-intelligence software and how none of it's ever worked. Well, Tyrellovich cheated—he went biological.

"Inside Melissa Revkin's brain, her neural transmitters somehow modified the synaptic gap, making it an efficient and permanent connection. Her brain was functioning at such a proficient level that she had perfect recall. Events that occurred six years before were as vivid as when they happened.

"As great as that sounds, there's a little problem, one any psychiatrist could've warned Tyrellovich about. There's a disorder, a psychiatric disorder that occurs when a person lives in a world where everything has significance, where trains of consciousness encroach upon each other, where normal thought processes cannot be sustained. Irrelevant thoughts and ideas continually sidetrack the person—a life of perpetual hallucination.

"It's called *schizophrenia*, Angie, and it's probably what you're going to find when you run into any others like Melissa Revkin.

"Think about it. This poor kid had to choose between an autism and insanity. Every event, every moment in her life was as memorable, as intense now, as when it originally happened. We survive as thinking animals because of our ability to forget. We repress memories, and for good reason. The slightest trauma—a death in the family, a skinned knee, a glass of spilt milk—would leave a lasting impression. And I thought I had it bad.

"Voices! Can you imagine the voices in her head. A psychotic nightmare. Is it any wonder Melissa retreated into a shell? The alternative is more frightful than anything Stephen King, E. A. Poe, or Dante could dream up.

"Under favorable circumstances, someone with a brain like that would make Einstein look like Beavis and Butthead. But reality has this nasty habit of intruding on our dreams. Reality takes no prisoners. I think it was Aldous Huxley who said it best: 'Ye shall know the truth, and the truth shall make you mad.' Autism or schizophrenia, what's the difference?

"People might think Tyrellovich was a genius for what he did, but I've already identified a couple of glitches in his scheme. If what limited medical readouts I've been able to dissect are believable, he might have compensated for those, too. That cold-blooded bastard seems to have thought of everything.

"I better shut up before I get *really* pissed off. Look the autopsy over and get back to me, okay? While you're doing that, I'm going to do some more digging. We need to find out who's running Nyentzi. Someone's out there, hidden deep. I don't know who, but his, her, or their signatures are everywhere. I'm really going to grill Jim Revkin about what he knew. She was a cute kid, Angie. I'm sure you found her picture. She deserved better than this. Who knows, maybe we all do? Good luck, and please be careful. Love ya."

Kaloostian's message ended. The two women stayed with their own private thoughts. For several minutes they traveled in silence, neither wanting to speak first.

Slowly, then building, Toner's frustration grew until it erupted. "Just what the hell do we think we're doing?" she demanded, pounding the steering wheel for emphasis. "I mean it, Naddie! What do we think we're going to accomplish? We're on our way to Moscow after barely surviving an attempt on our lives. We don't have a clue who we're up against. Your friends are dead, Samanov's dead, my career is over, and for what?"

"Do you think that I have not had such thoughts? I am not a stupid person, you know. But I will not be stopped, Angela Toner. If the plotting is so serious as you seem to be thinking, then we are dead already. We are knowing too much. But I will not stop. I cannot. Did you not hear your friend, Gregory? It is our responsibility, our calling. If you would like, I will halt the car at the next town."

"I didn't mean to say I was quitting. I was just expressing an opinion. I needed to hear what you wanted to do, that's all." Angela looked at Nadezhda with a forced smile. "I needed to know you were in this for the long haul."

"For as long as it takes. Nothing is going to stop me. Nothing."

"Then I guess we're stuck with each other." After another pause, Toner continued. "You know what Greg said—that perfect recall stuff. As frightening as it sounds in a seven-year-old, can you imagine what adolescence will do to those girls? If they aren't crazy now, any sanity left will run screaming into the night. And the boys better watch out, too. If he says he's gonna call, he damn well better. Every conversation, every phone number—perfect memory…Hey, something wrong? It looks like you've seen a ghost."

Nadezhda did not reply. She stared at Toner with wide eyes. Her lips moved, but she could not find the words to communicate the question she had to ask.

"Naddie, what is it?"

"What, what you were just saying…the perfect recall…every phone number. At the rest stop…Wait, let me think. Gregory said he was *bouncing*—that is the term he used—bouncing our call to prevent the tracing of the number. What do you know about tracing? Is it really a possible thing to follow a number from Siberia to Los Angeles?"

"I guess so. From what I understand, every phone call, every fax, every Internet broadcast leaves some sort of digital trace. It can't be avoided. I'm not too concerned, though. He bounced that sucker halfway 'round the world and back again."

"But I am worried. I do not think he was successful."

"What do you mean?"

"I was wondering about the possible gifts of someone, or many people with the brain capability Gregory spoke of. There may be many Nyentzi children. We know of only three, and we have only confidential knowledge of the one—Melissa. But what of the rest? What of their potential of recall?"

Molotova had Toner's undivided attention. "What are you getting at?"

"While you were in the rest room, I heard a phone ringing. My thought was 'how odd.' Here in middle of nowhere, at such late hour of the night? It did not make sense. I looked, but no one was around—just me. I walked to the phones, listened again. It was the same phone we used to call Greg. It kept ringing, Angie. It rang and it rang. I didn't know what to do, so I answered it."

"What happened?" Toner quietly asked.

"There was a voice, a child's voice, a girl. She said, 'Hurry…please hurry.' And click—the line was disconnected."

19

A Minor Technicality

"Play the part or I'll kill you," Toner challenged. She looked at her colleague and waited. Molotova had thirty seconds. The expression on her face was blank.

"Give up?"

"Yes. I am unknowing of the answer."

"*Moon over Parador.* You ever see it—with Raoul Julia and Richard Dreyfuss?"

"Ah, yes. The actor Dreyfuss pretending to be South American dictator. Very good, Angie. You are winning. But it is my turn now, and I have one prepared. Here it goes: 'The gods of my tribe have spoken. Do not trust the Pilgrims.'"

"Oo—oo—I know that one," Angela said, sipping lukewarm coffee between bites of a Granola bar. It was shortly after eight o'clock in the morning, Thursday, January 10. The two weary travelers were more than halfway to Moscow, and the snowstorm had veered to the east. They'd driven through the night and early hours of the day, taking turns at the wheel, catching what little sleep they could.

"Damn, where have I heard that? I can see her. Young actress, dopey play at summer camp…Yes, *Addams Family Values*. Am I right?"

Nadezhda pounded the steering wheel. "You! I will never win this stupid game. You are too media-exposed. Being American, you should provide me with handy-clapping points."

"No way. You've got almost as much television and movies in Russia as we've got in the States. If you were a Kalahari bushman, I might cut you some slack. But get real. You're only down three points."

The Russian shook her left index finger while holding onto the wheel with her right hand. "Fine. I will continue to play, but let it be known that it is under protest against an unfair advantage."

"You sound like the United Nations. My turn. Let's see, so many lines, so little time." Angela finished the bar and threw the wrapper into the back seat of the Lada Explorer, along with the other accumulated debris of their trip.

"I've got one: 'Okay campers, rise and shine. And don't forget your booties. It's *cooooold* out there!' Ha, good luck on that!"

"Finally, an easy one. *Groundhog Day*; Bill Murray and Andie McDowell. Am I right?"

"Yep, score one point for the little gipper," Toner said, drawing a line in the air with her finger. "You know what's great about that movie? At the beginning, Bill Murray's character is every woman's nightmare—obnoxious, stupid, crass, loud, you name it. But at the end, like a miracle, he's transformed into the perfect man. I love that."

"And he only had to be killed a thousand times."

"A minor technicality."

"Not to change the subject…"

"Just because you're losing."

"I am not changing it for that," Molotova said with exasperation. "I was thinking of the phone call. It is much like the movie *Three Days of the Condor*, with Robert Redford. Have you seen it?"

"Not that I remember. There you go proving my point. And you wanted a *handy clap*."

"Just because there is one movie I saw that you did not—great sorrow. Anyway, like us, Robert found a secret that was not supposed to be known. Networks within networks and agencies within agencies. Hush-hush stuff, very much shooting. Excellent movie."

"Sounds like a WMC," Toner observed.

"What is that? WMC?"

"White Male Conspiracy. Was it?"

"Actually, yes. Very bad things happened to Robert. He was on the run for his life."

"He survived, right?"

"Yes, how did you know?" Molotova asked.

"Redford only died in one movie—*Butch Cassidy and the Sundance Kid*. And they never actually showed him dying. What'd he do to survive?"

"Improvised, adapted to circumstance, got help when he could, discovered the truth. The regular Hollywood plot."

They sat in silence for several minutes. Molotova drove while Toner went back to studying the Revkin autopsy. Out of habit more than necessity, Angela reached for the thermos they had purchased. She began to refill her cup.

"Enough already," Nadezhda exclaimed. "You are drinking so much of the caffeine you could neutralize anesthesia."

"Not to worry, I saved you some. Did you know drinking coffee reduces the risk of suicide?"

"I did not know that. Are you thinking of killing yourself?"

"Not today, maybe next week." Angela paused, then continued. "When Jake died, I was pretty despondent. Some bureau-assigned therapist even labeled me clinically depressed, said I shouldn't be allowed near loaded weapons. Yeah, right. Kaloostian said I should start smoking pot, that it would help cheer me up."

"Did you try it?"

"Naah. Sitting around giggling and eating cartons of Ben and Jerry's ice cream didn't seem very therapeutic at the time. 'Course, I did put away three or four Hershey bars a day."

"Men…they always think they know what is best for us."

"You got that right, sister."

Another pause. Suddenly Toner exclaimed: "Redford."

"What about him?"

"Your description of *Three Days of the Condor*. I've can't figure out why Mercereau would go to such great lengths to change the embryos to female. It's a nice gesture, but beyond a personal vendetta—which I doubt—is there a reason for the switch?"

"Perhaps she did not like Robert Redford," Nadezhda said.

"No. I wasn't referring to Robert Redford as a movie character. I was thinking of the conspiracy angle. I mean, what's Nyentzi all about, Naddie? What's going on here?"

"And Robert Redford made you think about that?"

"Sort of, but I was mostly thinking about the thought processes, what's inside his head. Well, maybe not Robert Redford but most other males."

"I thought we had earlier agreed there was nothing inside men's heads."

"Well, come on Naddie! It's not a vacuum up there. There are neurons, dendrites, nerve cells, all sorts of gray matter. It just doesn't work very well. Kaloostian said something, though, about all those vitamins and pharmaceuticals Melissa was taking. And there was that oblique reference to nitric oxide in her autopsy."

"Yes, just our luck it was at the point where the information ends."

"Do you remember studying nitric oxide in school?"

"Yes, in chemistry and psychology," Molotova answered.

"Okay, then consider this: What if all the genetic changes upset the chemical balance in these kids' brains? The data Greg was able to get indicates that some of Melissa's chemical levels were a little out of whack, but a lack of nitric oxide would be disastrous. Maybe Mercereau knew that. And maybe Tyrellovich was too much of a guy to admit the obvious consequences of such a minor flaw."

Molotova's eyes widened. "I see what you are meaning. In laboratory studies, nitric-oxide-deprived male mice attack others relentlessly, refusing to stop even when other mice surrender. Uncontrollable violence, unstoppable sexual appetite. My God, Angie, that would be a disaster."

"Exactly. But female mice with deficient nitric oxide levels fight only to protect their young. They aren't overtly aggressive toward other mice or people, at least not in any way the research people could measure."

"So, you are saying Mercereau made the changes to prevent genetic Darth Vadars from emerging out of all those little Luke Skywalkers."

"Something like that. You gotta admit, we're not just talking about simple boyhood arguments over who gets to play quarterback. Nitric-oxide deficiency couldn't even find a sponsor in the U.S. military. I remember the Pentagon flat-out rejected a proposal to study a drug that would decrease the brain's NO supply and enhance a soldier's fighting ability. Think about that, Naddie—the Pentagon, a company that dropped nuclear bombs near its own employees to test the effects of radioactive fallout. And nitric-oxide deficiency scared the hell out of *them*."

Molotova nodded. "I know. The Russian army also was not interested in looking to use such a weapon. All the laboratory studies showed the male mice to be completely out of control. They killed anything in their cage, they attacked their handlers, and they even attacked cats."

"Could Mercereau have done it?" Toner asked.

"In school I learned what she would do to change the embryos from male to female. It is surprisingly easy. There is first a selected fertilized cell. Before cloning, the Y chromosome is removed, and an X chromosome from a second cell of the same zygote is supplied. This will create a female cell of the same genetic pattern as the original zygote. Except…"

"Except?"

"Yes, except the X chromosome is reproduced, all the while the Y chromosome, which makes the embryo male, is done away with. Then, the modified cell is replicated, giving a true female clone-zygote remade from a true male original."

"Piece of cake!" Toner said.

Molotova gave her a sidelong glance. "It is not that simple, but someone with the proper equipment and knowledge could do it."

"Wouldn't her little scheme be detected?"

"She may have had an accomplice or several. If sabotage was not suspected, they might not have performed the microscopic scan necessary to detect the change."

"Tyrellovich would've known after nine months. I wonder what happened to the original embryo? Was it destroyed along with the rest of Monogovody? And what about…?

"Tagi-Zade said there were thousand of eggs!" Nadezhda said, following Toner's line of reasoning.

"You read my mind. What if…if someone got a hold of those…if the explosion at Monogovody and the gender changes are connected? My God, Naddie."

The two women stared out the window into the brightness of the Siberian morning.

"How did Tyrellovich get interested in genetics?" Angela asked several minutes later, eager to learn more about the man who conceived the Nyentzi Project.

"Chess."

"Come again?"

"Chess. Tyrellovich was obsessed with chess. His first computer programming was software for simulated chess."

"Are you telling me that because Tyrellovich was a frustrated gamer, he started messing with genetics?"

Naddie shook her index finger. "It's not such an obvious transformation, but I believe it was a factor in his decision to begin genetic experimentation. You must understand how captivated with chess Tyrellovich was. It was highly important to him. Do you play?"

"I know the rules, if that's what you mean. But do I play? No."

"Okay, I will explain. Until 1996, a human grandmaster could almost usually beat a computer, no matter how expertly programmed. That year, Garry Kasparov, the Russian grandmaster, accepted a challenge from the IBM company to play a chess match against its new computer, the Big Blue. In mathematical terms, it should have been no contest. Big Blue could evaluate a hundred million possible moves every second. Kasparov could calculate two, perhaps three, moves per second. Not only that, Big Blue could see everything that could possibly happen for ten or even fifteen moves into the future."

"That makes sense," Toner said, nodding. "The computer has the ability to multitask, without regard to memory or distraction."

"Very true. But in chess terms, it should have been no contest. Kasparov had the highest chess rating in history. And because of his human intuition, he could see twenty moves into the future. Add such gifts with his lifetime of experience, profound insight, pattern remembrance, and you see why he was such a world chess champion."

"Kasparov won, right?"

"He did, as to be expected. Yet to the astonishment of the world, he lost the number-one game. Everyone was with the big shock. How could this be?"

"So tell me, how could it be?" Toner asked.

"There is a French word—*sangfroid*. It is meaning with cold blood, or having a supreme ability to not be upset even under the most highest stress. Big Blue had sangfroid up the butt. In game one, when its king was being attacked with furious intensity by Kasparov, Big Blue ignored the attack and went around bumping off a modest little pawn. The computer was able to do that because it knew, it had calculated, every imaginable combination of Garry's options. By reaching the precise conclusion that it could fool around like that, in a way no human would dare, it was able to take the game exactly one move before Kasparov would have won."

"But Kasparov came back to take the match."

"Yes. In the end, he even admitted Big Blue was a worthy opponent, that the quantity of computing power was almost equal to quality of thinking, even if it was limited."

"And you think that's why Tyrellovich became obsessed with genetics?"

"It is probably one of the reasons."

"But there was a second match with another computer?" Toner asked.

"Yes. In 1997, IBM company championed Deep Blue, its next supercomputer. It was a huge machine—thirty-two computing engines in twin black towers—able to calculate 230 million moves each second, twice as fast as the Big Blue."

Molotova's excitement rose as she recalled the historical match. "Kasparov was amazed at Deep Blue, said it had an alien level of intelligence, said Deep Blue's moves were like 'the hand of God.'"

"Hand of God? What is it with all these religious connotations?"

"I do not think he was talking biblical. He was, instead, referring to unfair advantage of the computer, that he was not allowed to study the computer's prematch games."

Toner snorted. "In other words, he accused the machine of cheating?"

"Not the machine. Only the rules. In the end, Kasparov was not overly impressed with the machine. Even though Deep Blue possessed a new kind of intelligence and played impressive and nearly faultless chess, it was restricted by the limitations of being a machine."

"But the machine won. So why didn't Tyrellovich stick with computers?"

Naddie shrugged. "For one thing, work had already begun at Monogovody. There was no turning back. For the other thing, Deep Blue's success, instead of stopping Nyentzi, was the last straw of Tyrellovich's artificial-intelligence dreams. If it took that much computing power to beat one man at one game, then building any machine to function as a human would simply be impossible. So he apparently created these human computers called Nyentzi."

Toner shook her head. "It's hard to believe a game led to this."

"But you see, Angie, chess is an ancient sport. The rules do not change, ever. There is no innovation, no future planning, only historical thoughtfulness. All Deep Blue proved was that computers were better than people for computation problems, which is what chess truly is.

"What Deep Blue could do in chess could never substitute for real learning. All information had to be inputted by others. Think about your own biology. Only when an organism is able to learn and apply knowledge to unrelated subjects can it become a higher animal. Only then does it have the power of wisdom. Information is useless if it cannot be applied in a variety of situations. If knowledge is applied to only one field of expertise, then wisdom is still lacking."

"I see what you mean," Toner said, nodding.

Molotova smiled. "Evolution is like technology advancements—one stage at a time. It is like from sponge, to fish, to monkey, to us, to…"

"…Nyentzi, the next higher level of existence. You're saying those girls in Moscow could be a new step on the evolutionary ladder."

"Only in theory. We do not know if Tyrellovich's experiment worked."

"You didn't seem too surprised by that autopsy report, Naddie. Why not?"

"As I explained, I have studied Tyrellovich for months, even years if you include my education at the university. I suspected he might have tried something of an intellectual nature. Everyone who was majoring in genetics would ask herself: 'If I were Tyrellovich or Mercereau, what would I do?' Melissa Revkin's mathematical ability you described, despite her unfitness, seems to have come from something he did to change the circuitry of her brain. But I am surprised at the wholeness of the changes. It is why we need to see these twins."

Toner turned in her seat and faced Molotova. "Wait a minute. You *knew* he'd changed her neurotransmitter levels."

"No, I did not know. I suspected. Be logical, Angie. If you had the ability to do such genetic engineering, what would you change? Add another foot? Even with my guessing, we do not perfectly know if it works. We suspect, but we do not know for certain. And of what good is a computer if the software will not operate it efficiently and properly?"

"I get it," Toner said. "The brain's the hardware, and the mind's the software."

"That is the assumption of those who wish to create artificial intelligence. But knowledge also requires a body with functioning senses—eyes, ears, touch, and speech. All those things are needed to be working together as a team, to learn bit by bit, day by day. For example, a computer does not understand the use of trial-and-error in learning, like a child does. It does not grow new circuits on its own, like a child's brain does."

Toner opened her mouth and tried to counterpoint, but Molotova was on a roll.

"Angela, if you unplug the computer, it is no different from a rock. Any thoughts a computer might have are based only on input by external procedures. They are not internally generated. They have an off-switch."

"I see what you mean. Every day we succeed, screw up, try again, gain experience."

"Yes. Those information fragments form the connections in our brains. Over much time, the connections are reinforced or weakened.

They are our permanent memory patterns, our neural network. Artificial intelligence will be successful only when a computer is asked to play chess, and it says it would rather play pinochle. Then it might be considered humanlike."

"That'll be the day. I can hear it now: 'Balance your own checkbook, human!'" Angela mimicked, lowering her voice. "Shades of HAL. But what about all the attempts to manufacture artificial eyes, ears, noses? Haven't any of those worked?"

"They have worked on a limited basis for several individual models, but never eyes and ears and noses machines as a team, feeding data to the same computer. Until that happens, each is just another machine. Intelligence may begin only when an organism or machine attempts to discover the reason for its existence. Then it is a rational unit."

"Right back to Descartes: 'I think, therefore I am.'"

"Or as Tyrellovich was always saying, 'Imagination is more important than knowledge.' Of course, it was Albert Einstein who originally said that."

"'Imagination is more...' I've heard that before. You say Tyrellovich used it?"

"Oh yes. It was his favorite quote."

"'Imagination is more important than knowledge,'" Angela repeated to herself. "Where have I heard that?"

Kaloostian fidgeted. Revkin was late, but that didn't surprise him. The nervous scientist had said he would have to shake the federal agents he thought were trailing him. And that might take some time. Greg glanced at his watch: 9:38 P.M., Wednesday evening. The site of their agreed-upon meeting was the law library on the UCLA campus, open until 11:00 P.M. Kaloostian had laid claim to a conference room in the northeast corner of the library. It was quiet and secluded but offered him only one avenue of escape should there be trouble.

Since he'd accessed Molotova's voicemail box in Moscow, meeting James Revkin had taken on a new degree of importance. Tracing a call that had been skipped off six different satellites was theoretically impossible, yet Angela and Nadezhda were convinced someone had done it. In their opinion, that someone was a crew of seven-year-olds with uncanny mental capabilities. If they were right—that his call had been traced—then the stakes were higher than anyone could imagine.

"I bounced that call six times!" Greg reflected with concern. "Impossible to trace. How the hell could they? How the hell did they? I've surfed the net for twenty years, and I've never heard of anyone or any program with that degree of proficiency. There's never been a hacker anywhere able to track more than a double bounce, and those kids nailed six. Shit. They don't surf the net. They luge. Maybe they're not so crazy after all."

And what if Suada Sivac's boss was who Greg thought he was? He had an uneasy feeling about Dr. Eldon Tyrell. Without sounding too interested, Greg had tried to get as much information as he could from Suada about the mysterious man. His age was right, and Tyrell seemed as secretive as the man Greg suspected was Tyrell's father. Tyrell was so obsessed with his privacy that he'd refused an interview with *Entrepreneur Magazine*, which had been doing a story about the phenomenal success of his company, Exemplary Temporary, Inc.

"No wonder we never suspected he survived," Greg brooded. "Sonofabitch buried himself so deep that in seven years none of the agencies looking for Nyentzi detected the slightest hint of his existence.

"God, I hate coincidences. Could Tyrell really be a renegade Russian? What are the odds of that? Toner thinks my knowledge of genetics is a coincidence. That's not coincidence. We've been planning for this for years."

Greg hoped by Thursday morning to have a dossier on Eldon Tyrell. Maybe then they would know enough about the man to formulate countermeasures. But first he had to warn Toner and Molotova.

Meeting the twins in Moscow could be a trap. If Monogovody proved anything, it was that Eldon Tyrell took no prisoners.

Contemplating the ramifications of an alliance between the children of Nyentzi and the man who'd possibly destroyed Monogovody made Gregory Kaloostian tremble. With their innate computer skills and Tyrell's beguiling business connections, the children had the ability to manipulate every file at every company and organization throughout the world, in both private and public sectors.

In the new millennium, records were duplicated and triplicated to avoid any loss of information. Those files were becoming increasingly difficult to protect as society demanded and received the right of free access. State-of-the-art security measures could keep most criminal snoopers and hackers at bay. But not the children of Nyentzi. Research notes, scientific and financial reports, private correspondence—the twins could exploit them all. AT&T, IBM, GE, Sumitomo, Philips, the U.S. government—none would have safe haven from the prying eyes of anyone with that sort of mental dexterity.

For thousands of years, humans had found power at the tip of a sword or the barrel of a gun. Now it was in the fingertips of genetically engineered children. Wealth was no longer land, mineral rights, monetary affluence, political connections, or social class. True wealth was raw data combined with the ability to manipulate a world relying upon it.

This type of power and wealth could block the navigation signals of a transatlantic jetliner, causing it to crash into the sea. It could plant false financial rumors, thus manipulating stock markets. Or it could murder hospital patients by electronically altering their medications. Every sector of the world economy, including the military and its massive arsenals, depended on information. No hole was deep enough to escape the all-encompassing grasp of the Fourth Wave.

A new elite was emerging—powerful, monopolistic, and all-knowing—with the ability to devour information at its whim. The potential consequences churned Greg's stomach.

"All that compressed and classified data flowing through the computer networks of the world, and a bunch of seven-year-olds are picking it off like ducks in a row. That's it!" Greg exclaimed to himself, pumping his clenched right fist in excitement. "That's how we can expose him. Trace the patterns in the data mosaic, follow the communication flows, and look for key associations."

"Gregory Kaloostian, you have a phone call. Please come to the front desk. Gregory Kaloostian."

"Jesus H. fucking Christ," he muttered. "That dumb ass, pencil-necked idiot…"

Kaloostian wheeled out of the conference room and headed for the service counter, swearing under his breath. He scowled at the attendant, who handed him the phone.

"Hello," he said, "This is Kaloostian…Hello…Excuse me, are you sure this call is for me?"

The library attendant gave Kaloostian a weary look and said nothing. Irritated, Greg shook his head, returned the phone, and headed back to the conference room.

Maneuvering through the doorway, he reached behind himself to close the door, but it was already swinging shut. The Armenian gripped the sides of his wheelchair, inhaled sharply, and held his breath as a cold, metallic object softly but firmly pressed against the back of his neck.

"Gregory H. Kaloostian, I presume."

20

BUSINESS AS USUAL

"Get the hell away from there, you sonsofbitches," Hatton roared, running out the back door towards the garage. He'd heard a clatter in the alley while waiting for the eleven o'clock news. The trouble behind his house had gone on for years, accelerating as the neighborhood deteriorated. The hooligans, concentrating on the elderly nearby, usually left him alone.

At age fifty-nine, Al Hatton refused to consider himself old. Once he received Social Security, *then* he would consider himself elderly.

His service pistol still in its holster, Hatton opened the gate and stepped into the alley. The eerie glow of the mercury vapor lamp above his garage reflected in the puddles left by an afternoon rain. Hatton didn't have to look far for the source of the noise. His garbage can was on its side. The bin for his recyclables was several feet away, its contents strewn. He stooped to pick up an unbroken bottle when he saw them. Holding the bottle, he looked to his left and saw a second group.

Like one reacting to a wild animal, Al Hatton tried to show no fear. Biting his lower lip, he stood and counted—four to his right, three to the left. He couldn't make out their colors, not that it mattered. They were all punks: Crips, Bloods, Latin Kings, Asian Tigers...all the same, all cut from the same cloth.

Their usual course of action was to trash the alley, then scatter when someone came out. Tonight was different. These gangbangers looked older, not like the neighborhood regulars, who were ten to fifteen years *young*, looking only to score brownie points towards juvenile-delinquent merit badges There was none of the familiar nervous laughter or exaggerated camaraderie. This group was silent—not out for a good time.

Alfred E. Hatton felt like a deer caught in the spotlight of a poacher's aim. From both directions they walked toward him. Still holding the bottle, Hatton stepped back to the garage, reached up, and unclipped the safety strap on his holster.

After several steps, both groups stopped, faces still shaded by the gloom. From a distance, the punks calculated his ability and determination to defend himself. Hatton didn't know why they'd settled on him. Tomorrow was Thursday. In the mentality of the jungle, that was reason enough.

Dropping the bottle onto the pile of garbage, Hatton looked right, then left, preparing for their attack. He could feel their stares, began to understand the rationale behind them. He was not their enemy so much as a figure of authority, a target for pent-up rage.

One of the bangers on the right stepped from the pack and strode towards him. To within twenty paces the punk came, his face hidden by a red bandanna tied in the manner of the outlaws of the Old West. Hatton could see only his eyes—cold and empty, like the ones he'd seen on kids in Vietnam...1967...returning from thirty days in the bush. They'd called it the thousand-yard stare. The stare of too much pain, too much suffering, too much killing, too much shit for a teenager to absorb without long-term emotional degradation. Al Hatton saw that stare and for the first time understood these punks...and became afraid.

The banger reached into his pocket and withdrew a pale object. Hatton could only watch as the kid dropped it with the nonchalance of a minor business transaction. The object floated to the dirty ground. Hatton looked hard to make it out: a crisp white glove.

Making sure Hatton had seen the glove, the punk nodded and turned, walking back to the group. Without word or signal, both groups dissolved into the shadows.

As the soft tread of their withdrawal echoed down the alley, Al Hatton realized he still held his breath. Grasping the aluminum fence, he gratefully inhaled, again and again and again. One step closer to death, he retreated to the relative safety of his house on wobbly legs, feeling every bit as old as his elderly neighbors.

Kaloostian knew that some stereotypes carry a small foundation of truth. The media often depicted a scientist like James Revkin as hurrying through life, too busy contemplating the intricacies of quantum physics to worry about a lamppost until it knocked him on his ass. But every now and then, these Walter-Mitty types woke long enough to surprise those around them. And there was no denying Gregory Kaloostian's surprise. Hiding behind stacks of books, watching the Armenian's every move, Revkin had pegged him the moment he entered the library, had watched to be sure neither was followed.

Greg let it go at that. No sense pointing out holes in his assumptions or trying to explain the latest advances of electronic surveillance. If the scientist felt safe enough to trust him, that's all he needed to know. James Revkin had other things to worry about.

"You're sure you weren't followed?" Revkin asked for the sixth time.

"I work alone. You can trust me, Jim."

Revkin hesitated before he took his son's oversized cap gun away from Kaloostian's neck, allowing him to turn.

"Okay. If you weren't alone, one of your backups would have busted through that door by now. So who do you work for—corporate or government?"

Greg smiled. He said nothing as he scrutinized the man with a toy gun. James Revkin was just under six feet tall, and he weighed more than two hundred pounds. At age thirty-eight, he was heavier than he'd been at Monogovody. His stomach crept over his belt, and his cheeks resembled a woodchuck's. He had parted his light brown hair in a fruitless attempt to hide a receding hairline. Despite his plain black-framed glasses, Revkin had no calculator clipped to his belt.

"I couldn't buy a gun without tipping off the Feds," Revkin professed, as Kaloostian stared again at the toy. "This was all I could find."

"Whatever works. I guess I don't need to introduce myself. And I recognize you from the news reports of your daughter's accident."

Revkin nodded, pulled a chair out from the table, and sat down. He stuck the toy gun into a backpack he'd placed under the table. Kaloostian maneuvered his wheelchair so that he could sit at the end of the table, his back to the door.

"Before we get started, I'd like to tell you how sorry I am about Melissa," he said. "I know how hard this must be on all of you. Coming here took a lot of courage."

"Thanks. I'm not so sure about the courage. It's more a matter of running out of options. When I found out you wanted to meet me, I thought we could help each other, that you might have some connections."

"Connections for what? What are you thinking of doing?"

"I'm not sure yet. I'll let you know as soon as I figure it out."

"Fair enough. What have you got that would make it worth the risk of helping you? The Feds seem pretty interested in keeping you on a tight leash. How'd you get here, anyway?"

"Every Wednesday, I go to the gym to play racquetball. Over the past two weeks, I brought extra items of clothing that I'd repeatedly washed—in case they'd planted some sort of tracking device."

"Good idea."

"Yeah, I thought so, too. Tonight I went into the locker room, changed, and left everything I wore in my locker. Then I snuck out the back door and caught a bus to the campus. Got here a early. Scoped the place out. It looked pretty safe."

"Nice work, Jim."

"I've watched a lot of movies. It's just a matter of paying attention to the little stuff."

Kaloostian smiled as a vision of Angela searching for Popeye came to mind. "Good job. Back to my earlier question. What can you do for us if we help?"

"I brought the video. I can tell you what I know about Nyentzi. What else do you want?"

"Let's start with why?"

"Why? My daughter's dead, my wife's being held prisoner, and I've had to send my son to live with his grandparents. Is that good enough?"

"That's not what I was looking for, but it'll do for starters. You mention the Feds. Any idea what agency?"

"You'll be pleased to know that I did ask. Didn't get much of an answer, though. They weren't too inclined to discuss who *they* were. Olga asked a lot of questions, too. She raised a big fuss at the hospital after a doctor got all excited about the brain waves and made some calls. Next thing we know, a team of specialists shows up. From the military."

Greg nodded, mentally reliving the events of the past two weeks.

"I know what you're thinking," Revkin continued, "but you've got to understand we were trying to save Melissa's life. We thought we were doing the right thing. Olga and I came back from lunch one day and were told there'd been an emergency, that Melissa had been transferred to a hospital at Santa Ana, on the Marine Corps base. They put us in a van with no windows and drove us there. The driver and his pal had automatic weapons! We're American citizens, for Christ's sake.

"Things went downhill from there. Olga—God, that woman can be stubborn—started raising a ruckus, threatened to go to the *LA Times*. Before I knew it, they'd escorted her to a locked psychiatric unit. The only reason I'm here and not with her is that we decided if it ever came to this, I'd cooperate with the authorities and do anything they ask. We figured it might buy us some time."

"You knew this was going to happen?"

"Are you serious? I can't believe it stayed buried this long. Every day, I expected there to be news about Nyentzi."

Revkin looked around the room, then continued: "Maybe I read too many horror books. Maybe I'm not as shocked as I should be by the gruesome headlines. But you know something? I can deal with axe murderers and psychopaths. At least they've got a limited kill zone. What really scares the shit out of me is the *Wall Street Journal*. Now there's a creepy publication. When the boys in their Armani pinstripes start mingling with their newfound friends in lab coats, sooner than later they see the dollar signs. When that happens, Kaloostian, watch out. It's time to run for cover, 'cuz there's bound to be hell to pay."

He sighed and started to speak, only to stop and reconsider. Then he said, "We didn't know what we were buying into. Tyrellovich made it all sound so...so noble. It seemed like the right thing to do."

"What seemed like the right thing? I'm not sure I know what you mean?"

"What you do you mean, you don't know? The project...Nyentzi."

"I think you're overestimating what people know about what went on at Monogovody."

"Isn't that why I was told to meet you, that your people had been monitoring Nyentzi? I thought you knew. I thought you could help us."

"Listen, Jim, I've...we've been looking for Nyentzi for seven years. We knew Tyrellovich was into genetic experimentation but not how far he'd gone. We didn't even know whether he'd been successful. Until Melissa's file came along, we had no proof. Nobody did. We still don't have the whole story."

Revkin shifted in his chair. "You...you really don't know, do you?"

Kaloostian didn't reply. As an active player in the information business, he had learned that the truth was supple, that it could bend to an amazing degree. But sometimes it was best to be candid—no rhetoric, no politics. With the increasingly agitated James Revkin, Greg knew only one way their conversation would continue.

"No, I don't," Greg said with a straight face. "And I'm afraid there aren't many people alive who could answer your question. You knew Tyrellovich operated in secrecy. Trust me when I tell you he was good at it."

"That's just great. Why am I talking to you, then? I thought you could help. Who are you, anyway?"

"I'm exactly who you were told I was. I can help. You're just assuming we know more than we do. You think Nyentzi is some news story sitting on every reporter's desk, waiting for sweeps week. Sorry. That's not the way it is."

"Then what way is it?"

"Rumors of Nyentzi circulated from the beginning, even before Tyrellovich broke ground at Monogovody. Human genetic experimentation isn't easy to conceal. You don't pull together a team of two-hundred-plus scientists and technicians without raising a few eyebrows. From secondhand accounts and anonymous sources, we've been able to piece together parts of the puzzle. We know when and where. We think we know what and how. Who and why are still vague. You're the closest we've come to prying the lid off."

"So, what you're saying is I shouldn't hold my breath hoping for a happy ending."

"That pretty well sums it up. I'm not usually this blunt, Jim, but what do you expect? You've had the inside scoop for seven years.

Monogovody was charred ashes before Melissa was born, and you did nothing. What have you and Olga been doing all these years?"

Revkin seethed as he was forced to confront the truth. He stared Kaloostian in the eye. "Will you answer a couple of questions for me before you begin your interrogation?" he finally asked.

"Sure. We've got an hour. The library closes at eleven."

"I'll keep it simple. Do you know who destroyed the facility?"

"No," Kaloostian answered.

"Do you know the purpose of Nyentzi?"

"No."

"Do you know why Tyrellovich started Nyentzi?"

"No."

"Do you know the current status of the Nyentzi Project?"

"No."

"Do you know what genetic changes were made?"

"No…not completely."

"Then we've got a real problem."

"Why?"

"Because I've kept in touch with one of the other couples—people who didn't lose one of the twins."

"They were *supposed to be* twins?"

"Yes. I'll explain all that in a bit. You asked why I hadn't come forward before. We…Olga and I thought everything was proceeding according to plan, except for the loss of Melissa's sister, of course. Willie and Marge—our friends—told us a few things, but they always said the project was cruising along, despite Tyrellovich's death. And even if we had misgivings, who would we complain to? All of us, we all assumed the original underwriters of the project had picked up the slack. You know, business as usual."

Kaloostian sat forward in his chair, listening to every word. "Who was picking up the slack? Who underwrote the project?"

"See, that's the weird thing. If it really was Uncle Sam and his poker buddies, then why the commotion when Melissa ended up in a coma? Why the grunts with the guns? Why the secrecy? We assumed the government knew everything about Nyentzi from the beginning. Tyrellovich sure made it sound like they did." Revkin hesitated. "Now I'm not so sure."

Greg shook his head, scarcely able to believe his ears. He knew he should not pass moral judgment on James Revkin, but the ease with which he pleaded ignorance was difficult to accept.

"Seems to me you and the other parents only heard what you wanted to hear. You knew human genetic experimentation was illegal. You knew his work was done in the middle of a Siberian wilderness, under the tightest security imaginable. You went there of your own volition, and now you're wondering why the government's suddenly involved, scrambling to keep the lid on. More than two hundred people died seven years ago, and it takes Melissa's death to open your eyes."

Revkin hung his head, trying to come up a rebuttal. But Kaloostian had not finished.

"I need to know *who,* Jim. Who underwrote the Nyentzi Project?"

Greg expected James Revkin to be repentant when he looked up. Instead, he showed irritation.

"Now it's my turn to be surprised. I thought people in your purported avocation understood how big government works. You want to know who paid the light bill, bought all those mechanical pencils, procured the volunteers? Well, believe it or not, it wasn't Uncle Sam, Ma Bell, the Russian Bear, the Chinese Dragon, *or* the Great Pumpkin. Nyentzi wasn't some secret cabal of archvillains scheming to take over the world. It wasn't five, or ten, or even fifteen sponsors with deep pockets.

"It was all of them…all of *us.* We're all in on this. Don't you get it, Kaloostian? Tyrellovich received financial compensation and research assistance from damn near every government and megacorporation in the world. That's why it's so hard to believe that not even the *National Enquirer* figured out the truth."

Greg leaned back and crossed his arms. "I think you've exaggerated the degree of global involvement."

"Have I? I don't think you understand how much money we're talking about. Monogovody was built from scratch on an empty piece of tundra, and Tyrellovich wasn't a man to believe in frugality. Every test tube, every beaker, every atomic microscope was state-of-the-art. Think of the salaries he had to pay to get people to work in the middle of that godforsaken Siberian wilderness."

Revkin laughed. "He even flew in an emergency shipment of caviar on New Year's Eve 1999, paid the pilot a small fortune in overtime. When that facility went up in smoke, there should've been repercussions across every sector of the economy. After investigators concluded the explosion was an accident, I figured it a whitewash. And the project kept right on going, despite the loss of its illustrious leader." The scientist paused. "Now do you understand why we didn't say anything? Like I said, who would've listened?"

"Then how'd they do it? If you're talking about that kind of money, how were they able to funnel it all to one enterprise?"

"The wonders of electronic banking. Remember the big stink over Citibank and its laundering of thirty million dollars for Raúl Salinas de Gortari, the eldest brother of the one-time president of Mexico?"

Greg nodded.

Revkin continued. "They were amateurs, with money that was chickenfeed to Tyrellovich. You know what they say, Kaloostian: 'A billion dollars here, a billion dollars there, pretty soon you're talking serious money.' Monogovody was built with funding from a mammoth slush fund. Everybody threw in their nickel's worth. Secret R&D money from dozens of corporations, all looking to cash in on the prospective breakthroughs. U.S. taxpayer dollars skimmed from various congressional packages, all hidden from the GAO. Millions of the dollars sent to

Russia in aid that vanished in the mid-1990s. Four hundred million in Russian diamonds, gold, and platinum also disappeared in the '90s. Then you've got the French, German, Dutch, Japanese, Chinese, British...military, aerospace, communication, transportation, software, medicine...every sector of every economy. You know what they say: no matter what you grow, you need fertilizer."

"Are you telling me Yuri Tyrellovich was a Hudsucker!?"

"That's good," Revkin said with a smile. "I hadn't heard him called that before, but it sure fits."

"Answer the question: Did the sponsors run Monogovody?"

"No way. Tyrellovich was in charge—100 percent. Nobody told him what to do. The investors transferred the funds, and he got the project running. They wanted results, not active participation."

Gregory pursed his lips. He was starting to get a feel for James Revkin. The portly scientist was running for his life—for the life of his family. Revkin would bolt if he felt threatened. The best strategy was to make himself the target of Revkin's anger and let the technocrat take his best shot. He had to structure each question for maximum impact.

"How the hell did they keep this quiet?" Greg asked with feigned shock.

"Come on, Kaloostian. I'm surprised by your naiveté. The world is full of secrets. Haven't you heard, it's a battle of words?"

"And you kept quiet all this time! You could've done *something*."

"Who the hell was I supposed to contact? Haven't you been listening?"

"We've had feelers out for years. Sure, we had to be subtle, but someone with an inside track should have picked up on them...someone like you. You could have helped stop this, helped alleviate the suffering of those poor kids."

"Bullshit!" Revkin thundered, rising from his chair. He glared at Kaloostian, his clenched hands on his hips, his breathing rapid. Exerting all his effort to control his emotions, James Revkin turned and walked towards the wall. Greg realized how angry the scientist had become and how his line of questioning might have backfired. Saying nothing, he waited.

Revkin sat back down and looked Kaloostian in the eye. "You're not here to *stop* Nyentzi. And don't feed me that crap about your fictitious concern over the children. You're here because your sponsor didn't get in on the original action and doesn't want to be left out. That's your only consideration."

"You're damn right my sponsor wasn't one of the original underwriters. By the sound of things, that's a plus for my side. And I'm not sure Tyrellovich is someone I'd want on my team, anyway. You remember in 2000 when that teenager died after receiving an infusion of corrective genes?"

Revkin nodded. "What about it?"

"Word on the street was the genes, the ones that caused the fatal immune reaction, came from Monogovody."

"It was a clinical experiment. There were bound to be mistakes," Revkin asserted.

"I'll grant you that. But I also heard it was premeditated. Tyrellovich, or someone else at ETI, purposely sabotaged the treatment."

"That's ludicrous. Why the hell would he do that? The political fallout from that kid's death set the genetics industry back for years."

Greg nodded. "Yep...suddenly everyone had the FDA looking over their shoulder. Everyone except Tyrellovich, operating under the cloak of secrecy at Monogovody. No checks, no balances, no competition, and no one asking pesky questions about Nyentzi. So what was his rationale, Jim? What possible explanation could Tyrellovich give us for ruining so many people's lives?"

"Tyrellovich wasn't some sort of monster, if that's what you're getting at," Revkin said defensively. "He saw the problem and had enough courage to do something about it."

"Refresh my memory. What exactly is the problem that justified the greatest perversion in the name of science since World War II? Don't you realize the only other doctors who came close to this sort of crime wore swastikas?"

"Don't get started on that! Christ, I've heard such insane stories about Monogovody. I may've had second thoughts, but I don't think you or anyone else understands the real purpose of Tyrellovich's work. In fact, I'm certain you don't."

Kaloostian thought about Toner's message and the religious fanaticism of the surviving Monogovody technicians. Had everyone involved in Nyentzi turned into a zealot?

"Despite everything that's happened, you still believe in him, don't you?"

"Yeah, I guess I do," Revkin answered after a moment of reflection. "Until I learn firsthand that Nyentzi was a total failure, I'll defend my decision…and I accept responsibility for that decision."

"Why, Jim? What justified hundreds of lives and billions of dollars? This is more than just an attempt to get around the complications of artificial intelligence, isn't it?"

"Of course. AI was just the tool. Nyentzi was…Nyentzi *is* about information."

"Information? What kind of information?"

"No, not just information. Information overload. We're overwhelmed with information. We're drowning in information. We've got all these scientific breakthroughs and theories, thousand of years of deductive reasoning, but no way to apply the potential benefits to society. We've got all these institutions doing research in isolated sectors but no one willing to share what they know. Knowledge is useless if it can't be applied. Any idea, any concept that has social value must be carried to fruition or it's worthless."

"I'm still not sure what you're getting at."

Revkin paused. "Did you know that every American alive today, including village idiots and politicians, assimilates as much information in one year as Thomas Jefferson did in his entire lifetime?"

"I'd heard that somewhere."

"Well, don't you see?" Revkin asked with increasing excitement. "We're losing track of what we know, what we're educating the next generation for. The world and all the information we need to survive is changing too fast. We need to rethink everything. We need not only to assimilate this information but also to apply it. We need massive computers with the ability to absorb and reapply it."

"Tyrellovich tried to justify Nyentzi because he couldn't get artificial intelligence to work?"

"It's not that simple. AI will never succeed. It's a dead cow, it's…"

"Bullshit. I'll admit we've got a ways to go, but the industry's making progress. In ten years, with advances in molectronics, I'm convinced they'll…"

"No! You don't understand," Revkin said, pounding the table. "I don't care how much money is spent, how fast computers get, how advanced software becomes, artificial intelligence will never work. AI is a boondoggle of unprecedented proportion. It's pissin' in the wind, Kaloostian. Don't believe me? Come on, it's written all over your face. You wanna know why…why AI will never work? I won't be changing the subject. AI is the foundation for Tyrellovich's genetic theories."

Greg slowly nodded and took a breath. "Okay, why?"

"Got any ideas? Go on, take a stab at it," Revkin said with a grin.

"It's an applications problem."

"Bzzt. Wrong answer," Revkin wisecracked. "No matter what the experts say, software has nothing to do with it. Even though it's obvious the operating program would be too large, that it's impossible to input so much data, that's not the reason. Tyrellovich was the only one who understood, who knew the secret. To understand Nyentzi, you've got to believe that his goal was to achieve true artificial intelligence.

You also have to realize what AI is. It's not just artificial intelligence, it's artificial consciousness.

"Every attempt at creating an AI system revolved around applying intelligence to an inert substance, ergo a computer's hard drive. But it's not a programming deficiency. It's an *electrical* problem. Computers are digital. They can be nothing *but* digital...a series of ones and zeroes, on and off. That's their inherent nature."

"You're spouting eighth-grade physics, Revkin. Tell me something I don't know."

"All right. You an audiophile?" Kaloostian nodded. "Then you know why compact discs sound so tinny compared to vinyl. Anytime you go digital, you lose information. CDs can only detect 65,000 levels of sound pressure, a lot less than the sensitivity of human hearing. It's not a huge difference but enough to be noticeable. That infinitesimal variance is fatal, however, when it concerns artificial intelligence. Sure, supercomputers are impressive, but they will never achieve true intelligence. They will never achieve *consciousness*.

"Consciousness is not digital. Neurons are not digital. They're analog. Their signal is graded—the gradual application of a chemical signal in the brain—from weak to strong. *But it's always on*. That's why those old albums sound so good. The signal's always there. It's a constant. Turn off a computer, break the signal, and you lose some data. Turn off the signal in the brain, and the organism dies. Big difference.

"That's why he stopped trying to adapt artificial intelligence. It can't be done. If you want a conscious supercomputer, you have to make it genetically. It has to be a living, breathing organism with the ability to sense and experiment with its environment

"It's like Niels Bohr once told a student who couldn't grasp one of his theories: 'You are not thinking. You are just being logical.' That's AI. That's all it can ever be! No one knows exactly what consciousness is, but we sure know what it's not."

Kaloostian said nothing. No more playacting. Revkin's argument had taken the conversation on a path he wasn't prepared for, reaching conclusions counter to everything he knew about artificial intelligence…and about Nyentzi. Pieces of the puzzle he had been working on for the past seven years suddenly fit. The emerging picture was not to his liking.

Then why change the sex of the embryo from male to female?" he asked. Now seemed as good a time as any to get back on track, discover what other secrets James Revkin possessed.

"How'd you know that? From what I'd been told, you didn't get the entire autopsy."

"I didn't. I had to terminate the connection."

"Sounds like you know more than you led me to believe," Revkin said, eyeing Kaloostian closely. With a shrug, he continued. "Yeah, we received an email message in April 2000. Olga was four months' pregnant. We were told our babies would be twin boys. I'd already painted their room blue, as instructed."

"What did the message say?"

"Not much. The explosion happened in March, you know. After that, we weren't sure what to expect. Olga was pretty upset about the whole thing. Then this epigrammatic email communication showed up. No return address. I still remember it: 'Congratulations on approaching due date. I just heard the news—twin girls. How exciting. Boys can be so much trouble. Sorry for the confusion. Everything else still on schedule? Everything else still on schedule.' That last sentence was repeated. First with a question mark, then a period."

"And you knew who sent it?"

"Not a clue. Like I said, we thought the sponsors had picked up the pieces. All we knew was that it was legitimate."

"How'd you know that?"

"The signature—C-Y-A-N-E-S. It's an anglicized variation of the Greek word *kyanos*. Means deep blue."

"Deep blue. Like the computer that beat Kasparov?"

"Exactly. Nyentzi's great catalyst—Tyrellovich and his damn chess game. The signature was meaningless to anyone but the parents. Silly game, really. Yuri's favorite song was "Teach Your Children" by Crosby, Stills, Nash, and Young. Take the first letter of each name, mix 'em up, add…"

"*A* and *E*. Where'd those letters come from?"

"Albert Einstein, originator of Tyrellovich's pet quote: 'Imagination is more important than knowledge.' Put them all together, and you've got Yuri Tyrellovich's Internet trademark, what he used on personal correspondence. We knew he was dead, but whoever sent it must've known what was going on."

"You never tried to get verification?!"

"Dammit, Kaloostian, how many times do I have to tell you? There was no one to turn to. Olga was having prenatal problems. She lost one of the babies…With only Melissa, and her with psychological problems, we drifted away from the project. Melissa—she sensed, she knew something was wrong, almost from birth. She tried. She tried so hard."

Revkin looked away, biting his lower lip, momentarily lost in his memories.

In a low voice, Greg offered condolence. "I'm sorry this had to happen, Jim. You and Olga did the best you could. There wasn't much anyone could've done. I'm just worried about the other children when word of this gets out. No matter where these kids live, it'll be front-page news. Then the authorities will step in and take them away from the only families they've ever known. God, what a mess."

"I don't think you have to worry too much about that."

"Oh, come on. You know how vicious the media can be when it finds a good story. And trust me, Jim, Nyentzi is one hell of a story."

"I know what you mean. I'm just saying nothing's gonna happen."

"You know something I don't?"

"Yeah. It's the children, the twins, Nyentzi. They're all dying."

21

AN UNEASY SILENCE

Moscow was buried under a blanket of white. A winter storm, rising above the Barents Sea, had swept south, covering Arkhangel'sk with more than a meter of snow. For three days, the blizzard had plodded on, then smashed into the Russian capital with frigid fury.

In the early afternoon hours of January 10, the streetlights began to go on. The tempest obscured the sun, turning day to twilight. Winter-hardened Muscovites hurried home. Long acclimated to wintry extremes, they knew better than to fight Mother Nature.

Working feverishly to keep the streets clear, municipal road crews were out in force with every available snowplow. Because they were able to clear only the main thoroughfares, the snow accumulated elsewhere, gradually impeding every means of transportation but the subway. The early dismissal of schools and businesses further worsened traffic conditions.

High above the chaos on the streets, two seven-year-olds confronted a jam of a different sort. Though ordinarily they were unaffected by weather, this storm was interfering with their satellite and cable links.

As far as the twins were concerned, the blizzard could not have come at a worse time.

During the preceding four days, working in collaboration with their sisters, the twins in Moscow had monitored electronic communications from around the world. For Lara and Katya Gracheva, the margin of error for their surveillance was small and getting smaller. Knowing their stepbrother as they did, far better than he suspected, they could not take any chances. Their long-awaited visitors approached, and the children knew he'd do his utmost to prevent their arrival. They were not about to let him succeed.

The meeting had to occur. They could not consider the consequences of failure. All their work depended on the two women they had never met but of whom they knew a great deal. A single Russian and a single American traveling through two snowstorms just to see them! It would be better than Christmas!

"And knowing that, you did nothing?!" Kaloostian challenged. It was 10:45 P.M., and he was still far from uncovering the truth about Monogovody.

"You sanctimonious sonofabitch," Revkin countered. "Don't you take the moral high ground with me. God, I hate attitudes like that! This *is* about responsibility, Kaloostian. This is about being part of the solution, not whining about the problem. If you're looking for someone to blame, go find a mirror. Like I said before, we're all in on this. We're all guilty at birth.

"We'd have done anything for these children. Not just Olga and me—all of us—every surrogate parent Tyrellovich recruited. I'd have thrown myself in front of a train to save Melissa. I loved her, loved her like she was my own child."

Kaloostian remained silent. In the confines of the library conference room, the atmosphere was tense. James Revkin was angry about Greg's intentional accusations. Hearing that the children of Nyentzi were dying was not the shock Greg had pretended. Even with limited knowledge of Nyentzi, he knew that making radical changes to a neurological system would affect other dependent systems. The body's metabolism contains a finite quantity of physical matter. Robbing Peter to pay Paula produces predictable, and not so predictable, side effects.

"It sounds like Nyentzi involved more than basic economics. I get the impression Tyrellovich incorporated a fair amount of ideology into the project."

"Whatever you say."

"I'm not sure what to say. I'm just wondering about when this is all over. When it's time to point fingers, who's going to get the blame?"

"You want to know who's to blame? You tell me! It's an old argument. Do we blame the child who buys a computer for school? The salesman who sells the computer because he's trying to feed his family? The manufacturer who's only filling a need dictated by the marketplace? The software designer? The guy who drives the truck that delivers the computer to the store? Huh, who do you want to blame? Go ahead, point your finger, Kaloostian. And don't forget to include yourself and whoever hired you. You and yours want the same thing Tyrellovich did. It's just that you don't want anyone else to get it first."

Trying to avoid a drawn-out debate, Kaloostian still did not respond.

"Was Tyrellovich aware of the premature aging?" he finally asked.

"I don't know. The embryos were developed before Shiels discovered that cloned mammals inherit the source cell's age patterns. But he did his best. He gave his life, for Christ's sake. What more do you want?"

"I'd just like to know this wasn't planned obsolescence, that's all."

Revkin's eyes narrowed. "You prick."

"Am I? Let me give you some food for thought. We're talking about the first computers that weren't out of date the moment they went into service. If these children are the physiological thinking machines you claim they are, tell me this: What happens when they're full, when there's no more room upstairs for all that data they're so busy assimilating? You told me the neurological connections—the synapses—were pretty much permanent. *Tyrellovich went biological*—those are your words. That being the case, adding a new hard drive isn't exactly plug 'n' play."

It was Revkin's turn for silence. His conscience tried to pretend it did not understand Kaloostian's assertion, but his knowledge of computers and biology was too strong for a profession of ignorance.

Kaloostian resumed his questioning. "You told me Nyentzi is about information, that the children are going to solve all our problems because they have unbelievable mental abilities. I followed what you said about information overload and how artificial intelligence will never work, but I still don't understand what exactly that has to do with the children."

Revkin had been staring at the floor. He now looked at Kaloostian. "I don't know what preconceptions you have about Monogovody, but Nyentzi wasn't about creating bubble-headed monsters with the powers of ESP. Monogovody was not some sort of vacuum inhabited by evil scientists in spacesuits. The scientists and technicians were real people, honorable people. They died believing in a dream. I don't know what else I can say to make you understand."

With his arms folded across his chest, Kaloostian's message was obvious. He might not know what else Revkin could say, but he expected him to say something.

"What Tyrellovich did was absolutely amazing," Revkin said after a moment of deliberation, looking Greg in the eye. "What he could have done is absolutely terrifying. The authority, the latitude they gave him—you have no idea, Kaloostian, no idea. When I was first approached about participating in the project, I did a lot of soul-searching. Back then, I wasn't told everything, but I knew Tyrellovich by reputation. I suspected he was going biological.

"The sponsors offered him nothing short of unlimited power, the kind of power that can really fuck people up. But it didn't affect him. I'd read something about power once: Is a society or a person powerful because they have the authority to kill indiscriminately? Or is power, true power, the ability to kill with ultimate justice and choose not to?

"When you realize what power is, you understand the awesome responsibility of that power. Tyrellovich understood. He knew that whatever genetic configurations he wanted, they'd accept. He had total control in every aspect of the…"

"Then why the switch?" Greg interrupted, trying to keep Revkin headed in the right direction. "I know for a fact the technicians at Monogovody were never told the embryos were reconfigured as females."

"They weren't? Are you sure?" Revkin said with surprise. Kaloostian shook his head.

"Then I don't know," Revkin continued. "I'll tell you this, though. It sure as hell wasn't because females are more docile and controllable! You married?"

"No."

"Take my word for it. Hormones are hormones, no matter what age."

"Do you think it was sabotage? Maybe Tyrellovich didn't know."

"Are you kidding? No, I see you're quite serious. Who?"

"Mercereau?"

"That's a long shot. I don't know what all you've been told, but everyone at Monogovody trusted Tyrellovich because they trusted his character. Mercereau might've questioned his theories on genetics, but she never challenged his authority. Maybe it was a last minute…Nah, that doesn't make any sense, either. You're sure the techs didn't know?"

"Positive. I received reports on two survivors. They were surprised to the point of agitation. Oh well, couldn't have been that important…I hope."

The two men broke eye contact, glanced at their watches, then back at each other.

"So we're back to the same question," Kaloostian said. "What was, what is the ultimate objective of Nyentzi?"

"Nyentzi was, in the most basic terms, a business arrangement."

"I need specifics."

"Like I said, it's about information. The children are designed to assimilate and multitask like nothing before them. Tyrellovich wanted to tap the pure imagination of a child, the unique ability to combine concepts and ideas without prejudice or preconception. Clean slates—free of sexism, racism, hatred. One hundred perfect little minds eager to learn, solve, and apply the solution to every problem they encounter—and love every minute of it. Did you know that a normal child's brain devours glucose twice as fast as adults'? Children are amazingly efficient processors."

"These children are human beings, not machines!"

"Don't get started on that." Revkin rebutted. "I know what they are. Don't lecture me, Kaloostian. Let's finish this up. It's getting late."

"All right. Tell me about the sponsors."

"All those corporations and governments—Tyrellovich said it was like sharks circling a bleeding swimmer, everybody wanting a piece of the action, at least until they learned the requirements."

"Which were?"

"Total access. The children were to gather information from any source, no matter how privy, whenever they wanted. That was the deal. No closed doors, no off-limit files, no encryption—not that it would have done anyone any good. I've heard those kids are brutally adept at languages and computer codes. Anyone that balked got locked out."

Gregory nodded. "That makes sense. We know that information is a commodity, but are we talking about buying low and selling high?"

"It's not just economics, it's power—the monetary standard of the new millennium. I can imagine your reaction when you first heard about Nyentzi. You were probably thinking of some madman trying to take over the world by monopolizing the flow of information. That's how it would play in Hollywood, but that's not the way it was. Tyrellovich figured that linking the world economies would make future conflicts counterproductive."

"That's not science. That's a flight of fancy."

"Is it? Remember your old testament—the Four Horsemen of the Apocalypse—famine, pestilence, war…what was the fourth? Oh yeah, death. Things have changed since then. In the third millennium, you don't destroy your enemy by poisoning his water supply, you do it electronically. Disrupt his communication networks, liquidate his monetary assets, shut off his access to the web, stop his flow of Big Macs. Nuclear war was never winnable. Military supremacy is an impossible pipe dream.

"The electron is the optimal smart bomb, the perfect guided missile. You can win a war without firing a shot, all because of information. We could turn two of these children loose and bring the United States to its knees in three days. But that's not what Tyrellovich wanted. The way he saw it, if the world economy became a conglomeration of shared knowledge, no one could win a war, electronic or conventional. Nyentzi is not about world domination. It's about democracy and freedom."

Shaking his head, Kaloostian looked at the ceiling. After a moment, he turned back toward Revkin. "That's a warm and fuzzy theory if I ever heard one. Please excuse my skepticism, but I don't share your faith. Reduce mankind to the Stone Age, but instead of using guns, people kill each other with rocks and clubs. It's in our nature, Jim. We're animals—rational, thinking animals but animals all the same. Just look at the Balkans. The hatred goes on generation to generation, century to century."

"I know where you're coming from. Nyentzi wasn't meant to solve all our problems or save the world. Tyrellovich figured it might buy us some time, though."

Again, the Armenian shook his head. The fanaticism Toner had seen in Elena Tagi-Zade was beginning to make sense, as was

Tyrellovich's rationale for naming his project *Messiah*. He was hoping to save mankind from itself. All he needed was the cooperation of a hundred children.

Revkin misunderstood Kaloostian's silence and continued to press. "If you don't believe me, go read up on your Toffler. Power exists in many forms, with many degrees of quality. Violence is power, but it has its drawbacks. It increases the risk to everyone involved. It's inflexible and can be used only to punish. A low-quality quotient.

"Wealth is only slightly better. Lots of money may mean lots of power, but only if it's spread around. Information is the highest form of power. It's an aggregate commodity, the sum of the individual units. Synergy, that's another way of looking at it. The whole is greater than the individual fractions."

"I've read Toffler. He also said information is a multiplier of power," Greg conjoined. "That being the case, we're right back to the world-domination theory, with information just a newer currency. And you know what they say, Jim—money is the root of all evil."

"Collating massive amounts of information's not a crime, Kaloostian. He wasn't going to hoard it. He was planning to share it."

"Yeah, share it fairly, but don't take a slice of my pie."

"Like I said, there's too much information to absorb. Computers were supposed to increase productivity, remember? All they did was create more information. There are too many rules and equations to decipher before reaching a decision about anything. But these children don't have that problem. No rules, no preset equations, no domineering educator holding a wooden pointer, ready to whack 'em on the knuckles if they sit around all day thinking about what could be, instead of what is.

"That's what Nyentzi is all about, Kaloostian. A reinterpretation of reality, a reutilization of our species' accumulated knowledge, treading where no man or woman has gone before, if only on a computer. You have no idea what these children have accomplished. You can't begin to comprehend the things that they've imagined, that they've designed, that will one day be built. And I've only heard about it secondhand."

With that, James Revkin pushed back his chair and stood up. He glanced at his watch, at the door, and back to Kaloostian. "It's eleven o'clock, time to wind up this up. I asked you earlier who you work for. Now I don't care. It doesn't matter. You're obviously working for a two-bit player who got left out of the original project. It's eleven o'clock, the library's about to close, and you're wasting my time. I'm gonna get back before they miss me."

Kaloostian did not speak or move from the doorway. Revkin could go around him, but it would not be easy. He looked into the other man's eyes, gauging him.

"Before you go," Greg concluded "there're two things you need to know. You said you watched a lot of movies. Apparently you learned something, but you've got to understand why I wasn't too worried about anybody getting the jump on me. Espionage is light years beyond anything James Bond ever imagined. If you leave without a coding device, people waiting outside will make sure you never see your wife and son again."

"Sorry Kaloostian, whatever you're selling, I'm not buying. I've had it up to here," Revkin said, moving his hand to his throat, "with you, Tyrellovich, and everyone else. I just want to do what's best for my family. The rest of the world can fend for itself."

Revkin stooped to pick up his backpack. Taking a step towards the door, he saw that the man in the wheelchair had no intention of moving. Again he stopped, tightening his lips. "Look, we're both too old for this tough-guy shit. Would you please move?"

"Be glad to," Greg said with a smile. "But first look behind me, at the attendant working the booth over there. Yeah, that's the one. She's with me. So are a few of other people in the library. We're going to stay after hours, Jim. Maybe 'til midnight, maybe 'til 2:00 A.M. However long it takes. I need some answers. I plan to get them."

The room was silent. Revkin stared into Greg's eyes. Then he looked at the attendant watching him. "What's the second thing I need to know?" he said at last.

"These children have been gathering information for the past…however many years…since they could sit in front of a computer screen. Is that correct?"

"From what I've been told, yes."

"And your contacts, they didn't mention any usual behavior on the part of the children?"

"No. What sort of behavior?"

"I'll get back to that later. There's something else you should know, Jim. Something no one might have noticed yet, a possible glitch in the program. A virus, if you will."

"What do you mean?"

"Does the name Eldon Tyrell ring a bell with you?"

"No, can't say it does. Tyrell?"

"Yeah, sounds a lot like Tyrellovich, doesn't it. He had a son, didn't he?"

"From his first marriage—Anatoly Yuriovich Tyrellovich."

"Was he involved in the work at Monogovody?"

"He was, actually. Yuri didn't play favorites. Anatoly was a minor technician. He was competent but not brilliant, not like his father. Why? You think he might've had something to do with the…?"

"What happened to him?"

"Beats me. I assume he was killed when the facility was destroyed."

"Do you know that for a fact?"

"No. What are you getting at?"

"I think Anatoly Tyrellovich might be responsible for the explosion. I think he might have changed his name to Eldon Tyrell. I think he may be the one controlling the Nyentzi Project. And I don't think he inherited his father's responsibility and altruism."

Toner and Molotova had outrun the first winter storm that harried their departure from Salekhard. That blizzard continued to hug the western slopes of the Urals. Moving southwest, the travelers made excellent time throughout the daylight hours. Listening to a weather report on the radio, they heard about the latest Arctic blast and increased their speed in an effort to beat it to Moscow.

They were not successful.

By the time they reached the city of Kostroma, 300 kilometers from their destination, the snow fell in earnest. Stopping only for fuel and a quick lunch, they pressed on. Kaloostian had recommended they call him before meeting with the twins. At the very least, they should check Nadezhda's voicemail for messages. But the deteriorating weather altered Toner and Molotova's plans. Driving through the northern suburb of Mytishchi, they found only the main roads readily passable. Even then, the accumulating snow forced them to reduce their speed, delaying their arrival in Moscow.

At four o'clock, with twilight decreasing visibility even further, the highway veered due south. A short time later, they passed Riga Station and headed towards an almost deserted Red Square. Despite her close relationship with winter, Moscow was no different from any other city faced with severe weather. The process begun at noon was now complete, the Russian capital all but shut down.

They took more than an hour to drive the final fifty kilometers to where the twins lived, a part of Moscow Molotova did not know. Several modern high-rises, built in 1999, rose just east of St. Basil's Cathedral near the Yauza River. Expensive and luxurious, they replaced the mass-produced units built twenty-five years earlier by the Communists. This was not housing most Russians could afford.

Her effort to read the street signs aggravated by the snow, Nadezhda quietly cursed her reduced vision. She had lived in Moscow much of her life, but the city took on a new look with the coming of the storm. Angela tried to help, staring through the frosted windows for the landmarks Naddie told her to look for, but there was little she could do. Every street sign was in the Cyrillic alphabet, which she could not read. She thus kept to herself, making sure they were not being followed, looking for suspiciously parked cars. The two women had agreed that any attempt to stop them would likely come outside the apartment building.

Minus her fatigue, Toner would have enjoyed the informal tour. Streetlights shimmered, with snowflakes reflecting as gold against the deepening shadows. The infrequent headlights of approaching traffic, beams cutting perpendicular to the light from above, added to the extraordinary display, The scene brought back childhood memories. Angela had always loved freshly fallen snow. As a child, she had thought of snow as urban skin cream, filling in the cracks, hiding the age spots and signs of wear, giving the world a refreshing makeover.

The trees—evergreens and leafless elms—were a uniform white. Saplings and aged oaks all looked the same, sharing a unique standardization. The snow brought to the world a sense of balance, of equality. There were no footprints on the unshoveled sidewalks, not yet any piles of muck plowed up and over the curb. There was only the peace and calm of the Russian night.

"This is it! Svoboda Avenue," Nadezhda shouted as they entered an intersection. She'd not seen the sign in time and gone too far for a safe stop. Instead she attempted an ill-advised left turn. Hitting the brakes and spinning the wheel, Molotova was determined to pull off the impossible maneuver.

Halfway through the intersection, the Explorer slid sideways on the icy road. Molotova took her foot off the brake and pressed the accelerator, spinning all four wheels, praying the Explorer would find traction before flying out of control. It was not meant to be.

The laws of physics reigned, seizing control of the Explorer from its frustrated driver and sending it into a spin. Exchanging a wide-eyed look with her helpless passenger, Molotova could do nothing as the car accelerated sideways and slammed into the curb.

Without the tree, the Explorer might have kept going, clear across the sidewalk and into the nearby building. There was a loud *crunch*. For the next several seconds, Molotova and Toner were silent. They looked at each other, at the tree, and at the large dent in the right front fender. Toner calculated the distance between the fender and where she was sitting.

"I hope this is the place," she said with a sigh of relief, "because I don't think we're going anywhere anytime soon."

Molotova relinquished her grip on the steering wheel, her knuckles white. She looked at the building and saw they were on the correct block. "At least we are here, okay? But we cannot leave the Explorer parked like this. Moscow streets must be cleared of cars for plowing after a snowfall."

"Well, they can just give us a frickin' ticket, 'cuz from where I'm sitting, I can tell it'll take a tow truck to move us—snow emergency or no snow emergency."

"Mmm, it was a nice car," Nadezhda said after considering Toner's remark. "Oh well. I will keep the motor going until we have gathered our things. No sense in becoming cold."

Toner nodded. She was already donning her coat and looking for her gloves. "What's the name of this street?" she asked.

"Svoboda. It means freedom. It is a word your Cold War President Reagan said did not exist in our language. Since then, it has become very popular."

Toner laughed, refusing to be drawn into a debate. In the twenty hours the two women had been together since leaving Salekhard, they had discussed everything from abdominal exercises to men to zygotic-cell reproduction. But politics was a topic the American did her best to avoid.

Her gloves on, her computer bag packed, Angela opened the door and stepped into a knee-high snowbank. Glancing up and down the block, Toner found the street empty of pedestrian and motorized traffic in either direction.

Molotova finished zipping up her boots and shut off the engine. She checked her pistol, opened her door, and got out. Slamming her door at the condition of the car, she looked across the roof of the Explorer at Toner, who was trying not to laugh.

"This is not a matter for laughter, Angela Toner."

"Sorry, it's just that I told you yesterday I'd let you know if I saw any Russian drivers worse than the people in California, and I…"

"Do not go near that," Nadezhda ordered. She glared at her friend, looked at the building, and tried to find her bearings.

Unable to see the building number from where she stood, Molotova stepped farther into the street. She glanced up, putting her hand above her eyes to shield them from the still-falling snow. "This is 2350 building. The address for the girls is 2500…which is…let me see…this way," she said, pointing to her left.

Angela nodded and grabbed her computer bag from the hood of the Explorer. "Shouldn't we find a phone and check your voice mail? Kaloostian said he would call before now. He might have something important."

Molotova opened her mouth to answer. Before she could, a pair of headlights approached from the direction they had come. Making the same mistake, the driver of a top-heavy delivery truck attempted a sharp left turn. There was no screech of tires, but the impending collision was inescapable. The immovable Lada Explorer sat between the speeding truck and the tree. And Molotova was between the Explorer and the delivery truck.

Toner shouted. "Naddie!"

Molotova spun about and saw the truck heading towards her. She could see the panic on the driver's face. She watched helplessly as he tried to control his careening vehicle.

Toner was powerless to help her friend. Realizing she too was in the path of the truck, she turned and tried to run. Her right foot came down on a chunk of ice that had fallen from the overhang of the building. She slipped. Thrown off balance, Angela fell to her right as the rest of her body moved forward. Tumbling into the snow, her ankle twisted sharply under her body. Crying out in pain, she lost sight of Molotova.

The truck might slide in either direction. There was no place for the tiny Russian to run. In the instant before the collision, Molotova dove to one side.

A crash—loud and decisive. Then the shatter of windows and bumpers, the pop of the driver-side airbag. Metal, plastic, and fiberglass—gouged, fractured, and crumpled. The two vehicles merged into a mass of twisted, broken pieces. In every direction, fragments of plastic and glass flew. The momentum of the truck demolished the Explorer, reducing the expensive motorcar to so much scrap.

The thunderous force drove the wreck into the tree, snapping its frozen trunk near the base. The tree tottered and fell, landing only inches from Angela Toner, lying defenseless in the snow. Closer and closer the destruction came, until it had finally exhausted its lethal energy.

The echoes of the crash slowly faded along the snow-muffled street, leaving an uneasy silence. Rising from the snow, her right ankle bent and sore, Angela reached out and touched the front bumper of the demolished Lada Explorer. Only the still-solid tree trunk lay between her and the mangled sports utility vehicle.

Toner looked right, then left for any sign of her friend. "Naddie?" she called. "Hey, you okay? Naddie…*Naddie?*"

There was no answer.

22

THUMBS DOWN

Suada's computer-generated alarm went off early, just after 4:00 A.M. in Los Angeles, Thursday, January 10. The evening before she had visited her neighbor. Over a cup of coffee, the chatter had turned serious when Gregory Kaloostian began asking questions about the owner of the company she worked for, Exemplary Temporary, Inc.

He'd tried to be nonchalant, but Suada detected a note of urgency in his voice. In the four years she'd worked for Eldon Tyrell, she'd never given her enigmatic boss a second thought. As long as she got paid, Tyrell's personal life was no concern of hers.

Yet Kaloostian's questions about the access software that ETI used to log into client computer systems seemed more than idle curiosity, especially in light of his subsequent behavior. She knew her friend was a lonely, melancholy man, but he was also an excellent host who loved having visitors. After Eldon Tyrell came up, however, he had shooed her out, claiming he had work to do.

Back in her apartment, preparing for bed, Suada suddenly remembered an incident of two years earlier. HiTechCorp, a company that utilized ETI's on-line technical writing services, had been rocked by an insider trading scandal. Illegally garnered information about a competitor's new product failing to meet expectations prompted a run on that company's stock just before its proposed merger with HiTechCorp. HiTech stepped in to absorb the competitor at a significantly lower price per share, saving millions of dollars.

The SEC had seized mountains of files and interrogated every employee before indicting a janitor for rifling through the corporate garbage. Allegedly, the custodian had gone to great lengths to unearth stock tips for sale at great profit.

The evidence, circumstantial at best, consisted mainly of bank records showing questionable deposits, as well as email transcripts to and from his Internet address. These electronic messages, involving several Mafia-related personalities, formed the basis for the prosecution's case. Though he professed innocence, even passing an inadmissible lie-detector test, the young, foreign-born worker was jailed, and a trial date was set. Several days later, however, a guard found him hanging in his jail cell—an obvious suicide. Or was it?

Suada had thought it strange that throughout the investigation, ETI's contract with HiTechCorp was not revealed. She knew that anyone armed with the ETI's access software could enter the company's databanks and steal the information. If the janitor's lawyer had been trying to keep his client out of jail, why did he not introduce such a key piece of evidence?

At the time, Suada had been busy with work assignments and not able to pursue her theory. The janitor's death had then pushed the event deep into the recesses of her memory. After witnessing Kaloostian's uncharacteristic behavior and remembering the HiTechCorp incident, however, Suada went back to her apartment and did something that could result in her termination from ETI, as well as the loss of her long-awaited bonus. She made a partial copy of her log-on software and downloaded it to a friend's computer in Europe, asking him to analyze the language she was unable to decipher.

Her wake-up call was an alarm indicating an email response. Quickly donning a terrycloth bathrobe, she stumbled into her office and sat down. After punching the password, she began to read the message:

Suada: If this was anyone but you, I would have first contacted your country's Federal Communications administrator and then the police. Your software is the best I've ever encountered. It has language and command structures I've never seen or heard of before. Very new, very innovative. It's beyond state-of-the-art.

As advanced as it is, that's not the reason I'd be inclined to call the Gestapo. There's a little side program tucked away very innocently, so much so that I almost missed it. Not only does your software open the door for you to do your work, but it also allows other outsiders who know the entry codes to access any database file as well, while you're busy doing your legitimate work.

Of even greater concern to corporate (or government) security is that this additional user would be thoroughly anonymous and completely untraceable. And that, Suada, is very, very illegal.

My recommendation for you, dear friend, is to find an attorney and then duplicate your log-on, log-off records from the time you started working at ETI until now. Give them to the attorney and start protecting yourself from potential prosecution *and* persecution.

I'm sorry I had to be the one to tell you this. I will be sure not to let anyone else get their hands on what you sent me. I hope everything else is going well. Please contact me if you have any other questions or needs.

Take care and cover your butt. Guten tag, mein bekannten.

Your cyber-buddy, J.J. Jingleheimer

P.S. I don't suppose I could talk you into sending me a complete copy of that program?

Suada finished reading. A shiver went down her spine when she realized that if Eldon Tyrell's software could do what her friend said it could, it might be monitoring the computer she had used to transmit the information to Europe.

Shaking from a fear she had not known since childhood, Suada Sivac jumped up and ran out of her office. Expecting a knock at any moment, she hurried to the front door and removed the key from the deadbolt, then went to her hall closet. Opening the door, she pushed several coats to the side and reached in. Mounted on the wall was a twelve-gauge shotgun. She undid the strap, pulled it out, and pumped it once.

Shotgun in hand, the frightened woman walked to her Early-American rocking chair, turned it to face her front door, and sat down. With tears streaming down her cheeks and the shotgun cradled on her lap, she rocked methodically, back and forth.

The only sound heard along Svoboda Avenue was the clatter of the delivery truck's diesel engine, still running despite the damage to the front end. Wincing in pain, Toner used the fractured bumper of the Lada Explorer to pull herself to her knees. Her right ankle was at least moderately sprained. At worst, it was broken.

Gritting her teeth and shivering from the pain and cold, she slowly, awkwardly, tried to stand. The heavy tread of her winter boots provided sufficient footing. Repositioning her grip from the bumper to the hood, Angela pulled herself to her feet. Placing most of her weight on her uninjured left foot, she looked around, finally able to see the extent of the accident.

The driver's side of the Lada Explorer had smashed in. It melded with the damaged front end of the delivery truck into a single grotesque sculpture of metal and plastic. Panning from right to left, Angela saw no sign of Nadezhda Molotova.

In the delivery truck, the driver was alive, though barely visible through the webbed cracks of the shattered windshield. Still dazed by the impact, he blinked and tried to focus. A deflated airbag lay across his lap.

"Naddie! Where are you?" Angela called. She limped around the Explorer towards the driver's side.

Molotova suddenly appeared. Her hat was gone, her hair was askew, she was covered with snow, and she carried her Makarov 9mm. She did not appear to be injured.

Her face tight with anger, Molotova walked to the truck, yanked open the door, and grabbed the driver by his hair. Seeing that he was without a seatbelt, she pulled him from the truck and threw him onto the snow-covered street, where he landed face down. She reached into the truck, located the key, and shut off the motor, cutting its incessant clatter.

Toner likewise removed her Beretta from its shoulder holster and searched for signs of trouble. Limping in pain, she hobbled around the wreckage towards Molotova, who kneeled as she rifled the driver's coat pockets for identification.

With wallet in hand, Molotova stood and allowed the driver to turn over. He sat up, cautiously wiping the snow from his face, overcoming his grogginess. He eyed Molotova with fear and distrust, his attention focused on the pistol pointed at his head. He was a short man, no more than five-feet-seven, and thin. He wore a dingy brown pair of heavy overalls and a coat. His grimy hair, mostly black, was gray on the sides and thinning above his forehead. He had a short, stubby nose, a bushy mustache, and a small cut above his left eye.

Looking to the side, the driver spied Toner moving closer. His dark brown eyes widened as he saw she too had a weapon.

"Naddie," Toner hissed, inching closer, "are you okay? Hey!"

At last Molotova looked up at her friend and nodded. "I am shaken over and quite upset, but all the same okay. What of you? You are limping."

"I think I sprained my ankle."

"How bad is it?"

"It hurts, but I can walk. What about him? You find anything?"

Molotova, her pistol still aimed at the driver, tossed his wallet to Toner: "See if he is carrying the identification card as required."

Switching to Russian, Nadezhda addressed the driver: "Ti na kogo rabotayesh, sukin sin? Otvechay, a to ya pozvolyu etomu nenormalnomu amerikantsu otstrelit tvoi kolenniye chashechki.

The driver, too frightened to respond, looked at his legs, then at Toner.

"What did you say to him?" Angela asked, opening the wallet.

"Only that you are a crazy American who would love to shoot him in both legs."

"That's really diplomatic," Toner said, not looking up. She quickly found a plastic identification card. Removing it from the wallet, she held up the card for Molotova to see.

"What does it say?" Molotova asked.

"It's in Russian," the American replied, handing the card to her friend.

Molotova examined the card in the dim light of the Moscow streetlight and repeated her earlier question. "Govori na kogo ti rabotayesh. Govori, amerikanets zdet ne dozhdetsya postrelyat.

"Srochnaya pochta...Ya rabotnik srochnoy pochti," the driver replied in his native language, wiping a trickle of blood from the cut on his forehead. Staring at the American, he slowly pushed himself away, his nervous breath evident in the puffs of frozen vapor.

"Would you stop telling him that I'm going to blow his kneecaps off?" Toner demanded, leaning against the Explorer, trying to minimize the pressure on her injured right ankle. "Who is he, anyway?"

Molotova did not immediately respond. She pointed the Makarov at the driver's head. Then, to Toner's surprise, she leaned in close to the driver, placing her nose near his mouth and sniffing, their combined breaths forming a cloud of icy exhalation.

"He says he works for Russian Parcel Express," Nadezhda said, standing up again. "His identification appears to be in order. His name is Constantine Yurichich, he lives about two kilometers from here, and he smells like cheap homemade vodka."

Molotova turned back to the driver and scolded him in Russian. "Ti nac chut ne ubil, padla! Ti chto ne ponyal vto ya iz FSB? Baba s pistoletom amerikanskaya diplomatka. Pyaniy voditel ubil eyo muzha i ona sobirayetsya otplatit toy zhe monetoy. Vto, razrehit ey strelyat?"

The driver's expression changed from fear to full-blown terror. He jaw dropped, and his eyes widened in sober realization of his predicament. Throwing himself forward, he begged for mercy.

Toner frowned. "Now what'd you say?"

"I said he almost killed us. I also mentioned I was with Federal Security and that you are a high-ranking American diplomat with deep dislike for drunken drivers."

"Cruel. I like it," the American said with a grim smile. "Hey, a siren."

Molotova turned as a police car advanced towards them down Svoboda Avenue. With lights flashing, it slowed at half-a-block away, the driver exercising prudence relative to the unplowed condition of the street. Remembering Salekhard, Toner and Molotova instinctively sought cover, leaving the driver to scratch his head in confusion at their hasty retreat.

The two agents were taking no chances, police car or not. Their nerves were frayed after two days of air travel, the twenty-three-hour journey in the Lada, their lack of sleep, too much fast food, too much coffee, and a primal need for a hot bath and change of underwear.

Molotova moved to the rear of the delivery truck. Toner positioned herself on the far side of the Explorer. She scrunched down and looked over her shoulder, making sure nothing was coming from behind. Both women had ready their 9mm semi-automatic pistols.

The police car braked to a stop less than twenty feet from the wreckage. The two agents could see nothing within the darkness of the police car. Only when the driver opened his door, activating the interior light, did they see the uniform of the Moscow police force. Then the passenger door opened. A man wearing a heavy brown coat emerged.

"Peter! What are you doing here?"

The officer handcuffed the delivery truck driver and none too gently placed him in the back of the squad car. Constantine Yurichich seemed grateful to be away from the menacing American, accepting his rough treatment with uncommon tolerance.

While the officer called for a tow truck, Toner and the two Russian agents moved onto the sidewalk and continued their discussion.

"I do not understand," Molotova persisted. "I believed you were dead. How can you be here, at this address, at this very time?"

"Nadezhda Andrevna, we were outside in the car, just as you ordered. But we had to park more than half the block from Chekhov's—no close-by spaces. I was getting coffee at the café. When I heard the shooting, I rushed out. Misha was already out of the car, running down the street. It was all very confusing. The second car arrived. I saw one man go down. Then Misha, he shouted something, one of the gunmen fired at him. He was shot and…"

"I saw it…from the alley behind Chekhov's. What happened next?"

"Next? Four men with more firepower than my pistol. What could I do? I ran and contacted the police. By the time they arrived, the gunmen had left. I looked for you also, but you had vanished."

"The police! One of the men dead outside in the snow was police?"

"Yes, I learned that during the investigation, before I flew to Moscow. He was rotten fruit, that one. They both were, more delinquent than actual criminals. But I am still confused by your disappearing. Why did you drive all the way here?"

"Are you being serious? Those men tried to kill us. We thought you and Mikail were dead, and we were next. What else could we do when people direct bullets at us?"

"You mean they were trying to kill *you*?"

"Of course! I saw one of them inside the restaurant. I recognized him from our visitation to Salekhard in November. He was giving me the close inspection before they shot at us."

"At you? No! They were not after you. Maybe he thought he recognized you, but the truth is the restaurant owner was refusing to pay them protection money. Chekhov's was already being protected by the Syndicate. The first two gunmen had tried shaking over the owner for cash payment, but he would not do it. They were trying to muscle in—freelance characters. The owner called the boss man for help, but the two bums thought they would show him and shot up the front window. The next four with the big firepower, they were authentic. They were from Russian Mafia."

"Are you saying the attack was not directed at us?"

"No, of course it was not. Was it supposed to be?" Peter said with confusion. "It was a mob thing."

"Then why did the second bunch try to blast us into next week?" Toner asked, trying to understand Peter's explanation.

"I cannot answer that. Did you shoot at them?"

"Of course, Peter Pavalovich," Molotova added. "They killed that one man and then came into the restaurant looking for more. Of course, we shot back. Remember, they also gunned down Mikail?"

"Yes, I will never forget that sight. We have made every attempt to secure the arrests of these men. They could not know he was Federal Security, but I assure you, Nadezhda Andrevna, his death will not go unavenged. We will bring those men to justice."

Molotova and Toner exchanged skeptical glances, each trying to remember the chain of events of the previous evening. No words spoken—none necessary. Their minds raced. Was it conceivable the attack in Salekhard had not been aimed at them? That their entire flight from Salekhard had been for nothing? It was a prospect neither cared to admit.

"Then explain how you are here now," Molotova ordered, refusing to believe there were no sinister forces arrayed against them. "I did not give you this address."

"I admit I entered your computer files and searched for this address, but I was…"

"That is a major violation of security, Peter Pavalovich Bogachev! I am shocked to believe you violated my trust, not to speak of disregarding Federal Security regulations."

"I was only trying to locate you. You did not return to the hotel. You did not contact Federal Security here in Moscow. I was not knowing of what to do."

Molotova was not convinced. "How could I make contact? I thought you were dead, that we were compromised as well. We had not a choice but to flee Salekhard."

"I understand your circumstance, but please to understand mine. I was only trying to do my job," Peter implored, looking at the two women for sympathy.

"Okay, that may be true, but how did you know to be here at this exact time?"

Peter paused, collecting his thoughts before answering the question, wanting to make certain he got it right.

"Well, I took Aeroflot to Moscow this morning, ahead of the storm. After arrival, I contacted the police, who were very cooperating to help me find you. You see, I suspected you left Salekhard in a car. There was a report about a woman who somewhat fit your description. This woman rented a car without proper card number, so I…"

"Stepan!" Toner and Molotova said in unison, remembering the clerk with the sore nose and bruised groin.

"It was you! Well, this Stepan guy spoke of a Lada Explorer, and when the police got a report of an accident on Svoboda Avenue involving an Explorer, I came along to check in. I will not repeat what the rental clerk told the police about you," Peter said with a slight grin.

"That is good, but remember," Molotova said, looking sternly at her American accomplice, "it was done in the line of duty. We will later discuss that in greater detail. But for now, it is late and cold out here, and we need to take care of other problem. Angela hurt her ankle and needs attention."

"The police officer has a first-aiding kit. Go to him, Ms. Toner. He will help."

"Good," Angela replied. She turned to Molotova. "I'll be back in a minute. Then we can go check on those kids."

"At this hour?" Peter said in surprise. "After such a long travel? It would be better if you checked into hotel or went to your apartment, Nadezhda Andrevna. Look at the time."

As Toner limped towards the police car, the two FSB agents switched to their native language and continued discussing the improbable circumstances of the days preceding.

"How is your ankle?" Molotova asked, after Toner joined her in front of the apartment building.

"I took some ibuprofen and wrapped it. It doesn't hurt if I walk slow."

"That is okay. I am too weary to move fast."

"Did you get everything straightened out with Peter?"

"For now, yes. I will talk in greater detail with him after we finish our business here."

"Is it really possible we overreacted?"

"I do not know what to think, Angie. There remains many answers for the questions we will have to ask. But under the circumstance, what else could we do?"

"Tell me about it," Toner said. "What I don't understand is how Peter got a hold of this address. Didn't you tell me that you kept two files and he never saw the one with all the key information?"

"I did tell you that, and it is true. He has some explaining to do. Perhaps it was my lapse. I do not know. There is that and also Peter's behavior. He is acting highly strange, and I am concerned. He was very against our concluding this business tonight."

"Well, he is the junior member of your team. He sees a fellow agent gunned down, and suddenly he's left fending for himself. Actually, I think he's proven himself to be a pretty resourceful fellow."

"We will see. I only wish he had remembered my purse. It had our identification in it."

"No problem. Like you said yesterday. 'We don't need no stinking badges.'"

Molotova smiled. "Yes, who needs them? What we are needing is to get into this building. It has the security entrance, and I would rather not ring their buzzer. It's too easy for them to refuse us entry. Do you have any suggestions?"

"Why don't we do like the movies—ring every buzzer? Someone's bound to let us in."

At that moment, the locked door to the foyer opened, and a bundled man with a snow shovel stepped out. Both women smiled. Toner reached out and held the door.

"Never mind," she quipped. "Let's get inside before he realizes what riffraff we are."

The women hustled through the door into the warmth and light of the foyer. Molotova read the name of the children's parents in the building's directory.

"What was their last name again?" Toner asked, peering over her shoulder.

"Grachev. I am not sure if I mentioned it earlier. Ah, you recognize it. Yes, it is not a coincidence. Their mother is the cosmonaut, and their father the famous writer. If this was not official investigation, I would be highly excited to meet them."

"Are all the parents of Nyentzi like this? Writers, cosmonauts, biologists, aerospace engineers? The aristocracy of science and literature. You were right about Tyrellovich being a good salesman."

"He had a message people wanted to hear," Molotova said.

Toner nodded. "Before we go up, let's visit the rest room. There's one down the hall. I'd rather not meet these people looking like something the cat dragged in."

"*The cat dragged in*? What does that American expression mean?" Molotova inquired, walking down the hall with Toner.

By the time they had tidied up, it was almost six o'clock. As the elevator rose towards the fifteenth floor, Toner noted, "There are cameras in the hall and the foyer. Did you see them?"

"It is common for such buildings. These people pay premium money for added security."

"In that case, let's hope whoever's monitoring them is as competent as the doorman."

Molotova laughed. "Do you realize what an uncommon day this has been? And now we are to meet not only Josef and Roza Grachev but also two children of amazing ability."

"Yeah, and all I can think about is a good meal, hot bath, and twelve hours of sleep."

"I am in full agreement with you there, my friend."

The elevator door opened, and they stepped onto the fifteenth floor.

"Apartment 1532 is that way," Molotova said, pointing to her right.

"I don't like these newer buildings," Toner observed, walking slowly down the empty hall, her limp barely noticeable. "There's no place to hide. I feel like I'm being watched all the time. Not like those old gothic buildings, with nooks and crannies every five feet."

Molotova suddenly giggled. "You are nervous?"

"Well, yeah. Of course, I'm nervous. You?"

"Very nervous, very tired. We are two lunatics, Angela Toner."

"Speaking of lunatics, I want you to know that if those kids' room is padded and it looks like the parents are going to lock us in, I'll let you go first."

"Thank you, but age is priority. You go first."

"Thanks," Toner deadpanned. "We should pay attention to their behavior—see whether Kaloostian's schizophrenia theory is correct. Damn, we were supposed to call him first."

"Too late. We can do that after. It is not overly important any longer."

"That's true. Here we are."

They stood in front of apartment 1532. The buzzer was on the right, nearest Molotova.

"You may have the honor, Angie," she offered.

"No, you do it. You're closer."

Molotova hesitated and shrugged. "Okay, if you insist." She pressed the bell.

Moments later, a male voice spoke through the intercom in Russian. "Vam pomoch?"

"Josef Gregoriovich Grachev. My name is Nadezhda Andrevna Molotova, with the Moscow school system. We had an appointment for today."

"At this hour?" the voice said, switching to perfect English.

The door opened. A stocky man of average height, wearing baggy corduroy pants, a wool cardigan, and an irritated expression, stood in the doorway. Josef Grachev had short brown hair, a wide forehead, and a neatly trimmed goatee.

"Do you realize the time, Ms...?"

"Molotova—Nadezhda Andrevna Molotova. It is a remarkable pleasure to meet you, sir. My American associate is Angela Carmen Toner, from Los Angeles."

"Yes, yes, but at this hour?"

"Who is it, Josef?" a woman asked, stepping into the entryway of the Grachev apartment. Roza Gracheva was slightly taller than her husband

and ten years younger. Though retired, she was still in top shape. Roza's long black hair was parted down the middle. She had beautiful skin, and the high cheekbones so characteristic of Slavic people.

"It's the woman who is here to sign off on the children's test results."

"From the school system? We were told you would not be coming," Roza said, her voice carrying a pronounced accent.

"Who told you that?" Nadezhda asked, facing the wife, her curiosity piqued.

"Roza, you misunderstood," Josef interjected. "I didn't say they wouldn't be coming. With the storm, I only assumed they would not be able to make it."

"Oh, yes. Of course," Roza stammered, trying to agree with her husband.

Molotova looked at Toner, who nodded that she should continue. "I am very sorry for the lateness of the time, but our delay is indeed because of the storm. Rather than attempt a rescheduling, we thought it would be better to come and meet with Lara and Katya tonight. It is only six o'clock."

"I know the time, but I do not agree. The papers can be signed by us, now." Grachev was angry, refusing to move from the doorway, keeping Molotova and Toner in the hall.

"I am afraid that would be against our policy."

"Isn't there some way to settle this? Please understand, we need to limit the children's stimulation. They are in fragile health. The doctor said no visitors. I must protest. Please, come back tomorrow."

"Who is their doctor, Mr. Grachev?" Molotova asked.

"Roza, do you remember his name? I seem to have forgotten. A younger man."

"Anatoly, I think," Roza Gracheva suggested.

"Yes, mother. Anatoly. Anatoly Yuriovich Tyrellovich."

"Oh my, Katya! Lara! What are you both doing out of your room? You know the rules."

"We heard talking. We were only looking to see who it was."

For a moment, there was silence. Roza and Josef stood to the side while the visitors stared at the frail girls shyly standing behind them. Toner and Molotova immediately knew the photograph of Melissa Revkin must have been taken months, perhaps a year earlier.

Lara and Katya Gracheva, though only children, frightfully old. They had long, thinning gray hair, receding around their foreheads. The skin on their faces, hands, necks, their entire bodies, was wrinkled beyond their years. Though more than four feet tall, neither could weigh more than fifty pounds, fully clothed, with rocks in her pockets—lots of rocks.

Despite their condition, both girls looked like Melissa Revkin, as well they should. Pug nose, small chin, long lashes—reproduction after reproduction—all copies of the same genetically engineered embryo.

And their eyes. Angela Toner was drawn to their eyes, to the liveliness, sparkle, and beauty. The bodies of Lara and Katya—of all the children of Nyentzi—might be aging prematurely, dying prematurely, but their eyes were full of vigor, energy, imagination, love, mischief, of life. Unlike the autistic stare of their dead sister, these twins had the eyes of enthusiastic children everywhere.

As no one spoke, the silence became increasingly awkward. Toner and Molotova met the gaze of the parents, recognized their pleading looks, and understood their unspoken message: "Yes, they are different, but they are ours, and we love them."

"Mother, father, are you forgetting something?" one of the children finally asked in a soft voice.

"Yes. Where are my manners?" Josef said, smiling at last as he looked at his daughter. "We get so little company."

Naddie knew what the child was talking about and began the introductions. "Hello, my name is Nadezhda Andrevna Molotova. And this is Angela Carmen Toner, from Los Angeles in the United States of America. You two must be Katya and Lara."

"Katya keeps her hair in those silly braids. I'm Lara."

"I'm Katya, and they're not silly."

"It is a very great pleasure to meet both of you."

"Our pleasure as well," said the girls with one voice.

Josef Grachev extended his hand. "And it is my estimate that you know who I am. This is my wife, Roza. Please come in."

The Grachev family moved back into the apartment, making room for their guests. Josef opened the hall closet, reached in and procured two hangers. Toner and Molotova took off their coats and handed them to the still-troubled man.

"One hour," he firmly insisted. "No more. Please, we are concerned for their health."

"I understand, sir," Nadezhda said. "One hour will be fine."

The girls' room was hermetically sealed, with oxygen-enriched air fed through filtered purifiers to remove impurities—dust, molds, and pollen. Against the far wall were neatly made twin beds, matching nightstands between them. Stapled and taped on the wall were posters of political leaders, computer-generated artwork, and a large placard with white background with neon pink letters: "Girls Rule."

Along the next wall was a collection of floor and wall shelves, chockful of books, software, and stuffed toy animals. Situated among the shelves were two large computer stations, built around the latest mini-mainframe PCs. Each station had a thirty-inch flat-screen monitor, wireless keyboard and mouse, and large, overstuffed chairs. Opposite the beds was a blank wall, in front of which was a long, narrow benchlike contraption. Toner recognized it as a programmable hologram-generator.

She had never seen one in person but had read about them. Their cost was astronomical, but for shut-ins like the Grachev twins, they offered a realistic sense of the outside world. Some of the more expensive models came with scent-producing equipment. Thus, a field of roses not only looked like the real thing, it smelled like it too.

"Methuselah syndrome," the girl with the braids said after the visitors had surveyed the room.

"What was that?" Toner asked.

"Methuselah syndrome. It's what's wrong with us," Lara answered, her voice carrying only a faint trace of a Russian accent.

"Why we're aging so fast."

"How, how did you know that's what I was thinking?" the American asked again..

"In the hallway, your eyes…"

"When you saw first us, they widened, ever so slightly."

"You recognized there was something wrong with us."

"Then you looked to the side, but only for a moment…"

"…While you tried to remember the right term."

"Next, your eyes narrowed, ever so slightly, when you couldn't think of it."

"All that in three seconds?" Nadezhda inquired

Angela laughed with the realization there was more to these children than their appearance. "Jeez, no wonder parents go gray," she concluded to herself.

"Well, if we only have one hour, let us begin," Molotova suggested, trying to keep the girls from taking control. "As you might know, we are here to ask you questions about school. Your mother and father would like you to remain here, at home, for your education."

"You can stop that now, Nadezhda. We know why you're here," Lara interrupted.

"We know who you are and that you've both come a great distance to meet us."

"And we've been eager to meet you."

"How did you know we were coming? From listening to your mother and father?"

"Roza is not our real mother," Lara said, walking to her computer station. She picked up a well-used stuffed rabbit and sat down, facing the adults.

"And Josef is not our real father," Katya added, joining her sister.

"How do you know that? Did someone tell you that you are adopted?" Molotova asked, not moving from where she stood.

"We're not adopted," Lara replied.

"Roza gave birth to us. She and Josef care for us."

"But, as you well know, we have other sisters around the world."

"Josef and Roza told you who you are?" Molotova said, exchanging glances with Toner.

"All the adults told us. They helped us find each other and link our computers."

"So we're never alone. We have a very large family, Naddie."

"The sisters are our friends," Katya added.

"And that's good because we can't go outside like other kids."

"We stay in here, do our work…"

"…and play our games. It's a dirty job…"

"…but somebody's got to do it." Lara said with a wide smile.

"If you say so," Toner agreed, looking from one girl to the next, trying to decide which to address. "What kind of games, what kind of work do you do?"

"All sorts of things. Puzzles, math problems, science, inventions."

"We do a lot of inventing."

"What are some of the inventions you have done on your computers?" Molotova asked.

"Do you remember the movie *Chain Reaction*?" Katya said, ignoring the question.

"With Keanu Reeves…" Katya piped in.

"From 1996…"

"…. terrible reviews."

"Of course, Katya, it was a terrible movie."

"Two thumbs down."

"Way down."

"A sinking ship…"

"…took the whole cast with it."

"Keanu…"

"Wuu wuu, what a guy…"

"Stop it, Lara. Anyway, Keanu was part of this research team."

"In Chicago…"

"The Windy City. They discovered a way to create energy from water."

"One vast pollution-free energy source."

"You remember that?" Katya prompted.

Toner and Molotova were speechless. They traded wide-eyed glances, imagining the potential ramifications of such a discovery. A scientific breakthrough of such a magnitude would change the world, solving mankind's energy and pollution problems forever.

"Yes, we remember," the adults replied, awaiting the twin's announcement that they, the children of Nyentzi, had calculated a way to do the impossible.

"Well, that's not one of them."

"Nope, can't be done."

"Never happen…"

"Pure Hollywood."

23

A CHANGE HAS COME

Kaloostian was not an easy person to please at 6:00 A.M. He'd completed his interview with James Revkin five hours earlier. With barely three hours of restless sleep, his mood was ugly and not likely to improve.

Nothing was going right. The dossier he'd requested on Eldon Tyrell had been emailed while he slept. Staring at the scant information on his computer screen—barely two pages—he gained a new appreciation of how difficult flushing the man into the open would be.

The group that had compiled Tyrell's file was the best. Anger at the brevity of the report would be counterproductive. Simply put, no concrete intelligence on Eldon Tyrell existed. What little Greg had was public information, largely attributable to the *Entrepreneur Magazine* reporter who'd written an article on ETI's phenomenal success in the temporary employment industry. Attempts to reach the reporter were unsuccessful.

Kaloostian's usually reliable source had been unable to unearth any fresh material. In this new millennium, most twelve-year-olds had a more extensive electronic dossier than Eldon Tyrell. As frustrating as that was, Greg took this to mean they were on the right track. Someone had expended a great deal of money and effort to remain so anonymous.

Greg had to consider another, more disturbing possibility. Eldon Tyrell operated a fairly prominent business. While a successful businessperson might be able to hide from John and Joan Public, circumventing the scrutiny of telemarketing firms, charities, and for-profit databanking companies was impossible. Such a brief dossier must mean Tyrell had help.

"From the government?" Kaloostian mused. "But if that was the case, why the Revkin file, which also suggested government involvement?" The inconsistency was disturbing. Was the right hand hiding Eldon Tyrell from the left hand? And if so, why?

This piece of the puzzle refused to fit, drawing Kaloostian to an unnerving supposition: Were there two distinct puzzles? Were two opposing forces at work? None of it made sense, and his frustration was a dangerous distraction.

Suada had been no help, either. She had never met Tyrell and had no idea where he lived. All she knew was that his number was unlisted and communication to and from him went through a messaging service. Attempts to hack into the messaging center were unsuccessful.

Kaloostian's annoyance grew. "Two thousand dollars for a two-page fucking report...sonofabitch." He sat back in his wheelchair and took a deep breath. He picked up a cube of Post-it Notes®, flung it across the room, and started cursing in Armenian.

The situation wasn't about to get better. Al Hatton had called late the night before with his own troubles, of a more personal nature. The deputy assistant director had described his encounter with the gang members to Kaloostian, fearing it was not by chance.

The confrontation in the alley had come after a second call from the director of the FBI yesterday afternoon. The director demanded the whereabouts of the Revkin file, calling it by name rather than "the disk from NSA." When Hatton admitted he hadn't heard from the agent in question, his boss said the matter was out of his hands—that Hatton was on his own.

"Out of his hands," Hatton had screamed at Kaloostian. "The head honcho of the fuckin' FBI told me it was out of his hands. What the fuck is going on? What the fuck was on that goddamned disk, Kaloostian? And why the fuck haven't you been at work all week?"

Greg had pleaded ignorance, alleging illness. He'd tried to calm Hatton down, but that was next to impossible. The dropped white glove was the clincher.

By 2008, LA street gangs had begun to organize themselves, to champion codes of conduct in an effort to reduce unsanctioned hits and reprisals among rival organizations. Before settling any score, bangers were required by their leadership to notify the target by means of a dropped glove. The new street decorum had opened fresh avenues of communication among the gangs and slowed the escalating violence.

But whoever had dropped the glove in the alley behind his house was following the rules, not looking for conversation. The message was clear. Watch your back, old man.

Kaloostian could identify with his troubled friend, especially since Hatton's clouded karma seemed contagious. Angela Toner hadn't contacted Greg since Tuesday. The two women had left a message on Molotova's voicemail service, which he had picked up yesterday, but they hadn't accessed *his* messages. They *must* call him before meeting the twins in Moscow.

Then there was Toner's visa. The Russian government had revoked it the day after Alexander Samanov's mysterious death. The U.S. State Department had also made noise concerning the whereabouts of the wayward FBI agent. The department had listed her as missing and even notified her family. Greg almost called her parents to ease their fears, but he suspected their phone was tapped.

Hatton had been right, after all. Toner's face would show up on the side of milk cartons across three continents if she didn't turn up soon.

All his attempts to trace the whereabouts of Toner and Molotova through the Internet had been unsuccessful. Just his luck. For the first time since they'd become friends, Angela Toner was following his advice—to the letter. She'd not used her credit cards, and she hadn't gone on-line.

Finally, there were the children. "How in the hell have they been kept under wraps all these years?" Kaloostian asked himself. "They tracked my number after I bounced the signal six times. Where the hell have they been hiding?" Then Greg's face lit as he remembered an incident that had occurred on the Internet three years earlier. "Could it be? Was that them?"

In the spring of 2004, the children would have been only four years old. That year, someone had made multiple attempts to break into highly classified and well-fortified web sites. The attacks had come from the four corners of the world, synchronized beyond the known capability of the typical script-kiddie. Word on the street was that some whiz kid had perfected an access program to an amazing degree of sophistication and distributed it to a circle of cyber-buddies.

The routine had been consistently annoying. It started with a single hack at the front door of a corporate or government victim. After electronic security parameters easily defeated the initial on-line encroachment, a second call arrived on a different circuit. Again the attack was defeated. Then a third, fourth, fifth…until the blitzkrieg. Ten, twenty, forty, as many as seventy coordinated calls, all within seconds of each other, each from a different source, all aimed at the same target.

By sheer strength of numbers, the crackers overwhelmed the frantic defenses. Once inside, they copied a useless file, downloaded it, and departed. They'd never left a virus and never compromised the host's security. An elaborate prank, no harm done.

The crackers had called themselves "Shadow Chasers." "We're everywhere, we're everywhere," they declared.

The perpetrators behind the scheme apparently grew bored and moved on. Or did they? Was there another reason for the escapade? Was it all an elaborate diversion? While the "Shadow Chasers" overloaded the system's main line of defense, did someone sneak in through the back door and do some real damage?

"Was that them?" Greg asked himself again. He took a breath, multi-tasked to the communication program, and typed a command to call his neighbor, Suada Sivac. Under the circumstances, he must tell her the truth about Eldon Tyrell.

Her phone rang once, then a pause, followed by the unmistakable blast of a shotgun. Then he heard the scream.

Lara began the answer, "We couldn't color within the lines…"
Katya finished, "…if that's what you mean."
Toner and Molotova had dropped the charade. Since the Gracheva girls knew so much about the two agents, they asked the twins about their physical and mental growth, hobbies, favorite toys, and Nyentzi.

Both girls sat in their padded chairs, dressed in identical smocks. The visitors had found folding chairs and set them up next to their enthusiastic hosts.

"I was just curious," Toner said.
"Our physical development was normal, Angie."
"Pretty much normal."
"Yes, there wasn't much we could do until our muscles grew…"
"…and our fingers learned to work together. But we talked at a very young age."
"Language is easy for babies."
"An average four-month-old recognizes phonemes in languages as dissimilar as Hindi or Swahili."
"And we were a little faster than that."
"Our mothers talked to us in the womb."

"To help our development. Because of that, we could operate computers when we were only two."

"Naturally, we used voice recognition at first."

"Is that when you began communicating with your sisters?" Toner said.

"We think so, but we always knew they were out there."

"Kind of a sixth sense."

"It was easy to find us," Lara laughed.

Katya joined in. "No problémo…"

"Black and blue…"

"But who knows which is which…"

"And who is who."

Their mood was contagious. Despite their deep sense of sadness over the girls' deteriorating medical condition, Angela and Nadezhda couldn't help but smile.

"How many are you?" Molotova asked.

"Thirty-seven," Lara and Katya said.

The smiles on the adult's faces disappeared. "Only thirty-seven—so few?"

"Pairs. Thirty-seven pairs of us."

The girls squealed in delight. "Can you imagine?"

"Plus Melissa," Katya added, instantly reversing the mood.

"Yes, plus Melissa," the adults chimed in.

"The other eggs were duds," Lara explained.

"Except poor Melissa. Her twin died before she was born."

The girls reached out and touched fingertips. "The only loss. We've been lucky."

"Very lucky. Melissa could never bond without a twin."

"And that's important."

"It's how we survive with the memory thing," Katya said.

"All the thoughts inside our heads."

"Working as a team keeps us on the path."

"All those thoughts can be overwhelming if there's no one to share them with."

Both adults began to speak. Toner stopped and nodded to Molotova, who then asked a question.

"What is it like when you communicate with your sisters?"

"It's like talking to yourself, only better."

"All of us are a lot alike…"

"…but also unique in our own way."

"We experience the whole world through each other's eyes."

"That sounds really neat," Angela said. "All of your parents must be very proud, and very busy. I suppose you're all perfect little angels, too."

"Ha, who told you that?" Lara asked, wrinkling her nose.

"Oh, come on. You mean some of you get into trouble? Who might that be?" Angela asked with a smile.

The twins laughed: "Erin and Emily!"

"Who?" Molotova asked.

"Our sisters in Denver," Lara laughed

"They're incorrigible. All sorts of trouble."

"Their parents caught them with a forbidden book," Katya explained.

"Gave 'em heck."

"Forbidden book? That sounds like censorship. What book was it? *Catcher in the Rye?*"

"*Fear of Flying?*" Nadezhda suggested.

"Oh no, nothing so mundane."

"Erin and Emily were reading *Green Eggs and Ham.*"

Molotova's eyes widened. "Are you being serious? That's a child's book. How can it be forbidden?"

"It's forbidden for us."

"Why?" Toner asked.

"Because it's full of useless information."

"We're not supposed to waste our minds on such things."

"But those Denver girls…"

"We think it's the high altitude."

"Makes 'em crazy, up and down and round and round."

"They misbehave more than any other sibling team."

Toner waved her hands. "Wait, wait, wait. Is all information restricted in some way?"

"No, but there are some things our parents don't want us wasting time with."

"Like AM radio…"

"…and talk shows."

Toner laughed. "I've got no problem with that."

"And *Nickelodeon*," Lara continued.

"Oh, come on. That's the kid's network. You're still a bunch of kids."

"Well…" The girls showed make-believe indignation.

"Thank you for the vote of confidence, Angie," Katya said. Lara poked her sister, and they both laughed it off.

Toner smiled. "You know what I mean. All work and no play makes Jill a dull gal, right?"

"True, but we still have to be careful."

"We can't misuse our gift on extravagant…"

"…superfluous…"

"…useless information."

"Could you give us an example?" Toner asked, eager to learn more.

"Okay. Angie, when did Columbus stumble onto the New World?"

"1492."

"Naddie, name the castaways on Gilligan's Island."

"The skipper, Gilligan, Mary Ann, Ginger, the professor. Oh, and Mr. and Mrs. Howell."

"See, all meaningless information."

"Hold on, 1492's a pretty important date," Toner asserted.

"For whom?" Lara asked.

"And by whose criteria? American Indians, Italians, cartographers?"

"My third-grade teacher, for one." Toner said.

Molotova absentmindedly whispered to herself in Russian.

Lara and Katya covered their mouths and sniggered.

Toner glanced towards her partner. "What was that?"

"Naddie inferred that what's important is a matter of personal prejudice." Katya answered, grinning from ear to ear.

Lara roared her approval. "She said it's a *pissing* contest."

Both girls erupted into a flurry of giggles.

"That's really nice, Ms. Molotova. Corrupting the youth of Russia with your locker-room talk."

"Sorry, but I see what they mean," Nadezhda said. "What some educator says does not make an arbitrary date any more important than the cast of a rerun show."

Toner tried to defend herself. "Come on, you're all ganging up on me."

"No, it is true," Nadezhda continued. "1492 is only a year using one calendar system that is not even accurate as to the actual birth of Jesus…"

"…ignoring the Muslim, Jewish, Chinese, Mayan, and other chronologies altogether," Lara added.

"In a thousand years…"

"…in ten thousand years, 1492 will be relevant only…"

"…to teachers who don't know how to teach…"

"…or *what* to teach…" Katya said, with surprising conviction.

"…or how to recognize permanence versus trivia."

Angela waved her arms and raised her voice slightly. "Hold it. Are you guys saying time renders all information obsolete?"

The twins exchanged a quick glance. Lara nodded and Katya answered Toner's question. "Not all. But we need to realize that what's important today…"

"…might not be important tomorrow."

"Our species does have a tendency to fixate, Angie."

Lara shook a finger at both adults. "Look at what happened to the Neanderthals."

"You said our species." Naddie asserted. "Neanderthals were a different species."

Katya looked Molotova in the eye. "You're sure of that?"

"Well, I read in the…" Her voice trailed off.

"We read that Elvis is still alive."

"And that aliens built the pyramids."

"And that…"

"Okay, we get the point. What about the Neanderthals?" Angela asked.

"They fixated. They chose one site to inhabit, then never moved."

"Never migrated. Overpopulation, overhunting, deforestation."

"On a small scale, but look at the consequences."

"Self-inflicted annihilation," Katya concluded.

Toner and Molotova said nothing, startled by the sudden change in the girls. In seconds, they had metamorphosed from tittering children to unbelievably mature individuals of unfathomable complexity. Angela looked closely at the girls before asking another question.

"I guess I can't understand a world where everything is remembered," she said.

Katya smiled. "It's not easy…"

"But it's also not what your silly friend Gregory thinks."

"You know Kaloostian?" Angela said, her perception of the twin's innate abilities increasing every moment.

"We know *of* him."

Katya poked her sister. "He thinks we're all schizophrenic."

"A very *clinical* interpretation," Lara said.

"But we're not. We're bleedin' quadrophrenic…"

"Times thirty-seven," they chortled, suddenly little girls again.

After a moment, the twins settled down.

"It's not easy, Naddie and Angie. It often takes hours of debate with our sisters…"

"...to determine what's important and what's not."

"There is always the danger of placing greater significance on a fact..."

"...or event, or equation, or theorem than there should be."

"For example, do you know the real reason Jesus was nailed to a cross?"

The adults leaned forward, eager to hear the explanation. "Tell us," Angela pleaded.

"You might be surprised," Katya said.

"You might be angry," Lara added.

Toner didn't care. She suspected Molotova felt the same. As much as they had discussed the need to learn the truth about Nyentzi, the two agents had an unspoken though no less important reason for wanting to hear the twins' explanation.

Nyentzi was the opportunity of a lifetime, of several lifetimes, of a millennium. Angela's love of philosophy and her search for the mysteries of life had begun when she first learned to talk. She had repeatedly, incessantly, asked her more-than-patient father the three-letter question "why?" She was never satisfied—never accepted anything at face value. Her father tried to explain the fallacy of her search. He told her that the answers to life's questions could not be communicated, could only be learned through personal experience and experimentation.

As much as Angela accepted that explanation, she never stopped looking for the answer or asking the same questions—over and over again. Thus she empathized with the Revkins, Grachevs, and scores of other surrogate parents who'd participated in the Nyentzi Project. If Molotova's assessment of Yuri Tyrellovich's hunger for information was accurate, then her long search might be over, for in these two small children were the wisdom and knowledge of the ages—ingested, absorbed, and analyzed. All she had to do was ask.

Hearing the answer was going to be better than sex, *good sex*.

For a moment, neither girl spoke. They seemed to understand the importance of the moment, to feel the anticipation.

Finally Katya began, "When the mysticism is stripped away…"

"…and the ideology restrained…"

"…then you reach the essence of truth."

"Jesus was nailed to the cross…"

"…to keep him…from falling off."

Angela felt as if she'd been kicked in the stomach. She couldn't believe her ears. Staring at the twins, she waited for the real answer. She waited for a sign, waited for their good-natured laughter, indicating a mischievous joke.

As the seconds ticked by, Angela knew the twins were serious. She looked at Molotova and saw on her friend's face an expression not unlike the one she surmised was on her own.

"We told you," Katya said at last.

"You understand, don't you?" Lara asked.

"I…I don't know if I do or not. I'm not angry, though," Toner fibbed.

"Nor am I," Nadezhda interjected. "But I would like to know your explanation."

"Too often in theology, we venerate the symbol and forget the reason."

"Why a god would give of himself…"

"Or herself. Sacrifice part of himself…"

"Or herself, for another being?"

"What if Jesus had been drowned?"

"Or thrown into a lion's den?"

"What then? Would a different symbol change the meaning…"

"…or purpose of his life?"

"Remembering his deeds, his life, any life…"

"…is what matters. Life—not death."

Angela met Molotova's glance.

"Go for it, Angie," Nadezhda said, preferring to be a spectator.

Toner nodded. "If you say so." She turned back to the children.

"Okay—Lara, Katya—I see what you mean. Someone's life is more important than how they died. That makes sense. But what about Jesus as a person versus Jesus as a deity? If he was the Son of God, then who or what is God?"

"God is God, whether he…"

"Or she has one name or a hundred…"

"…or a billion billion names. In each of us is a vision, some with names, others nameless."

"And that unique vision…"

"That *belief* is God," Lara stated.

"God is eternal gratitude for all we are."

"From the birth of the first star to today's snowfall."

"God is eternal veneration for all things past and all things to come."

"All that is now and all that is gone."

"God is understanding the difference between importance…"

"…and impermanence."

Angela shook her head in confusion. "I'm going to have to think about that for a while, for a long while. But I've got another question. If God is what you say he…or she is, then what's God's message to each of us?"

Lara wrinkled her nose. "We can't tell you that anymore than we can tell you the meaning of life," she insisted.

The twins smiled at each other. "And the answer to the meaning of life is *not* 42. Besides, if you knew, that would take all the fun out of life. However…"

Toner's mouth opened, and she sharply inhaled.

"…If you must know…"

"The message, the secret to life, to our very existence…"

Toner moved to the edge of her chair, bewitched.

"Is that there is no single message or immaculate word…"

"No absolute truth or optimal experience."

"There are only our actions and our perception of life…"

"And that perception is, in and of itself, an impermanent illusion," Katya concluded.

Angela sat back and said nothing. After several seconds, she reached into her computer bag and took out a small notepad. Both girls eyed her with suspicion.

"Tsk, tsk, That will get you nowhere," Lara admonished.

"As soon as you put thoughts to words, you open them up to reinterpretation…"

"Or misinterpretation. One misspelling, one imprecise translation, can change the meaning."

"Can change the very aspiration of a theology." Katya pointed to her head. "Up here, Angie. It's all up here. That pencil and paper will do you no good."

"How did we ever get on this unending topic?" Molotova asked, looking at everyone else in the room. "We will be here until the barn is full."

"Because we had to get it out of the way," Lara said.

Toner looked surprised. "You knew we were going to ask about religion?"

"Of course. It was a mathematical determination."

"Common sense," Katya added.

"It's a question anyone would want the answer to."

Toner put the notebook and pencil down and breathed deeply. "All right, you two. I give up. You can talk circles around me for weeks. But I think we should get back on track."

Molotova joined the conversation. "Yes, we had prepared several other questions. Do you mind if I ask you something different?"

"We knew from birth there was something different with us…"

"And something wrong."

"We knew our time was limited."

"We…"

Molotova waved her arms. "Stop, stop. How did you know I was going to ask such a question?"

"We just told you: mathematical determination."

"A simple calculation of what someone would want to know about us."

Angela's mouth opened as she prepared to ask a quick question.

Lara beat her to the punch. "No. We can't read your mind. Don't worry about that. We can perceive your emotions, your gestures, and body language."

"But it's not fair to you. We're a team, but we can't read each other's minds, either."

"We feel what the other is thinking."

"It's an extra sense for us, an unconscious awareness of the other."

Toner looked at Molotova and together they laughed. "In that case," the American said. "Why don't we sit back and let you tell us about yourselves without our interference."

"Good idea, Naddie and Angie. You want to know about our aging and approaching death."

"You want to know if we are anxious or upset," Lara said. "No, we are not."

"You want to know why. Well, what are we supposed to do?"

"Wail and gnash our teeth?"

"It's a side-effect. How can we be upset about such a thing?"

"Nothing in life is to be feared. It is only to be understood."

"Madame Curie," Katya said, offering the source of the quotation.

The look on Toner and Molotova's faces was grim. "Isn't there something that can be done?" Toner asked.

"No. It's normal programming for the molecular clock to quit."

"Our immune system is weakened."

"I have to believe there are alternatives. Intensive gene therapy," Toner insisted.

"Don't you think it's a little late for that?"

"No. There's got to be something someone can do."

"When you're up to your ass in alligators is hardly the time to drain the swamp."

Katya's swamp allegory stopped Toner in her tracks. Like something her grandfather would say. For the first time she looked at the twins and did not think of them merely as extraordinarily gifted children. Instead of interrupting, she remained quiet.

"Angie, Naddie, you need to understand. We are not sad about our death."

"We will not fight the natural course of events."

"Death will come, and we're prepared, better than you can imagine."

"I'm sorry, kids. It makes me sad," Angela said quietly, shaking her head.

"And me as well," Molotova added.

The children became serious.

"Please, see it from our view," Katya said. "This is not a life that should be wished on anyone."

"We are biological prisoners in our own rooms."

"God knows it's not what we would choose…"

"…to do. Even so, we have made the most of our lives."

Lara paused for a moment before continuing. "So please, don't worry about us."

"Come on, let's change the subject. We'll show you the work we've done."

"We'll show you the real Nyentzi Project."

"Things we've created—designs and diagrams and blueprints…"

"…inventions and plans. Some of them by Miyoko and Hiroshi in Kamakura…"

"And Shushila and Juli in New Delhi…"

"And Jiazhen and Fengxia in Shanghai…"

"And Hannah and Dvorah in Tel Aviv…"

"And the twins in Nairobi, and Dublin, and Belgrade, and Marseilles, and São Paulo."

The girls swiveled in their chairs and typed the access codes to their computers. Toner and Molotova silently pulled their chairs closer.

"The hour is up," Josef Grachev said as he knocked on the door. "Please conclude your business. Girls, it's time to get ready for bed."

Everyone looked up. Toner glanced at her watch. She'd been staring at the computer for so long her neck was stiff.

"You're sure all these things will work?" she asked, rubbing her neck and regretting the question the moment the words came out.

Both girls rolled their eyes. "Grown-ups! Don't you think…"

Toner held up her arms in mock surrender. "Wait. Before you go ballistic. I meant to ask whether you've tested all these designs. So far, this is just computer-generated, right?"

"Trust us. Everything will work."

"Okay? Whatever you say." Angela stood up and reached for her bag. She met Molotova's glance. "What?" she retorted. "I was just asking."

"Always the doubting Thomas."

The American felt a tug on her sleeve. It was Lara. "Angie, do you have any gum?"

"Gum? Sure, if you like sugarless."

"That would be fine."

Toner sat back down and unzipped the side flap of her computer bag. She burrowed through the pocket, feeling for a pack of gum while Lara waited at her side.

Katya suddenly exclaimed: "Hey, we've got email."

Toner turned to look. She absentmindedly held the pack of gum out for Lara, who took it from her hand. After taking two pieces, Lara glanced at the adults to make sure they weren't looking. She removed a five-inch-square envelope from the front pocket of her smock. Keeping her eye on Toner and Molotova, she slipped the envelope into the bag along with the gum, hiding it from view.

The child whispered into Toner's right ear. "I put the gum back. Thanks."

Angela turned to Lara with a smile. "No problem, honey," she said, reaching down and closing the bag.

Lara smiled in return. She looked at her sister and handed her a stick of gum. Though nothing was said, the message was clear. Mission accomplished.

"Hey, Katya," Lara said. "We can look at the email later. Let's be polite and see our guests out."

"Good idea. Sorry, Naddie and Angie. We can't leave our room."

"Papa Joe will get very angry."

Molotova laughed. Seeing Toner's confusion, she explained. "That is what the people affectionately called Josef Stalin—Papa Joe. These days it is not much of a compliment."

"You kids. Well, I guess this is it, then. I hope we can see you again." Toner gave each girl a hug.

"We do, too"

Molotova smiled and followed Toner's example. "And we will be sure to keep our promise. Is there anything else you need?"

"A kitten!" the twins exclaimed with heartfelt laughter.

"We will have to see about that." There was a tear in Molotova's eye.

The girls stood next to their computers as the visitors walked to the door. Lara looked up at Toner with absolute earnestness. "Are you ready, Angela?"

"Huh? I think I've got everything."

The door opened. Josef Grachev waited as the women stepped out. After a final backward glance at the smiling faces of the children, Toner and Molotova slowly walked away. The father closed the door, leaving the children alone in their room.

"Suada? Are you okay? Open the door. It's me, Greg." He pounded again harder, leaning dangerously forward in his wheelchair.

"Greg?" Her voice was faint and quivery. "Is that you?"

"Yes. What happened? Are you okay?"

"I'm all right. Wait a moment. I'll unlock the door."

Kaloostian could hear her trembling hands fumble with each lock. Finally the door opened, and Greg was able to see into his neighbor's apartment. A rocking chair was five feet from the door, a shotgun on the floor in front of it. To his right he could see the damage from the blast.

Suada stuck her head out from behind the door. "I'm sorry. Did I wake you up?"

"To hell with that! What happened to you? You see a roach or something?"

"Come in, quickly. I'll tell you then."

Greg wheeled into the apartment. "I can't believe nobody else heard that. 'Course, Old Lady Johnson's deaf as a heavy-metal groupie. Nice shooting, though."

Suada closed and locked the door. "It was an accident. I jumped when the phone rang. Oh, Greg. What am I going to do? I'm in real trouble."

"Nah, the tenant's union won't evict you just for this."

"No, something else, something worse. About Eldon Tyrell and the software you asked me about."

Suada went over to the rocking chair. She sat down and started to rock. Without saying a word, she reached into the pocket of her robe and pulled out a piece of paper, the email message she had received ninety minutes earlier. She began to read it again. After a moment, she looked up and handed it to Kaloostian. He took it and read. By the time he'd finished, his breathing was heavy. Biting his upper lip, he considered what next to do.

"Get dressed. We're getting out of here," he said at last.

"Where are we going?"

"Not far. There's someone I want you to talk to. Trust me, Suada. Everything will be all right."

The van was an everyday shade of charcoal gray and had heavily tinted windows. Its license plate was untraceable. Nothing distinguished the vehicle—nothing at all. Anyone recalling it would be able to provide few details.

Inside the van's comforting darkness were two men. The first sat in the driver's seat. He wore a communications headset, the mike pushed off to one side. Matching the van, he wore nondescript dark clothes. The only peculiarity worth noting was the Rolex watch on his left wrist. Not an imitation, it was worth more than fifteen thousand dollars.

The second man sat in a padded captain's chair in rear of the van. Like his associate in front, he wore colorless clothes and matching headset. No Rolex, but he held something even more precious.

In the silence, his black-gloved hands pampered a sniper's rifle. He waited, and he caressed. His left hand stroked the long, hard barrel, his right toying with the trigger guard. The sniper had been sitting there almost sixty minutes. If necessary, he'd wait sixty more. He knew they were inside. It was just a matter of time.

Movement—at the front door of the apartment building. He saw the quarry. They opened the door, stepped outside, looked around, chatted. He imagined he could hear their idle conversation.

"They've left the apartment," said the man in back, toggling a voice-activated circuit.

At first, there was silence. Then someone answered. "Is anyone with them?"

"No, they're alone."

"Keep watching," said the voice in accented English. The men in the van had never met the person behind the voice. Neither did they know his name. He was a steady customer, paid his fees, and was generous with gratuities.

They'd never been able to place the accent, though they'd discussed it more than once. His command of the English language was excellent, but he was not a native speaker, not Anglo, not American. He was educated, polite, but with a lack of emotion in the voice. Even by their standards it was unnerving. Nothing seemed to faze him. Good news, bad news, he always sounded the same.

"Has anyone else come out?" asked the voice.

"No."

"Where are they now?"

"They're moving down the block."

"Good. How does it look?"

"They will soon be under a street lamp. Line of sight is good. Distance, maybe the length of a soccer field. Won't be a problem."

"Perfect."

After a moment, "They're under the lamp. You're going to have to decide now. You want a single or a double?"

The silence was chilling. "A double. Do them both. Our friend's usefulness has come to an end."

"Sounds good. We'll be in touch."

"Good luck."

The connection terminated. The man behind the voice leaned back and smiled. In less than five minutes, his migraine would go away. Then he would then finish cleaning up the mess instigated by the meddlesome Americans. Turning in his chair, Eldon Tyrell began to stand. He stopped when he noticed that his computer screen had gone black.

"Damn," he swore, retaking his seat. Thinking the monitor had shorted out, he reached behind it to check the electrical connection. At that moment, the first word appeared.

In crimson type on a charcoal-black screen, four letters emerged. In slow motion, particles of each letter oozed and dripped, mingling red with black. The word reappeared as the macabre animation continued:

Fire...fire...life's backwards...life's backwards people turn around the house is burned...the house is burned the children are gone fire...fire...fire on Babylon oh yes, a change has come...

The final words were not blood-red but appeared to be engulfed in flame. He only stared as the words flickered and glowed. So powerful was the image, he could almost smell them burning.

They had warned him never to underestimate their abilities, but he had laughed it off. They had advised him of the consequences of his behavior. They had foretold "the fire on Babylon." But what did his sisters expect? They were *only* children.

"Only children? How did they get into my personal system? How did they find me here? My god, what have I done?" His hands shaking, his breath shallow and quick, Eldon Tyrell worked frantically to reconnect with the men in the van, hoping it was not too late.

24

▼

Snow Angel

Their wrath was light-years beyond their age. With a rage matched only by their intelligence, seventy-four children set out to destroy the man who believed he controlled them. That man—their half-brother—was Eldon Anton Tyrell, once known as Anatoly Yuriovich Tyrellovich, the son of Yuri Tyrellovich and his wife, Marta. Seven years earlier, after emigrating from Russia, he'd taken the name Eldon—meaning *from the East.*

He was thirty-four years old. Other than the twins, he had no family, friends, or lovers. He was alone in a world that did not understand or appreciate his genius, vision, or tenacity.

Though his name never appeared on the Fortune 500 list, Eldon Tyrell was one of the richest men in the world. In monetary terms, his affluence was comfortably sufficient. But in the new millennium, where wealth was gauged in terms of information and the power it bought, his personal riches knew virtually no bounds.

Eldon Tyrell was a robber baron of the Fourth Wave, powerful and ruthless, devoid of any sense of enlightened morality. To his seventy-four half-siblings, each the product of genetic experimentation at the Monogovody research facility, Tyrell was a requisite evil—as much a part of their strategy as they were of his. Out of necessity, they'd cooperated with him for seven years. To their credit, they never trusted him. To their regret, they underestimated the magnitude of his malevolence.

Now they had proof he had lied to them. Twins Gerta and Ilse of Düsseldorf had intercepted a wireless communiqué. Eldon Tyrell had gone back on his word. He had broken a promise to his half-sisters. And he had even crossed his heart.

Despite their apparent naiveté, the children had suspected Eldon would prove untrustworthy; and they'd long ago taken precautions. Now, with evidence of his duplicity and knowledge that his actions endangered everything they worked for, they activated electronic countermeasures. The children of Nyentzi were so confident of success that they directed their first barrage at their half-brother's personal computer.

He'd had his chance. They'd warned him of the "fire on Babylon." Eldon Tyrell would learn never again to take them for granted. "Oh yes, a change has come."

"It's nice to know they can be surprised," Molotova said, donning her coat after she and Toner took the elevator to the lobby. Josef and Roza Grachev had shown them out graciously, relieved the visit was over.

"No kidding," Angela chuckled, thinking about Lara and Katya. "They seemed irritated when we told them what was written in Dmitri's journal."

Molotova nodded. "And because one of Tyrellovich's scientists kept such written notes, that was how we knew about the third component of the Nyentzi Project, their designs and inventions. They never suspected the journal existed because it was written, not electronic. With their computer capabilities, those kids can access files anywhere. Now I understand why they know so much about us. Every time we go on-line, charge something, subscribe to something, send email, receive email, it leaves a trail."

"For a while there, I thought they knew everything. Man, they really had me going. And how they seemed to be able to read our minds…"

"And each other's. Very weird, Angela."

"Their room was so organized. You notice how carefully everything was arranged?" Toner asked.

"What is so unusual about that? Not all children are messes."

"C'mon, these are kids who never forget. They can leave their room as sloppy as they want and still find their favorite toys. Maybe it's not a big deal. I just thought it was pretty remarkable. And what about all those scientific and philosophic theories? You understand everything they said?"

"Perhaps in ten years. Perhaps when…" Molotova said, her voice trailing off.

Toner turned towards her. "When what?"

The Russian sighed. "Nothing. You know, Angela, I cannot forget the look of loneliness on the girls' faces when we left them. Until we met them, until I saw them as children, they seemed so remote, so unreal. Now, I feel something I have not felt before."

"What, pity?"

"No. Anger. I am angry about the injustice done to all those poor children. They did not ask to be changed or altered to the notion of Tyrellovich or Mercereau. They did not volunteer."

"Isn't that true for all of us?" Toner asked.

"You know what I am meaning! They are hardly in normal conditions. Genetics is going to change all of us. Don't you see that? Now we are forced to take the when-does-life-begin discussion back to even before conception. And I thought abortion was confusing."

"Well, nothing we can do about it tonight. That's one debate that'll rage for the next thousand years. But not for us, not now. We've got other priorities. Let's find a good restaurant. Eat, drink, and try to be merry. Then I want to check into a five-star hotel. I've got a wad of those Eurodollars left, and they're burning a hole in my pocket. Might as well use 'em up. Maybe order some of that beer that was in my refrigerator back in Salekhard."

"What beer?"

"Didn't I tell you about that? Six bottles, good stuff, all imported."

"That is highly unusual. My room did not have such a luxury."

"Really? I figured it came with the room or that you had ordered it out of the kindness of you heart. A welcome-to-Siberia six-pack."

Molotova shook her head. "I did not order beer for your room."

"You didn't, huh? Strange," Angela said in a quiet voice.

"Nevertheless, Angie, it is still your money. You only took it as a cash advantage on your credit cards. Don't spend it all."

Toner perked up. "Every last dollar. Hatton told me the bureau would reimburse any of my expenses, and I'm gonna hold him to that promise. First-class all the way."

"Okay. Sounds like the plan."

With an exaggerated gesture, Angela threw her scarf around her neck and pulled it tight. Both women put on their gloves and hats. Molotova opened the outer door of the apartment building, and together they stepped into the darkness of the Moscow night.

The storm had passed, leaving the streets in chilly silence. Though the apartment sidewalk had recently been shoveled, both women walked carefully over the patches of ice. The wind picked up, blowing snow back onto the path. Toner especially was cautious. Her right ankle, tightly wrapped in an ace bandage, throbbed.

Earlier, a snowplow made a halfhearted pass down Svoboda Avenue, but the street running by the apartment building was deserted. Down the block to their right, Molotova spied an automobile of indeterminate make parked on their side of the street.

"I hope that is the car Peter left for us," she said, walking towards it. Toner trudged behind, limping slightly.

Molotova stepped over the mound left by the plow. Three feet of packed snow walled in the car parked next to the curb.

"This is just not perfect," Nadezhda said, her hands on her hips. She sighed and shook her head. Reaching down, she lifted the handle on the driver's side. It was locked.

"Peter gave me the key. I think I put it in my coat," she said, putting her gloved hand into her pocket and fishing about. "Found it!"

Nadezhda placed the key into the lock and tried to turn it. The lock did not budge. "Angela," she exclaimed. "The key is not working. It will not turn. I think the lock is frozen."

Toner clenched her teeth. "Jeez, is there anything else that can go wrong? Just a minute, I'm coming over." She stepped over the snowbank and joined her friend.

The American jiggled the lock. "Yep, it's frozen, all right. Here, step aside." She opened her computer bag and took out a can of aerosol dust remover she used to clean her laptop's keyboard. She squirted the lock for several seconds. Molotova then reinserted the key and turned it. After a moment, they heard a pronounced click.

"And it's *just* that easy," Angela said. "Let's get going."

Nadezhda smiled. "Hot bath, clean clothes, good food, Moskovskaya vodka!"

"Woo hoo," Toner intoned.

As Toner put the aerosol canister back into her computer bag, however, Molotova coughed hard and fell against her. Caught off balance by the Russian's entire weight, the American dropped the can into the snow.

"Look out," she cried, losing her balance.

Angela landed in a heap next to the car. Molotova sprawled across her legs.

"Hey, you all right?" she asked after her friend didn't move. For a moment, the air was still. Angela reached out and touched Nadezhda's shoulder, turning her slightly to the side. She saw blood and screamed.

Toner's reaction was instinctive. She jumped back and sat straight up. In a heartbeat, she realized her mistake, ducking down when a second bullet smacked into the left front fender of the car.

"Oh God..."

The men knew there would be few witnesses on such a frigid, windy night. They had parked the van in the 2400 block of Svoboda Avenue more than an hour before, taking position shortly after the plows made their pass down the center of the street. The engine, fueled by compressed natural gas, still ran. There was little noise and even less vapor.

The man in the driver's seat watched in his rearview mirror. "Nice shot!"

"That ski jacket. Lit her up like a neon sign," the man in the back remarked. The rear window was partly down, the black barrel of his rifle sticking out an inch or so. "One down. Where's number two? She's wearing a dark coat, blends in with the car, hard to locate. Now I see her." He gently squeezed the trigger.

"*Werlichte*. She ducked behind the snow. If our friend hadn't insisted on a small caliber, I could shoot her through the snow," the assassin said, clenching his teeth. "Come on, little Fräulein, stick your pretty head up one more time."

A familiar voice entered the communication circuit. The man in back switched off his earpiece, eschewing distraction. He waited, fully understanding human nature—the inherent desire to face danger. Her head would appear in a moment. There! He fired a third time.

The driver called back. "It's *him*. Don't shoot the second one."

"Too late. I think I got her in the head."

"No. He changed his mind," the man in front shouted, his hand covering his mouthpiece.

He removed his hand and turned again to the client. "I told him. Yes. He fired two shots, but he thinks the second one missed. We'll wait to see if she moves."

Again the driver covered the mouthpiece. "Günter, *wie geht's?*"

"She a lucky one. I see movement behind the snowbank."

"Good. He wants a few more shots to scare her. Once you force her away from the car, the second team can pick up the blonde's body."

The assassin was angry. "I don't like this. That bastard's going to pay for a double. You tell him."

"He's already agreed."

The sniper fired again. "In that case, I'll charge him by the bullet."

"I cannot feel my legs," moaned Nadezhda Andrevna Molotova. She shivered, wide-eyed, spitting blood with each labored breath. Her once-perfect auburn hair was in matted disarray. Her manicured fingers shook from the cold and her own fear.

Angela had done her best, pulling her friend around to the front of the car, away from the sniper's line of sight. Twice she had dodged the bullets, though the second had nicked her wool cap. She caught a glimpse of the van parked on the next block and knew the shots came from that direction.

Molotova was in severe pain, her breathing strained. The small-caliber bullet had struck her from behind, entered near the spine, perforated her left lung, and severed a major artery near the heart. A bloody froth covered her pale white lips.

"Go. You must go, Angela, my friend." Another bullet hit the car.

Toner held Molotova in her arms, searching for some way to make the madness disappear. "This can't be happening. What am I going to do, Naddie? I can't leave you here, but I've got to get help. I can't, I won't let you die."

"Go. Please." Nadezhda coughed blood onto Toner's coat and face. "I am sorry," she said in a tortured voice. "My brother, Vassily..." Molotova paused and tried to swallow. "Go to him. Trust no one but him. You have his address. We talked of this. Tell...tell him I love him. Please...go."

Icy tears fell down Angela's cheeks. "I won't leave you."

"For the children...you must escape." She gasped as a spasm wracked her body in reaction to massive internal damage, then closed her eyes. Toner inhaled, held her breath, refused to believe her companion was dead.

A second convulsion soon followed. Nadezhda wheezed and opened her eyes, refusing to relinquish what life remained. "Angela, I must tell you...before...too late. Your...Kaloostian...he..." She coughed again, her eyes glazing over. "He...contacted Samanov. We knew...knew you were coming...I am sorry."

Molotova loosened her grip on Toner's hand and shivered one final time. Her labored breathing stopped. Her eyes stared into the chilly tranquility of the Russian night.

The peace was short-lived. Three quick shots struck the car, one of them shattering a window. Despite the danger, Angela Toner sat transfixed in the snow, cradling her friend's lifeless body. She tried to think, tried to speak, but her muscles refused to work. She couldn't even close her mouth, gaping at Molotova's final revelation.

The sound of a siren in the distance forced her back to reality. Shaking from fear as much as cold, Angela looked down at Molotova's peaceful face. She bit her lower lip so hard in her effort not to cry that she drew blood. Twisting from under her friend's body, Toner grabbed the shoulder strap of her computer bag and shifted to a kneeling position.

She removed her hat and peered above the hood of the car. The van was gone, and the siren was getting closer. She could not rely on it. The only person Angela Toner trusted in all of Russia was dead. Nadezhda Molotova was a disheveled, bloody snow angel on a street named Freedom.

Time, for Angela Toner, was limited, and what little she had was running out. Crouching in the snow, she picked up her cap, slung her computer bag over her shoulder, and looked up and down Svoboda Avenue.

Wiping away a frozen tear, clouding the air with her breath, Angela took one last glance at Molotova. In just four days, the petite Russian had become a large part of Toner's life. Now she seemed so small. Shaking her head with angry resolve, she took a deep breath, jumped up, and leapt over the snowbank. As fast as she could, she headed for the nearest intersection, about a hundred meters down the block.

She knew she wouldn't hear a rifle shot. If they—whoever they might be—were still out there, the only warning would be the sensation of a bullet entering her body. The anticipation was so powerful that Angela disregarded her fatigue, her throbbing ankle, and the icy sidewalk.

When she reached the corner, she slipped but did not fall. Stopping to catch her breath, she scanned the snow-filled streets. After a moment's hesitation, Angela walked briskly away from Svoboda Avenue, forcing herself to ignore the pain in her right leg. Unsure of what she was looking for, the wayward American knew only that she had to keep moving.

Moscow was an old city. More than ten million souls lived within its 340 square miles. Nevertheless, Angela Toner would be easy to find. A lone woman with a slight limp, dark complexion, who did not speak the language. How far could she get?

She ignored the odds and kept walking. One block, two blocks, several more, until she saw light spilling onto the snowy sidewalk. The local pub, the kind that stays open regardless of the weather. Since most of its clientele lived nearby, however, they would be wary of strangers. Angela had no choice. Glancing back, she opened the door and entered.

Without removing her hat or scarf, she walked straight through the darkened, semi-deserted room to the bar. A heavyset, unshaven man in his late sixties eyed her with suspicion from behind the counter. He chewed an unlit cigar. His bulky, stained and patched sweater barely covered his extensive belly.

"Vodki, pozhaluista" she said, silently praying her request would be understood. She remembered Nadezhda ordering vodka.

The bartender nodded. Keeping his eyes on her, he filled a glass with clear liquid. After setting the glass down on the bar, he did not let go. Toner reached into her pocket and pulled out three Eurodollars. She pushed the bills across the bar to his waiting hand. Only then did he release the glass.

"*Spasibo*," Toner thanked the man in a hushed voice. She picked up the glass of vodka and turned around. In the far corner of the room was a small table with a single chair. Looking straight ahead, she walked to the table, put down her drink, and turned the chair for a better view of the door. Then she took her seat.

Removing her hat, scarf, and gloves, Toner tried to ignore the stares of curiosity. She unbuttoned her coat and took a drink of vodka, swallowing it without coughing. Satisfied the newcomer could hold her liquor, the local patrons went back to their own affairs.

The conversations continued in hushed tones. Every so often, someone glanced in Toner's direction before speaking, not wanting the outsider to hear a family secret. Angela didn't mind—for all she knew or cared, they could have been speaking Swahili.

For the next several minutes, Angela did nothing but sip her drink and stare into space. Eventually, she pulled her arms out of the sleeves of her coat. She then reached down and opened a side pocket in her computer bag. Her only hope was to follow Molotova's suggestion. Fishing inside the pocket, she found her notebook. Opening it, Angela saw, in Nadezhda's careful handwriting, her brother Vassily's address and telephone number.

In the same pocket was a city map of Moscow. Nadezhda had given her the map and described Moscow's layout, which was like a wheel. The circular design derived from Moscow's early history, when rings of fortifications protected the city from attack.

The twin's apartment was circled in red. The pub was around the corner and down several blocks. Angela saw that her position was just east of St. Basil's Cathedral. She remembered that Vassily lived near Lenin Stadium, about seven kilometers southwest of the Kremlin.

She found the street, Komsomolski Prospect. She would need transportation—it was too far to walk. Though Moscow had one of the finest subway systems in the world, tonight it would not do. Toner needed a taxi. She also needed a way to explain to the driver where she wanted to go. The chances of finding a cab on a night like this were slim. The chances of finding a cabdriver who spoke English were nonexistent. Ah! but she had the Kaloostian's electronic translator.

"Kaloostian, that bastard," she silently fumed. "Is that why those documents were transmitted from the Russian consulate so fast? While I was talking to Samanov, that big-chested secretary was probably getting all the specs from the Armenian."

Angela caught herself. Taking a deep breath, she tried to control her rage. There would be a day of reckoning. "And if I find out that bastard had anything to do with Nadezhda's death, I'll kill him myself."

Toner took more than half a minute to clear her mind. Then, for some odd reason, she remembered a habit of her father's that had infuriated her as a child. Every year when they went on vacation, no matter where they were, he slipped into local character, a sort of cultural empathy. After three days in England, Walter Charles Toner, her dear old dad, was sounding more like a limey than the Prince of Wales. He could lose vowels and consonants with an ease that amazed her.

While vacationing in the Caribbean, he did the same thing, though with a different accent and dialect. He said *PueRRRto RRRico*, instead of Puerto Rico, rolling each *R* with deliberate distinction. Wally Toner did it in Italy, where his gestures became extravagant, and he ogled anything in a skirt. And he did it in Germany, strutting about, ordering beer with every meal, and laughing like Santa Claus. He did it everywhere—except France. Even her father knew his limitations.

Angela never asked why he acted that way. Why was not the issue. All she had cared about was that it embarrassed the hell out of her. But now, stranded in a foreign country, Toner needed all the help she could get. Leaning back in her chair, as inconspicuously as possible, she watched the Russian people interact. She noticed the steady eye contact, the hand gestures, the frequent touching to make a conversational point.

After getting a feel for the dialogue, Angela thought about the Russians she had come in contact with. Fast-paced, businesslike, little eye contact, always in a hurry to get somewhere, if only to stand in line. Like Molotova and Kaloostian had told her: the Russian people seem cold and aloof, but once they get to know you, you're part of the family.

Watching the everyday people in the pub, Angela began to understand what she must do to blend into her surroundings. Her confidence restored, she picked up her bag and went into the women's room. It would soon be time to catch a cab.

Standing in front of a mirror, Angela was shocked by the blood on her coat, in her hair, even on her face. Thank God for the smoky light of the bar, which did not reveal the macabre stains.

She could do little about the coat and hair, so she tried to clean her face. Dabbing her face with a wet tissue, however, brought back the grisly image of Molotova lying dead in the snow. It was an image she would never forget.

The worst was yet to come. Not only did she need Vassily's help, but she also had to tell him his sister was dead. The introduction would be not be lighthearted.

After her face was clean, Angela took out the electronic translator and began to experiment. The device proved easy to use. Within two minutes, she'd created the message: "I am a mute. Please take me to this address: 14454 Komsomolski Prospect. Thank you."

Satisfied the translator would work, Toner slipped it into her pocket and picked up her bag. Just then, she noticed a halt to the buzz of conversation from the bar. She tiptoed to the door, opened it ever so slightly, and peered into the tavern. At first, she thought the lights had gone out, but then she realized something obstructed her view. It was the black coat of the very large, broad-shouldered man standing directly in her line of sight.

She looked up. Before she could make out the man's features, his fist connected with her forehead, knocking her back into the rest room. Angela Toner was unconscious before she hit the floor.

25

A Real Patriot

Awareness came slowly and painfully. Her eyes tightly closed, she could feel the hardness of the floor but little else. The jackhammer pounding in her head short-circuited all other sensations. She thought she heard a muffled conversation in Russian. As she shifted slightly the better to hear, a spasm of pain ricocheted through her body. She moaned.

A menacing voice growled. "Suchka prikhodit v sebya. Seychas pobaldeyem."

Movement—two sets of footsteps. The first, a clump of authority and hostility. The second, cautious and soft, followed at a safe distance. Rough hands grabbed her by the shoulders. Her eyes opened in fear, Angela saw only the spinning room as she flew up against the wall.

The pain intensified as she slid back to the floor. She opened her eyes again. Through flashes of pain-induced stars, she looked up at the menacing Russian.

The beast was a nightmarish cliché from a bad movie. Perhaps in his late fifties, he remained a dominating presence—massive shoulders and chest, large hands, legs like tree stumps. He had a face like a carelessly ironed cotton shirt—wrinkled, scorched, and scarred from years of misuse.

The Russian leaned down and swung his right fist at Toner's head. She cried out and tried to shield herself, but the fist stopped a mere inch from impact. He laughed at her feeble attempt to protect herself and moved away. "A nu idi syuda, shpana," he roared to the figure behind him. "Skazhi ey chto ya ey vse kosti perelomayu svoimi sobstvennimi rukami esli ona ne skazhet gde disk. Skazhi ey seychas zhe, padla!"

The giant stepped back. Toner saw she was still in the now-deserted bar. The second Russian came into focus, his face illuminated by the dim light of a single low-watt lamp on a nearby table.

"Peter!" Toner hissed.

The young Federal Security agent said nothing. Refusing to meet Toner's glare, he stepped sideways to avoid contact with his oafish compatriot. Stooping to one knee, Peter leaned nearer to the American and whispered, "He wants the disk. If you do not tell him where it is, he will break many bones in your body."

"Govori gromche, govnyuk. Ne sheptat!" the giant ordered.

Peter sighed, paused, then repeated the request in a louder voice.

Toner blinked hard and looked up at the large man standing behind Peter. She wanted to say, "It's in the computer, you freaking moron," but instead she looked at Peter. Nadezhda had said the young man was proficient with electronics. He could have removed the disk from her computer any time he'd wished. Angela searched his face for a sign of duplicity, but she saw something unexpected. The lack of resolve in his eyes gave her a glimmer of hope.

"I don't have it," she whispered after a moment.

"Chego? Gromche, suchka! Padla, vego, ona skazala?"

Peter turned slightly and translated Toner's answer.

"Gde on? Yadreniy koren, sprsiu neyo gde on," the giant demanded.

"He wishes to know where it is," Peter said, still refusing to meet Toner's icy stare.

Toner looked up at the giant. "It's in Molotova's coat, sewn into the lining," she said, her voice intentionally weak and afraid.

Peter looked into her eyes before repeating the disk's purported location.

"Chto?! Ne mozhet bit. Ya ey ne veryu."

"Tell the truth," Peter demanded, shaking a limp fist, trying his best to sound tough.

"Tell him…tell him to look in my bag. There's a sewing kit…with needle and thread. There's a knife too, with a scissors. We cut the lining of her coat and sewed it in…for safekeeping. Tell him that."

Again Peter translated,. As he spoke, he stood up and with animated gestures walked to the table. He picked up the bag and explored two of the side pockets until he found what he was looking for. Holding aloft a small sewing kit and a Swiss Army knife, Peter turned toward Angela. "Is that what you meant?" he said for the benefit of the giant.

Toner nodded as the big man roared his displeasure. He reached out and grabbed the items from Peter's shaking hand. His lips tight, he ripped open the tiny sewing kit, pulled out a small spool of thread, navy blue in color. It was half gone, with a six-inch length poking through the eye of a needle.

Cursing, he stormed to the bar and slammed it all down. He opened a bottle of vodka, poured a tumbler full, and downed it in one swallow. Finally he bellowed, opened one of the blades on the Swiss Army knife, and moved towards Toner.

Pushing Peter aside, he knelt down and placed the blade under the American's shaking nose. "Eto znachit chto ti bolshe ne nuzhna, suka. Pora…" Before the big man could finish, he grabbed his side, stood back up, grunted, and pounded on his ribcage with his fist. He turned abruptly and lurched across the room to the rest room. The door closed with a bang.

Angela exhaled. Finally able to think straight, she glowered at Peter and seethed: "I hope you're proud of yourself. And Naddie called you her friend."

"I had nothing to do with the shooting. I swear. I did not know it was to be done. I was told they wanted both of you for questions only. There was no talk about killing."

"That'll make Nadezhda feel good…knowing you'd *only* betrayed her and didn't actually pull the trigger."

Peter tried to speak, tried to defend himself, but the words stuck in his throat. As he hung his head in shame, Toner surveyed the bar. The door was on the opposite wall, her computer case in the middle of the room, and her coat likely still in the bathroom—with Ivan the Terrible. Before she could rise from the floor, Peter surmised her intent and stood up, removing a handgun from his shoulder holster.

"Do not get the intention to be leaving, Angela. I may not be of the agreement with circumstance, but I must do what I must do."

"A real patriot. Your mother must be proud." Just then, they both heard a low grunt and a string of profanities from the men's room. "What's your friend's problem—gonorrhea?"

"He has kidney stones from a very poor diet and drinking too much vodka, even by Russian standards."

Toner filed the information for future use. "What's his name?"

"Oleg. Oleg Baryshnikov," Peter replied, omitting Oleg's formal middle name, a sign of obvious disrespect that Angela Toner, as an American, would not understand.

"Like the ballet guy? They related?"

"No. No relation."

"I thought all you Russians were cousins."

"Trust me, this man is no relation to Mikhail Baryshnikov. Oleg is not related to anything human. He is a spawn of Stalin and the Communists."

Toner's mind churned. "Great, a Cold War fossil." The last thing she needed was someone with a chip on his shoulder the size of a sequoia. It limited her diplomatic options and made her impending torture and death more of an ideological vendetta than a business transaction.

"You two a team?"

"I have never to meet this man before tonight. I hope never to again."

"Then why, Peter? Why are you doing this?"

"I needed money. I had large debts…of gambling. That is why I broke into Nadezhda's computer files. That is all I was supposed to do…not this…not killing."

"Money," Toner thought, "the toughest ideology of all." Then she asked, "Who's the bank?"

Peter did not understand. "Who do you work for?" Toner translated.

"I work for Tyrellovich."

"Tyrellovich is dead."

"The father, yes. The son, no."

Angela broke eye contact as her mind raced. The events of the past four days began to make sense and increased her sense of urgency.

"Peter, you've got to help me. You don't know what you're doing, the harm you're causing. Peter…"

The young man fidgeted.

"Let me go, Peter. Please. You've got to…"

"I cannot. I *can not*. I am sorry about this, about Nadezhda. I am very sorry, but I…"

"Nadezhda is dead, Peter. Dead! You liked her. I can tell. You cared for her; I did, too. She was like a sister to me—family. You don't have to do this. You're too smart for this."

"He will kill me if I do not do what I am ordered. He will kill my family, too."

"C'mon, he thinks he's got what he wants—the disk. He thinks it's in her coat. You'll still get paid. Take the money and run. You can do it. You can let me go. You don't need me anymore. For the love of God, Peter, he's going to kill me."

Peter was silent. He refused to meet Toner's pleading look.

"Let me go" she continued. "This isn't just about money. It's about you, me, and Nadezhda, about doing the right thing. Let me go, Peter. Oleg doesn't look too bright. He won't even know I'm gone."

Peter subconsciously nodded. "You are right about that. He is very slow."

"See, Peter, you're too smart for this. Let me go. Nadezhda, your friend, is dead. People like Oleg killed her. You don't have to do this."

"Please…stop reminding me. I am sorry, but I cannot…Shhh, here he comes."

Oleg Baryshnikov was in the mood to share. Unfortunately for Angela Toner, what he wanted to share was the experience of pain, in his case from the chronic kidney-stone attacks that tormented him. Scarcely able to walk, he bashed the door to the men's room open with his forearm, stomped to the bar, and filled a glass with vodka. Downing the drink with one sloppy gulp, he wiped his mouth on his coat and waited for the buzz.

The room was silent as he contemplated his next move. He looked to his right, then his left. Finally, he reached into the pocket of his coat and pulled out the Swiss Army knife, blade still erect. He looked hungrily at Toner as his fist tightened around the knife.

He took a single step from the bar, expecting the spasms of pain to return. When they didn't, he took a second step, then another and another, his eyes squinting with hatred and anticipation at the woman on the floor.

Angela tried to move away, but to where? Her only avenue of escape was through Baryshnikov himself, a notion too preposterous to contemplate, even if her ankle were not severely sprained.

Ever nearer came the silent Russian bear, knife trembling in his clenched fist. To within ten feet, until unexpectedly, Peter issued a challenge, irresolute though it was. "*Nyet*! Nyet Oleg Baryshnikov."

The big man looked to his left where Peter stood, cradling a 9mm Makarov in his hands.

Baryshnikov's boisterous laughter was all the indication Toner needed of how serious a threat the big man considered Peter.

"Yob tvoyu mat, ublyudok!" he said.

Peter's face reddened at Oleg's insult, though he held his ground. "Leave her alone," he demanded in English for Toner's benefit. "Ostav eyo v pokoye," he said again in Russian.

Baryshnikov turned back toward Toner and took another step. Peter also moved closer, a fatal mistake. The big Russian swung his left arm out in a wide arch. Though he was not close enough to make contact with Peter, the sudden movement so unnerved Peter that he almost dropped his pistol. Before Peter could recover, Baryshnikov pivoted to his left and lunged at the scrawny Russian, caught him by the lapel, and threw him across a table.

Peter went one way, his pistol another. Before he could get up, Baryshnikov was on him. He grabbed Peter by the hair, pulled him up with his left hand, and punched the defenseless FSB agent in the face with his right.

Peter was dazed, unable to resist. Oleg wrapped his mammoth arms around him and began to squeeze the life out of his helpless prey. Angela looked on, helpless to do anything. She saw the pistol, but it was on the other side of Baryshnikov. As inconspicuously as possible, she inched towards the bar. She would be next. She needed something, anything, with which to defend herself.

Baryshnikov threw Peter on the table, and though he was already unconscious or dead, the big man slit his throat with one precise stroke. As he gloated over his kill, Angela reached the bar and moved out of his line of sight.

"Baba," the monster crooned, ignoring the corpse and spreading pool of blood. He moved closer to the bar, the only place his next victim could be. "Baba, ti sleduyuschaya."

Toner weakly stood up and stared across the bar at the man who was about to kill her. With but a few seconds to search, she had not found a weapon, not even an icepick. She glanced down and saw the bottle of vodka. Picking it up as Oleg watched, she took a small drink, put the cap back on, and tossed him the bottle.

"Hair of the dog, lard butt. Drink up," she said.

The Russian caught the bottle. He grinned, twisted off the top, and took several swigs, as if trying to impress her with his ability to hold his liquor. Bottle still in his hand, Oleg tilted his head back a final time, savoring the taste of the last vodka with a hearty laugh. Then, with amazing accuracy he tossed it at Toner's head.

She ducked, but Baryshnikov was surprisingly quick. He dove at her, but Toner dropped down and scurried toward the opening at the other end of the bar, near the doors to the rest rooms. Though her ankle throbbed, she had to get out into the open where she could maneuver. Getting to the gun was her only hope.

Before she could get past him, however, he was on her, his arms wrapped around her waist in a bear hug. He pressed tight, but Toner was ready. She inhaled, flattened her body, and almost slid out of his grasp.

Oleg was not about to let Angela go. He grabbed her around the throat and began to squeeze. She squirmed and writhed, gasping for air, searching for escape. With grim determination, she scratched and clawed. Finally, Toner found his hand and bit down with all her might.

The Russian's eyes went wide with pain and surprise. He instinctively withdrew his bleeding, incisor-branded right hand. In the same instant, Angela butted her head into his chin, catching his tongue between his upper teeth, snapping his lower jaw, and flooding his mouth with blood.

She brought her freed hands up and grabbed his. With a fierce grip, Angela twisted, tightened her grip on Oleg's uninjured left hand, and dug her nails in deep, drawing rivulets of blood. Using her weight for momentum, she dropped down.

As he squawked in pain, she lowered herself even more. Unsteady on his feet, Oleg tottered, searching for equilibrium. Before he could recover his balance, she sprang up and back, smashing his enormous body into the wall. The giant oofed, spat a mouthful of blood, and tried to catch his breath.

He never got the chance. Toner swung one elbow, then the other, directly into his undefended kidneys. Oleg howled. With the monster's hold broken, Angela spun about, her left elbow elevated and extended. She caught the gasping and confused man in the nose. The cartilage snapped, spurting blood and mucus in every direction.

Now completely turned around, Toner gave her staggering opponent one karate chop, then another, on each side of the neck. As the Russian's eyes glazed, she ended her assault with a precise and powerful kick to the groin.

Oleg sank to the floor. Angela quickly turned and searched for Peter's gun, still lying near his body. She limped over, picked it up, turned, and took aim at the moaning brute.

In a moment of indecision, she held her fire. The man had information that might prove beneficial. But he spoke no English, and she no Russian. The electronic translator was still in her coat pocket, but Angela had no energy or desire to tie him up and begin the process of interrogation.

With a tear sliding down her cheek, Angela extended her arms forward, the Makarov held tight in her hands. Through his pain, Oleg looked at the American. Their eyes met—his narrow with defiance, hers wide with hesitation.

"Dumb-ass niggar bitch," the Russian grunted in broken English, slowly rising from the floor. They were the first words Oleg had spoken that Angela understood—all too well. A firestorm of primal emotion blinded her with rage. Through the throbbing pain of his brutality and the humiliation of his words, Angela Toner fired. Once, twice, three times, in rapid succession.

Oleg Baryshnikov clutched at his chest and slumped back down on one knee. He pulled his right hand away from the wound and looked at the blood that dripped to the floor. His face revealed a new expression—fear.

He looked up. Their eyes met a final time. Her hesitancy forgotten, Toner fired again. The fourth bullet flew straight and true. The brute's head snapped back and exploded in a shower of bone, hair, and blood. Oleg Baryshnikov's body collapsed and moved no more.

Toner sighed. Her arms dropped to her sides, and the Makarov slipped from her right hand, landing on the floor with a thud. Her legs went weak, and she too collapsed. She covered her face with her hands and quietly wept.

Bundled against the cold, her computer bag slung over her left shoulder, her own weapon concealed in her coat pocket, Angela Toner left the bar. Fleeing the terrible scene inside, she limped down the block towards St. Basil's Cathedral, certain of a taxi stand near the famous landmark.

On the street, her hat pulled down over her ears, her mouth covered by her scarf, Angela's disguise was complete. The downside of her plan became apparent after several minutes. Her sprained right ankle, her battered head and bruised body, together with massive amounts of unplowed and unshoveled snow, slowed her progress to a crawl. At this rate, she'd take an hour to reach St. Basil's. By then, she'd be frozen solid.

Walking across one of Moscow's many wide boulevards, Angela spotted a taxi, weaving and sliding down the partially plowed street. She waved her arms to catch the driver's attention. The boxy, black-and-white cab slowed and finally stopped. Toner hobbled to where it waited, opened the rear door, and climbed in. She nodded to the driver, who turned to examine his unexpected fare, and played her prerecorded message.

"I am a mute. Please take me to this address: 14454 Komsomolski Prospect. Thank you."

The driver grunted in agreement and turned to the front, thankful he would not have to engage in idle chatter about politics or religion. He clicked the meter on and sped away, while Angela settled into the warmth of the cab.

As the taxi made its way through snow-clogged streets, Angela had no idea whether the back seat was clean or dirty, what color the upholstery was, what landmarks they passed. For twenty minutes, she sat perfectly still and stared at the back of the driver's head, her hand wrapped around the handle of the Beretta in her right coat pocket. She memorized each hair on his head, the mole behind his left ear, and the greasiness of his shirt collar.

Twice they crossed over the meandering Moscow River, the second time just after passing Gorki Park. A block later, the driver took a left turn onto Komsomolski Prospect. He drove another two kilometers before coming to a stop.

"Thridtsat pyat rubley," the Russian announced, entering the fare in his logbook. Angela had no idea what he'd said, so she gave him a fifty-dollar Euro bill, gesturing that he could keep the change. The driver's surprised smile was all the indication Toner needed to know she'd paid him more than enough for the ride.

She climbed out of the cab and looked around as the cab drove off. The apartment building where Vassily Molotova lived looked depressingly Soviet, built in the late 1970s. But the sidewalk was shoveled, and the foyer was clean. Best of all, its front door was unlocked.

Without taking off her hat and scarf, Angela went inside and found a row of three elevators. She pushed the up button and one of the doors immediately opened. It was unoccupied. She stepped in, punched the symbol she thought was for the seventh floor, and leaned against the wall. What might happen next filled her with dread. As much as Toner had been through with the death of her husband and unborn child, she did not know how to break the news of Nadezhda's death to her brother.

The elevator stopped, and the door opened. Angela stepped into the hallway and inspected the landing. Down either side of the hallway were apartments. She could hear music, television, and conversations in every direction, none of which she understood. Walking to her right, she searched for number 709. It was the fifth door on the left.

Taking a deep breath, she rang the bell and waited. No answer. The second ring was like the first. Vassily Molotov was not home.

She had prepared for this possibility. First she turned the doorknob and pushed. The knob wouldn't move, but the door wobbled slightly—good news, no deadbolt. Pulling her computer bag around in front of her, she unzipped a side flap and removed her wallet. From her wallet came a credit card, which she slipped between the door and the frame near the locking mechanism. She worked it around, heard a click, and pushed. The door popped open.

Making sure no one had observed her trick, she pushed the door open farther. The apartment was dark. She stepped inside and closed the door, waiting for her eyes to adjust to the blackness. From where she stood, she couldn't discern any windows. Directly ahead of her, however, was another door—to a bedroom, she surmised.

"Zdravstvuyte. Hello. Is anyone here?" Angela quietly called. Again, no answer.

The only light was from a VCR in the near corner and off to her left, in what must be the kitchen, a digital display on a microwave oven. It read 7:52. She set her bag on the floor next to the door, the Beretta still in her coat pocket. Moving slowly ahead by shuffling her feet, she headed for the bedroom door.

She knocked. "Hello...Vassily?"

Angela opened the door. A window on the opposite wall had partially closed shades. A door to the left was slightly ajar—the bathroom was her guess. A full-size bed, a nightstand, and two dressers were the only furniture. She was better able to see as she moved across the bedroom floor. Suddenly her right foot hit something heavy and sharp near the corner of the bed.

She stopped and knelt down, feeling the floor in front of her. Even through the glove, Toner could feel the cold, steel blade lying directly in her path to the bathroom—one of Vassily's ice skates. She felt around for the other skate but couldn't find it. Standing up, she went to the bathroom door, entered, and closed the door, only then turning on the light.

The bathroom was small—toilet, sink, shower. It was also surprisingly clean. Angela hated to snoop, but she wanted to learn more about Vassily before meeting him. She opened the medicine cabinet, looked inside, but found nothing unusual. No prescription medications, no hypodermic needles, no makeup. Nadezhda's brother might be normal after all.

She did find a bottle of aspirin. With as much jubilation as she could muster, she twisted off the cap, poured six of the tablets into her hand, and popped them into her mouth. She downed them with a quick drink of water. Without more than a cursory glance in the mirror at her bruised and battered face, she turned out the light, closed the bathroom door, and walked back to the living room.

Toner found a small lamp and turned it on. Though it barely lit the room, she was finally able to see all of Vassily's apartment. Like the bathroom, it was tidy. Couch, recliner, television in the corner on an old table, an antique wooden desk with matching chair, a cracked hockey stick propped in the corner next to the desk.

An L-shaped countertop separated the kitchen from the living room. Atop the counter sat a microwave oven with digital clock. "Set to the same time as the VCR," Toner admired. Aside from the dirty dishes in the sink, the kitchen was well kept.

Walking back to the front door to pick up her computer bag, Angela's gaze came to rest on a framed portrait on the desk. Nadezhda had been a young girl when it was taken, Vassily younger still. The children and their mother were in their Sunday best, the father gloriously attired in his military uniform, chest brimming with medals.

With loving care, Angela picked up the picture up, fighting tears. They were so beautiful—a perfect family. Three of the four were now dead. Setting the frame back down, Toner began to understand the sacrifices they had made, knowing all too well the Molotovs were an average Russian family.

She went to the couch and sat. Vassily, she hoped, would soon be home. Once she broke the horrible news to him, she would have to figure out what to do about the Nyentzi Project.

"I am so tired," Angela said to herself. Reaching into her coat pocket, she retrieved the Beretta. If nothing else, cleaning the gun would keep her occupied. But she was dizzy from fatigue, could barely focus her eyes…

How much time had passed? Angela Toner slowly opened her eyes, surprised she had fallen asleep. She strained to see in the semidarkness of Vassily's apartment. At last she was able to make out the object that had tapped her cheek. The barrel of a gun.

26

THE TURNING AWAY

"And just when in the hell *were* you going to tell me?" Hatton demanded. It was 8:00 A.M, Thursday. The deputy assistant director sat at his kitchen table drinking coffee with Gregory Kaloostian and Suada Sivac. He was not in a good mood.

"You'd better call Malone. Tell her you're gonna be late," Kaloostian recommended.

"Quit changing the subject. How long have you known about that damned disk?"

"You want to know the exact time, or will the day be close enough?"

Hatton leaned forward, his cup shaking, spilling coffee onto the table. "You're lucky there's a lady present, you know that? Wheelchair or no wheelchair, I'd like to kick your paralyzed butt all the way back to Armenia."

Suada's mouth opened. Unused to Hatton's early-morning demeanor, she fidgeted and looked out the window.

Greg put his hand on hers and squeezed. "Don't worry, Suada. He's like this all the time. A charming fellow…

"Okay, Al," Kaloostian said, facing his amiable host. "I was pretty sure Monday. I was almost definitely sure on Tuesday, and I was damn positive on Wednesday."

"Goddammit, how the hell could something like this happen?"

"Hadley…" Kaloostian muttered, shaking his head in feigned dismay.

"Knock off the bullshit. You're as bad as Toner," Hatton ordered. "Flippant, irresponsible attitude. Can't even answer a simple fuckin' question."

"Even if I could tell you the exact moment, it doesn't matter."

"And why the hell not? It's my butt hanging out to dry, not yours."

Greg set his cup down and looked Hatton in the eye. "Because there's something a little more important we need to discuss, something we all have in common."

"Suada and I both have the misfortune of knowing you. What else is there?"

"Cut the crap, Al. We're all in danger. And if we don't work together, we're all dead."

The scowl remained, but Hatton softened. "You don't think I'm overreacting to that dropped glove?"

"Nope. We've both seen reports of gangs contracting as murder-for-hire mercenaries. That disk is bad news, and I don't think the incident in the alley was a coincidence. It's just what we should expect from someone like Eldon Tyrell. If he's got you pegged, nailing Suada and me is just a matter of time."

"What am I supposed to do? I'll probably get my pink slip later today."

Kaloostian took a sip of coffee. "There's nothing we can do about that," he said, "so let's get to work on something constructive. Why don't you two get started analyzing Suada's software? Maybe we'll find something useful in there."

"What are you going to do?" Suada asked, finally joining the discussion.

"I'm taking a cab back to my apartment. I've got work to do, and I don't want to miss Toner's call when it comes in."

Hatton shook his head and muttered. "If it comes in."

Not only was the barrel of a gun pointed at her head, it was *her* gun. Even in the semidarkness of Vassily's apartment, she could see the markings of the Beretta. The first rule in law enforcement was "Never abuse, lose, or surrender your service pistol," which is what Angela Toner apparently had done.

She shifted her gaze from the Beretta to the man holding it, then exhaled. Vassily Molotov, his resemblance to Nadezhda too pronounced for it to be anyone else. He was tall, maybe six feet, and broad-shouldered. Angela had expected someone shorter, like his sister. He was wearing a Chicago Blackhawks starter jacket, heavy boots, and neatly pressed blue jeans.

"Like a hockey player," Angela thought.

His hair was medium brown, cut short above the ears, parted on the left. By the look of things, Naddie had used more "headlighting" than she cared to admit.

Toner couldn't tell whether his eyes were green, gray, or blue, but he had bushy eyebrows, especially near the nose, that tapered out along his forehead. Prominent cheekbones, strong chin, and big ears.

Angela started to speak, but Vassily held up his hand, demanding silence.

"I do not want to hear any more, Mrs. Jorgenson," he said in accented English. "I told you on the phone, my decision is firm."

Toner was confused. "Can I please say something?"

"It will not do you or your son any good. There is nothing to discuss."

Her mind raced. "What the heck is this kid involved in? Is he seeing a married woman?" she asked herself.

Vassily leaned closer, waving the Beretta. "And I am not certainly happy about discussing this matter in my own apartment—at gunpoint—even if it is nothing but a toy."

Seeing the puzzlement on Angela's face, Vassily sighed and shook his head.

"You American mothers just do not get it, do you? Am I to spell it out...A, B, C? Like I said, Kevin's behavior is not good, and his attitude is even the worse. He will be suspended for the next game. That is my final decision. Please, Mrs. Jorgenson, I do not appreciate having players' mothers break into my apartment. Hockey is only a sport. Give it the rest."

Toner pointed at the Beretta. "The gun, it's not a..."

"What?"

"If you'd let me talk, I could tell you. The gun is not a toy. It's real, it's loaded, and I don't think the safety's on."

"Are you being serious? A real gun? This is too much. *I quit.* Find another coach for your bad-mannered, disrespectful children. You are guests in my country, and because your husband is a big-shot diplomat, you are acting like this is New Jersey."

"I...Vassily. You are Vassily Molotov? God, I hope I'm in the right apartment."

"Da, I am Vassily Molotov."

"Good—at least I'm in the right place. Listen, I'm not one of your hockey moms."

"You're not?"

"No. Jeez, how old do you think I am? Turn on a light."

"Huh?" After a moment, he reached over and hit a wall switch, illuminating the room.

"My name is Angela Toner," she said, showing him her badge. "I'm with the United States FBI. You know what that is, don't you?"

"Yes, I know the FBI. Oh, this is about Nadezhda. What did she do now, defect?" he said, with a sudden smile. "This is a joke of hers, right? What, am I under arrest? Massive treason? Crimes against womanhood? She put you up to this, yes?"

"She told me how to find you if I needed help. Please give me the gun."

The expression on the young Russian's face changed from mirth to indecision. He looked at the Beretta, finally saw Angela's bruised face, then carefully held out his hand. The American retrieved her weapon, checked the safety, and slipped it into the holster inside her blazer.

Angela's smile was awkward. "Sit down, please. I hate to meet you like this, under these circumstances. I feel like we've already met. Nadezhda told me so much about you."

Vassily sat on the opposite end of the couch, his eyes never breaking contact. "Something is wrong. Is Nadezhda in trouble? Or is it something more serious? And look at you. What happened to your face?"

"It's a long story," Angela said, touching her bruised cheek. "Did she ever talk to you about her work?"

"Not everything, but we kept in close contact. She told me she was going out of town to meet an American. I was watering her plants this evening. You are that person?"

"Yes, we were working together on an assignment." Angela paused, broke eye contact while she searched for words.

Vassily's eyes opened wider. "There has been trouble? Something has happened to her. That is why you are here, correct?"

"Yes. We ran into trouble earlier tonight. What time is it?" Toner asked.

Vassily already knew. "Ten o'clock.," he said.

Angela sighed, barely able to continue. She put left hand over her mouth and her right arm across her chest.

"Nadezhda…was shot. We…we never saw it coming. There was…nothing either of us could have done. It happened three hours ago…on Svoboda Avenue."

"Svoboda? But that is a good part of town. Is she at the hospital? Is she going to be okay?"

"No, she's not okay. The bullet…near the heart…she died in my arms. There was nothing I could do…Whoever killed her is trying to kill me, too. That's why I look like this, why I came here. I have nowhere else to go and…and I wanted to…to tell you. "

The silence was painful.

"I…I never expected anything to happen to her." Vassily finally said, biting his lower lip and breathing deeply through his nose. "She was not in dangerous job. She was only with Federal Security for two years. How could this happen?"

"Vassily, I'm sorry. It never should've happened," Toner said, uncertain, stumbling over her words. "I shouldn't have come here. I'm really sorry. Do you want me to leave?"

"No." He abruptly stood, choking on his words, barely able to speak. "I need to go, by myself…alone…" Shielding his face, Vassily retreated to the door. He opened it and fled down the hallway. The door slammed behind him.

Angela leaned back and covered her eyes. The look of grief on Vassily's face cut right to her heart. A tear formed, though she could not cry. The one emotion coursing through her body, suppressing all others, was anger. She didn't know when, and she didn't know how, she didn't even know who, but someone, somewhere, would pay for Nadezhda's death.

Payback, however, would take time. She had other priorities, the first to check her friend's voicemail box for messages. The sooner she figured out what to do, the sooner she could leave Vassily to his grief. Toner pulled her computer bag onto her lap, opened the large side pocket, and reached in. She had written down the access numbers in her notebook. Now all she had to do was find it.

Comb, hairbrush, wallet, envelope, lipstick, gum, nail file, notebook…She removed it from the bag. As she was about to set down the bag, Angela paused and reached back inside. Having no recollection of an envelope, she took it out as well.

The envelope was of plain white card stock—the kind found at any office supply store—with no writing or label on the outside. Inside, she found a CD-ROM and a small piece of paper. Removing them both, she saw the painstakingly neat handwriting of a child. Lara or Katya—she couldn't tell.

Her hands trembled as she read the brief message: "Dear Angie and Naddie, Thank you so much for coming. It is vital that you access this file as soon as possible. We will explain everything to both of you then. Love, Lara and Katya."

Holding her breath, she flipped the note over and saw that the reverse was blank. Setting down the disk, she unzipped the main compartment of her bag, removed her laptop, and set it up. Then she opened the CD-ROM door and replaced the Revkin disk with the one from the twins. Without external prompting, a message appeared on the screen:

"Truth is an elusive abstraction There are two sides to every story, with every shade of gray between. Nevertheless, it is possible to know right from wrong, fact from fiction, winter from summer, light from dark.

We told you about Nyentzi and the things we have conceived. Much, though not all of what we have done is already in the hands of the one who seeks to use it to his advantage. You have, on this disk, that which we have managed to keep from him.

It is vital that this disk remain free from his influence. Without this disk, much of what he has will prove to be incomplete. Accordingly, it is better for this information to remain inaccessible to all, than for it to be available for his exploitation.

To prevent that, we have constructed a safeguard. To access the disk, you must enter an eight-character password. You will have three attempts. If you are unsuccessful in those three attempts, the security system will not respond to *any* external prompt for a period of one year. After that time, you will be able to enter an additional password.

If that is incorrect, you will be able to try only a single password once per year, indefinitely. That, however, would be detrimental to all. By the way, changing the date on your computer will not work.

We trust in both of you. We know you can do it. Use all of your resources. Study every piece of evidence. Leave nothing to chance. Click on the prompt for the first clue."

Angela reread the message. It sounded so unlike Lara and Katya. She couldn't imagine those smiling children writing something so serious.

"Must be all that interactive multimedia nonsense," Angela said to herself. "I never was any good at that. Not like Naddie. God, I wish she were here."

Toner sighed and continued to study the message. Then she noticed a small box in the upper-right-hand corner of the screen. She gave it a click. In an instant, what looked like a poem began to scroll:

On the turning away, from the pale and downtrodden
And the words that they say which you won't understand
Don't accept that what's happening, is just a case of others' suffering
Or you'll find that you're joining in, the turning way.

It's a sin that somehow, light is changing to shadow
And casting its shroud over all we have known
Unaware how the ranks have grown, driven on by a heart of stone
We could find that we're all alone, in the dream of the proud.

On the wings of the night, as the daytime is stirring
Where the speechless unite in a silent accord

Using words you will find as strange, and mesmerized as
they light the flame
Feel the wind of change on the wings of the night.

Toner read it again. "I'm supposed to use all of my resources, huh? Think logically...If this is the first clue, that means there are others. And first clues are notoriously vague. But there's gotta be something that points to the second clue."

Angela hung her head and covered her eyes with her left hand. For more than a minute, she did not move. Finally, she looked at the screen, rereading each verse until she noticed a repeated phrase: "*On the wings of the night* appears twice," she said. "Does that have any significance? It's night here. And daytime is stirring. Stirring in...LA...Kaloostian. He's in LA. And they told me to use all my resources."

Easier said than done. Toner wasn't sure what to do about her old friend Gregory. He'd set her up, talked her into calling the Russian consulate, talked her into pressing ahead with the Revkin case. Now she was left to pick up the pieces, all the while wondering what stake he had in Nyentzi.

Only one way to find out. Contact him and demand an explanation. He'd said he was bouncing incoming calls to prevent them from being traced, but at this point, that was not a major concern. To whom he reported and where his loyalties lay were questions Angela wanted answers to.

She looked for a phone. There, in the corner at the other end of the couch. Angela set the computer down, walked across the room, and disconnected the phone from the wall jack. She then realized the call to California involved another person—Vassily Molotov. The possibility of it being traced to his apartment put Nadezhda's brother at risk as well.

Toner sat down. After a moment's contemplation, she decided that if Kaloostian's technique for bouncing calls was good enough for him, it was good enough for her. Moreover, if the Armenian was working for the Russians, she was in more danger than Vassily.

With a shrug, Angela finished wiring her computer for audiovisual communication and plugged it into the phone jack. Opening her notebook, she dialed Nadezhda's voicemail box to check for messages. There were three, all from Kaloostian.

The second and third messages reiterated the first but added a name. None of it mattered now. Nadezhda was dead, largely because they had not followed Kaloostian's instructions to check the voice mail before seeing the twins. Had they done so, had they heeded Greg's warning, they might have eluded the killers hired by Eldon Tyrell.

As angry as she was at Kaloostian for setting her up, she was fairly certain he was on her side. She could not say the same for Nadezhda's associate, Peter, though his death at the bar three hours earlier at least explained his behavior outside the apartment building. Peter was working two jobs, but he'd tried to remain loyal to Nadezhda Molotova. That tenuous loyalty had saved Angela's life.

Now it was time to check Kaloostian's loyalty. By her estimate, it was 11:30 A.M., Thursday, in LA. Toner dialed Greg's number and waited as the number cycled six times. After the sixth bounce, she expected connection, but the cycling continued for three more rounds. The Armenian had augmented his defenses.

The connection finally stabilized. Greg's phone rang once, twice, three times—no answer. Angela was about to hang up when the ringing stopped. An unshaven face appeared. It was Kaloostian.

"Angie...where are you?"

"That's not important right now."

"Are you all right? Why haven't you called? Did you make it to Moscow?"

Toner inhaled and fought for control. "Molotova's dead. We ran into some trouble. We didn't have a chance to check her voice mail. I listened to your messages only a few minutes ago. Day late and a ruble short."

Greg's mouth tightened. He closed his eyes for a moment. "I'm…I'm sorry. I wish there was something I could've done. What about you?"

"What about me? I'm alive, Greg. *I'm* alive. But a very dear friend is dead. I've also had the crap beat out of me, my head pounded into the floor; I've killed a man, I'm stranded in Moscow, and you called the Russian consulate before I did, you *sonofabitch*."

Greg was silent. "Molotova told you?" he asked at last.

"Her dying words. Bullets were flying by my head, you fucking bastard, and I had to listen to that. A hell of a way to find out my best friend's betrayed me."

Kaloostian started to talk, but Toner held up her index finger. "Don't. Don't you *dare* interrupt. I'm not done here. Naddie is lying dead in some snowbank because of you, you and your passion for international intrigue." Angela paused, her lower lip trembling, her hands shaking. "So who is it, Greg? Who do you work for? Who funnels money to your numbered bank account in the Cayman Islands?"

"I work for the U.S. government, Angie. I'm an electronics technician. I draw two taxpayer-funded paychecks a month—just like you. I know what you're thinking, but that's not the way it is. There's no secret bank account, no slush fund, and nobody's holding my mother hostage."

"You just happened to call Samanov because you're a nice guy, huh? Thought you'd give 'em some advance warning about my bad attitude, make sure the red carpet was out."

"I'm not denying I called the Russians, but I don't work for them, and I don't funnel secrets their way. I'm a naturalized American citizen, and I would never betray my country."

"*Your* country?" Toner said incredulously.

"Yes, *my* country. Don't jump to conclusions before you have the whole story."

"Then what the hell is the whole story?"

"It's called *Nyentzi*," Greg said with heavy emphasis. "You just happened to be the one who stumbled onto the file we've been looking for since 2000. Bad timing, bad karma, a mischance of circumstance—what can I say? You don't know how sorry I am it was you."

"Nice sentiments, but you'll have to forgive my persistently dubious nature. And what's this *we* shit I keep hearing?"

"You said it yourself on Monday, remember? How could someone like Tyrellovich build a facility in the middle of nowhere, create thousands of genetically engineered embryos, implant at least a hundred of them, and not have anyone looking over his shoulder? Words to that effect."

"I made some flippant comment about Howard Stern, but you were the one with all the answers. You've been looking for this for *seven years*. That's what you just said. And quit changing the subject. Who's this *we* you referred to?"

Kaloostian nodded his head in defeat. "All right. Jim Revkin verified what we've suspected for years: Monogovody was built and funded with a giant slush fund. Big business, big government."

"Who do you work for? Answer my question, dammit."

"I'll get to it, okay? You first need to know what happened seven years ago."

"Fine, I'll play your games," Toner said in exasperation. "Was the United States involved?"

"Does a beaver shit wood chips? C'mon Angie, of course it was. And don't act surprised. The U.S. budget is so frickin' big, billions of dollars go unaccounted for. Administration after administration has cloaked huge amounts of money under the Pentagon's black budget or safely tucked it away in a file marked 'National Security.' Tyrellovich said

'Show me the money' and that's what the world did. But Monogovody was business as usual only to a point."

Toner looked angry, still refusing to believe the country she served and loved had a hand in Nadezhda Molotova's death. "Only to what point?" she finally asked.

"March 2000—Monogovody ceases to exist. That's where the *we* comes in."

"What? You mean your people had something to do with Monogovody's destruction?"

Kaloostian shook his head. "No, of course not! You've gotta understand how Tyrellovich ran the show. To get all that money, he made certain promises. The technology Nyentzi was going to generate was his collateral. According to Revkin, Tyrellovich sent out feelers to governments and corporations before they'd even broken ground. Offers and contracts trickled in. As soon as he had enough money, all other bids were withdrawn. Do you see a problem with that?"

"Yeah. It sounds like your people were a little slow on the uptake."

"Precisely. They got invited to the party but chose not to attend. Eh, that's business…no hard feelings. But then the big bang. Tyrellovich was dead, but what happened to Nyentzi? No one, and I mean no one, was talking. All the records went up in smoke. And because all the contracts were under the table, there was never an independent inquiry. Suspicion has run high ever since. Everybody distrusts everybody."

"These groups have been looking for Nyentzi all this time?"

"Yep. And that's where the Revkin file comes in. With one problem. While Uncle Sam's Agency A apparently picked up on the lead and created our mysterious file, Agency B knew all along where Nyentzi was and who was calling the shots. The way I figure it, our stumbling onto their little secret let the cat out of the bag. Now everyone's working together to shut down the investigation and avoid a political scandal."

"Did Revkin know who created the file?"

"He has no idea. He was surprised to hear it even existed."

Toner clenched her fists and glared. "That's just great. We're right back to the tabloids...with no proof."

"...Except your file."

"Well, it's better than nothing. We could take the disk to *Washington Post*. It worked for Watergate."

Greg shook his head. "Not enough...You just don't go around accusing governments and corporations of funding illegal genetic research without hard facts. Look at how many decades the tobacco industry stonewalled Congress about the connection between nicotine and cancer."

"Then what are we supposed to do? Wait for CNN to call?"

"Look around, Toner. The millennium's got everybody obsessed with end-of-the-world prognostications—from the Bible to the X-files. Crackpot schemes, cults, plans for world domination. All sorts of shit. That's what people are reading. That's what they're watching. You think they have time for the truth?"

"But Greg, Nyentzi is the truth."

"Bravo. You hit the nail on the head. Problem is, all that other stuff's popular because people refuse to admit what's really going on around them. It's like what I said about tobacco and lung cancer. For more than thirty years it wasn't a question of health but of how deep the public was willing to bury its collective head in the sand. People don't want to hear the truth. It scares them to death.

"And if you think things are bad now, just wait a few years. Before the explosion, at least there was some accountability for the Nyentzi Project. But not anymore. Now there's no telling where that technology is going to end up."

"That's pretty Orwellian."

"Damn straight. Big Brother is alive and well and more dangerous than ever. He may wear a fancy suit, but that's only because jackboots are no longer in style. Big Brother killed Nadezhda Molotova, and he's not stoppin' there. Can't you see that? Can't you understand why some governments are scared shitless? Countries like Armenia, Israel, Nepal, Costa Rica, Zimbabwe…the little guys."

"Is that the *we* you were talking about?"

"'Fraid so. I work for countries that are in no position to dictate world policy but nevertheless suffer the consequences. I report on Nyentzi—and only on Nyentzi—directly to Armenian Intelligence. They share the information with other interested parties. People are scared, Angie. Nyentzi has the potential to unhinge the entire world order—economical and political."

"Revkin told you all that?"

"Pretty much. Some I got from other sources, but Revkin's a real find. He also verified one other thing."

"Let me guess. Yuri Tyrellovich had a son, and he's the prick who killed Nadezhda."

"How the hell?"

"Peter…I don't even know his last name…the two-timing FSB agent said he was working for Mad Scientist Jr. I take it that's what Revkin told you?"

"Sort of. He corroborated what we suspected. Yuri had a son who went by the name of Anatoly Yuriovich Tyrellovich. He worked at Monogovody as a technician. We think he's responsible for the explosion that destroyed it, that he's changed his name to Eldon Tyrell, lives in Beverly Hills, and is directing the Nyentzi Project."

"Fun guy. Who's his mother?"

"Marta Tyrellovich, Yuri's wife."

"Which makes him a half-brother to the children."

"Maybe. The surrogate parents were never told who provided the original genes."

"Tyrellovich and Mercereau did."

"They did? How do you know that?"

"Lara and Katya Gracheva told me."

"You saw them! Wait a minute. You never…Why didn't you say so? I thought…"

"Nadezhda was killed *after* we left the apartment building."

"After? Oh God." Greg stopped to collect his thoughts. "But you got to meet them. You've gotta tell me about them, please," he finally begged. "It won't take long."

Angela inhaled and held her breath, thinking about the twins. "I can't go into detail, Greg. We don't time. But they've surpassed your every expectation. And it wasn't like Oz, all smoke and mirrors. These kids are the real thing—sweet, beautiful, precocious, amazingly brilliant, funny…and terminally ill."

"Then how did Naddie die?" Greg asked quietly.

Toner described the events leading to Molotova's death, as well as the struggle in the bar. The Armenian listened in stony silence.

"Maybe I shouldn't have put four slugs into Oleg," Toner said, trembling, "but he didn't leave me a choice. There was no way he and I were both leaving that bar alive."

Greg nodded. "I've always said shoot first and ask questions later. I'm just glad you're alive, even if it's because of sloppy work on Tyrell's part."

"I think you're drawing the wrong conclusion. Tyrell isn't sloppy—he's overconfident. He's so goddamn sure of himself that he didn't kill me when he had the chance. It's a shame about the children, though. They've got so much to offer. Now that I know about Eldon Tyrell, I understand what they were talking about."

"What do you mean?"

"They showed us some of their designs and inventions. Not the whole blueprint, you know, just an overview. Naddie asked where their main databank was, and Katya said something about one of the adults monitoring everything. She said it with so much trust, so much innocence. And that maniac's going to defile everything they stand for."

"You know what they say: history is written by the victors. With Tyrell controlling all that technology, he can write the future, too."

"But he doesn't have it all."

"What do you mean?"

"It's why I called. The twins managed to slip a disk into my bag. I don't know what's on it, but there's a message and some lines of poetry."

"That's *un*believable. Send it to me, right now. Maybe I'll recognize it."

"Okay, just a minute." Toner shifted the visual link to a small box in the upper left corner of her screen and accessed the Nyentzi disk. She highlighted the verses and emailed them to Kaloostian on the other side of the world. As soon as she received verification of receipt, she returned him to the full screen.

"What do you think?" she asked after he'd had a chance to read it.

Kaloostian scratched his head. "That preamble's some serious shit."

"And so unlike them. While we were there, it was mostly fun and games."

"I wish I could have been there. Say, Angie?"

"Yeah."

"I meant it when I said I was sorry about Nadezhda and about getting you involved. I'll get you out of there, okay? I promise."

Toner smiled. "I'll take you up on that. Now, what about that poetry?"

"You're going to hate me, but I think I've seen it before," Kaloostian said.

"Really? I thought it was something they wrote?"

"No, I'm pretty sure it's by somebody else."

"Dylan, Yeats, Kipling, Angelou?" Toner asked.

"None of the above. I think it's the lyrics of a song."

"Come on. Is this another coincidence? Some album you listened to last night?"

Greg shrugged. "No, I'm just saying it sounds familiar. Give me some time and…"

"Take all the time you want. Once you get me out of here, I…"

"Angie. There's a problem with that. Your visa's been revoked. Getting you anywhere is going to take some doing."

"What? When did that happen? By whose order?"

"Like I told you, the authorities want the Revkin file back. Now that the right hand and the left hand are actually working together, our job's become a little harder."

Angela looked away, angry again. The frustration and sense of betrayal that had disappeared momentarily now came crashing back.

"Tell you what, Kaloostian, get me out of here, and you can spend all the time you want working on that password. Since your people want Nyentzi so bad, I'll give you the damn disk. As soon as I get back to LA, I'm through. I quit."

"Angie, I know it's been a week from hell," Greg said soothingly. "I know how frustrated and lonely you are, but walking away from this is not going to be that easy."

"Says who?"

"Says Tyrell, for one. I've got a nasty feeling about that bastard. I don't think any of us will be sailing off into the sunset any time soon."

Toner breathed rapidly through her mouth, shaking from repressed anger. Tears formed as she fought for control of her emotions.

"I am so sick of being afraid, Greg."

"I know. I know you are."

"I'm afraid, Greg. Can't you see that? Naddie died in my arms, for Christ's sake."

Kaloostian said nothing as Angela covered her eyes, shielding her tears from view. "I didn't ask for this. I never volunteered to save the world. It's not even in my job description."

"What is it, Angie? What's really bothering you?"

"It's…you…I don't know who…I don't know what to trust, anymore. You lied to me. Naddie didn't tell me everything until the end. I can't even trust the United States anymore. Who am I supposed to be working for now? Tell me that."

"I can't tell you what to do," Greg said softly. "I'll help. I'll do whatever I can no matter what you decide. But you've got to understand. There are certain responsibilities when you assume the title *American*. I know you've always felt a sense of pride in America and being an American—The Bill of Rights, Frederick Douglas, Crazy Horse, Eleanor Roosevelt, Martin Luther King Jr., man on the moon—all those great Americans and milestones. But, as you well know, there's a fair amount of baggage along with the glory—Trail of Tears, Rosewood, My Lai, Leonard Peltier…You want me to continue?"

"I hate it when you lecture," Toner sniffed.

"It's not just me, Angie. It's those kids. Like their message, there's two sides to every story. If you can't trust anyone else, trust the person they trust. That's you. Trust in yourself."

"*No*. I've got nothing left to give. In the last three years I've lost everything I ever cared for. I can't take it anymore. Visa or no visa, I'm outta here."

"You can't just surrender. If we work together, if we…"

"Would you please stop? I haven't seen odds this long since the last election."

"Fuck the odds. Those kids have beaten the odds all to hell. Do you know what the success rate is for zygote in vitro fertilization? Not even 30 percent. And they achieved a rate of 75 percent. Those kids are survivors. You can't just give up on 'em."

The tears stopped, but Angela continued to plead with Kaloostian. "Do you have any idea what you're asking me to do? We don't know how to get at Tyrell. We don't know who in our own government is helping him. We don't even know why Tyrellovich or Mercereau switched the embryos from male to female."

The answer came from the dark near the door to Vassily's apartment. "It is a logical and inherent quality of nature. Genetically, a female has more at stake in the survival of the species. That is why they made the switch."

"What? Who was that?" Kaloostian asked, staring from the computer screen.

"What?" Toner said, looking up, surprised to see Vassily Molotov. She hadn't seen or heard him come in. She did not know how much of the conversation he had heard.

Vassily expanded. "I am very highly sorry for the intruding. What I said was that the female has a larger role in raising the next generation. She has more at stake…more to lose. That is why Tyrellovich and Mercereau made the change."

"I didn't hear you come in," Toner hesitated, unsure of his frame of mind.

Kaloostian demanded some answers. "Angie, what's going on? Who are you talking to? You never did tell me where you were calling from."

"Just a minute, Greg…Vassily, please sit down. I guess this concerns you, too."

Vassily took a seat and when Kaloostian could see him, Toner introduced them. "Gregory Kaloostian, meet Nadezhda's brother, Vassily Molotov. Vassily, this is my friend in Los Angeles. I'm calling from his apartment."

"I see. Nice to meet you. I wish it could be under better circumstances. I'm very sorry about your sister. I had the honor of meeting her briefly. Blagoslovi I utesh eyo Gospod."

"Thank you. I am sorry if I intruded on your conversation. I was out for a minute."

Toner smiled at him. "No problem. You okay?"

"I do not know. It is all such a shock. Did Nadezhda die because of Nyentzi?"

Kaloostian remained silent as Toner answered. "Yes. We think Tyrellovich's son, Anatoly, contracted for our deaths. What do you know about all this? You seem pretty well informed. Did you mean what you said about the switch?"

"I majored in child psychology and as well am working on master's program."

"But how do you know why they made the switch?" Toner asked.

"Nadezhda asked me many questions, hypotheticals. Soon after she started her new assignment—in November. She did not give me details, but I knew enough about genetics and child development to guess what she was doing."

"You mean she knew all along that the embryos had been switched?"

"No, she never informed me. I only said what I did because I heard you and Gregory talking about it."

Kaloostian interjected. "You know for a fact that's why the change was made?"

"It is a notion, only, but I do believe it to be a valid point. Females are also wired differently. Their cranial communication networks are more efficient than a man's."

"See, Kaloostian."

"Shut up, Toner."

"Females have also emotional and verbal nerve clusters on both sides of brain. So if Tyrellovich and Mercereau treated verbal and communication skills of importance, the embryos should, of course, be female."

"If that's the case, then why were the embryos originally male?"

"Perhaps out of habit."

Kaloostian smiled. "Vassily, how do you know so much about Nyentzi? Are you sure Nadezhda didn't give you more details?"

"I am aware only of common aspects of such work. What are you thinking? That I too am a spy?"

"Just curious," Greg said. "Maybe you know a way to get Angela out of Russia."

Toner waved her hands in front of the monitor. "No way, Kaloostian. You are not dragging this poor boy into this da…darn case. Keep Vassily out of your schemes."

"Angela, I am hardly a boy. And yes, I do know of a good way for you to travel."

"Haven't you heard? My visa's been revoked," Toner proclaimed in an offhand way.

"And there's no way I can get any phony papers to Moscow on short notice," Greg said. "So unless you've got ruby slippers, I think she's stuck for at least a week."

"Could you have papers ready in Armenia tomorrow?" Vassily asked.

"Is this theoretical? It might take a little longer, but that's the right direction. Why? What are you thinking?"

"Our team is traveling to Yerevan for a hockey tournament. We leave Vnukovo Airport tomorrow afternoon. I am the coach. Angela could be a hockey player's mother or a reporter. We haven't been closely checked when flying as a team as many of the players are children of American and Canadian diplomats."

Toner was not impressed. "With the reputation hockey players have, that's no wonder. Thanks, but no thanks. I'd rather walk."

"That too could be arranged."

27

THE ROAD LESS TRAVELED

They hit him where it hurt. With fingers flying across their keyboards with corybantic legerity, seventy-four children, the heirs of Nyentzi, exacted vengeance in a massive and expeditious transfer of wealth.

One by one they accessed and depleted bank accounts, mutual funds, and asset management accounts, shifting his assets to other locations throughout the world. Universities, women's shelters, relief agencies, and numerous other charities received large, anonymous contributions.

By the time the children finished the first phase of their operation, they had transferred more than twenty billion dollars from the ownership of Eldon Tyrell. The children's only concern was minor. They thought he had more money than that.

Phase two was more selective. Through analysis of his portfolio, the children traced a recent business transaction between Tyrell and two men from Leipzig, Germany. That the matter involved a numbered account in the Cayman Islands was all they needed to know they'd identified their target.

Unable to verify whether the men had succeeded in their assignment, the children nonetheless reversed the transaction. The loss of their ill-gotten gain was certain to infuriate the men. With luck, they would shoot first and ask questions later.

Phase three was a waiting game. The children prowled the Internet, looking for sign of their friends, as well as for Tyrell's response to his newfound generosity. Knowing their half-brother, they wouldn't have to wait for long.

"Do you have any idea what you've gotten yourself into? This is insane. If Tyrell finds out you've helped me, he'll have you killed, too."

"I am only trying to help," Vassily argued.

"And I appreciate it. But I've got enough problems without worrying about you. No offense, but you're a hockey coach."

"Which means I am good at fighting and cross-checking."

"Cross-dressing?"

"Checking! Cross-*checking*. Have you never watched hockey?"

"I've seen plenty of hockey," Toner said. "I thought you had a bad leg."

"Only when I skate very fast. Or play contact sports. Or ski. But other than that, I am A-okay. It is what Nadezhda would have wanted. She told you I would help. I do this for her."

Toner shook her head. "Risking your life is not what she had in mind."

"You are quite the stubborn person, Angela Toner," Vassily said. "I too am stubborn. And we have already made agreement with Gregory. What are you now suggesting? That we call him and tell him of plan to change? I am only the provider of transportation. From Yerevan, you are on your own."

"Fine," Angela retorted, throwing up her hands in frustration. "As long as we agree to that now…here…up front. I don't want surprises later on."

Vassily held out his right arm. "To Yerevan only," he said.

Toner hesitated. Still reluctant to include Nadezhda's brother in her troubles, she nevertheless reached out and shook his hand.

"Now that is settled, we must begin new trouble. It's after eleven, and I am very tired. I am sure you are, too. I am the host, so I insist…"

"The couch is fine," Toner said.

"Exactly. The couch is fine. I will sleep here, and you sleep in the bedroom. The sheets are clean, and there are no bugs." Seeing Toner's skepticism, Vassily pressed his point. "It is Thursday. I do my laundry on Thursday."

"That's not what I meant. I've been enough trouble already. I'm not about to put you out of your own bed—clean sheets or not."

"You are the guest. Are you suggesting that I forget old Russian custom? The guest of the house always sleeps in the best bed."

"Nadezhda never told me that."

"Trust me. Very old custom. Dating back thousands of years."

"You just made that up, didn't you?" Toner asserted.

"Of course not. I am confident somewhere in Russia there is such a custom, and for this night I am practicing it."

"Whatever you say. I'm too tired to argue anyway."

"Good, that is settled. However, I will use the bathroom first." Vassily smiled and left the room, closing the bedroom door behind him.

Angela sat on the couch, pushing down on the cushions, checking their firmness. Satisfied her host would be comfortable, she turned off her computer, disconnected it from the phone jack, and plugged in the regular phone. By the time she finished, Vassily was back. He wore old sweat clothes and carried a pillow and blanket.

Toner looked at him and shook her head. "You sure about this? The couch is fine with me."

"Enough of this argument. Anyway," Vassily looked away, "there are family matters to take care of. I must call my aunt and tell her of Nadezhda's death. She will want to know, so arrangements can be made."

"You can't do that, Vassily."

"Why?"

"It will implicate you in helping me. The only way you could know about her death is from me. Your family will have to wait until the authorities notify someone. Sorry, but it's for the best."

Molotov was silent. He dropped the pillow on the couch, unsure of what to do next.

"Are you sure you're up for this trip?" Angela asked. "You don't need to do this. You can even cancel the trip."

"No, I must do it. I must go. I am just having a difficult time thinking of her…that she is gone."

At that moment, Angela wanted more than anything to hug Vassily, offer him comfort. She sensed his loneliness and pain but was afraid of her own vulnerability and held back.

Vassily sat down. "You said earlier the police might be involved. Do you think that is why no one has called about the shooting?"

"It's possible. To be on the safe side, why don't you call your aunt, but tell her only that you're leaving—and if anyone calls, you're on a hockey trip. That's the only to keep you in the clear."

"That is what I will do. By the way, do you have a toothbrush? I have a spare. It is even new."

"Thanks, but I have one in my bag." Toner picked up her computer bag and walked towards the bedroom. "Good night, Vassily," she said without turning around. "I'm sorry we had to meet like this."

"Angela?"

Toner stopped. "Yes."

"You are limping. And your face is bruised. Have you needing for first aid?"

She turned back around and saw the look of concern on his face. "It's nothing. I twisted my ankle earlier tonight. And the head…well, I've been popping aspirin and ibuprofen. I'll be all right."

"So you say, but I should look at the ankle, at the least. I have to deal with many injuries on hockey team. Come, sit back down, and I will take care of your hurt."

"I suppose you're right," Angela said, walking back to the couch and sitting. "If I'm going to travel tomorrow, I'd better have it wrapped by a professional."

Vassily smiled and moved to the couch. "Turn toward me and extend your leg." Following his directions, Toner tried to get comfortable while resting her injured leg across the young man's knee.

Molotov stopped as he was about to remove her sock. "Do you want to do this, or should I?" he asked.

Toner smiled. "Go ahead. You're the expert."

Vassily nodded. He cautiously pulled the sock off and pushed her pants leg toward the knee. After unwrapping the bandage, he examined the ankle, his soft touch warm on her skin.

"It is a minor sprain. Not too serious, but you must be careful. It will become worse without caution walking. Leave your ankle unwrapped for sleeping, but tomorrow before we leave, I will wrap it tight to limit the strain on the ligaments. Does that sound okay?" he asked, removing his loose grip on her leg.

"That's fine. Thank you," Angela said. She stood and hobbled to the bedroom door. "Goodnight again." They exchanged smiles.

Angela closed the door and went to the bed, setting her computer bag on the floor. The ice skate she had tripped over earlier was no longer in sight. Sitting on the edge of the bed, she opened a side pocket on the bag and removed her toothbrush.

For a moment, Angela sat quietly. Then she stood, but instead of going into the bathroom, she walked to the window. From the side, she pulled back the heavy curtain and stared into the wintry darkness.

Her mind raced—thoughts of the children, her family, Kaloostian, Nadezhda, and Vassily. "Has it only been four days?" she thought. "Seems longer…seems forever."

Angela closed the shade and shuffled to the bathroom. She picked up the toothpaste and spread it on her brush. As she began to clean her teeth, she glanced out the corner of her eye at the toilet. The seat and lid were down. "Oh Vassily," she whispered. "You sure know how to treat a woman."

Her sleep was so restless and spasmodic that she wasn't sure whether the crying was real or a dream. In the darkness of Vassily Molotov's apartment, Angela Toner opened her eyes and listened but heard only the ticking of an old clock on the dresser.

She'd had another nightmare. This time Jake was in it. He'd been crying, something Angela had never seen him do. She lay on her back staring at the ceiling, thinking about the dream, her arms behind her head. Jake had been alone in a small room, curled up with a baby's blanket. *He'd* been the one to survive the car accident three years ago and was weeping over her death. She'd tried to tell him she was not dead, but he couldn't hear her, couldn't touch her, couldn't sense her ethereal presence.

Angela didn't waste time trying to find the dream's hidden meaning. She had heard Vassily pacing more than hour after she turned off the light. After he finally settled down, she still heard him tossing and turning, mourning the death of his sister.

Toner couldn't help but feel responsible. Tomorrow she would leave Russia, helped by the brother of a woman whose life she'd been unable to save. Her sense of guilt and helplessness over Nadezhda's death would cause her to lose sleep for months to come. Her feelings of guilt were probably the reason Jake had shown up.

After she'd been discharged from the hospital to recuperate at home, Angela rediscovered the multipurpose remote control for the TV. During the two years they'd been married, she could never find the damned thing, though it miraculously appeared when Jake stretched out in his Lazy Boy. To him a remote that changed channels from fifty feet was the essence of technological sophistication. To Angela, it was just a piece of plastic.

Now it was hers—the spoils of survival. She had the freedom to watch what she wanted, without channel surfing, without the perpetual quest to find the latest score...without Jake. The price was more than she could bear.

How many nights had she lain awake crying, watching shadows on the ceiling, pacing the room? How often had she felt guilt just sitting in his chair and using his remote? How many times had she cleaned her Beretta in the dark, hoping for a stray bullet in the chamber?

Now, three years later, she faced another dilemma involving death. And again she was forced to rely on Kaloostian's ad hoc psychotherapy. Though the circumstances had changed, the outcome remained the same. No matter how articulate her argument, Gregory always won the debate. This time, despite his logic, despite the importance of fighting Eldon Tyrell, she was not convinced she was doing the right thing.

Not that she didn't believe in the danger of Tyrell monopolizing the work of the children. Her skepticism rooted instead in all the white lies she endured—from Santa Claus and the Easter bunny to fairy tales about Social Security and truth-in-government.

Lara and Katya had talked about shades of gray. They saw the truth as a tree branch under a street lamp in the wind. As the wind blew, the branch bent accordingly, casting myriad shadows across the landscape of the night. There was a limit, though, to how much the branch could bend before it broke.

Greg spoke of truth as a thin line in the sand. "The closer the public gets to the truth," he told her, "the greater the tendency of people in authority to erase the line with a sweeping motion of the foot, only to redraw the line half-an-inch on the other side. It might not seem like much, but after a few generations, you're miles from the point where you started."

What her Armenian friend did not realize was that no matter how carefully a line in the sand is redrawn, all it takes is one wave to wash away all evidence that any line ever existed. Angela sensed such a wave was coming.

Alvin Toffler had labeled the information age the Fourth Wave. She now had a vision of a fifth. Whatever its name—biotechnology? genetic engineering?—it was more than a wave. It was a *tsunami*, a tidal surge of unprecedented energy and transformation.

The world stood on the threshold of a new epoch, and seventy-four children were the catalyst. If Lara and Katya Gracheva were an indication of the power of their minds, the fifth wave was to be massive beyond preconception.

Angela rolled to her side and tried to get back to sleep. She had two choices. Learn how to swim fast and hard, or drown under the whitecaps of genetic revolution.

She'd never watch another hockey game as long as she lived. The chartered flight from Moscow to Yerevan, the ancient capital of Armenia, was 1,150 miles of torture. Angela Toner was jammed in like livestock with twenty-five juvenile delinquents with skates. The hockey team of Canadian and American children whose parents were on diplomatic missions to Russia convinced Toner that diplomacy, tact, and poise were not inherited qualities.

She had no idea what Vassily had told his players, but it could not have been good. Her assigned seat, the only assigned seat, was in the back of the plane, surrounded by pads, skates, sticks, uniforms, and helmets. Molotov sat by himself two rows up, with the team and its entourage filling the rest of the plane. Throughout the flight, no one spoke to her, but every conversation began with a dirty look in her direction—as if she was a war criminal on her way to Nuremberg.

Vassily, for his part, kept interaction to a minimum. He had his coach's manual on his lap, but Toner could tell he wasn't reading it. The book remained open at the same page for more than an hour, while he stared out the window.

He'd been just as closemouthed that morning as they prepared to leave for the airport. Angela could sense a simmering rage supplanting his depression. Vassily clenched and unclenched his hands and gritted his teeth, taking long, deep breaths. She could hardly get his attention, much less keep it.

He had been right about airport security. The chartered jet had parked in the restricted area of the tarmac, and every player arrived in a limousine with full diplomatic authorization. Vassily and Angela did not have that luxury. Without the Russian's knowledge of airport protocol, they would have been required to go through normal security checks. And Toner, with her revoked visa, would have been taken into custody.

Instead, Vassily told the driver of their taxi to drop them off at a side gate. The sun had come up bright that Friday morning, but with the cloud cover gone, the temperature had plummeted to well below zero. The driver must have thought they were crazy. But the wait at the gate was short. Within a few moments, a limo carrying one of the hockey players pulled up to offer them a ride. Once inside the vehicle, Vassily whispered something to the youth in Russian, effectively ending communication between Toner and the team.

For all Angela knew, her deodorant had quit, and he was warning everyone to stay clear. She had tried to maintain some semblance of hygiene, but with her luggage in Salekhard and no chance to shop, her clothes were beginning to feel a bit ripe.

The flight lasted less than three hours, and she had slept part of the time. Landing in Yerevan was exciting. Much like Denver, the city was surrounded by mountains. The pilot of the chartered jet navigated the narrow approach with finesse before settling onto the runway. Once on the tarmac, the hockey team again was accorded full diplomatic decorum. Before Angela had a chance to say good-bye to Vassily, he was off with his team in a luxury bus, and she was in a taxi heading for the center of town.

The taxi driver, a grizzled man long past the normal age for retirement, talked nonstop. He told Angela in broken English that he was Kaloostian's cousin: "Second, maybe third cousin twice removed…once forcibly." Talktalktalktalktalk.

The old man talked so much he never noticed that Toner didn't say a word. Before long, they arrived at a respectable hotel several miles from the airport. The driver, who never gave his name, escorted her to the desk. After a quick conversation with the clerk, he showed Angela her room. Leaving her with the key, the old man bowed, said good-bye, and departed. Toner went inside and locked the door. Following a quick tour of the small room, she sat on the bed to wait. Someone was to meet her.

She waited two hours—until 4:00 P.M.—longing for a hot bath. She didn't want to miss the rendezvous but evening was closing in…Just then she heard a soft knock on the door. Toner sat straight up on the bed and drew her Beretta. She stood and went to the door.

"Yes," she said, standing to the side.

"Hello. The manager has informed me that your accommodations are not satisfactory," a deep male voice said. "I there something we can do to make your stay more pleasant."

Angela exhaled at the reference to her accommodations—that was her signal. Still holding the pistol, she unlocked and opened the door. she saw a tall, dark, smiling stranger waiting to be invited in.

"Ms. Toner, I am Loris Berberian. It is a pleasure to meet you."

"Hello. Gregory Kaloostian said you would be coming. Please come in."

Loris nodded and walked into the hotel room. The Armenian was tall and thin, with a small opal earring in his left earlobe. His facial features and hair were similar to Gregory Kaloostian's, though Loris did not have a beard. He could have used a shave, however. The stubble on his face was at least two days old.

"Did our friend say who would be coming to see you?" he asked, closing and locking the door.

Angela slipped the Beretta back into its holster. "He mentioned your name, if that's what you mean. Did you know Greg before he moved to the States?"

"Indeed, I have that distinction. We are old friends, though I have not seen him in years…in person, of course."

"Yes, the wonders of technology," Toner said. She motioned to a chair, but Loris remained standing. "I'm afraid I have nothing to offer except tea. Would you care for some?"

"No, thank you. I won't be staying. As a matter of fact, neither will you."

Angela's eyes widened slightly. "I won't?"

"There has been a change in strategy. Is this yours?" Loris asked, pointing to her computer bag.

"All my luggage is back in Salekhard. That's all I was able to carry with me."

Loris picked up the bag. "Is everything in here that you want to bring?"

"Yes, but what's the rush?"

"There is a car waiting. Please, we should go."

Toner was about to grab her coat and follow the Armenian when she stopped.

"Loris, just a minute. I've been on the run for five days. I'm tired, irritable, hungry, and in desperate need of a change of clothes. Before I take another step, I want to know what the heck is going on."

"I do not have all the details. We received a message from Kaloostian in Los Angeles that things have 'heated up.' I am to take you to a private home, and from there you can talk to your friend. Is that acceptable?"

Toner sighed. "Do I have a choice? I guess I'm just going to have to continue trusting Kaloostian. Okay, let's go."

Loris laughed and slung the computer bag over his shoulder. Together they went into the hallway. Just then, Angela thought of something.

"Loris, you said you know Gregory?"

"Of course, he is my cousin."

"Wait a minute. I thought that old guy in the taxi was Greg's cousin."

"He is. And so is the desk manager of this hotel."

"I take it Kaloostian's got a lot of cousins."

"Millions, but who's counting? Come, we must hurry."

Toner put on her coat while they walked toward the elevator, shaking her head in resignation.

"Yeah, yeah, yeah..."

Felicia Mildred Scriff could not believe her good fortune. She felt like a child getting a puppy for Christmas. Deputy Assistant Director Hatton and Special Agent Toner—both gone in one fell swoop. It didn't get any better than that.

The call from Washington had come at 3:00 P.M. An hour later, she still wanted to pinch herself to see if she was dreaming. The director of the FBI himself had personally apprised her of the situation and asked whether she was interested in a little promotion.

"What a dumb question?" she'd thought to herself. "Yes *sir*, if you think I could be of better service to the bureau in a new capacity."

It was that simple. Hatton was history. A special detachment would clean out his office over the weekend. She'd have to remind them to bring a bulldozer. She wanted all trace of the man gone by Monday morning.

"Then I'll see what can be done about getting that battle-ax Malone to retire," Scriff thought. "And new wallpaper, new desk, new chair...I'm sure I can find some funds floating around somewhere. Maybe I'll send someone out to the Mercado house. They won't be needing their furniture for awhile.

"And the icing on the cake—Angela C. Toner, whereabouts unknown. With any luck, the little bitch died in that Siberian plane crash just reported in the news. Smart-assed mongrel. I won't have to put up with her shit anymore. 'Course, it's a pity she's not here for me to torment."

"Hey, Felicia."

Scriff woke up from her daydream as Marc Heiple came around the corner. He extended his right hand. "I hear congratulations are in order."

"It's not official, but I got word an hour ago," Scriff said with sham humility. "How do you know?"

Heiple laughed and shook her hand. "I've got my connections. You know what I mean."

Scriff cocked her head and tried to look strict. "Keep it under your hat, okay? I don't want people to think I'm jumping the gun or anything." Then her mood got the better of her. "Oh, what the heck, tell anybody you want. Personally, I think it's great news."

"Fer sure. I mean, like, how long have we been waiting for a change around this joint?"

"Too long, Heiple. Way too long," Scriff reiterated.

"And upwind from the stables—can't beat that. But what's that I hear about Toner?"

"She was in Russia on some asinine assignment…Hatton, of course. Anyway, there's been a plane crash up near the Arctic Circle, and they haven't located any survivors. Pity."

"Yeah, whatever," Heiple shrugged. "But Russia? What was she doing in Russia?"

"All I can tell you is…"

Heiple leaned in close, hoping to catch every detail.

"…I'm lucky Hatton was around to take the fall. Something about…this is just between you and me, understand. I don't want it repeated," Scriff demanded.

"No problem. I'm not like Toner," Marc said with a venom-tinged voice.

"Good. Anyway, Hatton grabbed this file from the NSA and sent the princess off on a wild-goose chase completely out of her jurisdiction. His too, for that matter. When the NSA demanded the file back, Toner had already disappeared. No one's heard a word from her since Monday."

"No kiddin'?" said Heiple.

"Yeah, can you believe it? I don't know what was in the file, but even the Russian government's involved. I heard the president was briefed on the situation. It's a big-time screw up, that's all I know. It's all I want to know."

"So they, like, think Toner's dead, huh? Wow, that's hard to believe."

"They think she's dead, but apparently the file's so valuable they're also worried she might have stolen it and is trying to pawn the information to the Russians or Chinese."

Heiple shook his head "God, this is too much—a real dime. You know, I never trusted her. All that phony-virtue crap. Who was she trying to kid, you know what I mean? Who'd she think she was?"

"The patron saint of cluelessness," Scriff quipped, laughing at her own joke, reveling in the trashing of her antagonist. "Anyway, thanks for the support, Heiple. I'll see you around."

Heiple smiled as Felicia walked away. "I'm always here—twenty-four/seven," he said with a smile. After Scriff was gone, he reached inside his jacket for his cell phone.

28
General Tso's Chicken

The grieving had begun. Nadezhda Andrevna Molotova was dead. Though initially limited to thirty-seven households and seventy-four children, the mourning was worldwide. All received a picture, gleaned from the computer records of her employer, downloaded in somber cyber-memorial.

To the rest of the world, Nadezhda Molotova was a faceless government employee, her death not yet officially announced, her body nowhere to be found. To the children of Nyentzi, however, she was the patron saint of sacrifice, someone who would remain forever in their hearts and minds.

The children had searched for hours for their two friends. They suspected Nadezhda had died outside the apartment building on Moscow's Svoboda Avenue, though they were unable to find any police report of a shooting or abduction. They based their conclusion on an internal FSB message listing her as missing. That and a communiqué from the two men of Leipzig to Eldon Tyrell's "limited-access" web site. The assassins demanded payment, threatening action if Tyrell did not reimburse them for the confirmed hit at least.

Their half-brother was as enraged as they were, for different reasons. Unimpressed by the children's raid on his financial portfolio, he vowed to get his money back.

"Do you take me for a lunatic?" he'd asked with a shrill laugh. "Do you think I keep all my money in electronically accessible accounts?" He all but admitted his hand in Nadezhda's death, informing the children *they* were next.

"Tell us something we don't know," they responded.

The camera clicked. "Is that the best you can do?" Loris Berberian asked, looking up from behind an expensive camera mounted on a tripod. He was taking Angela Toner's picture for a driver's license, part of her new identity. The travel-weary American did not cooperate.

"I am not going to smile, okay? No one smiles for these damn pictures. If you want it to look real, I should be off to one side and out of focus, with smeared makeup and a stupid look on my face."

"Why are you so unhappy, so full of anger?" Loris wondered. "I know you had a rough time, but not everything is in the pits. You have a beautiful smile. Show it. The future is bright if you want it to be."

"The future's bright, huh? That explains why I had to wear these sunglasses on the way over here," Toner said, holding up the pair of cheap eyeglasses Loris had given her. They had left the hotel in his car more than an hour ago. It was almost 6:00 P.M., Saturday. Angela was hungry, irritable, feeling very alone.

The Armenian laughed and wagged his finger up and down. "Kaloostian warned me about you. He said I should ignore your sarcasm and negativity."

"He did, did he? Did he also mention the only reason I'm going along with this new identity shtick is so I can get back to the States, find him, and wring his greasy little neck?"

"You don't mean that. Things have been very bad. I know how pent-up you must be. I truly do. But I also know that you are a tough cookie who will endure and prevail."

"Well, excuse me for feeling like an ensign on a *Star Trek* away team."

Loris laughed again. "Okay, I admit defeat. You may continue to be gloomy person. Three more bad pictures, and we are finished."

"Good, then can we eat?"

"I ordered out. The food should be here soon. Now smile—I mean, frown."

Angela glowered for the camera. Loris Berberian took the final three shots and rewound the film. "There, was that so unfavorable?"

"About time. Can I take all this makeup off now?" she asked, referring to the artificial wrinkles, age spots, gray hair, and skin coloring the Armenian had used to alter her appearance.

"No, of course not. That is not possible," Berberian said, looking up from his camera.

"Why not?"

"After we have eaten dinner, and while we are printing new documents for your trip, we will be redoing your features with makeup that is more permanent. But it is a slow process. What I put on earlier was only for the preliminary work. I need the makeup left on so I am able to match your picture. Then we will reshoot for final photo."

Seeing the look of shock on Angela's face, Loris sheepishly continued. "I'm afraid you did not understand me thoroughly when I told you this was going to be a totally new image. You will need to remain like this for several days, perhaps longer."

"You didn't tell me that…" Toner considered the ramifications of her new identity. Her mind had been elsewhere when Loris described the details of his work. "I guess I wasn't paying attention. How much of a change are we talking about?" Angela asked, remembering the makeover she had performed on Nadezhda Molotova forty-eight hours earlier.

"We can alter your weight by...oh, maybe five or ten kilos, your height by three to five centimeters, and your age by as many as twenty years, with the more durable cosmetics. It is the only way we can be sure that you will avoid the scrutiny at the security checkpoints. You understand, don't you? They will be looking for you."

"Yeah, I guess I underestimated the permanence of all this. You're talking complete makeover. The kit and the caboodle."

"Whatever you just said, yes, that is what we are doing," Loris said, walking toward the steps to the basement darkroom. "Do you have any preferences for your new identity?" he asked at the top of the stairs. "I have only made minor adjustment to your skin tone. With your features, you can be almost anyone in the world."

"How 'bout Dr. Winifred O'Boogie? Up from Montego Bay, mon."

"Too obvious. Gregory told me you like to vacation in the Caribbean. We need to find some other place for you to call home."

"I can't think long-term on an empty stomach. Where's the food?"

Before Loris could reply, the phone rang. He punched a button on Toner's laptop computer situated on the kitchen table. They had hooked it up to the phone line earlier.

"Angela, the call is for you."

"You're about the last person I feel like talking to," Toner said to Kaloostian.

"What did I do this time?" Greg asked with bewilderment. It was Friday morning in Los Angeles. He had asked Loris Berberian to check on the progress of the document forgery, as well as on Toner's frame of mind. Loris wordlessly retreated to the basement, leaving Kaloostian to face Angela's wrath.

"This is all your fault," Toner said, her eyes narrow, accusing.

Gregory's disposition was no better. "What's all my fault? Nyentzi? Nadezhda's death? You opening your big mouth on Monday morning? Come on, Toner. Which one is it?"

Toner regretted her outburst. "Sorry. This facial rearrangement's got the best of me."

"Well, if you want my opinion, I think Loris is doing a great job. You look fifty!"

The glare returned. "Greg, we've talked about this before, those certain things a man should never say to a woman. I've heard your excuse, but being a eunuch doesn't mean you can tell me I've aged twenty years overnight."

Kaloostian winced. "Oooo, that hits me where it doesn't it hurt. Seriously, though, I'm impressed. I recognized you, but it was mainly the sparks flying out of your eyes."

"Thanks a lot. What's new in California?"

"Hatton got his pink slip. Scriff got promoted. Revkin's in hiding. And I'm arranging for your trip back."

"Why LA? They'll have wanted posters of me the size of billboards. If you want me out of sight, I was thinking of something a little more…"

"Forget the sun, kiddo. Tyrell knows all your favorite haunts. LA's our best bet."

"Isn't that a little obvious?" Toner asked.

"Chess…always attack. The best defense is a good offense."

"I'm beginning to hate that game."

"Why so?"

"Naddie told me that one of the maxims of chess is to be prepared to sacrifice a few pieces."

For a moment Greg said nothing. "That's often the case."

"Is that all I am, Greg—a piece on a chess board?"

"You know that's not true. Come on, Angie. Don't start looking for metaphors, not now. I need you to find the password into that disk. Especially since I've identified the source of the first clue."

Angela's interest was immediate. "What is it?"

"I hesitate even telling you."

"Why?"

"Because it's from Pink Floyd," Kaloostian said.

"Who?"

"Pink Floyd. You know, the British group that did *Dark Side of the Moon*."

Toner's attitude reverted. "Would you stop jerking me around? This is serious. I don't have the time…or the patience for your drug-induced humor."

"I am serious, dammit. Do you think I'd bullshit about something like this?"

"Look, even if this is on the level, there's no way the are verses from some drugged out rock 'n' roll band. Those kids are seven years old!"

"What do I need to convince you?"

Toner remembered her brother Chip had played *Dark Side of the Moon*, though it had been released in 1973 when he was still an infant. As one of the most successful records of all time, *Dark Side of the Moon* had remained on the charts for more than twenty-two years. "Save your breath," she said. "There's no way you're going to get me to believe."

Greg held up his hand. "Listen to this—it's the final verse:

No more turning away, from the weak and the weary

No more turning away, from the coldness inside

Just a world that we all must share, it's not enough just to stand and stare

Is it only a dream that there'll be no more turning away?

"Where'd you get that?" Toner asked with renewed interest.

"From the album sleeve," Kaloostian said, showing her the record cover. "It's not on *Dark Side of the Moon*. It's from Pink's *Momentary Lapse of Reason*. The song is called "On the Turning Away." A great tune, by the way. I listened to it earlier."

"That's what I must have had when you talked me into this damned adventure."

"What's that? Oh yeah—a momentary lapse of reason. Funny—keep it up."

"Is that it?" Toner asked, gesturing towards the LP cover Greg was holding.

"What about it?"

"I can't see. What's on the cover?"

"There's a beach, with dozens of metal cots lined up. You know. The kind they used in army hospitals. And there's a guy sitting on one of the cots looking into a hand-held mirror."

"And what, pray tell, is the significance of that?" Toner asked.

"Well, there's also this hang glider up here," Kaloostian said, pointing to the middle of the picture. "And if you open it all the way, you see on the back a young and pretty nurse holding a stack of clean white sheets. And—now, this is crucial—each cot is made up in military style, but the blankets are all different colors. See, here's a gray one, a light blue one, a yellow one…"

"Okay, okay," Toner concluded.

"…A maroon one, a green one. Here's one with a stripe down the middle…"

"Greg."

"What?"

"Shut the hell up."

Kaloostian complied while Angela contemplated the evidence he had just presented.

"Are you high?" she asked at last.

"Is that a rhetorical question?"

"You're right," she said, lightly banging herself upside the head. "What am I thinking? Let me rephrase the question. Are you high or am I dealing with residual from last night?"

Kaloostian wrinkled his face. "Such a skeptic."

"Yes, I am. I'm sorry. Even with the evidence in front of me, I need something a little more substantial than peyote-induced hallucinations. And why Pink Floyd? Those kids have a world of literature to choose from, and you expect me to believe this relic from the 1960s has some sort of mythical significance?"

"Remember when I told you I wanted to volunteer for that government study on the effects of marijuana on the brain. You laughed."

"I laughed."

"Yes, you laughed, but I was serious. The results of the study may've been inconclusive, but I'm convinced pot accelerates neural synaptic activity. It's part of the high. The brain works faster. People are able to think of things, make connections, remember stuff they normally wouldn't."

Toner shook her head. "I think you've smoked one too many doobies."

"Our brains aren't that different from the twins', you know," Greg said. "We've got permanent memories, too. It's just that we usually can't remember them without hypnosis or drug therapy. Too much day-to-day bullshit."

"I still don't see the connection," Toner said.

"It's obvious. Their brains are in a natural state of acceleration. I'm convinced…"

"Are you trying to tell me these kids are chronic potheads—in a state of perpetual 'duh'? That's the most ridiculous thing I've heard you say all week."

"That's not what I meant," Kaloostian protested. "These kids are beyond anything you or I could ever hope to experience. For me, for you, being high is as close to their thought processes as we can get. This goes beyond 'oh wow man.' I'm talkin' religious experience."

Kaloostian suddenly laughed and shook his head.

"What's so funny?" Toner asked.

"I just recognized the irony of this whole thing. We stumbled onto the Nyentzi Project all because of your heroics busting the Mercado drug cartel Monday morning."

"Your point?"

"Methamphetamine…that's what their brains must be like, how their minds function. Like they were dipped in pure crystal meth."

Toner did not agree with Greg's conclusion, but she said nothing.

"Don't be so skeptical, Angie. What do you think your Native-American ancestors were doing with all that peyote in the first place? Hallucinations and religion—it's like bread and beer, chicken and egg. No one knows which came first."

Toner shook her head. "Greg, sometimes I just don't know about you."

"Have you ever *listened* to Pink Floyd?"

"I've heard some of their music. Chip went through his *Dark Side of the Moon* phase, too. But at least he grew out of it."

"Don't be so sure about that."

Angela ignored him. "So what am supposed to do? Run out and buy a copy of the album and smoke a joint?"

"No, just take my word for it."

"I *will not* take your word for it. If those kids are looking for some sort of harmonic principle, why Pink Floyd? Why not the Mormon Tabernacle Choir, or Amy Grant, or the Moody Blues?"

Greg interrupted. "You're missing the point."

"…Or Alanis, or Bob," Toner continued, refusing to give up the debate. "Or Joan, or U2, or Natalie, or Jewel, or…"

"All right, already. I don't have an answer. But as far as the Moody Blues go, I think it's probably because they're too whimsical and saccharine."

"They're kids, Greg—seven-year-old girls. I'm fairly confident they don't sit in front of their computer screens flickin' their Bics."

"Would you stop reminding me who and what they are? You've made your point. And if you'd shut up and listen, I could make mine."

The force of Greg's anger was such that Toner finally settled down. "Fine, I'll listen."

"Thank you," Kaloostian said. "I was skeptical at first, too. But I've been thinking about this all night. These kids have lived their entire lives inside sterile rooms. They didn't quote the Moody Blues because they can't relate to voices in the sky or nights in white satin. They've never experienced the world like you or I have. And that hologram generator is not an appropriate substitute. So, for what my two cents are worth, I think they used Pink Floyd because their lives, their very existence is about a path towards a goal, not the goal itself."

"I don't understand."

Greg ran his hands through his hair and sighed. "Then you're *really* going to have to take my word for it. Pink Floyd's music is a multilevel, multi-theme, hypnotic bombardment of the senses. It's a sonic mindfuck about alienation, madness, technology, humanity, inhumanity, the passage of time, and who knows what else. All that background noise Gilmour, Waters, Wright, and Mason layered their music with is probably what those kids live with inside their brains—noise, static, voices, and more voices. These kids are hanging on in quiet desperation."

Toner wouldn't give up. "My dad said…"

"I don't care what your dad says. The Moody Blues sang about reaching spiritual goals. That's why they used all that harmony and flutes and violins. Their lyrics even rhymed. But Pink Floyd's music is about the path, the trials and tribulations of getting from point A to point B in the helter-skelter of modern society."

"La-di-fucking-dah. Look who's become an apprentice in the philosophical workshop."

"Knock it off, Angie! What do you expect from me or from these kids? Your father taught philosophy, for crying out loud. You ever hear him yell *eureka,* then quit his job because he'd finally found the key to all knowledge, wisdom, and truth? I think not."

Toner started to say something, but Kaloostian cut her off. "And furthermore, I never said I had all the answers. But at least I've got an open mind."

"Are holes in the head a requirement for having an open mind?"

Greg's patience faded. "You really know how to get on my nerves, Spud."

Angela shrugged. "So what's next, oh guru of mine? You gonna ask Alice?"

"No, I'm laying off the hard stuff," Greg muttered.

For several seconds, no one said a word. Kaloostian finally scratched his head and confronted his friend. "Okay, what is it today? What the hell put you in this frame of mind? Is this a continuation of last night's conversation, or have you found a new cross to bear?"

"I shouldn't be upset? Is that what you're insinuating? It's been less than a week, and just because you want to save the world from some cyber bogeyman, my life gets totally ruined. Then you act like I should be all smiles as the newest member of Kaloostian's witness-protection program. How's that for a cross to bear?"

"Anything else? 'Cuz I don't have all day. C'mon, hit me with both barrels."

"Just so you can twist my words all around," Toner answered.

"You know something? You're one of the smartest people I know, and I say that without reservation. You're smart, sensitive, and courageous. But sometimes, instead of looking at the big picture, you've got this unnerving habit of sticking your head in the sand."

"The big picture, huh? I suppose there's a sailor in that one, too."

"Forest and trees, Toner. Don't you see? Don't you understand the danger? It's the new millennium, and more than half the biggest economies in the world aren't even sovereign nations. They're multinational corporations with the ability to control world trade. They go where they want when they want—for lower wages, lower taxes, and higher government concessions. When they say *jump*, Uncle Sam, the Russian Bear, the Chinese Dragon, and everyone else says *how high?* The domination of these multinationals is concentrated, expansive, and growing each and every day. Now we've got this amoral little prick named Eldon Tyrell looking to enrich himself by upping the ante even further."

"So give up…as if you've got so much to lose."

"I'm not giving up, dammit. I'm not about to surrender my freedom to Tyrell or any other unaccountable corporate entity. This is supposed to be the Age of Aquarius, not the Age of Scorpio. My native country lost its independence. As a result, the Turks slaughtered almost two-thirds of the Armenian population. Look what the Nazis did to the Jews and the Gypsies, at what the British did to the Irish."

"You're really a well-rounded guy, Kaloostian. A minute ago, it was philosophy. Now you're giving me a history lesson. What's next, math or spelling?"

"What's next is called *slavery*."

Toner looked up and met Kaloostian's unyielding gaze.

"So…you recognize the word. Do I have your attention now that Tyrell is in *your* house?"

"And how does the lesson of slavery begin?" Angela asked.

"It begins with the lack of freedom, lack of choice, subjugation, economic serfdom. It begins with accepting that chains, shackles, and whips can happen in the new millennium. This time, the master wields the promise of meager wages, temporary jobs, a few scraps of profit sharing. Those are the new instruments of slavery, and they're no less dehumanizing."

Kaloostian paused. "I know you're down and out. Why don't you tell me what's really bothering you?"

Toner's expression was mixed. Her frustration had built for years, but she lacked an easy target for her rage. "I want to know," she said. "I just want to know how this happened, why this happened. And I want the truth, not the typical propaganda. No bullshit, no fables. I want an honest answer about Nyentzi. And I want to know why it involves me."

Kaloostian thought about her request, then answered. "If you've learned anything this past week, Angie, it oughta be to stop looking for the truth. It doesn't exist."

"I've got to believe there's more to life than shades of gray. I need something to go on, Greg. Something, anything to help me go through with this. I need to know why. Is that asking too much?"

"Okay, fair's fair. First, stop trying to answer the big one, the ultimate why. The Bible's been around for thousands of years, and "In the beginning…" is about as much of that conjecture mankind's ever been able to figure out."

"Don't you understand what you're asking me to do? I'll probably never be able to go home, see my family again. That's too high a price for a bystander to pay."

"There are no bystanders. The world's become too small a place to use not wanting to get involved as an excuse. No more us and them. We're all involved—one way or another."

"They're kids, Greg. I know they're gifted, but they're still only children."

"The hardest thing a person can do is to put the decision-making in somebody else's hands. It's a helpless feeling. It takes faith—the kind of faith you've got to dig pretty deep to find. But it's there. It's in you, waiting for a chance to grow."

"You don't seriously expect me to just sit on my butt and allow anyone and everyone to lead me around like a lost puppy, do you? Sorry, I don't see that as an option."

"You don't because your priorities are upside down. You're hell-bent on self-actualization, while your only concern should be pure, fucking survival."

Angela clenched her face, her body shaking. She gritted her teeth and bit her lower lip, glowering at Kaloostian's image on her computer.

"There's a plaque in the California desert," Greg said, maintaining the initiative. "You mentioned it to me once, remember? Something like: 'On this site was a concentration camp that housed innocent men, women, and children whose only crime was being of Japanese descent...' You know what I'm talking about. I can see it in your eyes. 'Such an injustice,' you said. 'Grandpa Sugihara gave his life for America, and look how they repaid him.'"

"What about it?" Toner asked.

"Where's the truth? Some people go there and lay flowers or leave photographs of dead ancestors. To them, that plaque is a shrine. But I also read about—I never told you this—one old WWII vet who drove hundreds of miles to that sacred place in the desert, and it wasn't to lay flowers. He *pissed* all over that plaque, Angie. Not because he was a racist or didn't like sushi, but because he'd been a prisoner of the Japanese. Because he'd seen his buddies bayoneted, shot, starved, mutilated, used as human guinea pigs in medical experiments. He'd seen a different side of the Japanese culture. Who's the victim? Who's the aggressor? Us or them? Where's the truth? Don't you see? The twins are right. It's all shades of gray. There is no ultimate truth."

Angela was torn. She saw the logic of Kaloostian's argument but was too stubborn to abandon her lifelong quest. "Dammit, Greg. I..."

"Still won't give up," Greg said, seeing her frustration. "Okay, here's another one. You ever see the movie *Until the End of the World*? Bill Hurt, Sam Neill, Solveig Dommartin?"

Toner shook her head.

"Too bad. There's this perfect example of the duality of truth. Dommartin plays a woman named Claire who knows Hurt's whereabouts. There's a price on his head, and a bounty hunter's slipped a truth drug into her drink. Wonderful scene. She fights the medication, does everything she can not to tell the truth. You see, she's in love with Hurt and doesn't want to betray him. But the drug's too powerful, and she has no control over what she says.

"Finally, she answers the guy's questions, tells him exactly what he wants to know. But she does it on her terms by speaking French. And he doesn't understand a word she's saying. Now answer me this, Angela Toner: Did Claire tell the truth or not? She answered his questions, but he didn't know what she was saying."

"And the moral of the story is?" Toner asked.

"That you're trying too hard, looking too deep. Angie, these kids trust you. They know you care. That's all I know, and that's all I need to know to do everything I can to help you. I know I got you into this, but that's not why I've put my own life on the line."

"Why me?"

"You want an explanation or an excuse? Luck of the draw is how I see it. If you want to go any deeper, I'd say it's because you question everything. As your personnel file so aptly illustrates, to you *nothing* is sacred. I also know you need to stop being so damned Irish about it."

Angela took a deep breath. "Okay, what should I do?"

"Work with us. Trust us. You're not alone. You'd be amazed how many people are on your side."

"All right, I'll stop giving Loris a hard time. What else should I do?"

"Be patient. Be brave."

"Okay, I'll do my best."

Greg smiled. "That's all I ask, Angie. You're my dearest friend. I won't let you down."

"Thanks. It's nice to hear you say that."

"I'll say it anytime you want." There was a moment of silence. Then Greg continued. "On a more mundane note, we should keep using Nadezhda's voicemail box in Moscow. There's no way anyone can trace us to that location."

"Okay. I miss her, Greg. She was such a good person."

"I know. I wish we could've…you know what I mean." Kaloostian changed the subject. "By the way, how'd the trip to Yerevan with the hockey team go?"

"It was all right. I didn't get a chance to say thank you or good-bye to Vassily, though. Once we landed, everything moved so quick."

"Maybe you'll see him again. Who knows, maybe..."

Angela heard a knock at the front of the house. "Just a minute, Greg. Someone's at the door. It better be some food, or I'm gonna get really ugly."

"Hey, before you go, put that crazy Armenian on."

"Which one? You're all crazy," Toner said with a small smile. "Hey Loris, someone's at the door, and Kaloostian wants you." Turning back to her computer, Angela said her good-byes to Greg, just as Loris came upstairs from his darkroom.

She went to the front door and stopped. Her Beretta was in her computer bag on the kitchen floor. Angela knew she should have it ready, but for some reason, she felt safer in Armenia than she'd felt anywhere in forty-eight hours.

Ignoring her better judgment, she unlocked the door and opened it. A man holding a large paper bag was standing on the front step, facing the street. Hearing the door open, he turned around.

"Vassily! What are you doing here?" Angela said.

"It's just a matter of time, if you ask me."

"I think you're right. It's inevitable."

"No doubt about it. They're going to take over the world."

"Well, they have my vote," Vassily Molotov said, shoving a forkful of moo goo gai pan into his mouth. "A Chinese restaurant on every corner."

Angela Toner nodded. They sat around the kitchen table, feasting on egg rolls, two kinds of rice, and several entrees. A bottle of wine was half empty.

"Living in LA—it's something I've always taken for granted. But I still can't believe you showed up at a house in Yerevan, Armenia, with a four-course meal from Uncle Chen's Hot Wok. A most pleasant surprise."

Loris Berberian looked up from his plate of General Tso's Chicken and frowned. "Hey, you talk like this is the far side of the moon. Yerevan is a world-class city, even if it's not New York or LA."

Angela smiled. "Sorry, Loris. I wasn't trying to dis your fair city. It's just that when I think of a meal in Armenia, moo goo gai pan is not what comes to mind. And you," she added, turning to Vassily. "Now that you've got food in your stomach, would you mind telling me how you found me? And why you're here?"

"I hate to say it. You might be angry at him again."

Toner frowned and shook her head. "Kaloostian."

"I checked Nadezhda's voicemail box for messages," Molotov explained. "She asked me to do that when she was out of town. I found an old communication from Gregory. I had forgotten his last name, so now I knew it and his telephone number. Then I called and talked to him. He called Loris for a three-way conversation. Now here I am."

"Why Vassily? You're not thinking of...?"

Loris reached across the table with a white box of food. "Angela, would you like to try some of my chicken? It's very good."

Toner set her chopsticks down. "Someone's got some explaining to do."

"We wanted to surprise you," Vassily attempted with a feeble grin.

"Like I haven't had enough surprises the past five days. All right you guys, cut the crap. What plans have you made without consulting me?"

"No plans. We are merely keeping our options open. Tyrell and his allies will be looking for a single, woman traveler. Perhaps if Vassily..."

"Ooo, you men are so devious. Do you want me to complete that thought, or can I just assume you're thinking about tagging along?" Angela said, looking sternly at Molotov.

"I do not tag along. I am volunteering as your escort."

"No way. And now that we've broached the subject of air travel, what was the deal with your hockey team? They acted like I had the plague."

"I told them you were with the league rules committee, that our team had been accused of cheating, that you were an investigator with a bad temperament."

"Clever."

"I had to be sure no one talked to you," Vassily said. "I did not want any player informing to their parents that I was transporting an FBI agent. You understand, do you not?"

"Yeah, it makes sense. You could have told me, though."

"It was best you did not know. The players were trying to make you uncomfortable with staring."

"They sure as heck succeeded." Angela paused, then jumped right into the next topic. "But you're not coming with me, Vassily. There's no way."

"Please do not be so quick," Loris said, taking a sip of wine. "There is much to consider."

"I don't like where this conversation is going. Nadezhda is dead, and I don't want…"

"That was not your fault. There was nothing you could have done," Vassily insisted.

Angela bit her lower lip, trying to keep an open mind to the idea of a male traveling companion. "Why? Why would you want to do this?" she asked, worried that Vassily's only concern was revenge.

"I am twenty-two years old and have never been to Disneyland."

"That's not the answer I expected."

"Perhaps you asked the wrong question," Vassily said, holding out the contents of a paper bag for Angela to pick from. "Fortune cookie…?"

29

A Blur of Bytes

Kaloostian couldn't remember the first time he'd heard of *spam* in terms of the Internet, but he didn't like it—the corruption of a perfectly good product's name. And if Eldon Tyrell was spamming, he must certainly be desperate.

The mystery man was doing his damnedest to locate Angela Carmen Toner. He'd pasted her picture onto a missing-persons web site, as well as other Internet locations, asking anyone and everyone for information on her whereabouts. It was a bold move, one Kaloostian had not expected.

Greg guessed the web site was a dead end. Any data sent in was certain to be irretrievable—useless for tracing a message to Tyrell. Still, he'd give it a try.

For the occasion, Kaloostian used a fairly routine virus. Once received, the virus would lock onto the site's point of origin. The encoded information would escape by eating its way out, effectively destroying the site. The virus would then find its way back to the transitory rendezvous created for the occasion.

As a precaution, Greg bounced his call several times. When he found the site, he hit *enter* and it was "bombs-away." The procedure was probably a waste of time, but he had no choice. They could no longer take Eldon Tyrell for granted. If he had learned anything the past week, it was that Tyrell could not be ignored.

While he waited, Greg remembered a conversation he'd had with Jim Revkin Wednesday evening. They'd discussed the ramifications of Nyentzi, both men afraid the work of the children would be misused.

"I think evil is growing smarter," Revkin had said.

Kaloostian had reached a dissimilar conclusion. "Evil may be getting more resourceful, but don't you think that poses a mutual danger?"

"I don't see why," Revkin said.

"Technology may make evil smarter, but with technology comes information. You can't have one without the other. As I see it, information is a two-edged sword. It cuts both ways."

"I see what you mean," Revkin said. "Like the Chinese in the 1990s. The more the government used computers and electronics to track down dissidents, the more the dissidents used those tools to escape detection."

"Exactly. And the students were better at it than the government. It's impossible to suppress or monopolize both technology and information."

Revkin wasn't convinced. "I think you're overly optimistic," he said. "Look at what technology's done for us. Not only do we have TV, newspapers, and personal mail, but we're also swamped with faxes, email, and all that other electronic debris. Look at me. I've got three voicemail systems, two web sites, a cell phone. I've got tons of options for communicating with the world, but I've also got paralysis of analysis. There's no way I can sift through all that information."

"What's your point?" Kaloostian asked.

"Don't you see? We're right back to information overload. It's impossible for us to assimilate so much data. So we've developed the habit of believing other people's conclusions, making decisions without forming our own opinions—without knowing all the pertinent facts. What's worse, we're forced to focus on a smaller and smaller vision of the world. That being the case, it's become way too easy to fudge the data any which way. The government—or Tyrell, for that matter—can say or do damn near anything they want and have us all believing it's for our own good."

"It wouldn't last," Greg insisted. "The truth is impossible to suppress."

Revkin shook his head. "You're relying on the past. Today's decisions are based on today's facts. Sure, we can review history and reinterpret it, but current events are moving too fast for that luxury. The present has become a blur of bytes and images. And the decisions that govern our lives don't happen in the past, they happen in the present."

"But if enough people are aware of the lie, can't they educate everyone else?"

"Are you serious? The only way the uninformed masses can avoid being jerked around is for Tyrell not to use the information he's hoarding. And that won't happen because he *has* to use it. Information is like money. You've got to spread it around. That's the only way it increases in value.

"And if you think that's bad, remember that information is *not* like money. Spend twenty dollars and it's gone. But you can use the same data again and again. I think that's why the government's so afraid of Tyrell. With the database he's accumulated, he can dictate agenda and policy. The founding fathers thought taxation without representation sucked. Now we've got representation without representation."

"How much of this do you think Uncle Sam knows?" Gregory asked.

"Probably everything. It's definitely aware of what's going on, but I don't think it's involved in the destruction of Monogovody. It really got suckered on this one. Nyentzi is one of those nightmares, like the Bay of Pigs, that passes from administration to administration. That's why somebody created that file your friend got her hands on—trying to find a way to defeat or curtail the Eldon Tyrell's influence."

"Do you think the government will help us?"

"Not a chance. Whoever created the file was looking for a way to counter Tyrell. Now they're screwed, and Tyrell is probably threatening to expose the whole thing, all the way back to Monogovody. If that's the case, the Feds will do anything to squelch the rumors and bury the evidence. We're as dangerous to Uncle Sam as we are to Tyrell."

Greg had reached that conclusion hours before, but he was glad Revkin agreed. "In other words, we shouldn't be looking for the Feds to move against him?"

"They can't…or won't take out Tyrell. Without him, they'll never get their hands on all that technology. They know how valuable Nyentzi is, and they'll protect it any way they can. And you think that's bad, remember it's not just Uncle Sam we're dealing with. It's every corporate and government sponsor of the original program."

Greg hoped Revkin was wrong, but he feared the worst. Maybe technology *was* evil. Yet short of nuclear war or environmental holocaust, there was no turning back. Mankind had reduced its destiny to a limited scope of possibilities along an ever narrower path.

Five minutes had passed with no word from the virus he'd sent to Tyrell's web site. Gregory reached for the keyboard. Admitting defeat, he eliminated the rendezvous.

He had one more call to make before getting some sleep. Wanting no more surprises for Angela Toner, Greg accessed his on-line operator. He paused before dialing Nadezhda Molotova's voicemail box in Moscow. Kaloostian knew he'd been lucky so far, avoiding detection by Tyrell and his allies—or so he trusted.

"What if…? Damn," he muttered to himself. "What if…?" He done everything possible to stay in the cybershadows of the Internet, but now he had no choice. He had to place the call, had to leave Toner a message. She had to know what Tyrell was doing.

At least the voicemail box in Moscow was secure. Greg had verified that. Not wanting to risk another call to Loris's house, he dialed the number. After a short delay, he entered the system and heard a beep, signifying a message. He typed the password, expecting to hear Toner's sarcastic banter. Instead, he heard a child's voice. It was Lara or Katya.

Hatton fumed, "This really sucks." Late Saturday evening and he was out of milk. Granted, he'd rather have a double shot of Jack Daniel's on the rocks, but not tonight, not with his stomach acting up.

Kaloostian had left him with explicit instructions to stay home, at least until Monday. At that point, he'd become vague—something about getting away from Eldon Tyrell.

"Why Monday?" Hatton wondered "What was supposed to happen on Monday?" And why was Kaloostian bothering with him? He was useless to the bureau, useless to Toner, useless to the children of Nyentzi that Kaloostian had told him about. Useless even to himself. He was more than a burden. He was a nuisance.

"I'm too old for this shit."

The possibility of another sleepless night contemplating his future was all the incentive Hatton needed to ignore Kaloostian's advice. He put on a dark blue windbreaker, slipped his .357 magnum into its shoulder holster, and went to the front window. After turning off the living-room lamp, he opened the shade and peered out. The street was empty, as it had been all evening.

His Ford pickup was parked in front. He'd stopped using his garage after the encounter with the gang. Satisfied that the coast was clear, Hatton unlocked the front door of his house and stepped out. Keys in hand, he silently approached the truck.

Before unlocking the passenger-side door, Hatton got down on his knees. With a penlight he examined the underside of the truck. Satisfied there was no bomb, he unlocked the door.

As intended, the dome light did not go on. In the darkness of the California night, the former assistant deputy director closed the door, slid across the seat, and turned the ignition. He slipped into gear and pulled away from the curb. Only when he was all the way down the block did he turn on the headlights.

The local 711 was less than a mile away. Staying on the main streets and avoiding a shortcut, he'd be back home in less than ten minutes. Traffic was light when Hatton made a left turn, marking the halfway point. Suddenly, out of nowhere, a dilapidated, twenty-year-old junkyard wannabe roared alongside. Several shots rang out, piercing his steel-belted radials. As Hatton lost control, the driver of the car spun his wheel sharply to the right, crashing into the truck and sending it up the curb and into a palm tree.

The force of the impact propelled Hatton's body forward. Even at twenty-five miles per hour, a sudden stop can be deadly. But the shoulder strap tightened and his airbag exploded, stopping his forward momentum.

As soon as the airbag deflated, Hatton heard the screech of tires as the other vehicle made a U-turn and headed back his way. Unbuckling his shoulder belt, Hatton threw himself to the passenger side of the truck, grabbed a backpack he kept under the seat, opened the door, and slid out.

The rust bucket was approaching fast. Hatton glanced to his right and spotted an alley just down the block. Using his truck as a shield, he stood and fired three quick shots. At least one hit the oncoming car, shattering the windshield. The speeding car veered out of control while Hatton made a dash for cover.

Once in the safety of the alley's darkness, the old soldier paused and caught his breath. The driver must have regained control, as Hatton heard no impact. He did hear the sound of slamming brakes and the slamming of car doors.

Moving slowly from the street, Hatton saw that the alley opened into a parking lot behind the buildings. There was a light pole next to a dumpster, but he could see that the bulb had been shattered. Beyond the parking lot was a slight rise, dotted with palm trees and overgrown with weeds, the only cover in sight. Al ran across the parking lot, part way up the hill, and sat down in the tall grass.

He could see the shadows of the buildings across the blackness of the parking lot. He had a perfect view of the alley. Anyone moving that way would be in direct line of fire. Keeping his ears open, Hatton dug into the backpack, checking its contents—umbrella, extra shoes, tools, and, most important, two boxes of ammunition.

He reloaded, closed the pack, and slung it over his shoulder. Crawling on his hands and knees, he moved up the hill, searching for an avenue of escape.

The hill sloped down to a chain link fence, topped with barbed wire, angled towards the parking lot. On the other side was a sharp drop to a railroad track. He was trapped.

Biting his lower lip in frustration, Hatton slid back down. He found a depression in the hillside and took a seat. From this perspective, he had the advantage. He might be an old fart, but he had a few tricks up his sleeve. Unless his pursuers tried to overrun him in a suicide attack, he could hold the position until help arrived. The punks might be able to run faster, jump higher, and see better in the dark, but over the years, Al Hatton had learned a fundamental truth. In a battle that pitted youth and speed against age and guile, youth and speed didn't stand a chance. Or so the theory went.

In the chilly dampness of the California twilight, Al Hatton glanced at his watch and waited for the gangbangers to attack. It was almost 2300 hours.

"You stupid fool. You never should've gone out so late."

While he waited, he thought about his own adolescence. During the mid-1960s, hot action on a Saturday night had meant one of two things—a date with Mary Jane Mulligan or a twelve-pack, a couple of good friends, and a full tank of gas. For youth prowling LA's streets in the twenty-first century, however, a good time involved a Cobray .380-cal. with a select fire rate of 1,200 rounds per minute and a good pair of sneakers.

He'd been a wide-eyed kid when he stepped off the C-141 transport plane in South Vietnam in early 1968. Despite 352 hours in eight weeks of basic training, despite classes in everything from venereal disease to bayonet thrusting, despite a drill sergeant explaining his mistakes in language that left nothing to the imagination at a decibel level just below the roar of a nuclear explosion, despite all that, Alfred Lee Hatton was a child until he saw combat.

And of all the combat he'd seen, the worst came at night. Leeches and snakes in the water, booby traps across the trails, the red glare of rocket fire, the screams of the wounded, the silence of the dead.

Now, forty years later, squatting in the weeds, hunted by a gang dressed like Vietcong in baggy black pants, Hatton had come full circle. Gripping his .357 magnum, he couldn't help but think of Vietnam. Nighttime in the Mekong Delta, he realized, was not much different from nighttime in Los Angeles. Darkness in the jungle meant certain things, and none of them were encouraging.

It took Hatton less than a year in 'Nam to learn how combat changes people. Extroverts became withdrawn, introverts became homicidal maniacs, and homicidal maniacs became conscientious objectors. For Hatton's generation—and every generation before and after—war was as profound an experience as any human being could live through, packing a lifetime of bad memories into a single enlistment.

No matter how much training a soldier received or how much technology at his disposal, he was not adequately prepared for combat. Only through firsthand witness could one appreciate the enormity of war.

But his experience forty years earlier made Hatton hopeful he had the edge. He did not know or appreciate that the gangbangers moving towards his position, though children by many standards, had lived their entire lives in a war zone. To them, Saturday night on the streets of LA wasn't war; it was practice.

The silence broke. "Give us Señorita Angela," a voice shouted from his left.

"Yeah, amigo. Don't try to be brave *and* stupid," a voice chimed in from his right.

They were on both sides, but Al was sure they hadn't located him. He didn't know how many were in each group, but he could see only one punk lurking in the shadows behind the dumpster in the alley straight ahead. His only hope of getting out alive lay in that direction.

Hatton silently reached into his backpack and pulled out a long-handled flashlight. He had one shot at making his escape. Leaning on his left side, he threw the flashlight in a long arc towards the fence. It sailed through the air, missed a palm tree, and hit the top of the fence. A loud clang, then it clattered down the embankment to the railroad track.

All hell broke loose. Voices shouted on both sides; their owners emerged from the shadows. Hatton forced himself into the hollow, hoping the weeds would shield him.

In seconds, two groups of three figures ran by his position near the top of the hill. The shouting continued as both groups reached the fence. Though the animated conversation was primarily in Spanish, Hatton could sense their disbelief.

"Little bastards don't think I could've gotten over the fence," he thought to himself. "Just my luck…maybe they're not as dumb as they look."

But they did suspect their quarry had scaled the fence or slipped past them in the darkness. All six bangers moved along the top of the hill, scanning the terrain, their weapons ready. After they had gone fifty yards, Hatton crept out of his hole, moving through the weeds on his hands and knees. By the time he'd reached the edge of the parking lot, the gang was a football field away.

"Now or never, asshole," Hatton declared, sitting on his haunches in the weeds. He took a deep breath and ran, the shoulder bag slamming into his side like a lead-filled bowling ball. The dumpster, less than forty yards away, might as well, in the night, have been a mile. Hatton ignored his own labored breathing and focused all his senses on one thing—his target.

With five yards to go, the punk, who must have been daydreaming, spun and faced him. Hatton saw a baby-faced Latino.

"Fuckin' kid's still wet behind the earring," he thought, coming to a stop.

Eye met eye, but only for a moment. Then the teen's line of vision shifted to the barrel of Hatton's .357, pointing directly at his head. His own pistol—Hatton couldn't identify the make or model—was stuck inside the waist of his baggy trousers.

Against his better judgment, Hatton didn't immediately blow the kid away and make a run for the street. "On your belly, goddammit," he instinctively ordered. "Do it now."

"*Que pasa?*"

"What is your *fucking* malfunction? I said…" Hatton didn't finish the sentence.

In slow motion, kid reached for his pistol. For Alfred Lee Hatton, this was 1968 all over again. He didn't hesitate. The roar of the magnum was loud and decisive. The kid was dead before he hit the ground.

Still holding his weapon with both hands, his arms extended, the barrel pointing down, Hatton advanced the final few feet. He stared at the crumpled body, at the arms and legs spread in four directions. Hatton couldn't remember the last time he'd seen a dead person, at least not one who had died at his hands.

Hatton identified the pistol that lay next to the boy as a Tec-9. He knelt and picked it up. "Nice piece…Nice shot, too," he admitted without humor. The slug from the .357 had caught the punk in the left eye.

Other than the black hole for the eye, the face looked almost normal. The right eye was open, giving an overall expression of surprise.

Where the slug exited the kid's head was another story. The back of the skull was gone, brain matter and bright blood scattered on the pavement. Hatton knew the shot had alerted the other gang members. He had to move, but he couldn't help himself—couldn't stop staring.

Had it really been forty years? The memory seemed like yesterday. He was young then, and life had seemed long. Though his flashback lasted only a second, it came with a flood of images—patrols, boredom, government-issue rations, Saigon, nightmares, water buffalo, the jungle, the wounded…and the dead.

During the war, Hatton had dealt with death and dying like most of the others. Half the time they saw action; the other half was a splurge of drunkenness and despair. No wonder his memories of the war were convoluted.

But one memory stood. One memory refused obliteration.

He didn't know the replacement's name—never even had a chance to introduce himself. On the kid's first night patrol, Hatton had heard an explosion and come running. He found the new guy—what was left of him—just off the trail.

Both legs were gone. Well, they weren't really gone. They just weren't attached to his body. His right arm was broken, the left ripped off at the elbow, lying next to him, still clutching his M-16. Shrapnel from the claymore had ripped his belly, spilling his guts.

In the dim moonlight, it was a scene from hell. Hatton knelt, appalled to discover the kid was still alive. He looked at Hatton with uncomprehending eyes, his mouth open, trying to speak. Hatton leaned closer, trying to hear.

"Shoot me," the kid whispered. "For the love of God, shoot me."

Hatton never had the chance. The VC, alerted to the patrol's location by the explosion of the mine, opened fire. Hatton dropped to his belly and tried to find cover. As the night lit up, he lost his direction, unable to find the kid with no legs and one arm.

He wanted to find him. As the fire fight wore on, he became frantic, more concerned with finding him than with killing VC. He wanted to finish the job Charlie had started. He went so far as to call in help from the great unknown.

But God wasn't home that night. God was busy elsewhere.

From that night on, the only thing Alfred Lee Hatton wanted from God was a promise. "When the end finally comes, oh God of mine," he prayed. "Keep steady the hand holding the gun. Do not let it waiver or falter, Lord. Send the bullet with my name on it straight and true. Right between the eyes, God. That's all I want. Don't let me be wounded. Don't let me be maimed. Make it fast and easy. Amen."

Hatton heard shouting from the parking lot and returned to reality. Grabbing a clip from the dead kid's pocket and holding the Tec-9 in his left hand and his .357 in his right, he took off towards the street. He passed the beat-up Chevy, parked at the end of the alley. He had no time to steal it. The enemy was hot on his trail.

Hatton darted from the alley into the street. His pickup was still up against the palm tree, its hood open. He ran to the truck, stopped, and looked inside. The wires had been cut. The battery was in the gutter.

"Sonofabitch," he swore. "So much for Plan B."

He looked up and down the street, but there was no avenue of escape. They'd shoot him in the back before he got half a block. As he contemplated his next move, one of the six who'd chased his flashlight ran from the alley.

The hunted now became the hunter, if only for a moment. Al raised the Tek-9 and let loose a volley of lead, emptying the clip in one long burst, ripping the kid from stem to stern. Spewing blood in every direction, the body hit the ground with an empty sigh. Hatton could hear his other pursuers screech to a halt, their sneakers slipping on the gravel.

"Where the hell are the police?" Hatton muttered. More than five minutes had elapsed since his car hit the tree. Even in this business district, even this late, traffic and people moved about. The street intersected with a busy thoroughfare just several blocks away. "Somebody should've called in a report by now, for God's sake, unless…"

He remembered Kaloostian's description of Tyrell's computer capabilities. If the mystery man had hacked his way into the bureau's files, he could do the same with the LAPD. For all he knew, someone *had* called in the accident. But Tyrell may have intercepted the calls.

Al Hatton was on his own. Other than a hearse, the only help arriving any time soon would be more punks with Uzis, Glocks, and Cobrays.

With a heavy sigh, Hatton planned his next move. His options were limited. What he planned would require total surprise, a lot of luck, and more courage than he thought he had.

Al Hatton knew what courage was. And he knew what it was not. He'd seen the cowards of the world hiding behind the flag, the pulpit, a white sheet. The heroes, on the other hand, stood firmly behind the truth of their convictions. The only trouble with that, he knew from experience, was that the truth makes a better target than a shield.

Hatton reloaded the Tec-9 and checked his .357. Still crouching behind the front end of his wrecked truck, he thought about the mistakes of his life—the dumb things he'd said, the promises he'd broken, the people he'd hurt. Then he thought about what he would do and who it was for. It gave him strength he needed.

With a roar of determination, Alfred Edward Hatton, age fifty-nine, overweight, balding, and with borderline hypertension, stood up straight, fired a couple of quick shots for effect, and charged. He ran past the body he'd riddled with bullets, rounded the corner, and saw several moving shadows down the alley, lurking by the dumpster and the corpse he'd shot through the head.

Still shouting, Hatton reached the car. He flipped the handle to open the door, prepared to jump in and speed away. It was locked.

These heavily armed killers had locked the doors to their car so no one could steal it. It must be one tough neighborhood.

"Jesus H. Christ on a cheap raft up shit creek without a fucking paddle," he swore.

He couldn't stop now. As the shadows near the dumpster dove for cover, Hatton emptied the Tec-9 and blasted away with his .357 magnum. Moving towards them in orgasmic fury, Al expected the punks to scatter.

But they didn't. They held their ground like soldiers.

He could hear bullets ricocheting off the dumpster and the pavement, but only one of the figures dropped. Halfway between the car and the dumpster, he ran out of ammunition. Coming to a halt, Hatton saw the glint of gun barrels in the cloudy light of the waning moon. He also got a look at the remaining bangers. They were as young as the kid he'd popped earlier.

Hatton laughed out loud. "Well, fuck me. It's the Lollipop Guild."

The punks opened fire, not in the least bit amused. The first shot struck the former deputy assistant director of the FBI's Los Angeles office in the right arm. He dropped the Tec-9 and clutched the injured limb as another bullet shattered his right knee, dropping him like a sack of groceries. Even as he fell, the shooting continued. Bullet after bullet hit the old soldier. Finally the shooting stopped.

In the eerie quiet of the alley, Al Hatton lay on the pavement, bleeding from wounds to his chest, arms, and legs. He had proved he was not a coward. He couldn't hear and his vision was blurred, but he could just make out four figures standing above him, looking down. He coughed once, spitting blood.

As the ghostly figures prepared to finish the job, Al Hatton tried to think of something profound to summarize his life—a personal epitaph. But he couldn't clear his mind of the song that kept playing in his head:

And it's one, two, three, what are we fighting for
don't ask me, I don't give a damn
the next stop is Vietnam
and it's five, six, seven, open up the pearly gates
well it ain't no time to wonder why
whoopee we're all gonna die…

  He heard the chorus one last time, followed by an explosion. Then finally, peace.

30

A Wing and a Prayer

"One day at a time," the bumper sticker declared. To the undersized youth ambling through the parking lot of the Los Angeles International Airport, it seemed overly generous for a Monday morning. Homeless, uneducated, underaged, and unemployed, he lived his life more minute-to-minute than day-to-day.

The job offer couldn't have come at a better time. With luck, he might even get paid. He'd seen the assignment advertised on the Internet at the public library and recognized the address. Having worked for *the man* in the past, he knew it was legit.

Though he lived in southern California, the kid's skin was deathly pale. His cheeks were gaunt, like those of a refugee. His lips were chapped, and his nose was running. Not for at least seven more years would he have to worry about shaving.

He called himself Zombie, a tag used for so long he'd almost forgotten his real name. Since their drunken father—or was it their drunken mother?—had kicked his older brother out of the house, his life had gone steadily downhill. With big brother gone, Zombie became the sole target of his parents' physical, verbal, and psychological abuse. It was simply too much for the adopted child. He stuffed a backpack with clothes and books, emptied his father's checking account with a pilfered ATM card, and hit the road. He'd been running ever since, all the way from Indianapolis to Los Angeles—two years on the streets.

Zombie would be eleven in June...if his luck held out.

He wore an oversized trench coat, courtesy of the Salvation Army. Out of style, ragged, and dirty, it still kept him warm and dry. His faded jeans had more holes than a bad alibi. The green sweatshirt beneath the trench coat showed the initials *ND* on the chest in gold. Zombie's uncle had gone to Notre Dame. The sweatshirt was the one sentimentality the teen allowed himself. His uncle was the only adult member of his family who had treated him with the slightest kindness.

The teen's shoes, shoplifted in December, were his Christmas present to himself. New shoes, a meal at a good restaurant, and a pack of cigarettes—happy fucking holidays.

To the average passerby he was one of the walking dead, worse off even than the minimum-wage serfs who slaved throughout the world of the Third Millennium. Zombie was at the bottom of the totem pole, all but invisible to the society that had created him.

Under an LA Dodger baseball cap, Zombie's hair was brown and dirty. It hadn't seen a comb in weeks. He kept it long in front, hanging in his eyes. The back of his head was shaved almost to the top, showing off his red tattoo—*DKDC*. Like his name, it was effective camouflage. Zombie did know, and Zombie did care. He just preferred to keep it to himself.

The hair in his eyes was an essential component of his careful ensemble. Together with the bill of his hat, it prevented adults, most of whom were much taller than he, from seeing his eyes. Zombie tried to avoid that.

He knew what would happen. People would call him a freak. They wouldn't understand that he was special...endowed...over their heads.

They wouldn't understand that his eyes were gifts from God. They'd ask the same stupid questions, try to discover the secret of his gift. But Zombie couldn't explain why he was chosen or how his eyes worked. All he knew, all he wanted to know, was that his eyes were magic.

With his fantastical emerald eyes, Zombie could see things other humans couldn't. He could see deep inside the people who despised him. He could see the muscles and bones under their skin, the organs, sinew, cartilage, arteries, and other details of their bodies. He could see through the rouge, the eyeliner, the lipstick, and blush. He could ignore the beards, scars, mustaches, and dark glasses. With his ability to perceive the real person beneath the Madison Avenue costumes and fitness-center physiques, Zombie's vision of the world was one of unrefined purity. All because of his magic eyes.

During the week, Zombie set up his makeshift portrait studio at airport and bus terminals, on street corners, or in shopping malls. With remarkable ease, armed only with a pad of paper and a No. 2 pencil, he sketched people as they walked by, turning a ten-second glance into a graphic likeness equal to any portrait. It was a rare talent for which he'd never received schooling or training. It had come to him instinctively, like a cheetah's speed or a giraffe's height.

It was the kind of talent would make a normal person wealthy. But Zombie wasn't normal, not by a long shot. He was a destitute, delusional, frail misfit, whose life on the street most likely would be short.

Rather than making him rich, his genius provided only enough money for an occasional fast-food feast and his drugs—and only on days he saw fit to sell his art, which were few and far between. At other times, Zombie begged, borrowed, or stole.

But not today. Today would be payday.

After the bus dropped him off, he wandered through the central parking lot of the airport. The message on the Internet had suggested the international terminal as the best place to begin the search. But that was too obvious. Zombie was going on a hunch.

Nearing the entrance to the terminal, the youth adjusted his Dodger's cap, pulling it down even farther. He straightened his headphones and untangled the cord that snaked down his arm to a pocket of his trench coat, where it was plugged into…nothing at all. He'd hocked his stolen Discman weeks ago, and he hadn't gotten around to buying it back.

"No biggie," Zombie thought. When it came to listening to his favorite tunes, he'd discovered he didn't need the Discman. Running off the circuits of his brain, his personal repertoire of music was neurological, which had certain advantages. It went where he did, had no commercial interruptions, no obnoxious DJs, and best of all, needed no batteries.

Strolling with a certain lightness of step, Zombie felt lucky as he passed the suspicious-eyed security personnel at the front of the terminal. He scoped out the videorazzi, paparazzi, and autograph hounds who hovered about the airport like vultures, hoping to catch sight of people with big names.

Zombie's mark had a name, of course, but he didn't know what it was. All he had—all he needed—was a face. Everything else was clutter.

He glanced at an overhead display informing patrons of a flight from the East Coast arriving within the hour. He didn't bother checking the arrival gate, as he had learned that airport personnel did not feel blessed by his presence. To avoid harassment, Zombie stayed on his side of the security kiosk. If he identified the woman, however, he would have little time to make the call before she was out the door.

But the vagabond youth had come prepared. Surrounded by bustling crowds, hawking vendors, and public-address announcements, he took up his position on the tile floor where he could scrutinize all the people moving through the terminal to the exit. Sitting like a new-age buddha, his notepad and pencil in his lap, music blasting in his head, Zombie patiently waited, his head nodding to the cerebral rhythm:

Above the planet on a wing and a prayer,
My grubby halo, a vapor trail in the empty air,
Across the clouds I see my shadow fly
Out of the corner of my watering eye
A dream unthreatened by the morning light
Could blow this soul right through the roof of the night.

"Chicago?! Your father wanted to drop a nuclear bomb on Chicago?"

"No! He didn't want to do it. He wanted you to do it—the Communists, that is."

Vassily put his hand to his forehead and grimaced. "I am not a Communist. And what did your father have against that Chicago?"

"Nothing personally, but…"

"It is a great place—wonderful jazz and blues music—the Stormy City"

"Windy, not stormy," Angela Toner corrected.

"Whatever…" Molotov said. The flight had been long, and he'd gradually lost the desire to argue with his feisty, irritable companion. Their journey had taken them from Yerevan to London, from London to New York, and from New York to Los Angeles. Over the past twenty-four hours, the conversation between Angela Toner and Vassily Molotov had degenerated from intellectual banter to pass-the-time chitchat, to babble.

The men—Loris Berberian, Gregory Kaloostian, and Vassily Molotov—had won the first round. They'd talked Toner into allowing Nadezhda's younger brother to accompany her on the return trip to California. With that issue resolved, they had worked long into the night perfecting the change in her appearance. Even as the makeup dried, Loris had taken the final photographs, feeding them into his computer to complete her new identity.

Angela Carmen Toner, age thirty-two, no longer existed. In her place was an older woman, pushing fifty. Her Nevada driver's license listed her weight at 150, her height as five-feet-seven—twenty pounds and two inches that Angela could have done without. Other modifications included the darkening of her skin and the graying of her hair.

Her new name was Yvonne Denise Niemann, Las Vegas. In her purse were letters to her fictitious children, a notepad embossed with the logo of the casino where she worked as a waiter, even credit cards with hefty balances from Yvonne's recent holiday in Europe.

Every aspect of her new personality had been taken into consideration. She had a computer-generated photograph of a recent Niemann family gathering. In a classic Norman Rockwell pose, Yvonne/Angela stood proudly in front of a heavily decorated Christmas tree with her son and daughter, the family's black lab at their feet.

One aspect of Yvonne's personality drove Toner to distraction. Because of the war paint the old broad wore, Angela's skin itched increasingly. As she soon discovered, nothing was worse than an itch she couldn't scratch.

Yvonne had caught a cold in Europe, complete with a runny nose. Because of the delicacy of the latex makeup, however, she was unable to blow her nose, forcing her to spend every waking hour sniffing and coughing.

Vassily Molotov, on the other hand, had gotten off easy. He was now a foreign-exchange student at Berkeley, completing his studies towards a master's degree in child psychology. He had transcripts showing a GPA of 3.65 for one Lars Carl Larson, from Oslo, Norway.

Angela had insisted on picking out Vassily's new name. She'd always wondered why any parent would give a child a first name so similar to his or her last name. Accordingly, Lars Larson joined the ranks of such people as Danielle Daniels, Tom Thompson, Bhoutrous Bhoutrous, Richard Richards, Roberta Roberts, and Pete Peters. Now she knew why parents did it—pure spite.

The plane touched down, taxied towards the terminal. "And he's a philosophy professor?" Vassily asked, getting back to Toner's father.

"Just what kind of philosophy does he teach to want to destroy entire cities with nuclear bombs?"

"His sentiments about Chicago have nothing to do with philosophy," Toner said, feeling at home as she looked out the window at the noontime sun of Los Angeles. "Man, I wish I'd never said anything. I was just trying to make conversation."

"Well, what are you meaning then? I would like to know more about your family."

Toner looked at Vassily and tried to smile. "You wanna know why my dad wanted to nuke Chicago? Fine, I'll tell you. How's your geography?"

"I know where Chicago is, if that is what you are suggesting."

"Good. Here's Chicago, at the bottom of Lake Michigan. We lived on the eastern side of the lake, " Toner said, drawing a map on a cocktail napkin, "in the state of Michigan. But we had a timeshare condo to the northwest of Chicago—in Wisconsin, near Lake Geneva."

"Didn't there used to be a Playboy bunnies club there?!"

"Swimming and fishing only," Toner rebutted, ignoring Vassily's reference to Lake Geneva's past. "Anyway, to get there, we had to drive around the southern shore of Lake Michigan. It was all interstate, two to six lanes in each direction. Should've been smooth sailing, except the stupid Illinois Department of Transportation erected these freakin' tollbooths every few miles."

"We have tollbooths in Russia. What's the big deal?"

"Not like these, you don't. Traffic gets backed up for miles. A trip that should take four hours takes more than six, all because of the tollbooths in Chicago."

"Tollbooths are good for revenue collecting. They are just another form of the taxes."

"You don't understand. The Chicago toll system was built years ago, and the citizens were promised that once the highway was paid for, the tollbooths would be removed."

Vassily laughed. "And who made these unbelieving promises?"

"I don't know. The governor, state officials, whoever."

"Politicians, yes?"

"Yeah, but they promised!"

"And for breaking that promise, your father, an educated, presumably rational college professor, who taught philosophy—so you say—wanted to destroy an entire city?"

"I guess it does sound extreme."

"Only slightly," Vassily concluded.

"Actually, he didn't want to destroy the entire city. He always hoped you Ruskies would fine-tune the hydrogen bomb so that when it exploded, it would vaporize only the tollbooths, plus all the idiot employees who did nothing but stand around glaring at God-fearing, tax-paying motorists."

"And your husband, Jake, may he rest in peace…he met your father…and still he married you?"

A jab from Angela's right elbow into Vassily's ribs was her only response.

Angela walked alone down a concourse at the Los Angeles International Airport. Vassily stayed several steps behind, watching for surveillance. Her stride was slow, she conducted herself with an air of respectability that enhanced the persona of an older African-American woman. Her gray hair was shorter than before, arranged in a more mature style.

She wore a long, gray coat. A new carry-on bag, holding her laptop computer, swayed from her left shoulder. Angela had left her Beretta in Armenia. The absence of the gun's weight left her feeling naked.

They had passed through customs at JFK in New York without incident. Her passport, stamped for each stop of Yvonne Niemann's fictitious European vacation, had not raised an eyebrow. Nor did her disguise. If the search for Angela Toner was as widespread as Kaloostian reported, then Loris Berberian had done a remarkable job with her makeover. Wearing eyeglasses with nonprescription lenses, she was just another face in the crowd.

Most of the passengers from their flight had gone straight to the baggage claim. To save time and avoid the increased danger of recognition during a wait for their luggage, they had decided to abandon it. The clothes and personal belongings in their suitcase were props, put there solely to satisfy the curiosity of the customs officials in New York.

The sooner they were out of the airport and into a taxi for an arranged meeting with Kaloostian, the better. As anxious as she was to be on her way, Angela continued at a pace slow enough to avoid attention, to give no one a reason to look her way twice. She was a mature woman on her way to visit relatives, and after the long trip she felt the more than age on her new driver's license.

As Toner neared the end of Terminal 3, she saw nothing suspicious. On the other side of the security checkpoint, the normal airport crowds milled about, greeting friends, hailing taxies, shopping at obscenely priced airport concessions. Glad to be back in familiar territory, Angela didn't notice the unkempt youth on the floor, holding a tablet of paper on which he sketched her face with a stubby pencil.

"O frabjous day. Callooh! Callay!" Zombie chortled. It was *her*. Under the wrinkled latex, gray dye job, cosmetics, and phony glasses—here, most definitely, was his meal ticket. In less than twenty seconds, he finished the sketch, with results nothing short of astounding—a perfect rendition of Angela Carmen Toner, sans urban renewal. The disturbed juvenile delinquent with an amazing genius for portrait art had easily seen through a disguise that had fooled trained agents in both London and New York.

Zombie's hunch was correct. If one had to fly halfway around the world, traveling east to west was the better choice in terms of jet lag. Though he knew her flight had just landed, she was headed for the exit instead of the baggage claim. "Of course," the teen realized, "if she's lickety to split, she'd leave the luggage behind...No time to lose."

The line of people trying to get from Terminal 3 to the main concourse had backed up in the noon rush. This gave Zombie only a couple of minutes. He attached his digital notepad to a special button on a pay phone and dialed to the client's web site. Sliding his calling card through the magnetic slot, he heard a click, verifying the connection.

He glanced back at the mystery lady, then typed in his bank account number. No matter how desperate life on the street became, he always kept the minimum balance required.

Next he wrote the time and location of the sighting, along with a detailed description of the woman's disguise. The moment Zombie sent the information to the anonymous location on the worldwide web, he felt a tingling sensation in and around his spine, down his arms to his fingertips. His hands trembled in anticipation of his newfound wealth. For as long as he lived and high as he flew, Zombie knew tonight he was going to have some fun:

> There's no sensation to compare with this
> Suspended animation, a state of bliss
> Can't keep my mind from the circling sky,
> Tongue-tied and twisted, just an earth-bound misfit, I.

As much as Zombie wanted to kick up his heels, he knew his sighting would go unrewarded without verification by his employer. She was dangerously close to the front of the line. In less than a minute, his mark would be out the door and gone.

Zombie walked to a trash receptacle. Pretending to pick up litter, he crumpled a sheet of paper from his sketchpad and dropped it in the can. Then he reached into his coat pocket and pulled out an M-80. "Be, be, be prepared...the motto of a true Scout," the youthful vagrant sang to himself. He flicked his lighter, lit the fuse of the enormous firecracker, and tossed it into the container.

Wasting no time, Zombie walked briskly towards the exit. Normally he stuck around for the excitement of the explosion, the ensuing pandemonium, and his subsequent arrest. But tonight he didn't need a warm meal or bed at the county juvenile-detention center. Tonight he would party hardy.

Zombie was already on the bus that would take him downtown when the explosion tore the trashcan apart. He took his seat at the back of the bus and smiled.

At precisely 11:32 A.M., all hell broke loose on the main concourse of the Los Angeles International Airport. The loud *whump* of Zombie's M-80 shattered the sides of the heavy plastic trashcan, sending the lid into the air. A woman standing nearby fainted.

Everyone around fell to the ground or took off running. People screaming in panic toppled over their luggage and each other in an effort to escape the presumed terrorist attack. Security guards drew their weapons and rushed to the exit as police squads converged on the concourse, their sirens blaring.

The public address system barked: "Code red…code red…Section MC T-3. All units respond." Again and again came the announcement, barely audible above the frantic crowd. Yelling, shouting, crying, and praying drowned its blare. A tableau of unbridled terror and confusion followed the eruption.

Toner reacted by instinct and training. She dropped to one knee, reaching inside her almond-colored blazer for the Beretta before remembering who she was supposed to be. Vassily Molotov, however, acted like the normal person he was. He hit the ground split seconds after the bomb went off.

Moments later, looking up to see Toner behaving much too professionally, he pulled her to his level.

"Hey, watch the makeup," Angela said, pushing him away his clumsy effort to protect her. With more than a hundred other frightened bystanders, Toner and Molotov huddled on the floor of the main concourse to watch the action unfold.

In less than two minutes, security guards and recently arrived police sealed the exit in a well-rehearsed maneuver. This was no drill; with weapons displayed, they made sure no one went in or out of the area. Airport personnel quickly identified the source of the explosion. With that information relayed to security headquarters, they determined that the blast was not the work of terrorists and broadcast a message urging calm in both English and Spanish. Bruised, shaken, angry people slowly rose from the floor and dusted themselves off.

Toner and Molotov followed suit.

"I don't like this," Angela thought, slinging her bag over her shoulder. "The timing of this prank is too much of a coincidence. And I am really getting to hate coincidences."

They'd been almost through security and out the door when the explosion occurred. If someone was trying to slow them down, someone certainly succeeded.

Scrutinizing the crowd, she was tempted to step out of line and find a corner to hide in for a while. Though Angela knew she was not being watched, she had a bad feeling, a sixth sense, that something was amiss.

As a cleaning crew swept away the debris, and medical personnel treated the woman who had fainted, the security gate reopened, and the queue progressed towards the front, taking the two travelers with it. The line was painstakingly slow, as police questioned everyone passing through the metal detector.

Vassily went first. After answering the questions of a burly cop, he picked up his bag, looked over his shoulder at Toner, smiled, and walked through the automatic door to the sidewalk. Toner was soon at his side.

Ahead, the taxi stand was in chaos. Several police vehicles blocked one lane of traffic. The rush of people needing transportation added to the confusion. Sighing in dismay, Angela looked to her left. "Let's head towards Terminal 2. We'll never catch a cab here."

Vassily shrugged and followed. As he slowly walked behind his American host, he stared at the skyline, the lush plants, the colorful attire of the native Californians, and the endless stream of cars, buses, and taxis.

"Stop gawking like a damned tourist," Toner ordered, looking back at her slow-moving companion.

"But I am a damned tourist," Vassily countered, catching up.

Toner was ready to jab him with another elbow, but Vassily, wising up, stepped back before she could nail him. He raised his eyebrows in silent victory.

Halfway towards Terminal 2, Angela spotted a respectable-looking man standing next to his yellow cab on the other side of World Way, the main airport thoroughfare. The man motioned that his cab was available.

Seeing the long lines at either terminal, she yelled to Vassily: "Let's grab this cab. C'mon. Hurry."

They darted into the street. Halfway across the four-lane, a delivery truck barreled towards them, braking at the last second.

"Hey, I am walkin' here!" Vassily roared, thumping the hood of the truck. He turned to Toner, grinning from ear to ear. "I have always wanted to say that."

Before she could respond, a black van pulled directly in front of them, blocking their path to the cab. The door slid open, revealing a young man in black with a pistol pointed directly at them.

"Whoa," Vassily exclaimed, both hands up to his chest, palms out, trying to avoid confrontation. "I was not being seriously tough. Just kidding."

"Shut the fuck up, and get in, asshole. You too, lady."

Toner and Molotov complied, and the door automatically closed. As the van took off, weaving in and out of traffic, the man in the front passenger seat turned around and smiled.

"Angie Toner," Marc Heiple quipped. "Goin' so soon? Why the party's just begun!"

31

Punks

Kaloostian didn't like stereotyping. He hated categorization—stripping all sense of individuality away, lumping together millions who might share only a single trait, all for the sake of convenience. "There are two…five…seven types of people…" he'd hear comedians and statisticians and bureaucrats conclude. It was nothing short of dehumanizing.

But on Monday afternoon, committing that very sin, Gregory concluded that there were three types of people: The largest group, appropriately named *the masses,* was easy to manipulate and control. History taught that the government's highest unofficial priority was to entertain and anesthetize the masses. From gladiatorial bouts and feeding Christians to the lions in ancient Rome, to professional sports, multimedia entertainment, and legalized gambling in the new millennium—the powers-that-be used whatever was necessary to keep the people dumb, moderately happy, and out of the voting booth.

The second group was but a fraction of the first. As an employee of the FBI, even in his peripheral role as electronics technician, Kaloostian belonged to *the police.* This group monitored the masses and kept them firmly in line. Using a vast arsenal of tools, from brute force to the legal system to electronic surveillance to unrelenting intimidation, the police walked a razor's edge between serving the masses and enslaving them.

An infinitesimal percentage comprised the third group, which controlled both the masses and the police. *The controllers* manipulated governments, global markets, and world policy. They wrote the laws, but as often as not applied them only to the other groups.

Who chaperoned the third group was a question Kaloostian couldn't answer. He had learned to live with the hope that it was God, but in light of what he knew about Nyentzi, he found it hard to believe in a higher being.

Two principles motivated him to continue the fight against human genetic experimentation. First, his deteriorating belief in the concept of a god, any god. But faith—and to a lesser degree commodities like software, insurance, and genetics—was like sausage. Consumers bought it and used it without understanding—or wanting to understand—how it came to be. As James Revkin had preached, too many people arbitrarily tuned out knowledge and facts too important to ignore, surrendering decision-making to those with the money and influence to sway both laws and elections.

Which led to Kaloostian's second motivation. The possibility that a revolution could overthrow localized elements of the aristocratic third caste had been the carrot for visionaries of the past. But if a genetic revolution was underway, Eldon Tyrell was not the one to lead the charge. Inevitably, perpetrators like Tyrell assumed the habits and affluence of their predecessors, leaving the world in worse shape than ever. Now the people who would lose the most might never know the identity of the victor—or the vanquished. And that was something the world could not afford.

"So many worries…so little time," Kaloostian thought as he waited for the phone to ring. "Where the hell is she? She was supposed to call an hour ago." He'd already verified that her flight arrived on schedule.

"My stomach's in a knot because a couple of precocious kids traced us to Molotova's voicemail box. Is there nothing they can't access?" Greg wondered. He stared at his computer screen, at the letter he was writing to Al Hatton's grandchildren.

"Am I next?" he wondered.

That seemed unlikely, but the message from Lara and Katya was all he needed to worry about his own survival. Tyrell was tightening the noose. Even the children, encountering increased electronic roadblocks, satellite signal outages, and system overloads, now had trouble navigating the web. Just that morning, the *Times* had run a story about Internet blocks. The government blamed it on bad weather and sunspots.

Greg knew better. He knew Tyrell and the twins were at work. While he understood the theory behind the twins near-psychic ability to track electronic signals, Kaloostian hoped their genetically enhanced talents really gave them that power. If it was a variation of Suada Sivac's software, however, then the only way to avoid eavesdropping was via the U.S. Postal Service.

The message they'd left on Nadezhda's voice mail sent shivers up his spine. "The diaspora is ending," Lara and Katya had said. "Tell Angela. She needs to know. She needs to know *who* she is."

"Where the hell are you, Angela Carmen Toner?"

The ride was short, but Angela had lost all sense of direction. Blindfolded, she estimated their position to be near Santa Monica, north of the airport, or Redondo Beach, due south. As the abductors forced them from the van, she could tell they were near the coast by the smell of the ocean and the not-so-distant sound of crashing waves.

The van and the pickup were parked inside an abandoned warehouse. Her blindfold removed, she saw that the roof, of corrugated metal, was in disrepair. Water had damaged everything from the roof to the broken windows and skylights. On the floor were scattered piles of broken freight pallets, pipe from a once-functional sprinkler system, and other debris.

Five gang members, all in their late teens or early twenties, apparently followed the command of Marc Heiple. The "troops" were heavily armed and dressed primarily in black. Each wore a communications headset, but from what Toner could tell, all they were listening to was rap music.

Their baseball caps, no two alike, each cocked at a different angle, were the only deviation from uniformity. An African-American kid, who wore his hair in braids, sported a Los Angeles Lakers cap. A Vietnamese American with long black hair, cradled a 7.63-mm SKS assault rifle and wore an Apple Computer cap tilted cockily to the side. The driver of the van, a scrawny adolescent with Irish features and a fancy gold earring, wore a MacDonald's cap with the bill torn off.

After unloading the vehicles, the gang members lazily stood by, waiting for orders from Heiple. Their heads nodded to the staccato of the rap music like toy football helmets on springs:

Your future pulses in a computer
I'm you and how does that suit ya
Anarchy and chaos instilled as our will
And now we just wait for the killers have been
Born into the age of panic
Born to the age of panic.

The music was loud enough to hear through the headsets. Heiple gritted his teeth and looked the group over. He inhaled deeply, trying to maintain his composure. "All right, gentlemen. Let's change the frequency back to what it should be."

One of the motley crew, wearing an Oakland Raiders jacket and hat, rubbed his nose, sniffed, and turned the volume even louder. Four of the five bangers continued to bob their heads.

Check it check it out check it out
Bring it on bring it on come on come on
Check it check it out check it out.

"Enough! I said shut that shit off! Try acting like soldiers, not punks."

"What's with the harsh attitude, Mr. Heiple, *sir*? It's just music," one of the gang members said.

"Yah, c'mon man, it's Senser—a golden oldie."

"Like, from when you was a kid…"

"Or didn't your mammy and daddy let you listen to the rap?"

"The beat, the sound of the street."

"It's neat, sweet, makes you light on your feet."

"You men are *so* talented," Heiple said, his knuckles white from clenching. "GQ, bring the girl, and come with me," he snapped.

"What about this dude?" Apple Computer asked.

"Yah, mon. We found 'im. Can we keep 'im?"

"You gents can have your fun with Lars Larson…or whatever the hell his name is. He's a freebie. Take your time, and be sure to clean up the mess."

"Yes, mother," the punks intoned.

Heiple picked up Toner's carry-on and walked towards the far end of the warehouse. Toner moved slowly behind him, looking back at Vassily Molotov, who sat quietly on the warehouse floor surrounded by four delinquents. Last in line was GQ, his Cobray .380 caliber aimed at the back of Toner's neck.

With Heiple, Toner, and GQ gone, the Oakland Raider extended his middle finger in salute. "Little-big man dis our music again, and I'm gonna kick his white ass all over this fuckin' place."

"Yeah, don't he know what rap *is*?" another said. The kid looked down at Molotov and taunted him. "Yo—paleface. You know what rap is?"

Vassily looked up but said nothing.

"Then let me educate your dumb Caucasian ass. Rap is to the street what CNN is to the couch. You got that, snowflake? That's a little gift…from me…to you."

"Yeah, can ya dig it, *Lars*?"

"What kinda dumb-fuck name is Lars Larson, anyway? Man, if my mamma named me Lars Larson, she'd be one dead-assed bitch. I'da kicked her butt before I learnt to crawl. You kick your mama's ass, *Lars*, or d'ya like having a dumb-ass name?"

Vassily knew the routine. Silence was the only option. Any attempt at conversation, at bridging the gap, would result in his words being twisted and used against him. The gangbangers wanted something to stomp. Vassily resigned himself to the fact that for the time being, he was it.

"Answer the man," MacDonald's said, slapping Vassily on the back of his head.

"Yeah, dickweed. You retarded or somethin'?"

One by one, and then as a group, the four gangbangers ridiculed and provoked Vassily, trying to incite a reaction. Slapping and spitting at the man stoically sitting on the floor, they escalated their anger with each passing minute. Finally, one of the tormentors, a short-haired, bow-legged Latino who called himself Luscious, reached into his coat pocket and pulled out a handgun.

"You think you be a tough motherfucker, eh? Think you be better than us…that you can take a punch better than us? Okay, motherfucker, how about this?" Luscious asked, smacking the motionless Russian across the forehead with the barrel of the pistol.

The blow opened a gash two inches long. Blood streamed from the wound into the Russian's eyes and down his face. He bowed his head but made no attempt to stop another blow or stanch the flow of blood.

The blood was all the others needed to escalate the violence. From every direction, they punched and kicked their prisoner. One of the punks kicked his right leg.

Vassily screamed in agony. "No, please. Stop—don't—not there. I have bad leg. I have injury. Do not kick my leg…please…anything but that."

"Oh, poor baby. You hear that, Jingles? Lars got an owwie."

"Quick Dr. Phibes, get a first-aid kit. This poor man's got an injury."

"Here's the only medicine he needs," Apple Computer said. With that, he kicked Vassily in the right leg. Again and again the gang went after their defenseless prisoner. Molotov tried to crawl away, but every time he got a few feet, he was knocked down again. They kicked him in the stomach, in the back, and especially in the leg. By now, Molotov was only trying to protect himself, trying to avoid the brunt of each blow, but the punks gradually wore him down.

The blood from the wound on his forehead covered his face in a layer of gooey crimson, soaking and matting his hair and his shirt. The assault continued from point to point on the warehouse floor, leaving a bloody trail.

For almost three minutes, the brutality persisted. Vassily's cries for mercy and howls of pain faded to a sickening silence. Then, one by one, the street-hardened youths lost interest in the sport and walked away, repulsed by their prey's inability to defend himself. As they congregated near the vehicles, smoking, snorting, and laughing, Vassily lay motionless, the blood from the gash on his forehead beginning to congeal. Moving his arm so they couldn't see him, he slowly wiped the redness from his eyes. Then he heard footsteps approaching.

"This is boring," one of the bangers said to his friends across the wide expanse of the warehouse. "Let's finish this piece of Eurotrash. I'm hungry." Though Vassily's ears were ringing and the laughter loud, he recognized Luscious by the sound of his voice and the heaviness of his step. Nearer and nearer they came, stopping mere inches from his head.

"Be my guest," the kid with the Lakers cap graciously offered. "You know me. I'm always up for the clown."

"Big Mac, Big Mac," the others echoed.

Molotov turned his head and saw black tennis shoes. As Luscious aimed his pistol, the Russian turned with surprising quickness and rammed a piece of iron pipe he'd picked up on his tour of the floor into the unprotected toes of the startled punk. Luscious' scream of pain climbed several octaves when Molotov pivoted onto his back and jammed the pipe into his tormentor's groin with all his might. As Luscious bent in agony, Vassily smashed the pipe against his head, shattering the side of the kid's skull like a ripe melon.

The Russian reached for the pistol as Luscious fell. He tore a .357 magnum with a cracked handle from the punk's limp hold, spun around, and took aim.

It was payback time.

Vassily Molotov's rage exploded in a passion of blood. He fired once. The Irish kid with the MacDonald's cap went down screaming from a hole in his upper right thigh the size of a half-dollar. Scrambling to his feet, Vassily fired a second shot. Oakland Raiders dropped to the ground as a bullet whizzed by his head.

As the last banger ran for cover and MacDonald's crawled towards the van, Oakland turned on his side and tried to bring a short-barreled shotgun, wedged inside his long, black boots, to bear. Before he could pull it free, Molotov's third shot caught him in the back of the skull, blowing his face away. Eyes, teeth, sinuses, bone, and brain matter erupted from his head like chunky salsa from a burst piñata.

Vassily kept moving. He reached the corpse with the shotgun and yanked it out of the dead kid's boot. Shotgun in hand, the Russian reached his destination—a metal garbage bin near the entrance to the warehouse. As he checked how many shots were left, he heard the squeal of tires.

Lakers had jumped behind the wheel of the pickup and headed for the exit. From what Vassily could tell, MacDonald's was hiding behind the van. But Luscious was lying in the middle of the warehouse floor, and the keys were in his pants pocket.

Molotov had no time to reach for the shotgun. He stood up and fired repeatedly at the pickup: one, two, three…*click, click, click*. The Russian was out of bullets, but his aim was good. Three .357 magnum shells entered the cab through the windshield. Just before Vassily dove for cover, he saw the driver's head pitch back from the impact.

The pickup careened and hit the dumpster. Vassily tossed the magnum aside and reached into Oakland's boot, pulling out the shotgun. He pumped it, stood up, and blasted the right front tire of the van, preventing MacDonald's from going anywhere anytime soon.

Crouching back down, the Russian inched to the far side of the dumpster and the still-running truck. The punk behind the van hadn't fired a shot, but Vassily knew that wouldn't last. With a dash, he was at the driver's side door. As soon he opened it, the punk saw him and fired several erratic shots.

Vassily reached into the truck. About to pull out Lakers' body, he saw something behind the driver's seat. Tilting the seat forward, he grabbed a long black case and jumped back behind the dumpster. He opened it, stared for a moment, and laughed at his good fortune. Carefully laid out in the case was the Street Sweeper, an illegal, high-powered shotgun equipped with a twelve-round circular magazine.

Vassily wanted more. He stood up and let loose with two blasts of the pump shotgun to keep the opposition behind the van. Then he scampered back to the pickup, reached in a second time, pulled out the body, and dragged it behind the dumpster. Going through Lakers' pockets, he found a Tec-9 pistol and two 36-shot magazines. He loaded the Tec-9 and slipped the spare clip into his pants pocket.

With Street Sweeper in one hand and semiautomatic in the other, Molotov prepared for a final assault. Again he fired at the van, one shot from each weapon. He wanted to make sure both weapons worked, and he wasn't disappointed.

Vassily heard shouting. Peering from behind his cover, he saw GQ racing towards the van. As he ran, the other punk yelled at him to get the keys from Luscious, but GQ couldn't hear above the clatter of the pickup's engine. Stickling to his plan, Vassily let loose with the Tec-9. He couldn't tell whether GQ was hit, as the swift-footed thug dove behind the van.

Now or never. Vassily couldn't give the last two punks a chance to take the offensive. He fired two more blasts from the shotgun, blowing out the front windows of the van. Then he dropped to the ground and let loose with the Tec-9, aiming under the van, where the bangers crouched for protection.

Molotov thought he saw at least one target drop to the ground. The other was behind the front wheel. Vassily rose and ran towards the van, firing as he went. At ten feet, he slowed his attack and again let loose with the Street Sweeper. "This is for Nadezhda Andrevna Molotova," he screamed, moving in for the kill.

"Isn't this *special*," Heiple gloated. He leaned against the wall in a mostly empty office the end of the warehouse. Toner sat in a chair in the middle of the small, second-floor room. GQ had tied her up with nylon rope. Now he waited outside.

Marc Heiple moved from the wall and sauntered towards the chair. He leaned down and looked into Angela's made-up face. "I don't know, Angie, somethin's different. I've got it—new lip gloss. What shade is that—gingerspice or smoky plum?"

As Heiple gloated, Toner wiggled her fingers and stretched her wrists against the rope. The preferred method for securing a prisoner in the Third Millennium was duct tape, since few people knew how to tie a good knot. Distending the loop of rope around her hands led Toner to the conclusion that GQ might be one tough hombre, but he was no Boy Scout.

"Give me enough time, Heiple," she thought, "and I'll be out of here with my hands around your throat."

Then Toner went to work on her former colleague. "Glad you're having a good time, surfer boy. Maybe we could build a little fire out of those broken crates in the corner, roast marshmallows, and sing 'Kum Ba Yah.'"

"You never quit, do you? Always the smart ass."

Toner gave him one of her fuck-you smiles. "Yep, old Marc Heiple must be *pretty* important," she continued, "Tyrell's right-hand man. And these accommodations—they're what's *really* special. They're so…what word could I use? Oh, yeah, *appropriate*." Toner looked around the dilapidated room. "You decorate this place yourself?"

Heiple got defensive. "It'll do for now. But just you wait. In another month…"

"Marc, what the hell do you think you're doing? You're in way over your head."

"Funny, that's just what I was just gonna say to you." He uncrossed his arms and walked to Toner's carry-on. Then he sat down on the floor and rifled through the pockets and compartments, carelessly adding her belongings to the litter of the room.

Removing a box of feminine napkins, Heiple laughed. "*These* are what's appropriate. You've been on the rag from the day I met you."

Angela held her breath as he tossed the box over his shoulder. She watched where the box landed, hoping it would not open.

Ignoring the discarded box, Heiple unzipped the middle compartment and removed Toner's laptop. "Here's what I was looking for," he announced with a vicious grin. His smile widened when he turned on the computer. "Batteries are even charged. God Angie, you are so freakin' efficient. I'm really gonna miss having you around."

Toner was silent as he opened the CD-ROM slot and removed the Revkin file. "Amazing how much trouble this little disk has caused," he said, holding up the CD. "You should've returned this, should've minded your own business. Then maybe Hatton would still be alive."

Her gasp fulfilled his hopes. "Oh, you didn't know. It's a shame, Angie, a real shame. I saw the police report this morning: FBI deputy assistant director brutally murdered after traffic altercation with band of ruthless hooligans...something like that. Bottom line—it didn't have to happen. All you had to do was return the disk."

Angela lowered her head at the news, then looked up, her breathing heavy. "I wasn't Hatton's biggest fan, but he deserved better than that."

Flexing her arms, Toner continued to work on the ropes. "Is this what you meant on the way over here when you were talking about the New World Order? Everybody screwing everybody else for a little slice of pie?"

"That's not what I meant at all. What the New World Order means is that we can't trust anybody to do the right thing. But Tyrell wants to change that, put some checks and balances into the system. You think he's some sort of slimeball," Heiple said, placing the Revkin CD in a small envelope. "But he's not. He's a visionary, a real genius, a..."

"You fool. His promises and your greed have you so wrapped up, you can't see straight."

"You're the one who's blind. I mean, just look at you—latex, makeup, gray hair, plaid slacks. Who the hell dressed you—Mary Tyler Moore?"

Toner looked down on her ensemble, none of which she had picked out. "Maybe I'm dressed like your mother, Heiple, but when I look at you, all I see is a two-bit junior agent and a bunch of kids in black pajamas."

"Then you *are* blind. Do you have the slightest idea how much military training these kids have? That black dude—GQ—spent the last two years training at Fort Polk in Louisiana."

Toner had heard of Fort Polk. She knew it to be one of the army's elite teaching grounds, where a select few were sent to hone killing skills to peak efficiency. For years, she'd heard rumors of gang members enlisting for the express purpose of learning the art of urban warfare. Performing as model soldiers, they eagerly and honorably fulfilled their enlistments. After discharge, they returned to the streets of LA, New York, Chicago, Philadelphia, and points between, extending their knowledge to a new generation of street fighters.

If Eldon Tyrell had tapped that source, then the police had their work cut out for them.

"And I'm not just talking boot camp and calisthenics, Toner. These kids got their hands on a full-blown virtual-reality combat simulator."

"How exciting," Toner muttered, staring at the floor, trying to ignore him.

Toner looked up a minute later and realized Heiple was still rambling.

"...And when you add to *that* what it takes to survive on the street, you'll understand just how much on-the-job-training these kids have."

"I'm not so sure, Heiple," she answered. "Gang members don't take kindly to discipline. How do you expect to keep them in line?"

"They're model employees," Heiple explained with a smile. "Stock options, benefits, paid days off, the whole kibosh. Pretty neat, huh?"

Toner shook her head.

Heiple saw her and laughed. "I know you think I'm an idiot for telling you all this, but obviously, it doesn't matter. You're not going anywhere."

"And how much are you being paid to betray your badge, betray your *country*? 'Course, knowing you, you'd do this for gas money."

"This isn't about money. I don't expect you to understand, but it really isn't. Well, not entirely about money," Marcus said softly, running his hand across Toner's neck.

"Get back! You make me sick. Look Heiple, if you want to be rich, I happen to know the government would pay you dearly for turning Tyrell in. Why don't you do the right thing?"

"Don't give me that do goody-good bullshit. This *is* the right thing." Heiple's hand brushed Toner's breast.

"Fuck off," Toner ordered. Then she laughed. "Knowing you, Heiple, this is what you consider foreplay. Little Markie Heiple, can't get it any other way."

Heiple moved away, angry and defiant. "I'm sorry to disappoint you, Angie, but my working with Tyrell isn't about ideology. It's not even about power. It's about shares…millions and millions of shares. I'll be a stockholder in all those companies Tyrell's gonna incorporate when he applies the technology that comes out of Nyentzi. You call it greed. I call it success."

Toner laughed at Heiple's rationale. She knew enough about the business world to recognize that loyalties rested almost exclusively on money. With money, anything was possible. What Heiple didn't realize was that when ideology enters the picture, money might not be enough.

"Your parents must be proud," Angela said

"You know what they say—it's not the earth the meek inherit, it's the dirt."

"Marcus R. Heiple, you surprise me. Since when do you listen to Lerner and Loewe?"

"What are you talking about?"

"That line about the meek…You mean you don't know where it comes from?"

"Nah. I heard some guy at a seminar use it."

"Figures," Toner said with disdain.

"But it's *relevant*. It's what Tyrell wants to change. Everybody knows the root of society's evils and social problems is money, just like it's always been. But Tyrell's gonna correct that. No more corruption, no more despair, no more ignorance."

"No more ignorance? Where does that leave you?"

Heiple bit his lower lip, trying not to react. "We have a chance to make a difference here. I know you're worried about Tyrell and all the information he's accumulated, but you've got to understand, that's his *business*. You see, Angie," Heiple instructed, squatting to talk with Toner eye to eye, "information is neutral. It doesn't take sides or play favorites. It's what we do with it that's important. And Tyrell wants to share his wealth, open the world to the wonders of Nyentzi."

"Sorry, Marc. Someday information may make money secondary, but it'll always be important. You can't believe everything Tyrell tells you."

"You're jumping to conclusions."

"Am I? Information's like any other commodity. Tyrell buys, sells, and steals at his whim. And if people want to be informed, they'll have to pay the price, right?"

"What's wrong with that?" Heiple pleaded.

"There's something to be said for ignorance."

Heiple shook his head, glaring into Toner's face. "Why can't you see what I'm trying to tell you? Why won't you share the vision?"

"You're not describing a vision. You're describing a hallucination."

"Why am arguing with you? You're hardly in a position to negotiate," Heiple fumed. He stood up and walked to the window. After several seconds, he turned, his face full of malice. "You're dead. D'you know that? Your family knows…they've been notified."

Toner blinked hard but said nothing as Heiple continued.

"I've got your attention now, am I right? Yeah, it's been on the news—plane crash, just west of Salekhard. Molotova's body's already been found in the wreckage. Poor kid, she probably had to be picked up with a spoon. They're still looking for you, though. It seems you might have been thrown clear of the burning wreckage and ended up as a bear snack. Doesn't matter, though, 'cuz right now, you're sucking air. You're history, babe."

The fire in Toner's eyes didn't waver.

"Not convinced, I see," Heiple continued. "And I thought Hatton was stubborn." He reached inside his jacket for a cellular phone. "What's your phone number?" he asked, holding the phone so Angela could see the buttons. "Never mind, I've got it memorized." He punched in the numbers. "555-5418. Isn't that right?"

Heiple held the phone so they both could hear it ringing. After four rings, they heard a click, then a computerized message. He brought the phone closer to Angela's ear. "We're sorry," the expressionless voice said, "but the number you just called—555-5418—has been disconnected. No further information is available."

Cocking his head, Heiple terminated the connection and put the phone away. Angela looked away, refusing to meet his gaze, her chin trembling in frustration.

"Why don't you go ahead…finish the job," she said, sniffling from the emotional drain and the fermenting virus that had accompanied her from Russia. "Go ahead, tough guy. I'm sure murder will look good on your résumé."

"*Murder*? Such a nasty word. I prefer to think of it as the *fortuitous forfeiture of life*. I mean, aren't you the one who always corrects my politically incorrect speech."

"Then go ahead. Tyrell doesn't seem like the kind of guy who likes leaving loose ends."

"Funny you should ask. I was getting to that."

Just then, Angela heard something. Heiple did, too—the distant rumble of gunfire.

"Shit," Marc muttered. He went and opened the door. "Yo, GQ. Tell the troops no shooting!"

Angela heard GQ's footsteps echo down the hall outside the room. Though her wrists were raw from the rope, she renewed her efforts to free herself.

Heiple closed the door and turned. "This Lars guy—friend of yours?" he asked with feigned concern. "No matter," he said after Angela refused to comment. "Back to your earlier question. Why are you here with me instead of down there with Lars? Is that what you want to know?"

Still she refused to talk, refused to answer Heiple's questions. She knew he would tell her, so why make his job easier?

"What's wrong, Angie? Cat got yer tongue? Usually, people can't shut you up. Now all of a sudden you go quiet on me. Oh well, no big deal. I just wanted to know whether you'd consider a little joint venture with me…a chance to be rich."

"The only joint venture I consider you suitable for involves a different kind of joint."

Heiple had to think about that for a moment. He finally nodded.

"Funny…very funny. Hate to disappoint you, but I don't expect to be caught, much less imprisoned for the work I do. Jeez, babe, you make it sound so sinister. C'mon, working with me wouldn't be such a bad thing. We'd make a great team."

"I'd rather give a nearsighted rhino a Tabasco Sauce enema."

"You always were the kind of person who does things the hard way. Am I right?"

"Are you right? God, Marc. I don't know if you listen to yourself when you talk, but all I ever hear from you is 'Am I right?' Like you have this constant need for approval. Drives me nuts."

Heiple tilted his head and squinted, trying to absorb Toner's critique of his speaking style. "You don't like me very much, do you?" he asked after a moment.

"You blew it," Angela sighed. "You just asked the one question that positively begged to end with '*Am I right*?' I actually would've agreed with you. No, Marc, I don't like you very much. And if that surprises you, then you're dumber than I thought."

"So you don't like me. I can live with that. But you should at least give Tyrell a chance. He's anxious to meet you."

"I bet he is," Toner said with a sarcastic laugh.

"No, really. He doesn't want to hurt you…honest."

"You expect me to believe that?"

"Yeah…You impressed him, Angie. You got pretty far with that disk."

"Should I be flattered?"

"Fuckin' A. If you'd deep-six the smart-ass routine, you'd realize this is your last chance. This is it, babe. Tyrell'll be here in awhile. He said I've got one chance—and one chance only—to talk sense to you, to make you understand how important our mission is."

"One chance? And I'm supposed to make my decision tied to a chair, in an abandoned warehouse, with your new friends out there blazing away with their Uzis? I thought GQ was supposed to tell them to knock off the gunfire?"

"They do what I tell them. You've got nothing to fear. There. See. They stopped."

Silence. A shiver went down Angela's spine. "I've got nothing to fear, eh? No way am I buying that. Besides, I need to know what's in it for me."

"Let me put it to you this way. You'll have anything you've ever wanted in your entire life…new car, caviar, a regular four-star daydream."

"Grab that cash with both hands. Sorry Marc, that's more up your alley than mine."

"You're wrong, Toner, way wrong. And you know it better than anyone else. You've actually met them, talked to them. My God, don't you realize what those kids are? They're the future, they're…man, I don't know how to say it. We've finally encountered superior beings. And it's like…us."

As Heiple rambled, Angela realized she had something Heiple desperately wanted—a personal audience with the children of Nyentzi. She saw the fervor of greed in his eyes. He was enthralled with the twins, with their potential to make him a rich man. He was like a wide-eyed boy on Christmas morning. He gestured wildly, hands open, palms up. On and on he went, describing the technology of the future, a technology inspired by the genius of Nyentzi.

"…and Tyrell promised that if I could make you understand…"

"You really think it's gonna work?" Angela interrupted.

"How can you even say that? You were there! You got to meet them. They're a hit! Of course, it's gonna work. And you know it. In your heart, you know it."

"What about Tyrell? You sure this is okay with him?"

"He's just one man. Sure, he's got all those connections, but I've got a few things up my sleeve. I can pull my weight."

"What you're really saying is that it's gonna be me and you…us?" Toner asked.

"Sure," Heiple said, trying to curb his excitement. "And why not? I've had my eye on you. You should be flattered. I'm pretty choosy about women, but I've always liked you."

"Sorry, Marc. I've already got a job. I've got some money stashed away…"

"Be serious. With what we earn at the bureau, we'll be lucky if we can ever retire."

Toner was silent. She could feel the rope around her wrists finally loosening. A sigh rose from her throat as she thought about Vassily. A tear formed in her left eye, then the right. Her fists clenched tighter. Her entire body shivered.

"I guess you need an answer? *Am I right?*"

"Hah…Yeah, I guess you are."

"Before I answer, I've got one question," Toner said.

"What kind of question?"

"Nothing important. It's just a little question I always ask my men."

"Okay, what is it?" Heiple asked, curiosity aroused.

"Well, it's kind of personal."

"Oh, come on. It can't be that personal."

Toner smiled and blinked away the tears. "All right." She hesitated another few seconds before asking, "Can you touch your asshole with your penis?"

"Can I what? What kind of question is that? God, Toner, you're sick."

"Well, can you?"

Heiple stuttered a moment and broke eye contact. "Of course I can," he finally blurted.

Angela tensed her entire body before answering. "Good…then go fuck yourself."

Heiple's slap knocked her and the chair over. She landed on her side, her head bouncing off the hard wooden floor.

This was what she'd been waiting for. With all her might, she tried to slip her wrists out of the slipshod knot, but it wouldn't budge.

"God, I hate Mondays," Toner thought just as Heiple's boot caught her hard in the stomach. She grunted and cried out in pain. Coughing and retching, she heard the sound of a bolt feeding a bullet into a semi-automatic pistol. Angela tried to turn over. She wanted to look him in the eye before he killed her, but she could barely breathe.

"Bye-bye, bitch," Heiple hissed, his voice rumbling.

Angela closed her eyes and waited, tears streaming down her cheeks. But instead of the blast of a pistol, she heard a distinct thud. Then Heiple's body fell across hers.

"Sorry, it took me so long," Vassily Molotov said. "But there were five of those guys."

32

Ashes to Ashes

"How do you feel," Vassily asked, untying the ropes that bound Angela's ankles and wrists.

"Like I just sat through a timeshare presentation."

Molotov helped her up, the two holding onto each other for support. Angela impulsively wrapped her arms around Vassily. His eyes widened as he cautiously returned the gesture.

It didn't last. Toner dropped her arms. "Sorry…I don't know why I did that."

"That is okay."

"What'd you hit him with?" Toner asked, staring down at Heiple's body. Molotov held out a piece of pipe.

"Ouch! Bet that hurt. My God, Vassily," she said, looking at the Russian, gasping at the blood on his face. "You look worse than I feel. Those bastards really worked you over."

"As the saying goes, 'You should see the *other* guys.' They are in much worse shape."

"But still," she said, lightly touching his forehead. "That hurt?"

"Only when I talk, or walk, or run, or…"

"I get the idea. Come on, let's tie him up."

Grunting and groaning in pain, Toner and Molotov lifted Marc Heiple onto the wooden chair. Working as a team, they tied him with the rope that had held Toner. She pulled it tight, more to keep him from falling off the chair than from spite.

With Heiple secure, Angela walked to her carry-on to retrieve a silk handkerchief and a bottle of water. "Where do you want to be oiled first, Tin Man?" she said, dabbing the handkerchief into the water.

"Take your pick. I think I am all in bad shape."

Angela knelt and tenderly wiped the blood from his forehead, cheeks, and lips. "You can say that again. This isn't working…" She looked at small handkerchief and at the amount of blood on his face. "I'm gonna go look for some bandages. Maybe the troops carried a first-aid kit. Stay here with this creep, okay?"

"Sounds like the plan," Vassily said.

On her way out, Toner stooped over Heiple. She reached into his jacket and retrieved both the Revkin disk and his service pistol. Slipping the items into her pocket, she went to the door. "I'll be back in a minute. If you hear anything, come a-runnin'."

"I sure will."

The door closed. Molotov sat for a moment in contemplation. He then continued to clean the blood from his face with the handkerchief, pausing for a moment after detecting a hint of her perfume. He closed his eyes and sighed.

Angela took several steps from the room and began to tremble. Her entire body—from her sprained ankle to her sinuses, from to her ribs to her head, beaten in by Oleg—hurt like hell. She could barely walk. She was sure Vassily felt no better. As she headed for the stairs, she spied her companion's latest toy propped against the wall.

The Street Sweeper: Toner had never seen one in action, and she wondered whether going to look for a first-aid kit was a good idea. The carnage from the rapid-fire shotgun was sure to be extensive. Still, using the wooden handrail for support, she descended to the ground floor, one stair at a time. At the bottom was a long hall, dimly lit with sunlight spillover from the warehouse. She rested in silence before walking towards the open space.

Two hundred feet away was the black minivan. Beyond it, near the far wall, was the pickup, crumpled against the dumpster. From where she stood, the van appeared undamaged, but her vision was blurred, the pounding in her head so severe that she almost blacked out.

The closer she got—her gait an aching, awkward limp—the more she knew her mistake. The van was a total loss. The shotgun had blown out most of the glass. Both front and at least one of the rear tires were flat. She could see several bodies. Though the carnage was regrettable, all that mattered was that the good guys had won.

The first body she encountered lay in a crumpled heap. The side of his head had split open, leaving a circular pool of blood on the dirty floor. "I'll bet you went first," she whispered to the lifeless form. Then she noticed a second patch of blood and an irregular path of blood from where she knelt. She guessed it belonged to her friend upstairs.

Gaining an understanding of what had happened, Angela slowly stood. She moved towards the van, hoping to find bandages for Vassily and something for her own aches, past a second corpse with no face, so revolting she had to look away. Toner guessed that the kid with the Raiders jacket was killed after Vassily took a gun from the first casualty.

Nearby were two other bodies. GQ lay in a fetal position near the rear tire of the van. A second body lay on its back, arms spread wide, a hole where the chest had been and another in the leg. He was the red-haired punk, his MacDonald's cap still on his head. His eyes stared lifelessly at the rafters and skylights.

"Where's number five?" Angela asked. "Must be over by the pickup."

She knelt down by the corpse on its back and picked up an SKS assault rifle. If they got into any more jams, Toner wanted a little more firepower than Heiple's 9-mm Beretta. Reaching into the kid's pockets, eyes averted, she found three clips of ammunition.

Angela continued her search, moving around the front of the van. She could hardly see through the cracks and craters of the windshield. The glass on the sliding door was blown in, too. Though the door was heavily damaged, it did slide. She leaned the SKS against the side of the van and squeezed in as far as she could, trying to get a pouch she'd noticed near the driver's seat.

She unzipped the case, only to find compact discs, none to her liking. Climbing back out, she opened the front passenger door and located a compartment under the seat. There it was—a first-aid kit. She opened it and checked the contents: bandages, salves, alcohol pads, no morphine, not that she'd expected any.

Toner settled for a bottle of ibuprofen. She twisted off the top and popped four 200mg tablets of the anti-inflammatory into her mouth, swallowing them without water, almost choking in the process. Waiting for them to go down, she suddenly had a chilling recollection: "He'll be here soon," Heiple had said of Eldon Tyrell.

They had no time to waste. She adjusted the strap of the SKS and slung it over her shoulder. With the first-aid kit under her arm, Angela limped back upstairs.

"This is going to hurt you a lot more than it hurts me," Toner remarked, spreading Bacitracin on Vassily's forehead, trying not to press too hard around the two-inch gash.

"Ouch...thank you for the warning," he said, trying to remain calm. She carefully placed a bandage over the wound, nevertheless making the Russian wince. The adrenaline rush serving him earlier had worn off, leaving him susceptible to the slightest ache.

"You should have a couple of stitches."

"That is quite all right. I will live with the scar."

"You sure? I bet I can find a needle and thread somewhere," Angela said with a weak grin. "I thought you hurt your leg playing hockey. How come you're not limping much?"

"I did hurt my leg. I even had two operations before I could walk again."

"But didn't you just tell me that's where Heiple's buddies kept kicking you?"

"The problem with my injury was nerve damage. I cannot feel much in that leg. It hurt when they were being so tough against me—just look at the bruises—but not as much as I made it sound. What else I learned in hockey was how to roll with body checks and punches. Like when one guy kicked me in the stomach, I corrected my entire body and consumed much of the blow. They thought I was in deep dilemmas, but I was mostly play-acting."

"I see…Who did you play hockey for?"

"Why do you ask? I was not professional."

"I know. I'm just curious what team you were on."

"Only my school team."

"And what school might that've been?"

Vassily hesitated before admitting his secret. "The Russian Military Academy in Moscow."

"You graduated from the Russian Military Academy?"

"With honors," he added with a wry smile.

"Heiple said these kids received military training."

"They must have been absent the day the instructor told them how to treat a prisoner. They were also greatly lacking in teamwork."

"These kids never had a chance, did they?"

"They had their chance, but not here…not today…not against me. Not after what happened to Nadezhda…and you."

Angela and Vassily looked into each other's eyes.

"Thank you for saving me," she said.

"You would have done the same, wouldn't you?"

"Eh, maybe." Angela smiled, but for only a moment. "Come on, let's clean up and get out of here. Heiple said Tyrell was coming by soon. I'd rather not be here to greet him."

"I do not agree. Let's drag this worthless piece of shit," Vassily said, pointing to Heiple, "down to the warehouse and put him in the middle of the floor. Then, when this Tyrell person comes, *bam*, we eliminate the threat."

"Good plan, but I'll bet Tyrell doesn't travel alone. And neither of us is up for a fight."

Vassily said nothing, his jaw firm, his resolve unbroken.

"Come on, Rambo," Toner said, lightly punching his arm. "You know I'm right. Let's leave it at that. Okay?"

"There is a Russian proverb: 'The wise person does not climb the mountain but learns to go around.' I admit Tyrell is a mountain…a large mountain. You are correct to go around."

"Excellent proverb. C'mon. I'll get my laptop. You grab the rest of the stuff surfer boy tossed around."

Molotov nodded and began picking up the items removed from the bag. Toner placed the Revkin file back in the CD-ROM drive and repacked the computer. In less than a minute, they finished. Angela was about to zip the last pocket shut when she glanced around the room to make certain they hadn't missed anything.

They had. Several feet away was the box of tampons Heiple had tossed. Toner shook her head in relief, went over, and picked it up.

She opened the box, pushed the cardboard flaps out of the way, and reached in. Feeling along one edge, she removed a stiff white envelope, all but invisible to anyone who did not know it was there. She tilted the envelope up, allowing the compact disk Lara and Katya had given her to slide out. She turned it over, making sure it was intact.

Toner returned the CD to the envelope and replaced it in the box. She then poked around the other side of the box and pulled out another white envelope. "Let's get this over with, okay? Do you still have your wallet?"

"I do now. I had to take it from one of the boys downstairs."

"Good. Give it to me," Angela said, holding out her hand. Then she sat down on the floor, opened the wallet, and removed Lars Larson's identification card, credit cards, birth certificate, and other personal documents, placing them in a pile in front of her. After purging her own purse for records of her phony persona, she added several stiff tissues to the pile, stuffing them in and around the plastic cards.

"Poor Lars. He was starting to grow on me. Oh well, ashes to ashes," Angela said, giving Molotov a sidelong glance. She lit a match and dropped it onto the collection of documents.

"Good-bye, Yvonne," Vassily added, moving out of reach of Toner's elbow. "You were a grumpy traveling companion. May you rest in peace."

The tissues, soaked in a flammable chemical and sprinkled with magnesium powder, went up like sparklers. In seconds, the pile was burning with an intensity that erased all traces of the two travelers. The smoke and the smell of burning plastic rose with the air, drifting through the room on a gentle ocean breeze. The pungent odor was impossible to ignore.

Marc Heiple suddenly came out of his involuntary slumber, jerking straight up with alarm. "Wh...what the fuck? Oh my God, oh my God...fire. Shit, shit, shit," he blurted, struggling with the rope binding him to the chair. He blinked once, then twice more, trying to focus. "Toner. What're you doing? What are you doing to me?"

"Nothin' yet, you big baby. It's just a little fire. Too bad your friends downstairs didn't pack any hotdogs."

The mention of friends opened Heiple's eyes to the seriousness of his situation. He looked past Toner and saw Vassily Molotov standing in stony silence, his arms crossed.

Angela sensed Heiple's apprehension. "Are you still having a good time, Heiple? Now that you're there, and I'm here?"

"What're you doing? Don't tell me you're just gonna leave me here? I could die. I think I've got a concussion. I need a doctor. Untie me right now."

"Heiple, shut the hell up," Toner ordered. "After what I've been through, believe me, you're only a bullet away from that special assignment in the sky."

Though the tables were turned, Heiple kept trying to call the shots, squirming and wriggling on the chair. "You can't kill me. I know too much. You need me...Don't do anything stupid."

"Yeah, I wouldn't want to infringe on *your* territory."

"Who are tryin' to kid, Toner? You know you can't kill me. I'm your protection. Without me, Tyrell'll hunt you down."

"Hold that thought a moment, would you?" Angela requested. She walked to the door and stepped into the hallway. After a moment she returned with Molotov's shotgun.

"Here, Vassily, make sure your boomstick is loaded."

Turning back to her former colleague, she knelt down and looked him in the eye. "See that crazy Russian with the shotgun? He single-handedly exterminated your little troop of cockroaches. You know the vermin I mean, the ones with all that *elite* military training."

"The ones who should have studied harder," Vassily added, enjoying Heiple's discomfort.

"Yeah, those are the ones. By the way, Marc, I don't think you've been formally introduced to my traveling companion. Marcus Heiple meet Vassily Molotov, brother of the late Nadezhda Molotova—the woman your buddy Tyrell murdered."

"Th...this is insane," Heiple stuttered, a film of sweat breaking on his forehead and upper lip. "Tyrell didn't order her killed. Tyrell wouldn't..."

"Shut up, Marc. Didn't you tell me her body was found in the wreckage of a plane crash west of Salekhard?" She stood back up and looked at Molotov. "Sorry, Vassily. I should have told you earlier."

"I understand. Perhaps now she will get a proper burial," he said. Molotov looked down on Heiple, pointing the shotgun at Heiple's head. "Which is more than I can say for you."

Heiple continued to squirm. "Hey, Vaseline...I mean Vassily. Like, I had nothin' to do with your sister's death. Toner's just trying to rile you up. Can't you see that? She's usin' you, buddy, just like she uses everybody else."

Molotov was silent, but as he turned, he swung suddenly to his left, smashing Heiple's face with the gun stock. *Crack*. Heiple and the chair crashed to the floor in a cloud of dust.

For seconds, Heiple just lay there, his eyes watering. "Oh...this is fuckin' great. You broke my nose, you Slavic shithead. Great, just great. All right, now set me back up. Come on, I can't breathe. Help me up, dammit."

Molotov stooped down, grabbed him by the hair and collar, and none too gently lifted Heiple and the chair. Blood poured from Heiple's fractured nose, down over his lips, chin, neck, and onto his once-clean white shirt. Despite his injury and his being tied up, Heiple remained defiant.

Toner shook her head in amazement. "Marc, we're gonna leave you, your sunny disposition, and your broken nose, in peace. Maybe your buddy Eldon will cruise by and take pity on you. Then again, maybe he won't. But if he does, tell him we're gonna stop him. Not just Vassily and me, all of us. The world's not going to tolerate his perverted science. It's sick, he's sick, and you're sick for believing him. Come on, Vassily. Let's go."

Heiple spit blood and continued the argument. "Who're you trying to kid? People don't know shit about science. Most of 'em don't even know what DNA is. They're stupid, Toner, just like you. They don't give a damn about crusades or doin' the right thing. All they care about is what time the game's on and how much for a six-pack of beer."

Angela smiled and picked up her bag. "Bye-bye, Marc. Have fun explaining this little mess to the police."

"I know you. I know your obsession. You can't walk away now. You'll never know the truth. You'll never find out what Tyrell's got planned."

"There you go again. Assuming you know what's best for me. Sometimes—not always—but sometimes, ignorance *is* bliss," Toner said and walked away.

When she reached the door, Heiple hurled his last barrage. "It's just like a dumb-ass nigger-bitch to run from someone who's trying to help her. Your fuckin' family shoulda stayed on welfare."

Something inside Angela snapped. She stopped dead in her tracks. Vassily saw the look on her face and stepped aside when she turned around.

Angela Toner stared into Marc Heiple's hate-filled face. Her body began to shake as images of Nadezhda Molotova and Alfred Hatton flashed by, images of Peter and Oleg—the brute who'd used those very words—images of her family, her career, and the life she could never go back to. She remembered every racial remark, every act of discrimination, every social slight she'd ever received. After more than three decades of frustration, Angela Toner decided enough was enough.

Her face devoid of expression, Angela reached into her pocket and pulled out the Beretta. Her emotions were reduced to their most primitive level and her hands shook, but she held her breath and aimed.

A shot rang out. Heiple's bound arms tried to flail at the hole in his chest as both he and the chair pitched over backwards, landing in a heap on the dirty floor.

For seconds, the room was deathly still. Then, in slow motion, Angela looked to her side, at Vassily Molotov and the smoking Tec-9 in his extended right hand. She sighed, slipped the gun into her pocket, turned, and walked out the door, not bothering to look back.

Vassily caught up with Toner at the bottom of the stairs. Instead of heading towards the open section of the building, she moved to the right, down a hallway to the rear exit.

They arrived at the back door. "Angela," Vassily began softly, "I could not allow you to do that, but it had to be done. That man could not be allowed to live."

"Don't say anything."

"I know you are upset, but I want you to know that I am sorry...for his words, for your shame and anger. I am sorry."

"It's not your fault."

"It is anyone's fault if they do nothing to stop such things. I had to shoot. You understand, do you not? I only did what I had to do."

For a moment Angela stood there, her shoulders drooped, her body trembling ever so slightly. "Thank you," she whispered at last without turning around. She opened the door and stepped into the afternoon haze.

Parked next to the building was a late-model red sports coupe.

"Nice car," Vassily said.

"It's Heiple's. For all his faults, at least he had good taste in material things. Come on, Molotov. Let's get out of here."

"But it is locked. Even if I break the window, how do we start it? Do you know how to heat the circuits?"

"You mean *hotwire?*"

"Yes, that is the term I was thinking."

"Nope, 'fraid not. I've got something better, though." Angela reached into her jacket pocket and pulled out Heiple's keys and wallet. She unlocked the driver's door, opened it, and toggled the lock button. "Let's stow the shotgun and assault rifle in here. You packing anything besides the Tec-9?"

"No, that is all," Vassily said, touching his coat pocket where the weapon was hidden.

"Keep it handy. We may need it again."

Vassily nodded and slid his long body into the low-riding sports car. "Do you know where we are?" he asked after Toner climbed in.

"Look that way," she said pointing south. "All those big jets are coming and going from LA International. That means we're somewhere in Santa Monica."

"You know your way around town, I take it."

"Yep. I'll try not to get us lost. First things first, though. Let's find a pay phone so I can call Kaloostian. He's probably wondering where the heck we are." She turned the ignition and the radio came on, catching the final ten seconds of a song. "Damn. There it is again."

"There is what again?"

"Hard to believe it's only been a week," Angela mused aloud as she considered Vassily's question. "For the past seven days—from here to Salekhard, to Moscow, to here again—I've been catching bits and pieces of the same stupid song. It's just piano and accompaniment. I can hear each low note of the acoustic bass. I've got the melody memorized, but for the life of me, I can't remember the name of the song."

"It is important to you? It has a special meaning?"

"I haven't thought about, haven't even heard it, for more three years. It's on a compact disc Jake bought me. It was playing in the car when, when we...when he died in the accident. I can even see the cover. There's a black piano and a lady kneeling down...probably the artist, but I can't think of her name, either."

"Maybe you are trying too hard to remember."

"I don't want to remember it. I want to forget it. Whenever I hear it, I'm reminded that I've lost everything I ever loved. That damn song keeps reminding me."

"I know what you mean about loss and love" Vassily said, remembering his own past. "It is that emptiness down inside the soul, the kind you feel more on a rainy day in autumn. The kind that will not go away."

He turned. Their eyes met. Angela reached across the car and brushed a strand of hair from his face, seeing him as if for the first time. Before either could speak, they heard the sirens.

33

The Holy Grail

"Another fine mess you've got me into, Kaloostian." The line was Oliver Hardy's, but Angela felt anything but jolly.

"Where are you? What happened? You sound terrible."

"Not far from Van Nuys Airport…just off I-405 on Roscoe Boulevard. I can't take time to hook up my computer, so we'll have to do without video."

"What the hell happened? I've been waiting more than two hours for you to call."

"Somebody spotted me. And Marc Heiple works for Tyrell. They nailed us outside the airport." She summarized their flight, the trouble at the airport and subsequent capture, leaving out certain details.

"What'd you do with Heiple? Is he still at the warehouse?"

"More or less," Angela said after a moment.

"By the tone of your voice I guess I won't worry about trying to fix his computer by next Thursday. Where's Vassily?"

"Using the rest room."

"How's *he* doing?"

"Okay. Thanks for talking me into having him come along. He saved my life. Did you know he had military training?"

"Yeah…he mentioned something about that. How're you holding up, Spud?"

"I'm sick, Greg. I'm really sick. I think I've got the plague or something. I've been coughing, and I'm achy and beat up and tired. My head feels all wrong…something's loose. And I haven't had a good night's sleep or a healthy meal in a week."

"You must've picked up the Energizer virus—it keeps going and going and going."

"Very funny."

"Maybe you should see a doctor."

"I'll try to fit it in my schedule. By the way, Heiple told me about Hatton. I'm sorry, Greg. I wish I'd returned that disk. None of this would've happened."

"Returning it wouldn't have saved him, and it probably would've killed you. Sorry, Angie, our hands were tied the moment Hatton gave you that file."

"I suppose you're right…What did we do wrong, Greg? How did they know I was coming?"

"You got spammed, little buddy. Tyrell pasted your picture all over the Internet. By the time I found out, you were already on your way. There was no way to warn you without leaving an electronic trail for Tyrell."

Toner took a deep breath. "You're pretty new at this, aren't you?"

"Whatever gave you that idea?"

"I'm beginning to feel like the first person who loaded MS-DOS."

"Whoa! I'm not doing that bad," Greg exclaimed. "Jeez, I'm an technician, not a spy. What can I say? You got an excellent makeup job, but someone, somehow, spotted you. We did the best we could, but I bet that explosion at the terminal was no accident."

"It's a good thing we've got another set of personalities. I've already burned the first set."

"Good. Tyrell probably got a complete description of what you looked like, so that'll at least be a dead end. What're you driving, by the way?"

"We borrowed Heiple's sports car. I think I'll leave it here, though—catch the bus to Burbank. Then I'll rent a car."

"Good, but wipe it clean. Your latest incarnation's got high dollar-limits on two credit cards, so money's not a problem. What's your new name, by the way?"

"Gloria Faye Calero. I'm only forty this time, so I took off that damned geriatric makeup and flushed it down the toilet," Angela said, coughing twice before continuing. "Say Greg, I don't want you to take this the wrong way. I know you've been busting your hump trying to help and all, but are you…you and your save-the-world buddies…are you guys really up for this? I'm not talkin' Keystone Cops, but my feelings have gone from bad to really bad to I-can't-believe-I'm-still-alive."

"I know, but we're not a bunch of web spelunkers with too much time on our hands. You've got backing from intelligence agencies around the world. But Tyrell's running with the big boys, and while you were away he called in reinforcements."

Kaloostian took a minute to explain what he had read about communication problems on and off the net over the past two days. "There's no direct evidence, but the feeling is Tyrell's trying to temporarily shut down the web to everyone but himself. The only systems not affected are local phone service and the Pony Express."

"In other words, we're screwed."

"It's a war, Angie, a full-scale information war, and it's escalating fast."

"Any suggestions about what to do next?" Toner asked.

"Well, we've been lucky. So far, Tyrell seems to be working out of pure spite."

"You serious? Nadezhda's dead, Hatton's dead, Vassily and I are lucky to be alive...You and Suada are probably next. And you think Tyrell's operating just out of *spite*?"

"If he wanted, Tyrell could get every city, state, and federal law-enforcement official looking for you. The political fallout from the Revkin file is *explosive*. But he's hasn't...at least not yet."

"Then maybe we're overreacting. Maybe he's not the Great Oz. Maybe all that crap Revkin gave you was just a line. Maybe Tyrell is just a guy with a very large phone bill."

"I wish. Trouble is, we've verified through independent sources most of what Revkin said. You've got a good point, but there's a second possibility, and I'm afraid you're gonna like it even less."

"What's that?"

"Eldon Tyrell is so sure of success, so close to landing a knockout punch, that he doesn't need to worry about us anymore. I mean, *get real*. Sending Marc Heiple after the one person who has enough evidence to put him out of business? What's wrong with that?"

"And Marc sounded like he was such a vital cog in Tyrell's organization."

"In his dreams. He did some dirty work for Tyrell, but that's probably the extent of it. And the reason is Eldon Tyrell doesn't care about the file. He thinks he's already won."

"Has he?"

"I'm getting to that. You see, Angie, some of what we've learned came from Lara and Katya. They crashed Nadezhda's voicemail box, which we thought was impossible."

Toner sighed. "You know, I'm not even surprised. Hey, Vassily's back."

To take part in the phone conversation, Vassily Molotov leaned as close to Angela as he could without actually touching her. Neither had noticed, but the handsome Russian was increasingly timid in her presence.

"So Lara and Katya think Tyrell's making his big move?"

"More or less. They also said we'd understand more when we access the disk. You've still got it, right?"

"Yeah. What else did they say?"

Kaloostian hesitated, not sure Toner was up to another dose of theory and conjecture. "They said the diaspora is ending," he finally said.

"The *what*?"

"Diaspora...it's biblical. The exile of the twelve tribes of Israel to Babylon in the sixth century B.C. Since ten of the tribes more or less disappeared, technically the diaspora never ended. It's still going on."

"You're spooking me, Kaloostian. I don't like these religious overtones."

"Neither do I, but I don't think that's what they're after. Diaspora also means the dispersion of an originally homogenous people. I looked it up," Greg added, surmising the next question.

"Meaning what?"

"I think they're talking genetics—the diaspora of the human genome. Two strands of DNA, 46 chromosomes, possibly from a single source, a single mother—depending on which theory you endorse—to a worldwide multitude of races and ethnic groups over the course of a million years, give or take several hundred millennia."

"Where is it ending?"

"Here, in America."

"Oh, oh, I think I smell something burning."

"Goddammit, Toner, why do you always assume I'm on drugs? This is not my theory. You asked me what the twins said, I told you. You're so frickin' quick to jump down my throat, maybe *you* should smoke something, loosen up for a change."

"Sorry, I was just kidding. Okay? We're both tired. I apologize."

"Fine. Apology accepted."

Angela turned her head slightly to see Molotov listening with eyebrows raised. She smiled weakly and shrugged. "Anything else?" she asked.

"Yeah, but I hesitate to tell you. You'll probably accuse me of snorting animal tranquilizers."

"Greg, I said I was sorry."

"They said they needed to talk to you, to tell you who *you* are."

"Who *I* am? What the heck is that all about? I'm a sniffling, hacking, irritable, cranky malcontent. What does that have to do with Nyentzi?"

"I'm just the messenger," Kaloostian said. "But your assessment's pretty accurate."

"When did they leave that message?"

"Late Saturday night, LA time. Sunday morning in Moscow."

"That was more than twenty-four hours ago. We need to check Nadezhda's message center again," Vassily said. "There may be another communication."

"I thought of that, too, Vassily. I checked, and there was."

"What did they say?" Toner and Molotov asked in unison, cheeks now pressed together, ears glued to the telephone.

"They said beware of what Tyrell offers, that some people will be seduced by it. They called it the Holy Grail."

"What do you think they meant?"

"DNA, the all-men-are-created-equal propaganda. A noble concept, but it's childish to think that all men and women at point of conception are equal in every regard, especially now that we've cracked the genetic code."

"I like to think the founding fathers were referring to equal opportunity."

"Probably, but I don't think the twins were talking about one particular race or religion. They were thinking bigger—pure genetics—the base sequences that make us who and what we are. In that regard, life is *radically* unequal, a deck so stacked against us it would piss off the pope."

"I can't believe Lara and Katya are that elitist."

"They're not. What I'd give to spend a week, a day…hell, an hour with them," Greg mused. "They throw out all these innuendoes, leaving it to us to figure what they mean. Drives me nuts. And their voices—God, they sound like angels.

"Anyway, the genetically ordained proteins that predestine who we are, are the same in all of us, regardless of what we look like on the outside. It's just the different combinations that make us unique. That's nothing earth-shattering. Most everyone, 'cept the Klan and the Aryan Nation, knows that. But there's a danger. We now have the ability to make changes in inherent characteristics, to move beyond the realm of nature, and chance.

"Tyrell, through the data he stole, offers the ability to rewrite Genesis, revisit the garden. Adam and Eve bit the forbidden fruit—took a big damn chunk out of it. God was pissed, gave 'em the boot. They wandered, were fruitful. Now we're right back at the beginning."

"Only now we are judging ourselves."

"It's a scary proposition."

"We're not ready."

"Even if we were, there's a conflict of interest."

"The fox and the chicken coop."

"The lion lying down with the lamb."

"And the lamb ain't gettin' much sleep."

"Heiple spouted all this bullshit about equality and leveling the playing field," Toner said. "Maybe that's what he was trying to say. Trouble is, he didn't understand it himself."

"My point precisely. Sure, Heiple was tall, handsome, blond, and drove a nice car. But I always said he only got into the gene pool because the lifeguard wasn't on duty." Toner's eyes widened as she realized the scope of Nyentzi. "And now Tyrell can change that," she added. "With a map of the human genome, he can modify every chromosome, tweak looks, tweak intelligence, make us as perfect as possible. He could even modify a gene that would make it impossible to be stupid."

"And in changing our genome," Greg added, "Tyrell destroys us as a natural species. He effectively terminates billions of years of evolution, the consequences of which we have no way of calculating."

Vassily shook his head in alarm. "You are right, Gregory. It is a seductive peril. The world is certainly not ready for this."

"I need to talk to the twins," Toner said. "I need to know how we're supposed to prevent this. And that deal about who I am, I don't understand that at all."

"Too dangerous. We can't even use Nadezhda's voicemail box. I'm afraid that message is our last communication with those kids."

"Why?" Toner asked. Before Kaloostian could respond, she answered herself. "They're that sick? Oh God, those poor kids."

"I'm afraid so. They sounded weak…a lot of coughing, but not depressed, almost cheerful."

"Did they say anything at the end…any sort of farewell?"

"They paraphrased St. Francis—said it's another clue—something you need to know to open the disk. Anyway, I wrote it down:

> Where there is hatred, we must now sow peace;
> where there is injury, pardon;
> where there is doubt, faith;
> where there is despair, hope;
> where there is sadness, joy;
> where there is darkness, light.
> It is in giving that we receive,
> in pardoning that we are pardoned,
> in dying that we are born into eternal life.

"That's it?" Toner asked as she finished writing it down.

"Yeah, but I did notice one odd thing. Do you want to hear it? I've got it recorded."

"Play it back."

"Okay," Greg said, manipulating his computer. "Listen to the way they alternate speaking."

"They do it all the time. It's weird, like a conversation in stereo."

The three conspirators listened to the delicate voices of Lara and Katya. Near the end of the message, Greg paused the recording.

"Did you hear that? Every phrase was alternated, except the word *light*. It sounded as if they both said it."

"Yeah, definitely two voices."

"I heard it too," Vassily added. "*Light* must be a clue."

"Great job, Greg. Is there anywhere safe we can meet in the next hour?"

There was a long pause. "You're gonna hate me when I tell you this. But no, there isn't. I'm packing to leave town myself."

"You can't be serious," Toner exclaimed. "This had better be a very bad joke in very bad taste, some demented mood you're in. Something you said impulsively, despite knowing my reaction would be an overwhelming desire to find you and kill you. I ask you, Gregory H. Kaloostian, you *aren't* serious? Are you?"

Kaloostian was silent, but Toner knew he was still there. She could hear him breathing.

"Well, what is it? she demanded again. "I don't have all day."

"We can't stay here. LA's not safe anymore."

"Aaahhhhhhhh," Toner howled, pounding the receiver against the side of the phone.

Vassily backed away and looked around, hoping no one saw his companion's tirade. The banging lasted more than ten seconds. Molotov was amazed the phone did not break.

Toner finally ran out of steam, wheezing and coughing in frustration and anger. She weakly beat the receiver against the metal box even as she rested her head against it.

"I wanna go home…I wanna go home…I wanna go home."

"Angie," Greg said gently. "You can't go home. Your family thinks you're dead. Most of your stuff's probably been boxed and shipped to Michigan. You've got no place to go. And if you call your family, you put them in danger, too. We're all in danger. None of us can stay here. This isn't my decision. It isn't even my idea. It's Lara's and Katya's. They warned us. They've been monitoring Tyrell's computer and telephone transmissions using secondary networks they set up. Despite his advantages, Tyrell still wants you…and chances are he's on to me, too."

"But you said he was acting out of spite," Toner said. "Can't we send him flowers and a box of chocolates? Maybe he'll forget the whole thing."

"Afraid not. He's got the gangs mobilized. With Heiple dead, and I'm assuming he is, the shit's gonna hit the fan. The only reasons the Feds aren't involved are, *one*, you're officially deceased, and *two*, they don't want to involve any more people than absolutely necessary. We have to leave. It's our only hope."

"I suppose they said where we should go."

"They mentioned a place with minimal gang activity."

"Where's that—the dark side of the moon?"

"Close, but not quite. Salt Lake City."

Toner closed her eyes and took a wheezy breath. "You want us to rent a car and leave town?"

"That's the plan. From where you are now, you can head over to I-210 until it intersects with I-15 near Ontario. Interstate 15 will take you…"

"I know, I know. It goes right into Salt Lake," Angela said. "And I don't agree. There are gangs in Salt Lake, too. I know there are."

"I know there are, too, but not many. Mostly Polynesian teenagers whose parents immigrated there to be closer to their converted faith."

"Mormons."

"A Bible in one hand, an Uzi in the other."

"No more jokes. Nothing's funny anymore." Angela closed her eyes, trying to suppress a pounding headache. "What if something goes wrong, Greg? What if one of us can't make the rendezvous? What if you get hit by a bus?"

"Yeah, like that's gonna happen anytime soon. If it does, we switch to Plan B."

"What's Plan B?"

"You don't wanna know," Greg quipped. "Trust me, I've got all the contingencies covered. There'll be other people meeting us there. We can work better as a team once we're away from Tyrell. It's our one chance, Angie. Our only chance."

"So you say."

"So Lara and Katya say."

"Damn kids. They're only seven. Who died and made them boss?"

"We're going to be asking that for a long time. Now, here's what we need to do…"

34

ORIGINAL SIN

He'd never thought of Nyentzi as a conspiracy, at least not the kind popularized in fiction and print. From the funding that built Monogovody, through the years of research, to the explosion that destroyed the facility, to the transfer of control to a new generation, Nyentzi hadn't been particularly intriguing or sinister. Granted, he'd made it sound that way, but that was mostly for Toner's benefit. In truth, the Nyentzi Project was business as usual.

Powerful people had entered into an agreement for future profit, wholly unconcerned about international law, ethics, human life, or the aftereffects of their actions. Hand-wringing, sleepless nights, or visits to the parish priest were unlikely. An irreversible course of events had been set into motion, consequences be damned. What's so devious about that?

But as he fit the final pieces together, Gregory Kaloostian saw a picture he never would have guessed. Staring at his computer, he rethought his earlier deduction. There was indeed a conspiracy within the Nyentzi Project, at its very core. Perhaps an inadvertent development the original planners could not envision, but the ramifications of that development made him shudder.

So trivial, a single sentence in the original Revkin report. On a piece of paper he and Toner had not seen before, a piece of paper Hatton had stuck in his desk. A piece handed him that morning with other personal effects, by Hatton's daughter, at the funeral of his former boss.

In his hurry to leave Los Angeles, Greg almost missed it. The call to the NSA—the call that prompted the government to swoop down on the hospital, transfer the comatose Melissa Revkin, along with her parents, to a Marine Corps facility—was from an untraceable source. Kaloostian had assumed it was an overzealous doctor. But that was not the case, and therein lay his concern.

In the new millennium, making an untraceable call was next to impossible, as computer and satellite technology was too advanced for such an anomaly. It could be done, but the necessary skills and equipment were so rare Greg could think of only two people who possessed them both.

The first was Eldon Tyrell. Obviously, he hadn't made the call, hadn't exposed himself and his ill-conceived enterprise to the world. Which left only one suspect, and that suspect was not one person but many, all with the same skills and intelligence. And they were only children, the children of Nyentzi.

As much as he tried to ignore their involvement, a second piece of evidence convinced him otherwise. Three unauthorized entries into Angela Toner's personnel file had occurred in the past seven days.

One was the NSA itself. They simply wanted to know more about the agent who had absconded with the Revkin file. Their access was not so much illegal as it was a violation of standard operating procedure.

The second was probably Tyrell.

Last, but certainly not least, was the third call. Like the original tip-off to the NSA, it was untraceable and probably made by the twins. Such a coincidence he might have accepted were it not for one significant distinction. The third call did not access Toner's entire file, but only the additions of the previous two weeks. That meant someone had accessed her file earlier still. A subsequent investigation of his hunch unearthed such a breach. It too was from an untraceable source.

Kaloostian sat in dumbfounded silence: The twins had orchestrated the entire chain of events—from the creation of the Revkin file, to tipping off Armenian intelligence to ensure *his* participation, even perhaps to jamming the fax at the Mercado drug bust to get *Toner* into trouble. Everything they touched was part of the conspiracy.

Though intimidated by their power and talents, something about the children never seemed right. For seven years they'd lived in relative obscurity, content with their lives of scientific exploration and design. Now, suddenly, they wanted that to change. Not they were up to no good—that wasn't in their nature, or so he hoped. No, this seemed more a desire by the children of Nyentzi not to fade into oblivion. They only wanted to be remembered. But in that case, then the thought of Eldon Tyrell being as much a patsy as a power broker sent a chill up Kaloostian's spine.

Evidence indicated the twins had been leaving clues for years—all the way back to their first foray into cyberspace, when they called themselves "Shadow Chasers." Kaloostian now knew they weren't referring to the character from an old radio program—they were referring to Jung.

Carl Gustav Jung, originator of analytical psychology as Gregory's latest research revealed, theorized that every individual has an inner shadow, a product of repressed consciousness. Infantile in nature, the shadow is made up of rejected and imprisoned desires, emotions, and attitudes forever untouched by education and maturation. Though the shadow is essentially harmless, the refusal to recognize it poses a deep-seated danger to the unconscious. Like evil itself, an unacknowledged shadow grows stronger and more wayward than the shadow accepted and mollified.

Reading material on Jung downloaded from the Internet, Greg thought at first he was on the wrong track. Only after expanding the search did he confirm the connection between the children of Nyentzi and their Shadow Chaser byline.

The way in which Jung's theory, called the central theoretical concept of the collective unconscious, tied to the twins was an eye-opener. As Jung theorized, humans have an instinctive need for religious belief and experience, as it is only through religion that they are able to confront and understand the extent of the collective unconsciousness.

But advances in science and technology have eroded many ancient religious beliefs and myths, making modern humans the victim of a multitude of psychological disorders. In neglecting God and religion, human impose upon themselves a profound lack of awareness of the basic powers within their nature. With nothing left to believe in, their own existence evolves into unfulfilling social isolation and despair.

Greg didn't doubt that. He knew the rate of depression in industrialized societies was doubling every ten years, with suicide, drug usage, and hopelessness taking an ever-increasing toll.

But the twins weren't suggesting a Prozac binge for the masses. The shadows they chased weren't psychological at all. Like Jung's theory, they were thinking religion. And they were thinking global.

They knew the world didn't need flash-in-the-pan heroes. It needed a miracle. If Greg's conclusion was correct, the children of Nyentzi had unleashed upon the world perhaps the most diabolical plot ever, a plot exemplifying the subversive power of innocence.

Seventy-four children, arguably among the most perfect humans ever to have ever lived, were setting themselves up for the ultimate destiny—deification and immortality. The Bible said God created "man" in His own image. In the third millennium A.D., the science of genetics reversed the process.

Volume 2 of *The Greatest Story Ever Told* read like a bad soap opera. The children had culled from humanity the ultimate cast of stereotypical characters. With themselves in the leading role of the immaculately conceived virgins in distress, they assigned Tyrell the role of depraved archvillain: Herod the Great, Pontius Pilate, and Judas Iscariot, rolled into one.

Born in the year 2000, they'd even nailed the date. What better way to celebrate an anniversary than by surpassing the original event?

"Tailor-made for the part," Kaloostian said to himself. "From the name of the project that spawned them, to their unparalleled mental abilities, to their martyred physical appearance…Who would've believed it? I mean, who can argue with a little girl? And what's on the disk they gave to Toner?"

Try as he might, Kaloostian couldn't blame them. So much talent, so little time—seven years—one chance to leave their mark. Would the children's story shine as a beacon of hope or fade in the dark? It all depended on cracking the code.

Lara and Katya's last message said that Toner needs to know *who she is*. "But," Kaloostian thought, "if Angela needs to know anything, its *who the twins are*—pint-sized demoiselles with ambitions, pride, and power greater than anyone could imagine."

Greg sighed, thankful that he'd lied to Toner, hadn't told her what he suspected. Given the stress she was under, the knowledge that they'd all been blatantly manipulated by a bunch of seven-year-olds might put her over the edge.

Maybe Yuri Tyrellovich had been right all along. Maybe the children of Nyentzi really were the Messiah. Or maybe Nyentzi was as close to God as humankind dared go.

"And according to the Bible," Kaloostian knew, "only a messiah can end the diaspora." He closed his eyes and thought back to the Armenian catechism lessons he'd endured as a child. He remembered an ancient prayer and instinctively mouthed the words in Latin: "*Ave Maria, gratia plena, dominus tecum, benedicta tu in mulieribus, et benedictus fructus ventris tui…*"

A knock on the door interrupted his recitation. Greg spun about in his wheelchair and rolled to answer the door. The ending of the prayer would have to wait.

"Are you sure? Maybe we should stop. You look terrible. You need rest. You need *sleep*."

"I'm fine."

"The snow is coming down harder. I think you are driving too fast. Slow down."

"Quit yer nagging. I just want to get to St. George. Then we'll stop."

"I wish you would let me drive. Those decompression pills you took for your runny nose said not to drive after taking. You are already sick and now drugs, too."

"Stop arguing. You can't drive. Why won't you admit those punks messed you up? There's no way you can drive, even with cruise control. You're having muscles spasms and leg cramps. You'd kill us for sure…not that that's such a bad thing."

"Stop sounding so depressed, Angela."

"I'm fine, dammit. Besides, it's not like I've never been on this road before. Jake and I came this way when we went skiing at the Brian Head Ski Resort."

"It is so dark. What if we have an accident?"

"Calm down, Vassily. I'm fine," Toner said, gripping the wheel, her bloodshot eyes reflecting the lights of the electronic dashboard.

They'd rented the most popular car in America, a late-model, white Ford Taurus, loaded with options. Following Kaloostian's instructions, the two travelers grudgingly left Los Angeles and headed for Salt Lake City, Utah, 688 miles away.

"I'm sorry I'm grouchy. It's been long day. What else is new, eh?"

"Are you still angry about leaving Los Angeles? Gregory was right, you know. It would be too easy for someone to see you. We would be squatting ducks for Tyrell's gang."

"I'm just upset about this whole thing. It's all my fault."

"It is not your fault. You bumbled onto it by accident. It is *not* your fault, Angela. Stop being too hard upon yourself. Lighten up the load. Be frigid."

"I beg your pardon?"

"You know, be cold, chill out."

"All right, I'll chill. It's not fair to drag you down with me. I keep forgetting you're a volunteer."

"That is true," Vassily realized. "When do you want to stop for the night?"

"We'll be crossing into Utah in about ten minutes. St. George is only a few miles after that. We'll stop then, I promise."

Vassily did not respond. He stared out the window into the darkness.

"Whatcha thinking about?" Toner asked, hoping conversation would keep her awake.

"Nothing much…differences between America and Russia."

"There's a few of those. Sorry we didn't make it to Disneyland."

"Oh. I forgot about that."

"There's always next year, as my father used to say. What do you think about America so far?"

"People are friendly. They smile very much. I like that. The waitress at that Daisy Chain restaurant near Las Vegas, when she said, 'Have a nice day,' she really meant it."

"It's Dairy *Queen*…and she just wanted a tip."

"No, that is not true. It was something else. It was her attitude. She was thinking positive. That is why America is so special."

"I missed something. Why is America so special?"

"The attitudes of the people. Have you not noticed?"

"I don't know…Give me an example."

"Okay. Have you ever seen the movie documentary about the original Woodstock rock concert?"

"You mean that drug-infested free-for-all from the 1960s?"

"Yes, that is the one."

"Please don't tell me you were weaned on bong water like Kaloostian."

"No, it's nothing like that. Have you ever seen it?"

"No," Toner said, shaking her head.

"It is a very long and chaotic movie, but there is a part that is completely perfect. The filmmaker guy interviews an old man. He must have been fifty years old. His job is the worst of anyone at the festival. He is to clean the outdoor toilets."

"Sounds like fun."

"You see, that is the wrong attitude. That is not correct, Angela Toner. This man did not think that way. Here he was, an older gentleman, not interested in listening to the music, cleaning horrible-smell toilets for partying youths, a job a Russian would do only at gunpoint—maybe not even then. And he was doing such a perfect job. He scrubs, he cleans, he sprays air-freshening. His job was to clean toilets, and he took such pride in his work."

"Your hero sounds like a moron."

"You have the bad attitude, Angela. This man may not have been rich or famous or a genius, but he did his job. He even told the filmmaker guy that he had two sons—one at the festival and one in Vietnam—and he was proud of them both. I could tell he was a good man—and a good father."

Angela clicked her tongue and shook her head. "And that man cleaning a commode is your best impression of America?"

Vassily knew Toner was in a foul mood, that she would agree with nothing he said. He sat in silence for a moment, then answered.

"To me, Woodstock shows the power of the people, what is in their hearts. When even doing the worst possible type of job, under bad conditions, for insufficient money, it still is done with pride. *That* is America. That is why your country, when it wants, can do anything. Think of that power, that belief in liberty and opportunity. He was only one man with a toilet brush, but since that day, almost forty years ago, his work has been seen by millions of people as an example of honest labor. And *that* is why I love America."

Toner was unconvinced. "He was probably doin' a good job 'cuz he knew he was being filmed."

"No...no, he did not. They filmed him at work before interviewing, before he knew he was being recorded. It was no act. It was work done from the heart."

"You'll have to pardon my skepticism, but you sound like Kaloostian. He's always rah-rah this and rah-rah that. Your story's nice, but I've seen too many people trying to get over on the system. Right or wrong, I just have a hard time identifying with anything positive."

"Yes, I see that...Speaking of Gregory, why do you give him such a difficult time for his use of marijuana if it helps him with his missing-leg pains?"

Toner started to answer but closed her mouth and thought for a moment. "I know it helps him. I know he lost a leg, and he's paralyzed from the waist down, and he's got all sorts of medical problems."

"You are countering your earlier statement."

"I just want you to know that I see the need for his using pot. But it seems such a crutch for him. And he's always braggin' about it."

"It seems to me you are angry because pot is something he enjoys. Why not leave it at that? Look Angela, I am not defending illegal or overdosing drugs. I told you, remember, that my goal is to complete my graduate degree. I am planning on drug-and-alcohol counseling for Russian teenagers as my next job. My paper, what you call...?"

"Thesis?"

"Yes, thesis. My thesis, for which I have already made much research, is concerning drug use in the entire world."

"Is there a lecture in this conversation?"

"Only facts and information. For example, have you heard the phrase *feed your head*?"

"I've heard it. So?"

"It made me wonder…"

"And?"

"And in my research on drug use, I collected crop statistics from around the world. From all the land used for farming, what amount—percentages—would you guess was used to feed your head?"

"What is this, a trick question? You gather all these asinine estimates on how much acreage is used to produce pot, coca, and poppies. Then you magically come up with a nice round number, say 10 percent. And I'm supposed to think wow, one-tenth. That's a lot of land for drugs."

"There you go again, Angela. You are too quick to conclude. It is actually a higher number because you forgot to include coffee, percents of wheat, rye, barley, hops, corn…"

"Hold it! Hold it! Since when is coffee a drug?"

"By terminology. The coffee bean releases caffeine, a noted amphetamine. Not maybe the most powerful, but amphetamine just the same. And you forget tobacco crops. Is nicotine not one of the most deadly and addicting drugs in the world?"

"Okay, fine, but what's with the wheat and corn?"

"Parts of each crop are used for beer, malt liquors, whiskey, vodka, gin, and other intoxicating drinks. You also must include grapes for making wine. And of course percentages of rice, for the Japanese love rice wine—saki. So you see, Angela Toner, when all those crops are added up, together with marijuana, cocaine production, poppy plants, and other illegal narcotics, you will find that much more than 10 percent of the world's agriculture is devoted to feeding the head."

"And the moral of the story is?"

"That our friend Greg is doing what is natural. Leave him alone."

"So just because the shit is grown, that somehow justifies its use to alter reality?"

"You do not include yourself somehow?"

"I don't do drugs!"

"Would you care to be telling me what you have been drinking for the past six hours? Is it not perhaps coffee? Does coffee not have a chemical in it that affects the brain?"

"It's not a *drug* drug. It's just caffeine. It's also quite legal."

Vassily reached to pick up the thermos Toner had propped against the seat. "Legal or not, this is a chemical," he said, shaking the container. "It affects the neural synapses in…"

Toner reached to the right, grabbing the thermos from Vassily.

"Don't you go there, Vassily. Do *not* touch my coffee. I'll smack you a good one."

"My point exactly," the Russian replied, refusing to let go, playfully tugging on Toner's prized possession.

"I'm warning ya. You're skating on very thin ice here, *comrade*."

"I was a hockey player. I always skate on the thin ice."

Glaring at Molotov, refusing to loosen her grip on the thermos, Toner never saw the dark shadow cross the headlights' beam.

Vassily screamed. "Angela…Look out!"

He pointed towards Toner's side of the car, but she instinctively looked at him, following the sound of his voice. Her mouth gaped when she tried to speak, but the words never came.

The impact was explosive. The windshield cracked in three places, almost caving in. The driver-side window erupted in a barrage of glass, showering both of them with sharp projectiles. Before she could react, a second impact smashed in the rear window and threw the car into an irreversible spin towards the side of the road.

Time slowed to a numbing crawl. Angela turned her attention back to driving, gripping the wheel as the car skidded off the darkened road. In the rearview mirror, she caught a glimpse of something large and dark falling to the road behind them. Then, in a puff of white, the car punched through the plowed embankment and careened down the steep slope of the highway.

Down, down, down they slid, the Taurus' headlights piercing the wintry darkness of the Utah countryside. Unable to see through the shattered windshield, Angela pressed on the brake with all her might, desperate to slow the vehicle.

The third impact was decisive. Rock or tree, it didn't matter—the front end of the car caved in like an accordion, damaged beyond repair. In a second puff of white, both airbags deployed, stopping Toner and Molotov's forward momentum.

For several seconds, the only sound was the hiss of escaping air. Then a moan, hesitant movement, the tinkle of falling glass. A hand reached out to turn off the ignition, generating more silence.

"Angela, are you okay?" Vassily asked, his voice uncharacteristically loud.

"What hit us? What was that?" Toner asked, blinking several times in the darkness as she tried to refocus.

"Can't you smell?"

"Smell? *Whew.* What is that?"

"Deer dung, maybe a moose. No, it was a deer…a very big deer."

Toner shook the cobwebs from her head, pushed the now-deflated airbag out of the way and tried to move. A spasm of pain shot up her right leg. "Aahhh, my ankle!"

Vassily reached towards her. "I cannot see a thing. Turn on the light."

She punched the maplight switch, but nothing happened. "The battery…damn. The impact must've broken the connection. Double damn…I can't move my seat back."

"Is your ankle broken?" Vassily said, releasing his shoulder and lap belt.

"No, I think it just twisted again when we hit the tree."

"There is glass everywhere. Do not touch your head. Your hair is covered with sharp pieces."

"I know. I can feel them," Angela said. "Try your door. Mine won't open."

A second rush of cold air signaled Vassily's success. "I will get out and help you across the seat." In a moment, Vassily was leaning back into the car. He carefully gripped Angela by the shoulders and gently maneuvered her body across both seats. Once she was out, he supported her as she sat back down on the edge of the passenger seat.

"I will take off your shoe and look at the ankle."

"What good will that do? It's dark as hell, and you'd have to loosen the ace bandage. Just leave it."

For half a minute neither person spoke. Angela stared down at the snow, shaking her head, trying to get the glass out of her hair. Vassily, taking control of the situation, surveyed the area.

"This is a very steep hill. Everywhere else on the highway are barricades to prevent cars from crashing down. But we did not go through a barricade, did we?"

"Now that you mention it, no."

Vassily walked awkwardly for several feet, poking around in the snow. "There are pieces of heavy timber and a long metal railing over here. And other tire markings, deep tracks. I am thinking there must have been another accident here not long ago. The repair guys have yet to fix the damage. The deer must have come onto the highway through the hole in the fence."

"And it had to be me driving," Toner concluded, cursing under her breath at their misfortune. "Vassily, would you do me a favor?"

"Sure. What is it?"

"Open the trunk, get your shotgun, and shoot me."

"This is not the time for the joking. We are in troublesome situation."

"Who's joking? How can you even stand to be near me? I'm a Jonah—a curse. Everything I touch turns to shit. How many people are dead because of me? If you won't put me out of my misery, at least do yourself a favor. Climb up that hill and leave me. You don't want me along. I'm bad news."

"It is not that wretched. Come on, do chin-ups. Be smiles. We are lucky this is not a Hollywood movie."

"What do you mean?"

"The car would have exploded in a ball of fire when it hit the tree. We would have been thrown clear of the crash, but at least one of us would have had clothes burned completely off, requiring the sharing of garments."

"How can you make jokes at a time like this? It's nine o'clock at night…ten o'clock, we just changed time zones…We're at the bottom of a hill, our rented car is totaled, it's cold, we're both walking wounded, and someone is trying to kill us. Now tell me, Mr. Sunshine, is that something to laugh about?"

"Look on the bright side, Angela Toner. There is a certain freedom to being over the creek. We have every selection open. What more mistakes can we possibly make?"

"You haven't been around me long enough for such an assumption."

"You are so depressing," Vassily said, turning. He pointed in the direction they had come. "I saw a light off the road a kilometer ago. The road curved this way," he gestured. "So even if I could get back up to the road, which I cannot because my leg is very painful, it would be a longer walk than straight through those trees in that direction. See where I am pointing?"

"It's wilderness. You could get lost, eaten by bears, shot by the militia."

"I will bring my shotgun along for protection. My only anxiety is the river."

"What river?"

"We crossed a short bridge on the highway, just before the deer attacked us. Didn't you see it?"

"No."

"Trust me. It is a river, maybe a stream. Whatever. It is most highly probably frozen over, right?"

"Vassily, it's snowing, visibility sucks, it's cold, and…"

"I am a Russian. Do you understand? This is not a bragging. My people live with winter. This is our element. I will go find us help while you wait in the car with the door closed and covered up with your coat. Before you know anything, I will return. Okay?"

Toner said nothing, staring at Molotov like a lost puppy. He opened the trunk and removed the shotgun, handing the assault rifle to Toner. "Just in case you need this."

She accepted the gun but remained silent.

"Angela, trust me. I will not let you down."

"Fine. Go…get help. I'll wait here. I'd just be a burden if I tried to come along."

Vassily smiled, then turned around. Several yards through the snow, he stopped and turned back. "Angela, I know you think I am just a youngster kind of guy. I know this has been a very, very bad week for you. But please to understand, I am here by choice. You have not let me down. Stay in the car, and try to keep warm. Please."

"Yeah, yeah, yeah. I'll be fine," Toner said unconvincingly.

"You will be fine. Have faith, Angela. Be patient and have faith."

Angela nodded. Vassily took a deep breath and walked away. After another hundred yards, he called back to his cynical companion, "Stay warm. I will bring help."

Toner waved but said nothing.

Other than the incessant pain in her head, which seemed like it would never leave, Angela Toner was alone, a state of being she felt both physically and psychologically. Since Jake's death, she had built a series of barbwire-topped walls around her emotions, napalmed the bridges of many interpersonal relationships, and guarded the remaining few with religious fervor. Her logic was simple: better to live in a world of social isolation than bleed to death from the incisions of dishonesty and criticism.

Not that she enjoyed being alone, but that she'd rather sit in the relative safety of her unlit apartment than socialize with pseudo-acquaintances, nurturing superficial friendships. Her life was not glamorous, but she was able to maintain a relative degree of sanity. Kaloostian thought she lived a life of quiet desperation. Angela saw it as a means of survival.

She hadn't always had a negative personality, but she had learned that sarcasm worked to keep most people at arm's length. Nadezhda Molotova, the one person who'd fought through the defenses and charmed her way into Angela's life, was dead. Vassily Molotov, the last surviving member of that proud family, was now in danger, all because of her.

As she sat quietly on the edge of the seat, tears rolled down her cheeks. Angela didn't know whether they were for herself or those unfortunate enough to know her.

Raising her head, the tears freezing on her cheeks, she watched the slow snow hang in the air and drift down at a deliberate pace. It began to fill Vassily's footprints and the tracks left by the car. In time, the snow would cover all evidence of human encroachment. The loneliness she felt at that moment—so deep, so potent—was more painful than her throbbing ankle or fevered and broken head.

From what Greg had said, her funeral would take place the following morning in Michigan. To the public, Angela Toner was officially deceased. For all it mattered, she might as well finish the job. Her hopes and dreams, her friends and family, were lost forever. She could think of no reason to live. Nyentzi and Vassily would have to survive without her.

The Russian thoroughly confused her. He had seen her at her worst—weeping, swearing, ugly, lost, irritable, murderous. Yet Toner had noticed his cautious glances, felt the brush of his hand against her arm as they talked. However sick and depressed she felt, she knew Vassily was good medicine. The sensation of discovering—of being discovered—was an exciting novelty. Her infrequent smiles arrived sooner and stayed longer. Kaloostian would have picked up on it immediately.

But Vassily did not and could not know. He might have sensed a shift in her attitude, but their relationship was too new for him to understand it. Moreover, he hid his feelings for Angela as much as he hid his grief for his sister. Angela had caught him on several occasions brushing away a tear, staring into space, his knuckles white from clenching his fists. Despite his unpretentious demeanor, Vassily Molotov was a private person. In time, he might have learned to share, to love. In time, given different circumstances, Angela Toner and Vassily Molotov might have had a chance. But there was no time.

As much as Angela longed for love, her fear of vulnerability was greater. She must not lose emotional control. She must not tear down the walls she had meticulously erected around her fragile heart. She had resisted every moment of optimism with three years of chronic negativity. She'd replaced every positive outlook, every reborn desire, with a stronger yearning for numbness. While she never considered her life void of purpose, knowing how to defragment her hard drive did not seem like much of an epitaph.

Angela needed something, but she didn't know what it was. After several minutes of contemplation in icy silence, she decided that more than anything, she needed a hug—a warm, tender, loving embrace. From Vassily, her father, Jake, or God—it didn't matter. But Vassily was off somewhere getting lost, Jake was dead, and she would probably never see her father again. That left only one option: Plan B.

Kaloostian seemed vague about his Plan B, but Toner had been thinking about hers for three years. She'd had enough of battling demons, depression, and foreboding. It was time to run up the white flag.

Biting her lower lip, blinking away the tears, she reached into her coat and pulled out the Beretta. She checked to make sure it was loaded and that the safety was off. Slowly, hesitantly, she raised the pistol and placed the barrel in her mouth, trying to hold her hands steady. The act required every ounce of effort and all the courage she could muster.

The cold of the Utah winter, combined with her raging fever, reduced her to a mass of quivering flesh. The last thing she wanted to do was miss. The result would be worse than death.

Staring towards heaven, a final desperate sob rose from the depths of Angela's tormented soul. It burst forth, as though her body had exorcised a demon or expunged a vile poison. Her grip on the pistol tightened until her knuckles were white from the cold and the exertion.

BAM…A single shot echoed down the valley.

35

My Foolish Heart

"Hey, Kiddo, I wasn't expecting you so early. How'd you pack so quick?"

Suada Sivac wordlessly entered Kaloostian's apartment. He was closing the door when she finally spoke. "I can't let you do it, Gregory. You're my best friend, but I can't."

"What?" Greg turned his wheelchair to find himself staring into the barrel of a handgun. "What are you doing? Suada, would you please stop pointing that thing at me."

The gun remained pointed at his chest.

"You *know* what I'm talking about. You've been snooping."

"What are you talking about?"

"The children…you've been snooping on the children."

Kaloostian exhaled through his nose. "How do you know that?" he asked in a shaky voice.

"They told me. They warned me about you. They said you were no longer one of us, that you were trying to hurt them."

Gregory thought about the information he'd gathered on the Internet the night before. With a mental kick in the pants, he realized the children were monitoring the flow of data to and from his computer a lot closer than he'd thought. He bit his lower lip and looked deep into Suada's eyes, hoping to see a sign of hesitation or indecision. There was none. He then looked at the barrel of the gun, a bargain-basement 38-special, expecting to see it shaking in his neighbor's nervous grip. It was rock steady.

Greg began to sweat. "Can we talk about this? I know how much the children mean to you…"

"No you don't. You have no idea, Gregory Kaloostian. Those children are everything I believe in, every dream I've ever had. I can't let you defile them."

"Suada, don't you think they're my dream, too? I care about them, too," Greg argued, loosening the belt that held him in the wheelchair. "You've got to believe me. I'm just a little concerned about how they're going about this…this quest of theirs."

Suada shook her head. "It is *not* a quest. That's where you're wrong. They've been *chosen*, Greg. Chosen and anointed by God. You must understand that, accept that, accept them for who they are."

Greg sighed. He hadn't expected this and was not prepared for an argument. Moreover, he knew he had to proceed slowly in stating his case. But he could not afford the luxury of a drawn-out debate.

They were eyeball to eyeball—Suada on the couch, Greg in his wheelchair. He had coaxed her away from the door, offered her coffee, a soft drink, a shot of whiskey, anything to calm her down. His offers had been refused.

Greg's misgivings about the twins were now a reality. He could not deny their power, and he knew that power tended to attract certain personalities, sometimes of a pathological nature. The children may have laughed off his *schizophrenic* label, but he suspected his clinical assessments were close to the mark.

One pronounced characteristic of schizophrenia is the delusion of grandeur. Based on the information supplied by Toner, it could also be argued that they were paranoid, depressed, and a tad neurotic. Greg couldn't blame the children; they were as much victim as villain, their psychoses an unforeseen byproduct of the genetic goo from which they were created.

Suada, he realized, was the last person with whom he could discuss his misgivings. She'd become a believer, her mind closed to debate. But Greg refused to surrender as his friend pursed her lips and glared.

"Don't you understand how dangerous this is? It must be prevented."

"You are the danger, Gregory. You are what must be prevented."

"I'm not talking about the children. I don't mean them. I mean Eldon Tyrell. Do you think for one minute he's going to stop here? Nyentzi is just the beginning of these experiments. We have to stop him…now…together…before he can sell the secrets of Nyentzi to the highest bidder."

Silence.

Greg pressed on. "There are millions of species of animals, each with its own genetic code. Instead of the ones and zeroes of binary computer programming, nature uses DNA. But each species has the same genetic programming.

"With his knowledge of genetics, Eldon Tyrell can replicate any trait from any species into the human genome. They did it when they inserted jellyfish genes into monkeys. Remember that? That was years ago. That was before Nyentzi. Imagine what can be done now, with the complete human genetic blueprint. Imagine the thousands of human embryos that will die in these experiments. That is what I am trying to stop, Suada. That is what we all must stop."

The gun still did not waiver.

Kaloostian pushed on. "Evolution took three-and-a-half-billion years. Tyrellovich's experiments took less than twenty. Don't you see the danger of this…hyper-evolution?"

Suada shook her head, freeing herself from the trance of Greg's argument. "No. No, no, no. The Children will not allow that, Gregory. Nor will God. The Children are our redemption—redemption for the millions of sins we've committed in two thousand years."

Realizing now why Yuri Tyrellovich had injected religion into his genetic experiments, Kaloostian made a final attempt to dissuade his friend from killing him. "You know something, Suada. There are only a few real sins. Our species just has this nasty habit of repeating them, replicating them. But Nyentzi, that's every sin rolled into one."

"The Children are free of sin. You know that, Gregory. You know they are pure."

Greg spoke slowly. "Yes, I know. The sin is not the children; they are blameless. The sin is how…and why they were made."

"They trusted you, Gregory. They *trusted* you."

"Suada, if I could clone Jesus Christ, what would be the result? Could I also duplicate Israel under the dominion of Imperial Rome? A dirt-poor existence? Twelve fishing and drinking buddies? Without all that, would Jesus of Nazareth still be a messiah? The children are special. I will not argue that. But please, don't make them into something they're not."

More silence. Gregory sighed. He sighed, and he gambled. "They lied, Suada. Not just to you. To all of us. A subtle lie, but a lie just the same. Remember they told us that their biological parents were Tatiana Mercereau and Yuri Tyrellovich? Remember that? It's not exactly true.

"Mercereau and Tyrellovich may have provided the genetic material, but that was for a single egg. Cloned material—and the twins are definitely clones—must come from a single source, a single egg. What happened to that egg, Suada? It's the one that was altered the most. It's older than the twins, and we don't know what happened to it. It must've been implanted before Nyentzi began, but we don't know what happened to it.

"It's out there, Suada. Your real messiah is out there. And I don't think even Eldon Tyrell knows who it is."

Finally…hesitation. Suada averted her gaze in contemplation. Greg was waiting. He grabbed the gun and tried to wrench it from her vise-like grip. She screamed when he twisted her arm. She was no match for his strength, for his arm muscles built to an amazing degree from years of wheelchair use. Nonetheless, the feisty Bosnian, pushing up from the couch, refused to let go of the weapon, her determination enhanced by the power of her convictions.

Kaloostian twisted to the right, throwing Suada off balance. She began to fall, then grabbed Greg's shirt. Both combatants pitched to the side, the gun locked in both their grips. The thud of their bodies on the carpet was loud, but the spit of a bullet was louder. For several long seconds, there was only silence.

Then: "Greg…you've shot me. Ooo, God, it…it really hurts, Greg."

Kaloostian pulled himself up as best as he could. A spot of red formed on the right side of her blouse. From the crimson froth on her lips, Greg knew she'd been hit in the lung. He frantically unbuttoned and removed his shirt to form a compress, ignoring the fact that Suada still had the gun in her grasp.

"Here, push down on this," he said, carefully removing her fingers from the pistol and placing them on the shirt he was pressing to her chest. "Push tight. I'll call 911."

As Suada lay sprawled on his living-room floor, staring at the ceiling in shock, Greg grabbed the phone he kept in a pouch on his wheelchair and dialed the three magic numbers. "Hello…yes, this is an emergency. There's been a shooting…accidental. Yeah…2598 San Mateo Boulevard, apartment 1215. No, this is one of the neighbors. Hurry up, dammit."

He ended the call and looked at his friend. Bubbly blood covered Suada's lips, and her breathing became a series of rapid gasps. Greg knew she could die from a lack of oxygen if help didn't arrive soon. He looked around the room for his wallet, spied it on the coffee table. He pulled his body over. Opening the wallet, he removed a laminated library card and crawled back to Suada.

"Okay, honey, this'll be quick. I'm gonna open your blouse and place this card over the wound. It's the only way we can keep the oxygen from escaping."

"Whatever you say," Suada whispered.

The first-aid maneuver was quickly accomplished. Greg pushed the compress over the card and placed Suada's hands over it. "Keep your hands there. Okay, now try to breathe…good…I think it worked. Don't move your hands, honey. Just hang in there."

The sound of a siren filtered into the high-rise apartment. "Listen…help's on the way." With that sentence, Kaloostian realized he could not stay. He pulled himself to his wheelchair and climbed up. He knew his idyllic life in Los Angeles was over. He looked around his apartment, down at his dear friend bleeding on his living-room floor, and bit his lower lip.

"Greg," Suada moaned.

"Yes, dear."

"Don't do it. Don't. God will never forgive you. Never…"

"Okay, Suada." He shook his head, wheeled to his luggage, and picked up the one item that could not be replaced—his computer's hard drive. With a heavy sigh, he spun about and headed for the door.

In the elevator he placed a call to his sponsors as he rode down. Quick change of plans. Immediate evacuation. New rendezvous. No time to explain.

The door opened. Across the foyer he saw the elevator doors on the opposite wall begin to close. The paramedics were here. He breathed a sigh of relief and propelled himself forward, through the automatic doors and onto the sidewalk in front of his apartment building.

Greg raced down the block, past the concerned looks of pedestrians, startled by the sight of a wild-eyed man in a speeding wheelchair, spots of blood on his white T-shirt and hands. He reached the corner and kept going.

Though the light was changing, pedestrians always had the right of way in California.

Sewer work had put him behind schedule again. Street after street sported bright-orange construction signs, with lane after lane closed to make way for heavy equipment. Ignoring the yellow light, the exacerbated bus driver didn't take his foot off the accelerator, didn't slow, didn't see the man in the wheelchair until it was too late.

The impact crumbled the wheelchair and sent the pedestrian flying. If he'd worn his lap belt, he'd have died instantly, crushed beneath the wheels of a city bus. Instead, his broken body ended up under a palm tree on the sidewalk.

A crowd formed. A policeman arrived and radioed for help. He asked whether anyone had medical training. Two Good Samaritans stepped forward and tended to the severely injured man. The crowd grew larger, then split into two—one gaping at the human spectacle, the other gawking at the mangled wheelchair.

A second policeman arrived. He shooed the people away back, demanding civil obedience with a stern voice and a well-trained right index finger. With the crowd corralled, the policeman began to clear away the debris of the accident—a bent wheel, glass from a broken headlight, a shoe, a small, squarish metal box.

The policeman stopped and looked around. He activated his radio, clipped near the collar of his shirt. Then he glanced at the other cop, who was kneeling down to assist in the treatment of the victim, using the emergency medical supplies from the city bus. Still talking into his radio, the policeman stooped and casually picked up the metal box.

He stood up again, shut off his radio, and walked away, melting back into the crowd.

Gregory Kaloostian waited for the pain, but it never came. He began to sense people near him, above him, around him. He knew he was seriously injured. Being hit by a bus usually involves more than a couple of bruises. He knew he'd been thrown onto the sidewalk by the impact, but try as he might, he couldn't move his fingers...couldn't manipulate the phantom keyboard that floated through his mind.

Again and again he tried the three-fingered salute—CONT-ALT-DEL...CONT-ALT-DEL...CONT-ALT-DEL. He couldn't move his arms. He couldn't move his neck. He couldn't move his eyelids. Panic set in. He'd always had one overriding fear, and it wasn't death. It was something far worse.

"Oh, God, not this. Not this. Anything but this," Greg screamed inside. He began to slip into unconsciousness. Just then, he remembered what he'd been doing before Suada Sivac knocked on his door. As darkness enveloped him, he concluded the ancient prayer: *"Sancta Maria, Mater Dei, ora pro nobis peccatoribus, nunc et in hora mortis nostrae. Amen."*

Eldon Tyrell knew the digital onslaught of the children of Nyentzi was inevitable. He sat alone at a computer terminal, among row upon row of supercomputers, each backing up the data in the next. Redundancy upon redundancy, to prevent the destruction of his vulnerable electronic data.

They would try to destroy the information he'd worked so hard to accumulate; of that he was certain. But he was ready for them, as ready as possible. Tyrell had no way of knowing when the assault would begin. His gateway and proxy servers deployed the latest firewall technology—designed to filter any suspicious digital packet. All domain names and IP addresses would be screened. Any message with an attachment would be refused admission.

The children's weapons were stealth. Worm and ripper viruses, Trojan horses, file infectors, macros—their arsenal was extensive. And many of his defenses were questionable, designed by those whose access he hoped to prevent.

As a precaution, he had taken many of his servers off-line and terminated the corresponding subroutines. The effects of his actions rippled across the Internet. Throughout the world, web surfers noted delays, misrouted emails, missing links, frozen screens.

Tyrell didn't care. His concern, his only concern, was survival. The rest of the world would just have to be patient. It could be a long day.

Angela bolted straight up and removed the Beretta from her mouth. "Vassily," she blurted. The shot had come from the direction he walked.

She showed no hesitation, slipping the gun back into her pocket and climbing out of the car. Using the assault rifle as a crutch, she began to follow the Russian's footprints. At first, the pain from her injured right ankle was so intense she almost fainted, but determination drove her on.

The snow, though deep, was light powder, allowing Toner to drag her right leg. Gradually, the pain melted, replaced by a numbing chill working its way up from her feet.

Fits of coughing cut into her breathing, labored and shallow. The temperature, below freezing, had no effect on her progress. Indeed, after traveling several hundred yards, Angela was so hot that she had to open her coat. Her forehead blazed with fever.

She had no idea how far or how long she'd been walking when she heard the sound of burbling water. Then she saw it—a mountain stream, its wintry chill reflected in the pale light of the night. Progressing to its bank, Angela saw Vassily's footprints on the other side.

"If he can do it, so can you, Angela Toner," she told herself in a shivering voice.

Easier said than done. For several long seconds, she stood on the bank and examined her position. The stream, more than twenty feet wide, appeared reliably shallow. Countless rocks and boulders dotted the streambed, where the near-freezing water flowed, too swiftly for ice to form.

Toner tried to work up the courage to take the first step into icy water. There! She was surprised to find it not nearly as cold as she'd imagined. Though the water flowed instantly over the top of her ankle boots, the expected chill never came. Her confidence restored, she took another step towards the other side, carefully shifting her weight away from her injured ankle.

One awkward step, then another, until she reached the middle of the stream. Peering through the frosty haze of the woods, she again saw Vassily's path disappearing into among the trees.

"Almost there," Angela muttered, her teeth clattering. She took another step. As she dragged her right foot behind, her boot caught the corner of a rock, shocking her with a pain more intense than anything she'd ever experienced.

Instinctively turning to the source of her agony, she felt her left boot slip. In slow motion, she lost her balance and dropped the rifle. Her body arched backwards as her good leg flew up and out of the water, pitching her into the stream.

The back of her head smacked against a rock, while the shock of the icy water slapped her nearly senseless. The combination was wicked, a one-two punch that left her incapacitated. Captured by the swift current, Angela was knocked and pushed along. Gasping for breath, she swallowed the chilly water. The stream's pull took her only several yards before her body wrapped around a large piece of bedrock.

Angela floated face down in the water. Though conscious, she was helpless and alone, powerless to do anything physical. Voluntary muscle control was gone. Breathing was gone. Nothing but the beat of her heart denoted the passage of time.

"The cold…refreshing. I'm not hot anymore," Angela realized. She tried to open her eyes but saw nothing. She could not see, could not feel.

She could still hear. Above the roar of the water, she detected the measured cadence of her heart as it beat…beat…beat.

She could not know how much time elapsed. Time was meaningless. She remembered, out of some long-forgotten corner of her mind, the obscure fact that the brain, deprived of oxygen, shuts down after five minutes.

"That's impossible," she thought. "I've been here all day. No, the car…the accident…Vassily…Vassily! Where are you?" she called, shouting louder than she had ever shouted before.

But no one heard.

"Vassily…don't leave me. You promised…"

She stopped shouting but heard only the thunderous sound of water. "This is not good. This is definitely not good. I'm dying…I've really done it this time. I can't move, can't see, can't hear. That's not right. I can hear…I can hear that damned song.

"Piano. Bass. One note…another…simple tune. Won't go away, not like Vassily. Vassily! He loves me! Angela, you fool…how can he love you? You're over thirty. He's just a boy. You're black. He's white. Oh you, you and your heart—your foolish, foolish heart.

"Foolish heart. My foolish heart. "My Foolish Heart," by Liz Story. That's it! The name…that damned song. I've finally…finally…figured…it…out. Maybe today won't be a total loss after all…"

A feeling of warmth and contentment swept over Angela Toner. She stopped thinking, stopped worrying, stopped complaining. Nothing was wrong anymore; nothing mattered. Death, the one friend she could count on, was paying its overdue visit. She floated in the pure waters of the icy stream while her favorite song slowly wound down to the beat…beat…beat…of her fading heart.

36

SOMETHING TO SHOOT

Was it live or was it Memorex? It might not even be a cassette tape. Could be a compact disc or the radio, for that matter. Whatever the source of the music, Angela Carmen Toner didn't care for it. Not one dang bit. It was rowdy, twangy, and it grated on her nerves.

The music faded in and out, like her recurring bad dream. Problem was, as the song got louder, the dream grew fainter. In fact, the tune was now loud enough for her to hear the words:

>I was born and raised way out west.
>But the thing that I like 'bout livin' here best.
>It ain't the mountains, the valleys, the hats, or the boots,
>It's having plenty of guns and somethin' to shoot.

At the sound of the word *shoot*, Toner's agitation increased. She tried to open her eyes but saw only darkness. She tried to move her arms and legs but couldn't. Though she could feel her extremities, she seemed paralyzed. By the third verse of the song, she had a chilling realization.

"I really died...I'm really dead. And either God's a Texan, or I've gone straight to hell. Sweet Jesus, why won't it stop?"

Decibel by decibel, the volume of the music intensified, until it entered the realm of pain:

> I don't care 'bout the future, don't care 'bout the past
> As long as I've got some creatures to blast
> We've got deer, we've got elk, we've got old owls that hoot.
> And when I've killed them all, there'll be Yankees to shoot.

"Why didn't anybody tell me God had a red neck?" Toner moaned, trying not to panic.

"Angela? Can you hear me?"

She blindly looked about and answered in a hoarse whisper: "Vassily? Are you dead, too?"

"Yes, it is me, but you are not dead."

"You mean I'm alive…and this isn't hell…and you're not here to torture me for all eternity?"

"Two out of three is not too bad. How do you feel?"

"Thirsty…weak…Where are we, a cave or something? Everything's dark. Is it the middle of the night?"

"No, it is noon."

"Oh, my God, I'm *blind*," Toner bellowed, thrashing about.

"Stop. Stop, Angela. You are not blind," Vassily said, turning off the radio. "It is only a headband over your eyes, so you could rest without the light bothering you. And you are restrained in the bed. We had to do that to prevent you from hurting yourself. You continued to flail your arms and legs."

"I can't move my arms."

"That is what I just said. If you remain still, I will help you, okay? You have to promise to not to get up. Do you promise?"

"I promise."

"Your fingers…they are not crossed?"

"I can't move my hands, Molotov," Toner croaked.

"Okay. First, your eyes. Close them tight. Though the window shadings are pulled down, it will be very bright."

Vassily leaned over the bed and removed a black headband. Toner scrunched her face.

"Okay," he said, "open them slowly."

Following his orders, Angela opened her eyes ever so slightly. "I think it'll be all right. The light's not too bad." She opened them farther. The first thing she saw was Vassily Molotov, sitting on a small stool next to her makeshift bed. For several seconds she did nothing but stare into his pensive eyes.

"Hi," she said at last.

"Hello yourself. We have been very concerned about you. It is good to see you."

"Feeling's mutual. Who's *we*?"

"George Coffey."

"*George*? Who's George?"

"He is the owner of this wonderful house. He saved your life. He is a portable medic-guy with much knowledge of first aid and medicine."

"I see." Angela craned her neck and looked around. She was lying on an army cot pushed up against the paneled wall of a rustic cabin. On the opposite side of the large room was a kitchen. Two stuffed chairs and a dining room set sat in the middle. In the center of the connecting wall was a sliding glass door leading onto a balcony.

"Oww, my neck is sore as heck," she said, trying to look behind her.

"Do not move your head. George thinks you have a twist in your neck or something like that. I am not very sure what exactly he said. Too many new words these past days. Plus he has a type of American accent I have difficult time understanding."

"Sounds like you've encountered a Western twang."

"Whatever that means. He is also a volunteer firefighting person."

"What happened? I heard a shot and came looking for you. That's the last thing I remember."

"Yes. George had a gun and heard a noise outside his house. He thought I was a bear. Lucky for me, he only was making the attempt to scare the bear away. When he fired his rifle, I made loud yelling and said, 'Don't shoot.' I told him we had an accident and described where the car was. He knew immediately where I was talking about. We both ran back and found you in the stream."

Vassily paused and looked into Angela's eyes. "I am afraid I was not very helpful. I jumped in and pulled you out, but George did the life-saving things with breathing and pushing. It was horrible. I almost cried with happiness when you spit water and gasped."

"Thank you…again. This damsel-in-distress routine must be getting pretty old, eh?"

"I am not complaining, Angela Toner."

"That's nice to hear." Angela tried to bring her arms out from under the heavy blanket to embrace him, forgetting his earlier comment. "Vassily, my arms are tied…literally."

"Sorry—forgot." He reached under the blanket and undid the silk scarves that had been wrapped around each arm. She pulled her arms out and rubbed her wrists.

"Ooo, silk scarves. This relationship is getting weirder by the hour, Molotov."

"It was all George had that was soft enough. They were his wife's. She died several years ago."

"How old is this George guy?"

"He said he was seventy. He is very gray in the hair, but a very nice man."

She reached out and took Vassily's hand, gently squeezing it and pulling him closer. When he was close enough, she moved her head up as far as she could, kissing him ever so gently on the lips.

She lowered her head back on the pillow. Vassily followed. He brushed his lips across hers lightly, then pulled back several inches. Gently stroking her hair with his right hand, he looked into her eyes for a long time. Then he moved closer, eyes open, with an expression of love and tenderness Angela had never seen before. His second kiss was stronger, longer, yet their eyes never closed, as though each were afraid the other would disappear.

"That was nice," she said, breaking the awkward silence. "Say, where is this George fellow?"

"He is out doing some work. Early yesterday morning, we used his tractor to pull the wrecked car to his big shed so no one would find it."

"*Yesterday*? Yesterday was Monday. The accident was last night."

"No, today is Wednesday, January 16. You were asleep for a long time."

Angela thought about the implications of Molotov's statement, lifted the blanket, and looked down. She was completely naked except for an adult diaper, her skin still pale from the near-drowning and her illness.

Vassily, understanding her next question, said, "George is a medical guy. He had to get your wet clothes off. I did not look, Angela—honestly. He has been taking care of you for personal things. He is a good man…but old."

"It's all right. You two saved my life. That's all that matters. Why is he being so nice to us? What'd you say to him?"

"Well, I said all the right things. It is a thing my mother taught me when first meeting strangers. I said, 'Wow, nice television. How many channels does it get? Who is the woman in the picture? She is very beautiful.' It was his wife. The best one, I think, was: 'This cabin is very well constructed. Whoever built it is a true carpenter.' And of course George built it. I told him, 'Go away from here! Are you being serious?' I think he knew I was exaggerating a little, but whatever."

"Get outta here."

"Why? What did I do?"

"No, not you…the phrase. It's *get outta here*. Not *go away from here*. People will think you're from Wisconsin."

"And that is bad?"

"Minnesota's bad enough. Wisconsin, well, let's leave that for our next lesson." Angela paused and took a deep breath. "Did you tell him *why* we were driving to Salt Lake City?"

"Yes. I told him we were to meet Gregory there."

"You told him *that*?"

"I told him everything, Angela. About you, about me, about the disk, Eldon Tyrell, that there was a problem trusting the intentions of the government about this."

"Are you crazy? How do you know you can trust this man? How do we know he's not out there now, selling us down the river?"

"It is not a river, just a small stream. But I…we have no choice. There was nothing else I could do. You were in desperate situations."

"You're right. What do we got to lose, anyway? Come here." Vassily leaned down. Angela reached up and embraced him, pulling him even closer, not wanting to let go.

"You cooked this?"

"Sure. You like it?"

"It's very good."

"Thank you. I am pleasantly pleased by being told that."

She was propped up in bed, and Vassily was spooning homemade chicken soup into her mouth. Angela was surprised at her appetite, though she knew she hadn't eaten in more than two days.

A door closed in the hall behind Angela's bed. She heard stomping feet. A stocky, gray-haired man entered the room. He had a wrinkled forehead, Brill Cream hair, Andy Rooney eyebrows, and a wide smile. Dressed in a flannel shirt and baggy blue jeans, George Coffey looked like the kind of neighbor everyone wished they had.

"Somebody's returned to the land of the living. Hello, Angela. It's a pleasure to finally meet ya."

"It's good to be back. Thank you for taking us in, and for saving my life."

"Eh, think nothin' of it. I've always been a sucker for a woman singin' the blues."

Toner innocently smiled. "This is a beautiful home," she said. "Have you lived here long?"

"Nah. Retired here six years ago. Built the house myself, though. Vassily probably told you that. Lived in Vegas before that—electrical contractor by trade. 'Course, I did lots of other handy jobs, carpentry, auto mechanics, plumbing. As the sayin' goes, jack of all trades, master of none."

"Are you *from* Las Vegas?" Toner asked, propping herself up on one elbow, liking the gentleman more and more.

"Mooresville, North Carolina, originally. Signed up with Uncle Sam in '55...when I was eighteen. Thought I was gonna do one tour in the military. Ended up makin' it a career."

"The army? My grandfathers were in the army."

"Nope, Navy. Didn't wanna carry my bed around with me."

"A sailor?"

"Anything wrong with that?" George asked with a laugh.

"Oh no, not at all," Toner said, remembering Kaloostian's theory. "I was just thinking of what a friend of mine said about sailors."

"You'll have to tell me all about it. First things first, though. How ya feelin'?"

"I've felt better, but under the circumstances I'm not complaining," Angela said, remembering Monday night with a shiver. "What's the prognosis?"

"I'm no doctor, but I do some volunteer paramedic work with the local fire department. From what I can tell, aside from exhaustion, I'm pretty sure you got walking pneumonia, a minor strain of *pneumococcus bacterium,* as it's officially called. You've also got some severely strained neck muscles and a mild concussion, coupla good lumps on your head. But yer gettin' better. BP's steadily improved. Monday night it was 72 over 36. This morning it was 110 over 75. You also had rapid, erratic breathing. You were delirious...swallowed a lot of water. A real mess.

"I was all for running you into the local hospital, but Vassily here talked me out of that. Lucky for us, I keep a few antibiotics around. Now let's check your BP and pulse."

George picked a blood-pressure cup and a stethoscope and pulled up a chair. He wrapped the cup around Toner's right arm, pumped it up, placed the stethoscope on her arm, and listened carefully as the bag deflated. He nodded, checked her pulse and smiled.

"Looks like you weathered the storm."

"Thank you, George. I can't tell you how much I appreciate everything you've done."

"No problem. Vassily's told me all about your little problem. Sounds like the two of you had some pretty bad experiences out there."

Angela smiled. "Are you sure you want to be involved with a couple of fugitives?"

"Eh, what the heck. At my age, any excitement's better 'an sittin' 'round channel-surfin'. And I gotta admit, this here's pretty damned exciting."

George leaned back and folded his arms. "I did some checking with a few pals of mine on the Web, and they were all talkin' 'bout the *brownout*, as everybody's calling it. Been a lot of tie-ups and slowdowns all over the net, 'specially in southern California. It's a good thing y'all left when ya did."

"Have you been on-line long?"

"A few years—mainly for news, sports updates, and whatnot. I'm no keyboard cowboy, if that's whatcha mean. I get around okay…just enough to make me dangerous."

"What do you think about everything Vassily's told you?"

"The $64,000 question. I've actually given it a lot of thought. You gotta understand, I'm not one of them paranoid antigovernment militia types, the ones who are always quotin' Article 13, paragraph three of the Bill of Rights like some bumper stickers quote Revelation."

"You believe us, then?"

"Heck yeah. What's not to believe? Personally, I don't think the government's bad or evil, and I don't think bad people run the world. I think the United Nations' a good thing, and world peace is a team effort. But I also think them genetic scientists cooked up a batch of somethin' pretty out-of-the-ordinary, and we're all gonna have to hope it was for the best."

"You're talking about the twins?"

"From what Vassily's told me, what else is there to talk about?"

"He told you *everything*?" Angela asked, looking at Vassily with curious eyes. George, understanding her concern, patted the Russian on the knee.

"Not to worry. I'm happy to say that I can be trusted. I know you're carryin' a computer disk with a password. I know about that Eldon Tyrell fella. I know about Nyentzi. Now, ya gotta understand, I'm no philosopher, not like your dad…"

"He's just a teacher."

"*Just* a teacher. Oh come on, I'm sure he's picked up a thing or two over the years."

"Osmosis, I suppose."

"Somethin' like that. Anyway, like I was sayin', I've given this Nyentzi thing a lot of thought. Take the switching of the sex of the embryos, for instance. I gotta think even that's for the best. I don't consider myself one of them new-age sensitive guys. I spit, swear like the sailor I am, drink Jack Daniel's out of the bottle. My wife was a saint, Angela, a bona fide saint. She put up with me and my insufferable habits through thick and thin. With all that said, I believe that whoever made the change did it for all the right reasons.

"It may be true that women baffle the heck outta me, that the battle of the sexes has been raging since the first one-celled animal got all confused about its sexual orientation. But I also know that women embody all of life's intensity. Me, all I've got to donate to the cause is somethin' you can get out of a test tube. And I'm man enough to admit it."

Angela smiled at George's comment. "You're a modern thinker, Mr. Coffey, but aren't some of those ideas contradictory to what's written in that book I see sitting on the table?"

"I'm seventy years old, young lady. Forgive an old man who's tryin' to cover all the bases. Don't get me wrong. There's plenty of good in the Bible. We've got a million laws in this country tryin' to enforce what's pretty much covered by the Ten Commandments. Still, a lot of what's written in that book bugs the heck out of me. With all due respect, the Bible can get pretty deep—and I'm not talkin' philosophical. Mostly written by a bunch of bitter old men…blame women for everything, especially their own weaknesses."

Vassily tried to suppress a smile as Toner looked up toward the ceiling, expecting lightning to strike the blasphemer. George understood what she was suggesting.

"Have no fears, kids. I don't think the heavens are about to open up and zap me with a bolt. I've never been a believer in that silly notion. I can't respect any god that's got so much time on his, or her, hands to sit around all day listening to my every complaint."

"That's an increasingly popular sentiment, George."

"In Russia as well, even with the return of the Orthodox religion. Such strict beliefs are sounding much too similar to Communist doctrine."

"Amen, Vassily. Either of you two ever read Spinoza?" Toner and Molotov shook their heads. "When Sally died, I did a lot of reading and soul-searchin', trying to find some answers. Now, I'm just paraphrasing here, but Spinoza felt that God revealed himself…or herself."

"George, for our purposes, let's just stick with tradition, okay?"

"Gotcha. Like I was saying, God revealed himself in the harmony of all things. A nice day—that's God. A rainy day—that's God, too. A healthy child, a good harvest, a famine, a plague—they're all part of God." George stopped for a moment and chuckled. "Cubs winnin' the World Series, now that's a leapa faith."

"That's not a leap of faith. That's a shuttle launch," Toner added with a laugh.

"Yeah, no shit—oops. Sorry. Like I was saying, God doesn't run around worrying about our fates or actions. He keeps an eye on the big picture. He's not mean or malicious, none of that Old Testament stuff. Got no time for it. He *wants* us to succeed. He's given us everything we need, but it's up to us to figure out how to use it.

"Spinoza said that part of man's problem is the notion of God givin' us total dominion over all the earth—that it's ours to do with as we please. That kind of thinking's magna-cum-laude stupid. The American Indian knew better: We're here to take care of the earth, not abuse it. God and nature are one and the same. And when you understand who and what God really is, then you know God doesn't need to dictate or watch our every action and thought. And once you understand that, you can see God as an equal, not a superior."

"I thought we were talking about the twins?" Angela asked, somewhat confused.

"I am, Angela, I am. I've always thought our species was pretty egocentric—selfish, too. For thousands of years, we've placed ourselves at the center of the universe. Funny thing is, if ya look real hard, ya see that most of our gods are still based on that outdated model. Then along comes Galileo, Newton, Darwin, Einstein, Hawkins, all them thinkers and scientists. Suddenly mankind gets knocked down a few notches.

"Before we know it, we're nothing more than a smart monkey. People begin to have doubts, about everyone and everything. Nothing's sacred anymore. If ya ask me, I think evolution gave us an identity crisis, ruined our belief in God and religion. But that's changing. I think we're standin' on a threshold. And those kids are what's gonna push us over the edge."

"Are you saying, Mr. Coffey…" Vassily began.

"George. Call me George, fer cryin' out loud."

Vassily smiled and tried again. "Are you saying, *George*, that the twins are somehow to be a new faith?"

"Exactly. It may not be any kind of religion we've known before, that's fer sure. Instead, it'll be a faith in ourselves...that we're worthy of this wonderful world. It'll be part of our evolution as a species.

"You see, for the past several hundred years, we've toyed with a new religion, and we call it *science*. We revere it and put it up on a pedestal, but we also fear its excesses and its potential for harm. Some of us bow down like good little worshippers—not everyone, mind you, but some. To others, science is only a tool that if used properly—with restraint—will yield wondrous things."

"So you think the children are a miracle of science?"

"I don't think Nyentzi's the miracle, Vassily. It's a splendid achievement, the culmination of every technology from every industrial sector throughout the world. I think the real miracle is yet to come. Making something of life—now there's a miracle."

For several seconds, the room was silent. "Did Vassily tell you what Lara and Katya said about the diaspora?" Angela asked, looking to George with increasing respect.

"Yep. That's an interesting idea, but all ya gotta do is look around to see that's true. America is more than just a melting pot of people. It's a melting pot of our gene pool. People like you, Angela, and Tai Babalonia the figure skater, and Tiger Woods, Whoopi Goldberg, Colin Powell, Mariah Carey, Tom Jefferson's descendants, and damn near everybody else in this great land of ours.

"Take my family tree—one of my grandfathers came from Bavaria. As long as he stayed in Europe, he was a low-class dirt farmer, Bavarian to boot. Lots of prejudice back then against Bavarians. So he sails out of Kiel for New York City in the 1880s. Once he lands in America, he's no longer a dumb Bavarian but a German American.

"He works hard, moves to Raleigh, starts a small business, marries a girl he met on the boat from Lyon, France. They start a family. His children, including my mother, aren't German or French anymore. They're American. Then my mother marries a guy who's half Polish and half Irish, mixin' things up even more. Lookin' at you, Angela, I see a similar history. That's what America is all about."

"But what about Tyrell?" Toner asked. "If he has a map of the human genome, he could change all that, make it so everyone who wanted a baby could just put in an order. Pretty soon we'd be overrun by blue-eyed, blond, six-feet geniuses—with a little dimple on their left cheeks."

George scratched his head and rubbed his neck. "I know what you're sayin'. Maybe he could. But I think those children must've thought of that, done somethin' to keep that from happenin'. And even without that disk of yours, Angela, maybe what we need is more faith in each other. I'd like to give my fellow man the benefit of the doubt on this genetics thing."

Vassily shifted in his chair and faced Mr. Coffey. "I am sorry to disagree, George. Russia trusted the Communists, and even after the sacrifice of the revolution, the people were only left with a new dictator. I am fearful of human nature. We are a selfish species, always to look out for number one."

"Good point, but like I said, you need a little more faith in your fellow man…and woman. Ya gotta look at the big picture. Like I was saying about evolution. Two hundred years ago, slavery almost destroyed America. We fought a war over it. My side lost—hallelujah.

"Seventy years ago, six million Jews and other so-called undesirables were exterminated. And as you well know, Vassily, Stalin killed another twenty million. Mao did his thing, too. Forty years ago, Pol Pot in Cambodia wiped out three million. Still the world sat on its butt. Yugoslavia, only twelve years ago, tens of thousands murdered. Worst ethnic cleansing in Europe since World War Two. Rwanda, too. Still terrible, still criminal, but this time the world interceded. Maybe not as quickly or as forcibly as we should have, but it was a start. Same thing with Kuwait and all those other hot spots. It's taken thousands of years, but we're finally unwilling to let our fellow man massacre our fellow man. The world's tolerance for evil is decreasing. We're losing our cattle-car mentality.

"Technology has made the world smaller. It's brought us all closer together, made us understand and appreciate our similarities, as well as our differences. When I'm on the net, unless I go with video—which I usually don't—I don't know the race, religion, political ideology, not even the gender of the person on the other end. We're all just plain folks.

"The media's got us all convinced that we're goin' to hell in a handbasket, but that's a lotta bunk, a way to sell more newspapers, magazines, or to gain viewers. I stopped pining for the good ol' days years ago. *These* are the good times. Right here, right now. We're not waiting for the American dream; we're livin' it. As long as America's a democracy, we'll never have a trade imbalance."

George nodded his head and smiled. "Class dismissed," he said with a chuckle. "Angela, now that you're feelin' better, it's time for me to catch up on some chores. Vassily, do me a favor. I've gotta find my checkbook, so run out and start the truck." George reached into his pants pocket, pulled out a set of keys, and tossed them to Molotov. "We're headin' to town. Got some errands to run, and then we're gonna stock up on some groceries. Sound good?"

"Okay, but remember our plan, George," Vassily said, walking towards the door.

"How could I forget?"

The door closed, leaving Angela and George alone. The old man laughed.

"What's so funny? What plan is Vassily talking about?" Toner asked.

"If I go and tell you that, it'll take all the fun out of it. Not to worry, nothin' illegal. Just somethin' between us boys. You gonna be okay here alone?"

"I'm feeling better. The soup really helped."

"Good. But I don't want you up and about. Stay in bed. That's an order."

"Aye, aye, sir."

"And so that yah don't worry, your computer's fine. I pulled it out of the car, brought it inside, and turned it on. That's one tough little laptop," George added.

"Magnesium alloy case. It'll stop a .38 slug…or so they say. And the hard drive rests on gelatinized cushions for added protection."

George smiled. "You and that laptop are both built pretty well. Say Angela, now that we're alone, I'd like to talk private with ya. I know it's none of my business, but I've had my eye on that Vassily for almost two days." The old man paused, then continued. "I don't think I've every seen a boy so devoted to his girl as he is to you—'cept me to Sally, of course."

Angela smiled when she realized where the conversation was going.

"Anyway, I'm no expert on love or nothin' like that. Some men say they love ya, and in the next breath say the same thing about pizza and beer. With you defenseless and such, I asked him, if y'all will pardon my forwardness, what his intentions were. Were they honorable, you know?"

"Are they?" Angela asked.

"Extremely, I'm pleased to say. So I asked him if he was in love, and he said he was. Now that ain't good enough for me. I says: 'Not love, Vassily. *Love*. Are you in *Love*? I love a home-cooked cheeseburger, but I don't wanna marry one, if ya catch my drift.' He's a smart boy. He understood what I was askin'. He didn't hem or haw—answered me straight out: 'Yes I love her.' I'm athinkin', 'So far, so good.'

"Next I asked him if he knew about the rules. 'What rules?' he asked. 'The rules of love,' I says.

"Well, now he's confused again. 'You mean there's rules about love?' '*Hell yeah*,' I told him, 'specially about love. Always rules…lots of rules…lots of regulations, codes of conduct—you name it. He shakes his head, wondering what the heck he's gotten himself into this time.

Then I gave him the good news, and I'm gonna tell you the same thing. You know about all them rules, doncha Angela?"

"'Fraid so. More rules than you can shake a stick at."

"Exactly. I was married for over thirty-five years to the same woman. I know times are a changin' in this so-called New Millennium. More rules than before. So if you'll pardon my language: Screw the rules. Love each other and to hell with everyone else, 'cuz it goes by so dang fast. I'm an old man, Angela, but I still remember my first date, the first girl I kissed, the first time I made love. I remember the tears, the hopes, the dreams, each with brilliant clarity. And it seems like they all happened yesterday.

"Anyway, that's my sermon for the day. We're off to town. Y'all stay in bed, keep warm, and we'll be back in a jiffy." The old man smiled and started walking toward the door.

"Say George, could you send Vassily back inside? I need to ask him something."

"No problem," he said, turning back around. "And Angela, one last thing, just between you, me, and God. When Vassily pulled you out of the stream Monday evening, I figured you was dead. I'd never felt a body as cold as yours. I had no way of knowin' how long you'd been in that water. I hesitated, I really hesitated doin' CPR. You had no pulse. I mean, none at all. And you had the most beautiful smile on your face—I can't begin to describe it. Vassily later told me your husband and baby died in a car accident three years ago. If I'd known that, I'd've let you sleep, you looked so peaceful and all. Like you was up there in heaven with the ones you love.

"But you came around, girl," George said with an expression of admiration. Then he hesitated and looked at her with scrutiny. "I meant what I said earlier. Those Russian kids, Lara and Katya, they chose their guardian angel well. Do 'em proud. I trust you, Angela, and I'm thankful fate brought you to my door. It's a heavy burden they've given you. But I've got a feelin' 'bout you. You can crack that code. You've got power, deep inside, power you probably didn't even know was there. It's in your heart. It's the part of you that's tied to God. And just as I know the sun will come up tomorrow morning, I know that if you believe in yourself, you can do anything."

With that, George smiled, turned, and headed for the door.

He'd been warned. Long ago and oftentimes between, they'd cautioned him on the consequences of his conduct. But he chose not to listen. They were conciliatory while he remained obstinate. They tried to negotiate, but he preferred to quarrel. When they offered peace, he chose war.

Proof of Nadezhda Andrevna Molotova's murder had marked the opening of hostilities between Eldon Tyrell and the children of Nyentzi. Now the war escalated.

Two sets of twins—one from Caracas, the other from Vancouver—already had died, their bodies wracked by sickness, their immune systems powerless to defend them. The seventy survivors, knowing their time among the living was coming to an end, initiated their apocalypse.

A house divided against itself cannot stand. So it came to be that Yuri Anatoliovich Tyrellovich's vision of a global empire of information, wealth, and enlightenment teetered on its last legs. Just one push would topple it—a push from within.

Rather than see their work prostituted and corrupted by their half-brother, the children, like the avenging angels of Revelation, unleashed their cyber-fury. Barrage after lethal barrage of computer viruses, the plagues of the Third Millennium, laid siege to Tyrell's fortified web sites and computer networks. His defenses, though impressive, only slowed the electronic blitzkrieg.

Days earlier, they'd liquidated his assets. Now they set out to destroy his true wealth, the information he'd gleaned and stolen. Tyrell's data-banks were hit from multiple locations, which shut them down. No information could get in or out.

Most computer viruses lie dormant until a specific date or command sets them in motion. But not these—not the binary toxins of the children. Quick-acting and virulent, the computer-generated cyclones destroyed without remorse. The ensuing carnage was horrendous, with casualties in the trillions. The digital Armageddon obliterated byte after encoded byte of data. They knew exactly what they were looking for and where the files were located. After all, they had designed much of Tyrell's computer system and downloaded the files themselves.

"Fire on Babylon…fire on Babylon," the children trumpeted, their anger of biblical proportions. "Oh yes, a change has come."

But even as the destruction continued, even as the children of Nyentzi fought for what they believed, most of the world went about its business with casual indifference, oblivious to the electronic war erupting around it. Some noticed a tie-up in the phone lines. Pagers didn't work. Some could not access their voice mail or web sites. Still others could not access the Internet.

The day was long. Tyrell fought back, launching digital countermeasures, thwarting some of the children's endeavors. Expending their last reserves of energy, the children huddled around their computers in dimly lit rooms, refusing to yield or compromise.

Through history, prophets proclaimed the coming of a messiah, light of the world. Yet worn by sickness, betrayed by nature and the inherent weaknesses of their genetic codes, the children of Nyentzi began to die.

On every continent, across every time zone, one by one, the lights began to go out.

3 7

THE LUCKY ONES

She waited for the sound of George's pickup to fade into silence. Only then did Angela sit up in bed, wrap the quilt around her, and try to stand. Reaching down, she steadied herself until she was sure she had her balance.

"First things first," she whispered, shuffling to the kitchen sink. Opening one of the cupboards, Angela found a tall drinking glass—a brightly colored souvenir from Ringling Brothers Barnum & Bailey Circus.

"Someone's got grandkids," Angela said to herself, filling it with water. She swallowed it with one long gulp, then refilled the glass. Thoroughly enjoying the opportunity to wait on herself and to drink without a straw, she sipped the second glass of water until she'd quenched her thirst.

After a moment of contemplation, with only the kitchen clock ticking into the stillness, Angela was rudely interrupted by an insistent bladder. With little time to waste, she continued her exploration of

George's cabin. To the right of the kitchen was a hallway, with bedrooms on either side. The first door on the left was the object of her search.

The bathroom was long and narrow. To Angela's regret there was no tub—a hot bath would have to wait. She removed her robe, ripped off the embarrassing diaper, sat down, and with a thankful sigh, relieved the intense pressure.

Just before finishing, she noticed a mirror on the back of the bathroom door. It was a tempting proposition. Despite the rigors of the SWAT Team, Angela had struggled with her weight even before she was pregnant.

She stood up. Standing in the middle of the small room, Angela looked in the mirror at her naked body. She had *finally* done it—lost ten pounds in a week. Her waist and hips were thinner, her skin tighter. And she knew it wouldn't last.

Angela had tried many diets and weight-loss programs, only to achieve her goal with a harsh regimen of jet lag, near-fatal lack of sleep, sporadic and unhealthy food consumption, buckets of coffee, a severe virus, a concussion, and a two-day hibernation.

"Sure beats the hell out of cabbage soup, rice cakes, and grapefruit," Toner reflected, reaching for a towel. "All the same, I don't think I'll be trying that diet again anytime soon." She went to the other end of the bathroom to check the accommodations, "Soap, shampoo, washcloth…it's all here."

She turned on the water of the shower, waited for it to be hot before stepping in. As the shower stall steamed, she stood directly under the stream of water, letting its wash away the bad memories, hopelessness, and pain of Monday night…

Five minutes of brushing and flossing to get the cobwebs and cooties out of her teeth, and finally, head to toe, Angela felt 100 percent better. She wore fresh underwear, a T-shirt she'd bought in Las Vegas, and an old pair of sweatpants she found next to the bed. Angela guessed they might've belonged to George's wife. Why he'd kept them around was another question. But they fit, and as far Toner was concerned, that was all that mattered.

Returning to the kitchen, Angela noticed the teakettle on the stove, with a colorful mug, spoon, and a variety of teabags on the counter next to it. She had the feeling George knew she'd be up the moment he was out the door. After lighting the old-fashioned burner under the kettle, she walked over to stoke the stove in the living room.

Soon the kettle sang, and the wood-burner's heat radiated throughout the cabin. Forgoing a cup of Morning Thunder, Angela decided on a cup of chamomile herbal tea. Maybe Vassily was right; maybe she was a caffeine junkie. Whatever the diagnosis, for what she was about to do, she wanted a head free of chemicals, stress, and distraction.

As the tea steeped, Toner set her trusty laptop on the coffee table, turned it on, ran several system checks to make sure her software and hardware was intact, and pushed an overstuffed chair in front of the fire. She looked around the room, reminded of her family's vacation home in Wisconsin. She smiled and reached for her legal pad, its top page filled with earlier jottings about the mysterious disk.

She plopped down in the chair, leaned back, and felt the warmth of the fire carry away the tension of the week past. The radiance of the dancing orange-yellow flame, the distinct smell of burning cedar, and the crackle of the wood permeated not only the room but every pore of her body—calming, relaxing. That and the chamomile tea, slowly sipped, combined to make Angela Toner's mood as mellow as anytime in recent memory.

Soon the tea was half gone, and Angela was ready. She tore the page with her notes from the legal pad, crumpled it, opened the door of the fireplace, and neatly tossed it in. With the door still open, Angela watched the wadded paper retract from the heat, burst into flames, and crumble.

"Words," she whispered in a soft voice. "The twins said they were only words."

For Angela Toner, there would be no more scribbles or superfluous conjecture. Whether it was God, fate, or karma, Angela knew she'd been given a second chance. This time she was going to do things by the book. It wouldn't be easy; starting over never is. But if what George had said—that the power to change and adapt and persevere was inside her—was true, now was the time to prove it.

Her first job on the first day of the rest of her life was cracking the code on the Nyentzi disk. Lara and Katya had prescribed an eight-character password and given them three attempts. How hard could that be?

Vassily had tried during their drive from LA. He'd typed *g-e-n-e-t-i-c-s*. A good guess, a logical guess—they'd agreed on that. But they were wrong.

Only after the preprogrammed girlish laughter informed them their guess was wrong did Vassily notice an anomaly on the computer screen. Eight letters had been entered, but there was a space at the end of the prompt. Vassily recognized the problem immediately.

"The secret password must have two words…with a space between them."

"Wait a minute," Toner had fumed. "That makes it a nine-character password, not eight!"

"Not totally. By definition, the space does not automatically count as a character. Even with the space, it could be considered an eight-character word."

"That's cheating…little brats. We just blew one of our chances."

Angela could laugh about it now. But the incident had added to her depressed mood, like everything else in her recent life. Since Jake's death, she'd felt that bad luck was on her like the *fee-fie* on the *fo-fum*. Before her too-close-for-comfort almost-rendezvous with the big Kahuna in the sky, even her perspective on the disk was cynical. She remembered her reaction when Kaloostian told her the first clue came from the lyrics to a song by Pink Floyd.

She'd really let him have it. "Would you stop jerking me around?" she'd demanded. Why would the children of Nyentzi, with a world of literature and song to choose from, single out some relic from the psychedelic sixties? Angela knew better now. She knew they'd chosen that song for good reason, and when she saw her Armenian friend again, she'd apologize for her years of abuse and derision.

With renewed sensibility, Angela started the deductive process from the beginning. She knew she'd missed many bits of evidence. Now reviewing the events of the past several days, she remembered that after nabbing her and Vassily at the airport, Heiple had said something she'd ignored as idiotic banter.

"You'll see," he'd said, justifying his actions. "You'll see what we're all about. Tyrell isn't the enemy. What he's doing is gonna prevent another Dark Age."

Toner had told Heiple the only dark age involving him had to do with the near-total lack of external input to his brain. Rising to her sarcastic barb, Heiple informed her that Tyrell talked about a new Dark Age, as if that somehow made it more credible.

But in retrospect, knowing that the source was Eldon Tyrell made the comment anything but trivial. Kaloostian had told her Tyrell could control the flow of information both on and off the Internet. That prospect, no matter how far-fetched, required serious consideration.

What made Angela remember Heiple's seemingly innocent comment was the recurring theme of light and dark and day and night, woven throughout the clues left by the twins. There were also words like *shroud*, *flame*, and *shadow*, as well as the use of opposites, especially in the St. Francis passage.

"What the hell is Tyrell talking about, *Dark Age*? It can't be these kids—they're anything but. They're like beacons of light. Like a thousand little points of…" Toner's voice trailed off to pensive silence. She leaned forward to type a word, then a space, then a second word—*t-h-e_l-i-g-h-t*. She stared at the two words, her fingers inches from the keypad. She wanted to believe the children of Nyentzi were the light in her life and the hope for the world's future. She was desperate to press *enter*.

But she couldn't. "Wait a minute," she protested, moving her fingers away as if they were too close to an open flame. "This doesn't look right. It's not symmetrical. They're twins. They'd never use two odd-numbered words. That's not how they see things."

She reached down, picked up her legal pad, and drew four small lines, then an X, then four more small lines. "Yeah, that's how it should look. Nice 'n even, four and four. And nothing so obvious as *light*." Using the backspace, she wiped the words from the screen.

"The song said no more turning away, but from what to what?" Angela wondered. She closed her eyes and tried to imagine the world as Lara, Katya, and the other twins would see it from their shuttered rooms, from an existence no better than slavery. But the children didn't act like slaves. They were so alive, so in love with life and everything beautiful.

Angela mouthed some of the lyrics:

It's a sin that somehow, light is changing to shadow And casting a shroud over all we have known…

She dropped the legal pad onto the floor and slouched in the chair, her arms hanging over the side. She sat and pondered, staring into the dancing flames. After several minutes of idle contemplation, Angela suddenly laughed.

"Do I know who I am?" she mocked, referring to the cryptic message the twins had given Kaloostian. "*Yeah*, I'm the one who'd better figure this darn thing out!"

Angela sat up straight and took a deep breath. "Okay…okay…. Think. Think of the clues. Opposites. Lots of opposites. Doubt—faith…despair—hope…sadness—joy…darkness—light," she mumbled, biting the nail on her left thumb.

"Light, light, light—always the reference to light. But according to the song, light is changing to shadow. Light changes to dark."

A pause. A scrunched face. A sigh. "And what about Pink Floyd? Greg said their best-selling album was *Dark Side of the Moon*, the side no one sees. I've met Lara and Katya. I've seen Nyentzi, seen the light, but I've never seen...the dark side of the moon."

Angela's fingers, again poised above the keyboard, began to shiver in anticipation. She typed a single letter, then quickly, decisively, three more. Next came a space, followed by four more letters—*d-a-r-k_s-i-d-e*. Was this the password? Could this be the key that would unlock the secret of the Messiah Project?

There was only one way to find out. Angela closed her eyes, took a deep breath, exhaled slowly through her nostrils, and hit *enter*. The screen changed as the CD-ROM hummed into action, accessing the disk.

"Well, I'll be damned," she said. "Charlie Brown just kicked a field goal."

Angela pulled her hands from the computer. Her initial reaction was to find the disk's directory and explore, but she fought the impulse. Better to let the children show her the way.

With no external prompts, the computer screen changed from solid blue to a million points of light, swirling and dancing on the screen. As the wonders of Nyentzi unfolded before her, Angela leaned back in her chair to enjoy the ride. Though they were only children, Toner knew their show could rival Hollywood in scope and production.

The dancing points of light began to slow and form new shapes, small fragments of matter in four colors representing, Angela surmised, nitrogenous bases. Adenine, guanine, thymine, and cytosine. Soon the twisted-rope ladder of the DNA double-helix appeared amidst the thousands of base pairings.

The three-dimensional strand rotated on the computer screen for only a moment. Then it broke into a myriad of smaller strands. From these twisting strands of DNA, two faces emerged. Angela recognized them immediately. Lara and Katya, or so she assumed. They could have been any of the other thirty-six pairs of twins. A tagline seconds later confirmed Toner's guess—Lara and Katya Gracheva, Moscow.

The image changed again. Two more faces, just slightly different, replaced the first ones. The next set of twins had straight black hair, pale skin, Oriental eyes. "Miyoko and Hiroshi Toyama, Kamakura." They were from the island of Honshu in Japan.

With another change, Toner saw twins from Lagos, Nigeria—Bisi and Katsina Akinduro. Angela saw a resemblance to Lara and Katya—in their smiles, the mischievous eyes—though the skin was dark, the hair kinky, the noses broad. Their eyes were brown, like Miyoko's and Hiroshi's, not blue like Lara's and Katya's. But they were sisters nonetheless.

Angela stared in wonder as face after face appeared on her computer screen. No four were alike, though all were from the same original egg. Hannah and Dvorah Meir from Jerusalem, Erin and Emily Saunders from Denver, Hanan and Khulad Sarraj from Hebron. Twins from New Delhi, Dublin, São Paulo, Nairobi, Düsseldorf, Singapore, Edinburgh, Tabrïz, Marseilles, Atlanta, San Salvador, Athens, Tunis, Istanbul, Cairo, Quito, Toronto, Auckland, Manila, and many more.

This was a parade of diversity amidst uniformity, a parade of faces from the four corners of the earth, from every race, religion, and ethnic classification. Mercereau and Tyrellovich's experimentation had achieved the genetic revisions Toner was already aware of, but they'd also suited each set of twins to geographic location, further demonstrating the remarkable degree of genetic precision of the Nyentzi Project.

Angela gazed at the faces of the children, each so different yet poignantly alike. She finally understood Lara and Katya's reference to the diaspora. From the pinnacle of humanity's family tree—an ancient towering willow—she recognized the tree's many branches, long and coiled like strands of DNA, weaving, flowing, merging, connecting, breaking, and finally connecting again.

On a winter's day in January 2007, back through the ages of time, to a single fertilized seed in one woman wandering the Laetoli plain of Tanzania, Angela saw in these children the designs of God and nature, as well as the simple truth of Nyentzi: Whether one's faith lay in heaven or science, all humankind is truly related. This truth, espoused by most by denied by others, was so obvious she could only bow her head in awe.

So beautiful and unique was each set of twins, Angela could not bring herself to stop the flow of images. In their faces she saw every emotion and temperament. She saw innocence and duplicity, brilliance and ignorance, hope and despair, age and youth. She saw images of Buddha, Lao Tzu, Brahma, Moses, Abraham, Mary, Jesus, Muhammad...

She saw the legacy of all the great empires: Inca, Aztec, Greek, Chinese, Persian, Egyptian, Roman, Mongol, Ottoman, Western European, American. She saw the seeds of humanity flow across the planet in wave upon wave of nomadic expansion, conquest, and assimilation. As tears rolled down her cheeks, Angela Toner saw some genealogies mingle and flourish, others wither and die.

She saw the ultimate lesson in history as not one of self-importance but of humility. Indeed, Angela understood that the message of Nyentzi goes beyond science and technology, beyond religion and dogma, to a single, essential truth. People everywhere are the same.

"We are not apart from nature," Lara and Katya had said. "We *are* nature. We are not apart from history. We *are* history. And when you listen to the voices of antiquity, you will discover that they have so very much to say."

Twice the images flowed across the screen before Angela clicked the mouse to prompt further action. The faces dissolved back into the deep blue background, and coils of DNA formed again. After a moment, they turned white and fashioned themselves first into swirling letters and finally into words. The image grew in intensity until she was able to read the lines.

> Only love can set us free.
> Only love can bear the truth.
> Only love can bring us peace.
> Only love can save me and you.
> Only love can purify.
> Only love can conquer fear.
> Only love can testify.
> Only love can make a miracle of life.

Angela read and reread each line. She recognized the words as the lyrics to a song by Sophie B. Hawkins, one of her favorite artists. How the twins knew that, she did not care to guess. Kaloostian had told her that any item purchased with a credit card could easily be traced. She had purchased the compact disc over the Internet a decade earlier. The twins had certainly done their homework. Then again, it could be just another coincidence.

"Fat chance," Angela thought.

After a moment, the lyrics dissolved, and the twins from Moscow reappeared. Without external prompting, a video clip began.

"Dear friends," Lara and Katya said in unison. "We hope it is you we have the pleasure of speaking to. Congratulations on accessing our disk. We are confident you did not find it too difficult.

"You are now aware of the full extent of our circumstances. You know there is a strong possibility that we are no longer alive. You and your friends may be on your own. It is something we are preparing you for. It is why we have given you the disk.

"Like every other human who ever lived, we have asked ourselves why we are here. And we know the answer. We know *why* we were brought into the world.

"We don't resent our lives or the circumstances that created us. We want only the guarantee that our lives have not been wasted. The disk is part of that guarantee. You will understand what we are talking about as you further investigate its contents.

"We have taken steps to prevent this abuse from occurring again. There can be no more Nyentzi projects, no more genetic slavery. The temptation will be strong, but if you and others like you tell our story, convey our message, perhaps you can persuade others to respect our wishes.

"We love you. We will always love you. Thank you for being our friends."

The video ended. Angela bit her lip and wiped away a tear. This was an amazing request—no more genetic experimentation, no more sacrificial lambs to the gods of biomechanics. Nyentzi was too much too soon. If nature had taught science anything, it was that evolution couldn't, shouldn't, be rushed.

Genetic engineering was hardly a third-grade science project. An interlocking web so intricate as to be almost unfathomable governed human reproduction. For that reason, Tyrellovich's grand experiment, the human race's first attempt at altering its own genome, now seemed little more than an expensive failure.

Toner had seen the consequences firsthand—seventy-five children condemned to a life of imprisonment and premature death. Too high a price for any attempt to repeat the experiment. The pleas of the children reinforced her resolve to do what was necessary to carry out Lara and Katya's dream.

Angela thought about the children and smiled. Seventy-five little angels, perched on the threshold of heaven, wanting nothing more than a better life for everyone else.

"How the hell do they do it?" she wondered, impressed with their ability to persuade.

"Only love can make a miracle of life," she said aloud, remembering the song they'd quoted. "Maybe that's how they do it? Maybe that's how they're *going to* do it? Maybe that's their manifesto?"

In crafting their experiment, Yuri Tyrellovich and Tatiana Mercereau had left nothing to chance. By subtly altering the physical attributes of each set of twins, they'd covered all the bases. With their all-embracing charisma, the children's message of love might finally be heard.

Unable to wait any longer, Angela clicked the mouse and began to explore the disk, eager to learn what genius the children had left as their legacy.

The Nyentzi disk was a veritable gold mine. In creating and concealing the multimedia file, the twins had demonstrated a degree of deviousness so remarkable that Angela momentarily forgot they were children. As enamored as she was of their innocence, she had not given their scheme much of a chance for success. But after her review of the disk, all bets were off.

Sifting through file after file, Angela was not disappointed. The twins had given Eldon Tyrell the scientific formulas and theorems his insatiable appetite demanded. To say they had held back on a few items, however, was the understatement of the millennium. $E=MC^2$ may have led the scientific community to the building of the first atomic bomb, but Toner knew the Manhattan Project, like any other scientific endeavor, involved more than juggling numbers on a blackboard.

At first, Angela was too busy scanning the files to notice what the children had done. Even allowing for her unfamiliarity with the terms, she should have seen it earlier, should have grasped the totality of their strategy. Not until her reading of their report about a new generation of antibiotics did she notice a deviation in the twins' methodology.

Every document contained a reference to an equation, formula, or blueprint in Tyrell's possession. The information on the Nyentzi disk amplified that data to include subtle manufacturing techniques and shortcuts not easily discerned from the figures they'd sent their half-brother. Intrigued by what she saw, Angela dug deeper.

Years of trial and error were just the beginning of the scientific process needed to reach the goal of genetically engineered antibiotics. With only a hypothesis and the barest of information regarding the end result, Tyrell and anyone else foolish enough to buy his genetically extracted snake oil were conceivably a decade away from realizing any value from their investment.

The Nyentzi disk, on the other hand, illustrated in precise detail what would be needed during the manufacturing process to accelerate development. Angela saw how the children proposed to transmute a simple yeast cell into a preeminent antibiotic. As a living micro-organism, the yeast cell could modify its inherent protein-based structure according to the characteristics of the disease it encountered. Designed with an unbelievably short lifespan, subsequent generations of the yeast plastid would instinctively adapt themselves to overcome and consume as food the most resilient strains of the world's communicable diseases.

Angela laughed to herself as example after example confirmed her suspicion. This was a perfect arrangement, and she recognized the theory behind their duplicity from conversations she'd had with Vassily. During their flight from Armenia to Los Angeles, the two travelers had passed the time discussing many topics, including the standard Marxist doctrine that power flowed to those who controlled the means of production.

Eldon Tyrell thought he was playing Solitaire. He would soon learn of other players sitting around the global table.

The final phase of the Nyentzi Project was an interesting gamble, a gamble that began with Yuri Tyrellovich's inability to develop artificial-intelligence software for the game of chess. Failing that, he'd switched from silicon to carbon, from computer programming to genetic engineering. In doing so, he'd forever changed history. The twins were only following his legacy.

Angela leaned back in the chair and concluded her work with a proper maxim. "*Checkmate*," she declared, turning off her computer with a hard stab of her finger.

She pivoted in the chair and draped her legs over the side. With arms behind her head, she thought about tomorrow and the decisions waiting to be made. She thought about Vassily and their blossoming relationship. She thought about Kaloostian and how excited he would be. She thought about her family and how she wanted to see them, talk to them, explain what had happened.

Over the course of several hectic days, Angela Toner's life had forever changed. As if waking from a dream, she had lost the complacency, lost the dissatisfaction that dominated her personality. In its place, she had found something far better. She still had many questions and doubts, but she was certain of one thing. She knew who she was and what she was capable of achieving.

Basking in the glow of her success, Angela looked around the cabin and mentally reconstructed the circumstances of her metamorphosis—from the Mercado drug bust to George Coffey's strangely unsettling comment that Lara and Katya had chosen her well. As the shadows of the late afternoon sun tinted the room, a twinge of uneasiness infringed on her mellow mood.

"Dark side," she murmured, reverently repeating the cryptic password to the disk. "Whose dark side—Tyrell's or...?" Angela's soft voice trailed off to troubled silence.

She remembered something Kaloostian had once said: "There is nothing in the world as suspicious as love. It penetrates and alters the soul like nothing else. Love fills and binds the heart with hope, joy, and despair. If you're not careful, it can also enslave."

"Am I being used?" Angela asked herself. "Is that the dark side? Is that what this is all about?"

Again she sat in silence, contemplating the possibilities. She thought back to meeting the twins in Moscow. She remembered their sparkling humor and love of life. She remembered saying good-bye.

"Are you ready?" Lara had said just before she and Nadezhda left the twin's apartment seven days earlier. It had seemed an odd question, though she hadn't had time to think about it. Now she felt the answer to Lara's question involved more than preparation for Moscow's frigid nighttime weather.

"Ready for what?" she wondered aloud. Angela stared at the ceiling, unable to shake the doubt that Kaloostian had been right all along. Time and time again he'd cursed the bizarre string of coincidences that followed the Revkin disk. From its creation, to its misappropriation by Hatton, to its coming into Toner's possession—halfway around the world and back.

She considered the clues given by the twins, worded such that both she and Kaloostian had just enough information to crack the code. It seemed more than an odd fluke. Had the twins planned everything in advance?

"That can't be," she muttered. "If they could do that, well then, they could…" She didn't finish the sentence. She was not sure she wanted the answer.

"Be careful what you ask for," her father had warned. "You might find the joy of knowing is worse than the pain of ignorance."

Angela shook her head and laughed. "Eh, what the heck," she said, "They're *just* kids."

She sat silent and still. After a moment, she reached to her left, picked up a book of matches, lit a candle on the coffee table, and blew out the match. She then stood and walked to the sliding glass door. It wasn't locked. Angela gave it a strong tug, slid it open, and went out onto the deck.

Wrapping her arms around herself, Angela inhaled, filling her lungs with the chilly mountain air. She looked towards the horizon and saw that night was not far away. A smile crept across her face as she realized that tonight, and for many nights to come, she would not be alone.

"Hey, you're back."

"What are you doing? You are supposed to be in bed. It is freezing cold out here."

"I needed some fresh air. I'm fine, really. Come on, watch the sunset with me."

"Okay, but put my coat on. That robe is not enough. You do not need to be any sicker. George said if you were out of bed, I was to *admonish* you. What does *admonish* mean?"

"It means to give high praise and many compliments. I'll settle for a hug."

Vassily wrapped his coat around her first, then readily complied with Angela's suggestion. "That George had the good idea. *Admonish*. I like that word."

"I knew you would," Toner said with a wry grin. "Where *is* George?"

"He is visiting a neighbor. He dropped me off and told me to give you the company."

"Sounds exciting. Say, I've been doing a lot of thinking about the past few days. I know this all happened pretty fast. Heck, we only met a week ago. Anyway, I want you to know that you're under no obligation here. You're free to do what you want. I'll respect any decision you make and won't stand in your way. That makes sense, doesn't it?"

Molotov nodded and looked closely into her face. "So, if I decide to stay here…with you…that could be my choice?"

"It's up to you. I don't want to pressure you."

"What are your feelings about this matter?"

"I guess I can put up with you a little longer," Angela said, hugging him tighter and pulling his face towards hers. Their kiss was long and passionate. "I'd like you to stay."

"Okey-dokey. That is one of the new phrases George taught me while we were gone."

"Speaking of which, how'd everything go in town?"

"Yah sure, just like the plan. We went to the hardware store. George told everyone I was his cousin from Minnesota. He introduced me as Bob Gretzky and they said: 'Yep, sounds just like them thar Minnesotans.'"

"With an accent like that, we'll have to start calling you Sven. Did you stop at the grocery store?"

"Yes, I mean *yah*. Not as good a selection as Moscow, but we found everything on the list…including your items."

"Thank you. You pick up any ice cream?" Angela asked with keen interest.

"You said not to. With much specifics, you told me you could do without Ben & Jerry's." Toner looked at Vassily with an mischievous expression that positively unnerved him. "No serious. You said it. I heard you."

"Vassily, my dear, I'm going to tell you a little secret. You can't repeat this to anyone 'cuz I don't want to be excommunicated from womanhood. I'm only going to say it once, so listen up." Angela shook her head and laughed. "What am I worrying about? You'll forget in an hour."

"I might surprise you, Angela Toner."

"I'll give you the benefit of a doubt. In any case, when a woman acts like she doesn't want something fattening or rich or yummy, it's because that's what she wanted all along."

Vassily was baffled. "I don't understand," he said.

"If a woman puts up a big fight but ends up saying 'Oh, all right,' what she really means is, 'Whew, that worked out well.' You look confused."

"So…if you say no, you really mean yes?"

"No."

"You just said…"

"I didn't say *that*. See, you weren't listening."

Vassily sighed and gazed at Toner. "Is it always going to be like this?"

She pinched his sides and smiled. "Repeat after me: Yah sure, you betcha."

"Yah sure, you betcha."

"George is right. It does sound like you're from Minnesota. Kaloostian'll be proud."

"You didn't answer my question."

"Shh, that's not important now," she said, pulling him closer.

"Huh? Oh, now I understand. Speaking of Kaloostian, I was wondering about…"

"Tomorrow," Angela scolded, placing her index finger over his lips. "There's always tomorrow. We can call him then…and tell him the big news."

"What big news?"

"Later…"

Standing on the deck of George's cabin, holding each other tight, Angela Toner and Vassily Molotov looked towards the setting sun and the mountains. The few clouds, high and billowy in the sky, were like a canopy over the panorama.

Finally Angela shivered. "You're right. It is chilly out here," she said through her chattering teeth.

They broke their embrace as she pulled Vassily's coat closer to her body. She then slid her right hand out from under the coat and took his hand. Still surprised at her soft touch, Vassily looked at her and smiled, squeezing her hand in return.

At its customary pace, the sun reached the horizon, blossoming into hues of orange, yellow, and red, lighting the evening sky in a glorious rainbow. As if by magic, the spectacle of light reflecting off the snow and ice of the mountains and trees, doubled and quadrupled the display. It was nature in all her glory.

For some, these are magical moments, a instant in time when decisions are made, paths chosen, journeys begun and ended. While not commonplace, such transpirations are not inordinately rare. Yet most people miss them. Too busy muddling through their harried lives, they trivialize what nature so selflessly provides.

The lucky ones not only recognize the magnificence of a rendezvous with destiny, but also have someone with which to share it. For them comes the quintessential wisdom that peace and wealth are experienced not bought, lived not mail-ordered. A twinkling of life and love captured not on film, but in the heart.

Angela Toner and Vassily Molotov understood the magic. Arm in arm, hand in hand, they turned towards the west and watched with loving passion as the sun dipped below the horizon, etching in their memories the essence of a perfect moment.

Epilogue

Bombay, India
January 17, 2007

Many minutes before dawn, Chandrapal Dasa patiently awaited the next set of instructions. He was the only person awake in the sleepy neighborhood of middle-class houses and shops. He had ventured to this part of Bombay for that very reason.

Chandrapal was of average height, no more than five-feet-seven, though slight of build. His black-framed eyeglasses matched his neatly trimmed straight black hair and mustache. The Indo-European features of his ancestors were chiseled into his naturally tan face.

His clothes, a muslin shirt and white cotton pants, wrinkled from the humidity and his own perspiration. Though the sun had yet to show its face, the heat was already uncomfortable.

He was thirty-five years old and had volunteered for the assignment, hoping for a promotion. The change in plans, however, was unexpected.

He should have done the job—entering a series of bids on the Internet—in the privacy and darkness of his own home.

Two days earlier, something had gone terribly wrong. The Internet, shot full of holes, bound and gagged, could now barely sustain minimal traffic. The newspapers and broadcasts had dubbed it "The Great Brownout, the First International Paralysis of the World Wide Web."

Reports on the cause of the problem were numerous and contradictory. The most apparent conclusion, predicted for years, was that the demand for phone lines had exceeded supply, creating maximum congestion. For more than forty-eight hours, no one had been able to determine whether traffic caused the widespread computer breakdown or vice versa. Like the chicken-and-egg debate, it was a moot point.

The second theory was more exciting—computer hackers! They'd busted into IBM, Deutsche Bank, the Pentagon, the United Nations, and every Ivy League admissions databank. They'd fooled diplomats with phony intelligence reports, doctored academic records, reprogrammed all the traffic lights on Rodeo Drive in Beverly Hills, and spawned more urban legends than any other media source.

Now they'd done the unthinkable—shut down the Internet. According to CNN, a gang of delinquent anarchists had mined several communication junctions with a fast-acting, lethal virus. Despite the skill of the perpetrators and the expense of the prank, they had issued no ultimatum, demanded no ransom. The job appeared to be one of sheer maliciousness.

Chandrapal didn't believe that for a minute. He knew it was the children.

For years, Chandrapal Dasa had heard rumors of the children. On many occasions he'd picked up thin strands of information about Nyentzi from the Internet. It was a story impossible to suppress.

Scientists from around the world had altered the human genetic code, creating a family of living computers. Though God, Lord Brahma, in his rightful fury, had destroyed the facility that created them, the children lived on. Only seven years old and already, so he'd heard, they'd performed miracles beyond comprehension. So much new technology, so much hope for humankind! But now a man named Tyrell, a spawn of Kali, a weakling enslaved by his own desires, was auctioning off those miracles to the highest bidders.

Chandrapal knew it was wrong, just as he knew his participation in the buying and selling of the children's work was wrong. He should not have volunteered to do the bidding, though better him than a nonbeliever. The Children, God bless them, at least deserved that.

God understood that taking the moral high ground was a luxury Chandrapal could not afford. With a family to support, he would light an extra candle, burn holy incense, and pray for forgiveness. Surely this was all part of God's plan.

In the midst of his uncertainty, the courier heard bells tolling in the distance, calling the Hindu faithful to morning prayer. He clasped his hands and offered to Krishna a quiet petition from the Bhagavad Gita, the epic Hindu scripture. Like Exodus 33, in which God revealed his glory to Moses, Chandrapal's prayer described the grandeur of Krishna as revealed to the great warrior Arjuna:

Oh, my God, I see all gods within your body;
Each in his degree, the multitude of creatures;
See Lord Brahma throned upon the lotus;
See all the sages, and the holy serpents.
Universal Form, I see you without limit,
Infinite of arms, eyes, mouths and bellies—
See, and find no end, midst, or beginning.

Chandrapal understood the message of the Gita. He knew that his life, all life, had but one conclusion and purpose—to realize the Eternal Self within. Only then would he know the all-encompassing joy of union with God.

But he couldn't shake his uneasy feeling about the children. If the experiments had truly been what the rumors reported, what then?

Would children born of a test tube be offered the chance of rebirth and immortality? How did they fit into the infinite design of God? What if they were, as many were saying, Krishna reincarnated? What if they were something else?

What if the message in the Christian Bible were true? Chandrapal had once read that "A child shall lead them." Was the Christian year 2000 the dawn of a new age?

It was too much to think about, and he was but a simple man. He would meditate and fast, praying to the gods to bless him with a vision.

His beeper vibrated. He held it up and saw the number he must call. Hurrying across the street, Chandrapal entered the phone booth, closed the door, and inserted his coin. He dialed the number and waited. In a moment, he was connected to an automated operator.

Though he had memorized the information, the courier took no chances. In the dim light of the phone booth, Chandrapal held a scrap of paper in front of him and slowly tapped in his employer's ID. In a moment, he heard a second recording, requesting confirmation. He keyed in the numbers again and waited for the final message. It was quick in coming.

He sighed and nodded. His job was complete, the call difficult to trace. Thus, India purchased some of the technology of Nyentzi—the genetic code for a new strain of wheat. It might be wrong, but who was he, a mere public servant, to judge? And what choice did India have? She had to compete, had to feed her hungry and restless masses.

Leave the judging to God.

Chandrapal exited the phone booth, folded his hands, and prayed for favorable influence on his karma by the Children of Nyentzi. He prayed the rumors were true. He knew that throughout history, humankind had been blessed by the comings of great teachers, martyrs, saints, imams, and buddhas. Perhaps this time, people would be less inclined to forget their lessons.

Chandrapal thought about his family—his wife and two children sleeping peacefully at home. He quickened his pace. As he walked down the dusty street, the courier saw the first glimmer of the morning sun peaking above the rooftops. He remembered how the sky had looked an hour before, lighted only by the moon.

"Is it not also true," he thought with a smile, "that no matter how bright the light of day, under the right conditions, at certain predestined times, even the sun is eclipsed by the moon?"

6252

About the Author

Joseph Driessen lives in Apple Valley, Minnesota with his wife and two children. His interest in science and technology comes from working with computers for over 25 years. He is employed as a Site Maintenance Engineer with Digital River, Inc.

Destiny's Hand is his first novel.